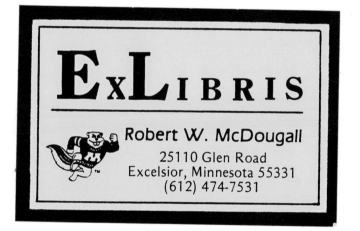

FAINT PRAISE

A Jane Lawless Mystery

Ellen Hart

Seal Press

Cover and book design by Clare Conrad
Cover art by Debbie Hanley

Library of Congress Cataloging-in-Publication Data
Hart, Ellen
  Faint Praise / Ellen Hart
  1. Lawless, Jane (Fictitious character)—Fiction. 2. Women detectives—Minnesota—Minneapolis Metropolitan Area—Fiction.
3. Restauratuers—Minnesota—Minneapolis Metropolitan Area—Fiction. 4. Lesbians—Minnesota—Minneapolis Metropolitan Area—Fiction. 5. Minneapolis Metropolitan Area (Minn.)—Fiction. I. Title.
PS3558.A6775F35   1995   813'.54—dc20   95–14852
ISBN 1-878067-67-2

Printed in the United States of America
First printing, November 1995
10 9 8 7 6 5 4 3 2 1

Distributed to the trade by Publishers Group West
In Canada: Publishers Group West Canada, Toronto, Ontario
In Europe and the U.K.: Airlift Book Company, London, England

For the two new men in my life,
My grandson, Avery Kruger-Williams
and
My son-in-law, Tom Gibson.

And, as always, for my beloved Kathy

CAST OF CHARACTERS

JANE LAWLESS: Owner of the Lyme House Restaurant in Minneapolis.

CORDELIA THORN: Artistic Director of the Allen Grimby Repertory Theatre in St. Paul. Old friend of Jane's.

ARNO HEYWOOD: Host of "Eye On Minnesota," a local TV show on WTWN-TV. Owner and resident of Linden Lofts.

AMY McGEE: Secretary. Friend of Jane's.

ROZ BARRIE: Promotions Director for WTWN-TV. Resident of Linden Lofts.

MARK THURMAN: TV News anchor on WTWN-TV. Roz's boyfriend.

KELLY HEYWOOD: Daughter of Arno Heywood. Resident manager of Linden Lofts.

JOHN MERCHANT: Gay lawyer found murdered in Loring Park. Childhood friend of Kelly Heywood's.

BERYL CORNELIUS: Jane's aunt.

EDGAR ANDERSON: Bridge Club friend of Beryl's.

ERIC LIND: Arno Heywood's nephew. Manager of antique store in Minneapolis. Resident of Linden Lofts.

TEDDY ANDERSON: Writer. Resident of Linden Lofts.

PEG MARTINSEN: Psychologist. Resident of Linden Lofts.

MABEL LIND: Arno Heywood's sister. Eric's mother.

BRANDON VACHEL: Artist.

JULIA MARTINSEN: Peg Martinsen's daughter.

Damn with faint praise, assent with civil leer,
And, without sneering, teach the rest to sneer.
— An Essay on Man, *Alexander Pope*

FAINT PRAISE

1

On the day after Thanksgiving, the first floor of the Foshay Tower in downtown Minneapolis was packed with carolers ushering in the Christmas season. Earlier in the afternoon, Santa himself had put in an appearance. In all the commotion and good cheer, no one paid much attention as an elegantly-dressed woman entered from Marquette Avenue and moved quietly to the elevators. The small but exuberant choir had just begun its rendition of "It Came Upon a Midnight Clear" when the ornate metal doors opened and the woman, clutching a tasteful gray leather purse to her side, stepped on.

"We're going all the way to the top!" exclaimed a small boy proudly as the others in the elevator looked at him with amused smiles. The boy's father quickly put a hand on his shoulder to quiet him. Silence returned to the small compartment as it sped upward.

On the twenty-fourth floor, the woman got off, turning briefly and giving the boy a conspiratorial wink. Then, squaring her shoulders, she proceeded to an office on the northwest corner of the building where a young man was waiting. She nodded a greeting, at the same time taking in the almost empty white room. A single chair sat in the corner. Stepping to the windows, she could see that the view of the downtown landscape was everything she'd hoped for. Historic St. Anthony in the distance. James J. Hill's famous stone bridge spanning the Mississippi. The newly gentrified warehouse district. It was all waiting for her, buried in a white winter coating. There was no doubt about it, this had been the right decision. Standing in the quiet office, she felt a shiver of anticipation, a heightened sense of her own mission.

She turned and faced the man she'd come to meet. Clearing her throat, she asked softly, "How much does this office rent for?"

The man smiled. "You like it then?"

She nodded.

"It's a perfect spot for your travel agency. When you called me on Wednesday morning to set up this appointment, I knew you'd like it. It's two thousand a month. Twenty-four hundred if you want the small office adjacent to it for a reception area." He hesitated. Then, perhaps thinking he needed to sell the location a bit more aggressively, added, "It's centrally located and has a prime downtown view."

The woman turned back to the window. "I can see that. Actually, I've been here before, Mr. Bennett."

"Really?" He slipped his hands into his pockets. "When was that?"

She looked up at the sky. "When I was six. My father brought me here for my birthday. It was just before the war."

"The war?"

She gave a faint smile. "World War II. We took the elevator to the thirtieth floor, then walked up to the observation platform. It was the first time I'd ever been to a big city." Her tone had grown reverent.

"Where are you from?"

"For the first seventeen years of my life, I lived on a farm in southern Minnesota. It doesn't really matter because that day my entire world changed."

"How was that?"

"I fell in love, Mr. Bennett. I knew I had to live in Minneapolis, had to make my life here."

He folded his arms over his chest, taking her in for the first time. "That's quite a story. You know, you do look kind of familiar."

"Do I?" She turned briefly, allowing him to view her face in profile. Then, very calmly, she removed her coat and tossed it over the chair. Underneath, she was wearing a gray silk blouse with matching silk scarf tied around her neck—almost the same gray as her hair—and a navy skirt. Her earrings were pearl. With a dismissive glance she said, "Right now I need to spend some time in here alone. I have a strong sense of place, Mr. Bennett. I expect that comes from my first visit to the Foshay Tower. My surroundings are very important to me. Before I sign your lease, I have to be absolutely positive. I have to sit in here and let my senses make the final decision."

With some hesitation, he responded, "Of course. Just take your time. My office is down on the fourth floor. When you get off the elevator, turn right. You'll see a sign that says Foshay Tower Rental Information. I'll have all the specifics waiting for you."

"Thank you." Her voice was formal.

"Just close the door and turn off the lights when you're done."

She nodded and then watched him walk to the elevator. After he was gone, she turned again to the window as if drawn by some inner compass. The winter light was beginning to fade. Taking a pack of cigarettes and a gold lighter from her purse, she lit one as she stood gazing down at the town that had sustained her for all of her adult life. Now wasn't the time for second-guessing. Doubt had been the enemy for far too long.

Leaning against the window frame, she whispered the words, "Foshay Tower," remembering that the man who had built it back in the late twenties, Wilbur Foshay, had called Minneapolis, "This new Cannan. The promised land." She'd felt exactly the same way when she'd viewed it for the first time. So much promise. Such energy. And just like the tower, a building which was meant to symbolize the optimism and the exuberance of the roaring twenties, her life had taken on the same quality of failed dreams. She hadn't lied to the young rental agent. A sense of place *was* terribly important to her. This office was perfect.

Noticing that the cigarette tasted unusually bitter, she glanced around the room for an ashtray. Unless she wanted to use the seat of the chair, nothing was available. She reached up and disengaged the lock, opening the window wide. A gust of cold wind hit her square in the face, momentarily disorienting her. Twenty-four stories was a long way up. There weren't even screens on the windows. Peeking her head gingerly over the edge, she flicked the half-smoked cigarette into the abyss, watching it sink out of sight.

Then, her eyes fixed on a single building in the distance, she hoisted herself into the opening, and jumped.

2

"Can you beat that?" said Todd Nelson, the new evening bartender at the Lyme House. He was leaning over the mahogany bar reading from the front page of the Saturday *Star Tribune*.

Jane Lawless, the owner of the restaurant, sat on the other side of the counter, sipping from a lager and lime. "Beat what?" she asked absently. Her mind was elsewhere. Another month and it would be Christmas, the busiest time of the year. In front of her rested the guest register. Most of next weekend's dinner slots had already been filled. Business had been good all year. Tonight, since it was after nine, the upstairs dining room had cleared a bit, but the downstairs pub was packed. Celtic music—a hammered dulcimer, harp and drums—wafted through the crowd. The group, one she usually booked around the holidays, was called Stonehenge. It was the perfect background music for a room that glowed with the ancient luster of burnished copper. Two fireplaces, one in the main room, and one in a more intimate back room, helped ward off the cold of a bitter Minnesota night.

Todd pointed at the page and shook his head, bringing Jane's thoughts back to the subject at hand. Not that she knew what the subject was. "What's it say?" she asked.

He picked up a soft cloth and began polishing a glass. "You know that woman who jumped from the Foshay Tower yesterday?"

She nodded.

"Well, it says here it wasn't a woman after all. It was a guy. His name was —" He drew his finger down the page. "—Arno Heywood."

"Good lord!"

"You know him?"

"Doesn't everybody?"

"I'm new in town, remember? Anyway, it says here that he hosted a local TV show on WTWN. Unless he was on the SciFi Channel, I wouldn't have caught him."

Jane was stunned. "You say he was in drag?"

"Dressed like a woman."

She shook her head in amazement. "He's kind of an institution around here. He's been on TV forever. It's funny someone didn't recognize him." As Todd was summoned to the other end of the bar by a waiter, she pulled the paper in front of her.

The front-page story featured a picture of Heywood, and a caption which said, Local TV personality commits suicide at 63. The story revealed little about the actual death. A note had been found at the scene, but no information about its content was available. His daughter had been contacted by a reporter, but was unable to shed any light on her father's state of mind before the "unfortunate incident."

Jane picked up her lager and lime and finished it slowly, wondering what kind of pain a man would have to be in to end his life so violently, and so enigmatically. As she thought about the drag part, she realized he could have pulled it off fairly easily. Arno Heywood was a small man. Sandy-haired. His beard wasn't heavy. And even if it had been, there were ways around that. Still, Jane had never overheard any scuttlebutt around town that Heywood was a cross-dresser. She'd been to more than one drag ball in the Twin Cities and his name had never come up. She even had an old friend who lived in a building he owned. Perhaps her friend could shed some light on what had happened.

Jane pushed the paper aside. She needed some fresh—if freezing—air. She'd felt claustrophobic all day and this news only made it worse. Grabbing a winter jacket from the rack in her office, she sprinted up the stairs to the deck just off the main dining room. In the summer, it was a favorite spot for her customers to sit and sip a glass of wine, or linger over a cup of coffee while listening to the music making its way across the lake from the bandstand on the opposite shore. Tonight, it was empty except for one lone Adirondack chair. The chair Jane kept outside just for herself.

The deck had been swept of snow. Christmas lights and decorative pine boughs adorned the wooden railing. As she sat down, pulling on her mittens and snuggling into the folds of her wool pea coat, she watched the colored lights twinkle. The lake itself was covered by several inches of ice. Since there was no wind, it was a beautiful night to be outside. She took several deep breaths, trying to put the image of Arno Heywood's shattered body out of her mind. In a few days, perhaps the police would be able to shed some light on the mystery of his suicide, as well as just why he'd been dressed as a woman. The national tabloids would probably pick up the story. It was too juicy to pass up. Jane grimaced at the thought, realizing her own interest went beyond the realm of good taste.

Changing gears, her thoughts turned to a personal problem, one that had been occupying her mind for several weeks.

"As God is in Her heaven, I can't leave you alone for *five* minutes!" roared a voice from the steps leading down to the parking lot.

Jane turned to find Cordelia, her oldest and dearest friend, trudging up the walk. She was wearing a red wool cape, black boots and a black, fake-fur Cossack hat. All that was missing was a rearing stallion breathing steam.

"How did you find me?" called Jane, cracking a smile.

"I know your habits. Such as they are."

"And why is it you can't leave me alone?"

Cordelia puffed to a stop, leaning her large frame against the railing. "I should think that would be obvious. You're brooding again, dearheart. Leave that to Young Werther, Baudelaire, and the drama freaks in those Hesse novels you like so much."

Jane started to laugh.

"You were thinking about your aunt Beryl, weren't you?"

The fact was, three months from now, her English aunt's visa would be up. After the death of Jane's partner, Christine, many years ago, she'd lived alone. Since her aunt's arrival, she'd slowly gotten used to living with another human being again. It was a civilizing experience, one Jane had learned to value. And she'd come to count on Beryl's companionship. It was simply too depressing to consider that in a few months her aunt would be gone, taking her warmth and her silly hats with her.

Feeling something hit her chest, Jane looked down and saw that Cordelia had thrown a snowball at her. And she was preparing to throw another.

"There's more where that came from," smirked Cordelia, nodding to a huge snow bank. "Being pelted by snowballs is one of the only known cures for brooding. That and reading *The Fall* by Camus all the way through in one sitting, diving head first into a lake in the dead of winter, or eating an entire lemon meringue pie. What doesn't kill us, makes us stronger."

Jane held up her hand. "I'm not brooding, I'm just . . . thinking."

"Right. And I'm Helen Hayes. It's a fine distinction."

"I thought you were supposed to be at the theatre tonight."

"Well," said Cordelia, tossing a particularly hefty snowball from one gloved hand to the other, "I left early. The stage manager called an important meeting for after the show, but as I am *only* the Artistic Director, my input was not deemed necessary."

"Do I detect a note of sarcasm?"

"Why ever would you think that?"

Jane brushed the snow off her coat.

"Actually, I've come to invite you and Beryl and that new friend of hers—the one she met at her bridge club —"

"Edgar Anderson."

"Right. I want to have you all over for dinner. Mugs is going to be out of town for at least ten days."

Mugs—otherwise known as Mary Katherine Lonetto—was Cordelia's newest love. She was also a home security expert who traveled to conventions all over the country.

"That's a great idea," smiled Jane. "I'm sure we'd all love to come."

"You can bring someone too," said Cordelia, wiggling her eyebrows suggestively, "If you like. How about that . . . *unusual* person you invited to Thanksgiving dinner?"

"She was *not* my date. I made that perfectly clear." Jane knew she was protesting too loudly.

"Of course, Janey. I would never suggest you were attracted to someone who looked like they'd starred in *Beach Blanket Bingo*."

Jane rolled her eyes. She'd met a woman recently at Cordelia's "*Richard the Third* bash," a party Cordelia gave every year in honor of her first directorial triumph, Shakespeare's *Richard III* at the Blackburn Playhouse. Amy McGee had come with one of Cordelia's long-time friends, but had spent most of the evening sitting alone in a corner, not talking to anyone. Since Jane had never been one for boisterous partying either, she'd gone over and introduced herself.

The more they talked, the more Jane sensed that Amy was a lost soul. Except for a rather shy comment about being a lesbian, she seemed unusually private about her life. She wasn't unattractive, but her clothes did look as if they belonged in a beach party movie from the fifties. Lots of pinks and blues and feminine fluff. Bunnies appliqued on her sweater.

White bobby socks and flats. For any woman in the nineties, she made a bizarre fashion statement. Amy had explained that she was planning to spend Thanksgiving at home with a microwave dinner and a romance novel. Jane couldn't help but feel sorry for someone in such an awful predicament, so, on a whim, she'd invited her to her father's house in St. Paul for dinner.

However, before the grand day arrived, Jane made it clear to one and all that Amy was *not* her date. She hated it when all the happy couples in her family clucked their tongues over her unfortunate singleness. She'd dated here and there since Christine's death, but nothing had lasted long. Even though she'd taken her partner's death very hard, she was now enjoying the single life. As a matter of fact, it felt great, so why analyze it to death? As expected, that assessment cut no mustard in a family so heavily into self-analysis it could have traced its ancestry back to a Viennese couch. Jane was weary of trying to educate the entire clan about the joys of single-hood. And Cordelia didn't help with her little whispered asides about "The lady doth protest too much, methinks." Sometimes Jane felt the urge to stick a dish towel in Cordelia's mouth.

Cordelia tossed the snowball over her shoulder. "Maybe you could all come over some night next week. I'm going to fix my famous filet de sole Veronique. I'll have my social secretary check my extensive calendar and get back to your social secretary."

"Fine," said Jane.

Cordelia hesitated. "You're okay, aren't you dearheart? I mean, I know you're upset about Beryl's going back to England in the spring. That's all it is, right?"

"I'm fine. I wouldn't be human if it didn't make me a little depressed."

"Well, look on the bright side."

"What bright side?"

Cordelia considered the issue.

"There is no bright side," said Jane. "Face it."

"You'll have an extra bedroom."

"Yippy. An extra *empty* room."

Cordelia shrugged. "Maybe you should buy an aquarium."

"Replace my aunt with a *fish*?"

"Well, two or three fish."

Jane glared at her.

"A hamster?" she said, weakly.

"Look, I appreciate the concern. Really I do."

"Always, Janey. You call if you need anything."

"I will."

"Well," said Cordelia, pushing away from the railing, "I'm off. Mugs has prepared a late dinner and I'm supposed to pick up the wine on the way home."

Jane checked her watch. "Afraid you're out of luck, kiddo. The liquor stores closed half an hour ago."

"You're kidding."

"Nope."

"Well . . . hum. I guess I could stop at the neighborhood grocery and buy some strawberry soda. That wouldn't be too bad."

Jane tried not to gag. "Listen, just go inside and tell Todd to get you a bottle from our cellar."

"Really?"

"It's on me."

Cordelia walked over and gave Jane a huge bear hug. It was the only kind she knew how to give. "I'll just take something . . . simple."

"Good thinking."

"A fresh little Beaujolais with a poignant insouciance. Something banal, yet murky."

"You read too many wine columns."

"Say, how about that Chateau Malartic-Lagravière 1945 you said was so ridiculously expensive and so fabulous? I'm surprised I can even remember the name. It falls trippingly off the tongue, don't you think? Chateau Malartic-Lagravière 1945. Makes me feel like I'm in a David Niven Movie."

"Try a California red, Cordelia. 1994 was a good year. That way you might make it to your car alive."

With a mischievous grin and a goodbye wave, Cordelia disappeared inside the restaurant.

Once again, Jane was left alone with her thoughts. Out of the corner of her eye, she thought she caught a small movement near some pine trees that bordered the lake, but when she turned to look, the woods and the path leading up to the deck were quiet.

She shrugged off the vague sense that she was being watched, and glanced around into the main dining room of her restaurant. Viewed from outside, it was an inviting scene. Linen-covered tables and fresh flowers set against a backdrop of rough log walls and a roaring fire in a stone hearth. Jane had worked hard and created a unique dining experience in the Twin Cities. She'd even published a cookbook last fall and it was selling well. She was forty years old and life was good. So why had she felt so damnably restless lately? Cordelia was right. She was brooding too much. But since she was in the mood, she might as well brood away.

Jane was positive her current restlessness was a separate issue from the depression she felt over Beryl's impending departure. But if that wasn't the cause, what was? She refused to believe it had anything to do with her recent birthday. She'd finally crossed the great divide into middle-aged land. But she didn't feel over-the-hill, stodgy, jaded or left in the dust by her younger friends. She was much too midwestern to be impressed by some of the bi-coastal sleaze which passed for cutting edge culture. She'd always been singularly unimpressed by what was "in." She knew gays and lesbians were part of the new chic, and while she appreciated the visibility and, hopefully, the understanding it would bring, it nauseated her to be part of anybody's flavor of the month.

So, she didn't feel out of date, she was healthy. So what was it?

"Hi, Jane," came a soft voice from the edge of the deck.

Jane turned to find Amy McGee standing about ten feet away. She was holding a small box. Her red hair was pulled back loosely into the hood of her coat.

"Well, hi," said Jane. "What are you doing here on such a cold night?" She stood, not quite knowing what to make of this unexpected visit.

"I brought you this." Amy held out the package.

Jane walked over and took it. It was a box of chocolate-covered cherries. The dime store variety.

"It's just a small thank you for inviting me to your father's house on Thanksgiving."

"Amy, you didn't need to do that."

She looked down at her feet. "I know. I wanted to."

Jane could sense the woman's discomfort. "So, how've you been?" she asked kindly.

"Oh, all right I guess. I worked on my coin collection all day yesterday. But, see I hoped . . . well, I mean—" She looked up at the stars. "I thought maybe you'd call."

Jane didn't know what to say. It had never occurred to her to get in touch with Amy again. Surely she realized they had very little in common. Most of their conversations were a struggle. Mainly, they talked about old U.S. coins. Jane could only talk about the Denver Mint so long.

"Hey Janey!" came a boisterous voice from the doorway leading into the dining room. "What the hell are you doing out here?"

Jane turned to find a former roommate from her days at a University of Minnesota sorority smiling at her. "Roz," she said, her surprise evident. This was great timing. Roz Barrie was the woman who rented an apartment from Arno Heywood. Maybe now, she could ge some first-hand information.

"You got a couple of minutes to talk to an old buddy with a problem?"

Jane glanced back at Amy who stood rigidly by the wooden railing, her hands stuffed into the pockets of her coat. She looked angry.

"Amy, I'd like you to meet—"

"That's okay," said Amy, cutting her off. "I've got to get going."

"Are you sure?" said Jane. "If you want to wait, we could have a cup of coffee later."

"No. Thanks. You're too busy." She turned and rushed down the path to the parking lot.

Jane watched her fling the car door open, slam it shut, and then gun the motor and roar out of the drive. Her personality was so generally subdued, Jane was amazed to see how aggressive she was behind the wheel.

"What was all that about?" asked Roz, her breath swirling like steam in the bitter night air. She took several steps out onto the deck.

Jane shook her head. "Beats me."

"Well, what about it then? You got a few minutes for an old buddy, or are all your brain cells frozen?"

Jane grinned. "As long as we talk in my office, in front of the fire, with a cup of hot cocoa, I think they'll thaw."

"Great. Lead the way."

3

Roz Barrie was in her late thirties. She was tall, fashionably, but to Jane's mind excessively thin, with short dark hair, a boyish freckle or two, and an open, friendly face. She'd worked for WTWN-TV in Minneapolis for almost ten years, first as a writer and part-time reporter, and then making her way through the ranks until her recent appointment as the station's promotion director.

During Jane's sophomore year at the University of Minnesota, she'd joined Kappa Alpha Sigma and shared a room with Roz on the third floor of the sorority house. Initially, they'd had little in common. Roz was straight out of high school, boy crazy, and willing to party at a moment's notice. Jane was almost two years older, a serious student, and definitely *not* boy crazy. Yet, over time, they formed a strong bond. Even though their adult lives had taken them in different directions, they still managed to get together at least once a month for a long dinner or late-night drink. Roz loved to gossip about the old gang, and Jane, much to her chagrin, listened with undisguised alacrity.

As they entered the office, Jane found that she was concerned, and also a bit intrigued by Roz's unexpected appearance. She bent down and lit the paper under the kindling and logs she'd built in her office fireplace several hours ago. Moving over to the desk, she called the kitchen, asking for two mugs of cocoa to be sent down to her office. Finally, she joined Roz on the sofa. The fire was just starting to catch. The only other light in the room came from a reading lamp on her desk.

Roz had squirmed out of her heavy coat and was rubbing her hands in front of the warmth. "So, how've you been?" she asked with an amiable twist of her head.

"Fine," said Jane. "Nothing really new. The cookbook is doing well."

Roz raised an eyebrow. "You're *such* a celebrity these days. I just bought a copy. It's on my kitchen counter even as we speak."

Jane knew there was a certain knack to accepting a compliment gracefully. It was a skill she hadn't quite mastered. After stumbling over a polite thank you she changed the subject. "So, what's up?" Even in the dim light, she could see the question made Roz's cheeks flush with color.

Without even a moment's hesitation, Roz answered, "Everyone thinks I'm crazy! That I've gone off the deep end."

Before Jane could ask why, a knock drew her attention to the door. Rising quickly, she ducked around the back of the couch and answered it, taking the tray from the waiter. "Thanks," she said, closing the door behind her and returning to the sofa. She poured the steaming cocoa from a thermal carafe into two mugs, handing one to Roz.

"I don't know where to begin," said Roz, taking a sip, "but I figured you'd be the perfect person to bounce this off of. You tell me what you think."

"Sure," said Jane. She gave Roz her full attention.

"Something strange is going on at the loft where I live."

"Define *strange*."

"Well, you remember a couple years ago I moved from that condo out near Lake Minnetonka and began renting a loft downtown. You've been there."

"Twice. Once for a dinner party. And then for your birthday last year."

"It's a great spot."

"You won't get an argument from me. And hey, correct me if I'm wrong, but didn't Arno Heywood own that place?"

She looked down at her hands. "He died yesterday, Jane."

"I know. I'm very sorry. Were you two close?"

She gave a sad nod. "I think the main reason he bought that old warehouse and turned it into six of the most beautiful lofts in the city was because he wanted to live with people he cared about—his family he called us. He'd have potlucks in his place the third Sunday of every month. We all got to know each other. It was great, Jane. Really great."

"Does anyone know why he did it?"

"To be honest, he'd been kind of down lately, but it never occurred to me he might take his life."

"Have you heard what was in his suicide note?"

She shook her head.

"How about the reason he was dressed like a woman when he jumped?"

She took out a tissue from the pocket of her sweater and wiped her

15

eyes. "Well," she sniffed, "the police came and talked to Kelly—that's his daughter, she manages the apartments for him—yesterday evening. Apparently he'd scheduled a meeting with a rental agent at the Foshay Tower on the pretext of looking at some office space. The police thought, since his face was so recognizable, he was probably trying to disguise himself. Otherwise, there might have been too many questions. He asked for time alone in the room. When the agent left, he jumped." She sniffed again into the tissue, shaking her head. "I'm going to miss him."

"You say his daughter lives in one of the lofts?"

"Yeah. She's his only child. Arno was divorced many years ago. Never remarried. I suppose she'll inherit the place now that he's gone. The will is going to be read early next week. Actually, that's what I came to talk to you about."

"Heywood's will?"

"No, my loft."

Jane remembered her cocoa and took a sip.

"It all started about six weeks ago. I came home one night—you know me, I'm a neat freak—and found this mug sitting on the coffee table. I have no idea how it got there. It certainly wasn't mine. I sniffed it and discovered it was mint tea. Mint tea! I *hate* mint tea, Jane."

"I don't understand."

"Neither did I. But as I thought about it, there was only one explanation. Someone had been in my apartment. There was no sign of a break-in, so I decided they must have had a key. The next day I went to talk to Kelly. I wanted to know if she'd let a workman in. Sometimes she does that, but in the past, she's always come and asked me for permission first. And she says she stays with the workman the entire time. Anyway, I talked to her and she said she hadn't been in my apartment for months. I told her what had happened and she said maybe I'd had a memory lapse. That I'd had a guest and hadn't noticed that they'd left the mug there."

"Is that possible?"

"Absolutely not! Well, I'm almost positive. Peg, the woman from the top floor, had been down briefly that night, but she wasn't drinking anything. I'm sure of it."

"Who has a key to your apartment?"

"Well, Kelly does. I suppose Arno did. And then Mark Thurman "

"Thurman?"

16

"My, uh, boyfriend. Actually, we've been dating for about five months. I know you're going to tell me this is really dumb, but he works for the same station I do."

"Not Mark Thurman, the new anchor?"

"Yeah. Him." Roz held up her hand to prevent any further comment. "Don't say it. I've robbed the cradle again. I realize he's a good ten years younger than me."

"You think I have a problem with *that*?"

"Well . . . no, not really. But frankly Jane, it has been kind of a problem. We broke up about a week ago. It's a long story. I don't need to go into that now, but you asked about keys. Thurman has a key."

"But he gave it back."

"He's going to. We talked about it today. He said he'd drop it off." She fidgeted with her gold necklace. "But let me finish. There were more strange occurrences. My favorite magazine is the *Utne Reader*. When I get home in the evenings, I generally pick up my mail before taking the freight elevator up to my loft. One night, I was too tired to read through the stuff and just let it sit—neatly—on the kitchen table until the next night. The new issue of the *Utne Reader* was in the stack. When I came home, it had been moved over to my piano bench and the brown paper cover was gone. Someone had been reading it!"

"Creepy."

"I know!"

"Have you called the police?"

"And tell them what? There was an odd mug in my apartment? I hate mint tea? Someone broke into my loft to read the *Utne Reader*?"

"I see your point."

"But yes, I called them."

"And?" Jane sat forward in her chair. This *was* an odd set of circumstances.

"They asked me if I'd been under a lot of stress at work recently."

"Have you?"

"Oh no you don't. You're my friend, you little termite. You *have* to believe me!"

"I do believe you, Roz. But cut them some slack. It wasn't an entirely illogical question." Roz was one of the most anal-retentive people Jane had ever met. She even had the vegetables in her freezer arranged alphabetically. If anyone would know if something was out of place, it was Roz Barrie.

Roz tugged on her sweater. "Well anyway. So I talked to Kelly. I said I wanted to get the locks changed on my doors. This was about three weeks ago."

"How many doors?"

"Two. She said she'd talk to her father about it."

"Did she?"

"It wasn't Arno that was the problem, Jane, it was Kelly. She's a good kid, but she's cheap. She's always hurting for money. I think Arno gave her so much per month to run the building. Anything that was left over she kept. So, what else could I do? I had the locks changed myself."

"Good for you."

"When I gave Kelly the new key, I also gave her the bill. She was furious, but I don't think she'll challenge me on it."

"Has anything happened since you changed the locks?"

"Not until last night. I got home late—it was after midnight. My car was in the shop, so a friend dropped me off after a late movie. As I was coming in the door, I heard the phone ringing. I raced to answer it. It was my sister with her usual litany of romantic angst. Her boyfriend had left her and she didn't know if she could go on. After about fifteen minutes of this, I told her I was dead on my feet and had to go. I took a quick shower and then hit the sack.

"Around three A.M., I woke to the sound of a door closing. I figured it must be out in the hall—my neighbor coming home or some such thing. I tried to get back to sleep, but I couldn't. I just had this really icky feeling—like some evil presence was right next to my bed. For a few minutes there, I was almost too afraid to breathe. But finally, I screwed up my courage and crept out into the living room. I saw immediately that the light had been turned on next to my desk. I was positive it hadn't been on earlier. The only light I leave on at night is a small one in the kitchen. I know you're going to think this is dumb, but I grabbed a knife from the kitchen counter, raced to the front door and flipped on all the lights."

"Maybe you should simply have left."

"Right. In my nightgown, looking like a freaking zombie?" She gave Jane a disgusted look. "When nothing happened, I started to search the

18

apartment. Thankfully, I found nothing. That's when I sat down be-hind my desk." She shivered as she looked down into her mug. "See, most every night before I go to bed, I have a glass of wine and write for a few minutes in my journal. It helps me relax and put the day into per-spective. Some nights I write more than others. I keep the notebook on the right hand corner of my desk. When I sat down, I saw that it had been moved to the left. And it was crooked, not straight the way I always leave it. There was only one explanation. While I was sleeping, someone had been sitting there reading it! I was in a panic. I mean, here was proof that someone *was* in the apartment—or at least had been! When I looked up at the door, I realized I'd forgotten to put on the chain or throw the bolt, the ones I'd just installed. Like a dummy I'd answered that stupid phone call from my sister and never given another thought to my secu-rity precautions."

"You're human, Roz. You were tired."

"But look what happened! Someone came into my apartment last night, Jane. While I was *there!* I could have been killed!"

Jane wasn't so sure. If this person, whoever he or she was, had wanted to harm Roz, there had been ample opportunity. Then again, if Roz had surprised the intruder, it might have been a different story.

Roz squeezed her eyes shut. "I'm terrified to stay there alone. In my own home!"

"I hear you. And I think you have good reason to be frightened. But tell me, what did you do after you found the journal?"

"I poured myself four or five stiff shots of brandy. I knew I'd never calm down without them. Another dumb move, right? I finally fell asleep around four and woke up with a hangover the size of Brazil. I can't live like this, Jane. I mean, would you want someone prowling around your place while you're sleeping?"

"Of course not."

"Then what can I do? I can't prove my suspicions. I just know what I know!"

"I wonder why the police don't seem to think you've got cause for alarm."

"They said they can't do anything unless an actual threat is made. A threat! Some officer came up last week and checked out the place. It was a woman. She asked if I'd ever had any problems with PMS. These idiots think they're freaking psychotherapists!"

"What do you want from me?"

Roz shifted in her seat, running a hand over her face in an effort to regain control. "As much as I resist this, I'm convinced my intruder is one of the other tenants. I'm gone most of the day. Anybody who was watching would know exactly when I'm home and when I'm not. The security in the building is tight. Nobody can use the freight elevator or get into the stairwell without a key. There was no sign of breaking and entering. I think the likelihood that this intruder is a complete stranger is pretty small. See, every loft has rear windows that look directly down onto the parking lot in the back. When my car is gone, so am I."

"And your car was gone last night?"

"Exactly. I think someone jumped to the erroneous conclusion that I wasn't home. It's got to be one of four or five people."

"So, what do you want from me?"

Roz's expression grew even more confidential. "Look, I wouldn't have come tonight if I didn't know you were good at, you know, solving problems. You've done it before. So, here's the plan. I want you to come and look the place over. And then I want you to figure out who's doing it— and why."

Jane's eyebrow arched upward. Roz certainly knew how to get to the point.

"You'll help me, won't you?"

"What you're asking may be impossible."

Roz glared.

"What do you think this . . . *intruder* wants?"

"How should I know? All I can say is that I woke up this morning feeling like I was being watched. To be honest, I've felt it for weeks."

Jane took a gentler tack. "Look, Roz, you have to bear in mind that I have a full-time job. I can't just take off anytime I want."

"But you could do it at night. See, last September Arno decided to move in with Peg, the woman across the hall. They'd been dating for several years and I think they just thought it would be nicer to live together. I know he liked the view from her loft better than his, so it was an easy choice. Kelly has been trying to rent out his place, but so far she hasn't had any luck. The lofts are kind of expensive. Arno knew it would take time, so he left a lot of his furniture in there, hoping it might help to offer it furnished. Here's what I was thinking. I'd be happy to rent it for you. I could even stay upstairs some nights. It would be like a slumber party! Like our old days back at the sorority."

At that small allusion, Jane's stomach turned over.

"You'd love Arno's place. There's a skylight, a raised loft bedroom and bathroom. And just because you're a friend, I'm not going to take advantage of you. Oh no. I'd pay you. I know what the going rates are."

"You do?"

"Jane, I'm desperate. You've got to help me. If you don't, I'm going to have to move out. I've never loved living in a place more than I have Linden Lofts. It's my home. Those people are my friends—at least most of them are. I'd be happy staying there until they take me out feet first. I just don't want that to happen before I'm forty!"

Jane could see Roz was in a real bind. She also knew her aunt Beryl wouldn't mind taking care of the house and dogs for a few weeks. She'd done it before. "Dear lord, protect me from myself," she muttered, her eyes cast upward to the ceiling.

"Then you'll do it? You'll help me?"

"Well, my aunt is leaving, going back to England in the spring, so I'll want to spend some time with her."

"But?" She sat up eagerly.

"I'll stay at Linden Lofts for exactly one month. I'll devote what time I can to getting to the bottom of this. If I can't resolve it in that period of time, you'll have to find someone else to help."

Roz grabbed Jane's hands. "You'll figure it out."

"I hope I can. But if I can't, you might want to consider looking around for a safe little bungalow in the suburbs."

Roz made a sour face. "What an absolutely revolting idea. If those are my only options, I think I'll take my chances with the local thieves and muggers."

4

The following Tuesday night Jane parked her car about half a block from the Linden Building and got out, leaning for a moment against the front fender. It was just as she'd remembered it, located on the northeast end of the warehouse district; a massive, six-story brick building. On the front side of the first floor were a series of over-sized, arched doorways—many times the normal size—now partially bricked up and replaced with windows. If she remembered correctly, the structure had been built back in the late eighteen hundreds as a livery, a place that cared for and housed both horses and delivery wagons, renting them out to various local businesses. Later, in the early nineteen hundreds, several more floors had been added. Now, the ground level was home to a popular Greek restaurant—Athena's Garden. The second and third floors contained a printing company. Only the top three levels had been made into apartments, two lofts per floor.

Jane knew that in the last thirty years, people had begun to show more respect for their urban past. An appreciation of the city's architectural heritage had led to the desire to preserve it. Still, it took an unusual person to want to live in what was essentially a grungy environment. The view of the Mississippi river and of St. Anthony beyond might be awesome from six stories up, but down on the street, the urban aesthetic, as Roz called it, wasn't all that appealing. Neither were the dark alleys, the gang graffiti or the grime. This was a rough area. Not far from here were some of the seediest bars in town. This kind of home had nothing in common with the manicured suburbs or the nicer areas of the inner city. Yet there was something oddly invigorating about the area. As Jane made her way to the restaurant entrance, she wondered what kind of commitment it would take to refuse to allow a building like this to die.

Athena's Garden was only moderately busy. Jane assumed it was because of the weather. The wind chill, at last report, was twenty-five below zero.

Only lunatics and Minnesotans would be out on such a thoroughly unpleasant evening. As she recalled, there were two ways to get to the freight elevator which would take her up to the fourth floor. One was by parking in the back and using the loading dock entrance. The other was by walking through the restaurant to a wide hall which led to the elevator.

The smell of garlic and lemon made her mouth water as she snaked her way though the oilcloth-covered tables. The decorations might be tasteless, but the food here was wonderful. Jane envied the loft dwellers for having a restaurant on the premises. Roz didn't have to brave the arctic winds just to eat out.

Standing at last next to a jumble of mailboxes, Jane rang Roz's apartment. A second later she heard a voice. "Jane, is that you?"

"Half an hour late. Sorry."

"No problem. Take the elevator. The stairs are for mountain goats. I'll buzz you."

Jane waited. She could hear the elevator moving up from the bowels of the basement. It sounded like some prehistoric beast coming to life. A second later a small red light came on. She heard a buzzing sound and knew it was her cue to grab the metal handle and pull it up, separating the horizontal doors. She lifted a wooden gate underneath and stepped on. The interior was scuffed and dingy, but it felt rock solid. After pressing number four, she waited for the elevator to begin its ascent. When it stopped, Roz was there to greet her.

"I thought you were never going to make it."

"Problems at work. My apologies."

"Never mind." She led the way down the hall to an open door. "I was hoping you'd get here before Thurman arrived."

"Thurman's coming?" said Jane, stepping inside. Just as before, the sheer physical space stopped her dead in her tracks. "This is amazing. The room must be sixty feet long."

"Eighty." Roz closed and locked the door behind them. She slipped a heavy bolt into place, then an even heavier-looking chain. "I'm not taking any chances."

Roz's precautions barely registered. "And the ceilings," said Jane. "What are they? Ten feet?"

"Fourteen."

This vast expanse of hardwood floors, rough brick walls, long rows of windows, exposed radiators and webs of pipes was like some strange interior prairie. Structural wood columns were scattered here and there. Roz had used area rugs to set off different parts of the room. It was as if there was a living room, dining room, a music area complete with grand piano, even a library. Several wallpapered screens enclosed the bedroom, with a bathroom off to one side. The south end was dominated by a high tech kitchen—black laminate and white marble counters surrounded by a long bar. It was all Jane could do not to drool. "You've changed the layout since I was here last."

"Do you see why I love it so much?" Roz ducked into the kitchen and poured herself a cup of coffee. "You can do anything in here. It's big enough to house the State Fair carousel!" She held up the pot. "Want some?"

"Sure," said Jane. Anything hot appealed on such a bitter night. She took off her coat and scarf and sat down at the bleached-wood dining-room table. "Anything happen when you got home from work tonight?"

Roz handed her the mug and then dumped herself wearily into a chair across from her. "Nothing. Thank God."

"Why is Thurman coming over?" The coffee tasted great. You had to give these yuppies credit. They knew how to use a grinder.

"He's going to drop off the keys. I figured if you were here, there would be less of a chance he'd stay. I don't want to get into any more fights."

"Say, not to change the subject, but why do you always call him *Thurman*, instead of Mark?"

"He insists. He hates his first name. He was named after some uncle he loathed."

Jane nodded. She wanted to hear more about Mark Thurman, but this wasn't the time. Roz's consistently terrible taste in men had been the topic of more than one conversation over the years, but this was different. Surely Roz understood that after the locks were changed, only Thurman and Kelly Heywood had access to the new set, and hence access to her apartment. From Jane's limited understanding of events, that probably meant that one of them was responsible for the strange goings on in Roz's loft. Jane would meet Kelly later in the evening, but for now, she put her money on Mark Thurman. He seemed the most likely suspect in this game of terror.

Jane heard a buzzer.

"That should be him," said Roz, hurrying nervously to the door. She stood next to it, adjusting and then readjusting her light blue cashmere sweater and gold jewelry.

A minute or so later, Jane heard the elevator clank to a stop. Roz opened the door just in time for Thurman to breeze in. He glanced briefly at her, then turned, glaring at Jane. His TV-anchor smile was noticeably absent.

"What's she doing here?" he asked, removing his gloves and tossing them onto the table near the door.

He looked just like he did on TV, only a bit thinner, and not as tall as Jane had imagined. Dark hair. Slight widow's peak. Well dressed. Dimple in his chin. He'd always reminded her of a Ken doll. Male anchors usually did. She could ask Roz later if he was anatomically correct.

"Thurman, I'd like you to meet Jane Lawless. She's an old friend of mine from college. Kappa Alpha Sigma. I told you about her."

He turned to Jane and nodded. "You're the dyke, right? The one who owns the restaurant?"

It now occurred to Jane that there was another difference between Thurman's anchorman persona and the real thing. His vulnerable sensitivity was also noticeably absent. She smiled at him. "Yes. I guess that's me. Although I prefer the simpler term *pervert*. Don't you?"

"Jane!"

Thurman held up his hand for quiet. He was about to make another pronouncement. "You're prettier than I thought you'd be."

He hadn't come to make peace, Jane was sure of that. Again, she smiled. "What's the world coming to when dykes are pretty and fairies are manly?"

"Hey, what do I know? I'm just a good old boy from Oklahoma."

"Is that what you are?" She held his gaze. She'd rarely met anyone quite this hostile. She knew it wasn't directed at her, but at Roz. And from the look on Roz's face, it had found its target.

Roz held out her hand. "The keys, Thurman."

He eyed Jane, then Roz. "I thought we might have a few minutes to talk."

"We've got nothing to talk about. Just give them to me." Her hand shook slightly.

Slowly, he reached into his pocket and drew them out, dangling them enticingly off the end of his finger.

Jane just knew he wasn't going to give them to her. He was going to toss them somewhere. Drop them on the floor. Pitch them into the kitchen sink. Anything but cooperate.

"You won't even give me five minutes?" He held the keys out like bait.

Roz was on the point of tears. "Don't make this any harder than it already is."

Thurman shot Jane one last disgruntled look and then very gently placed the keys in Roz's outstretched hand. Without another word, he left, closing the door behind him.

So much for Jane's infallible understanding of human nature.

Roz crumpled onto the sofa.

Sensing her friend's need to talk, Jane fortified herself with another sip of coffee and then got up and settled down next to her. "You want to talk about it?" she asked softly.

Roz shook her head.

Jane blinked several times. Strike two. Why did people think she could solve anything? Her people skills were waning by the minute.

"It's my fault," said Roz, beginning to cry. "He's a good man."

"Sure. Good. A little tactless, perhaps. A smidgen homophobic —"

"Oh, he's just hurt because we broke up." She took out a tissue and wiped her nose. "Hey, look at the time! We're supposed to go upstairs to meet Kelly in her loft at nine. She's going to discuss the lease with you and then I'll take you up to see Arno's loft."

Jane finished her coffee.

"Here's the deal. I told her you were a friend. That you owned a house in Minneapolis, but were thinking of selling. You thought you'd take it for the month of December and see if you liked it. She's already agreed. She'll take the month's money and try to rent it out from under you."

"That's all right, Roz. I won't be staying."

"Huh? Oh, right." She stood, rubbing the back of her neck. "My life seems so out-of-control right now. I know you're going to help. You've got to."

"I'll do my best, kiddo. But you've got to remember. I don't work miracles."

"Sure you do," said Roz. "I have it on the best authority."

"Really? Whose?"

"Cordelia Thorn's. When I was uptown this morning I ran into her. She assured me that with her help, we'd get to the bottom of this in no time flat."

"*Her* help?"

Jane wondered if it was really a chorus of angels singing, or merely her blood pressure rising.

5

"Have a seat," muttered Kelly, motioning for Roz and Jane to sit down. "I was sure I had the lease right here." She paged aggressively through a stack of folders on her desk.

Jane's first impression of Kelly Heywood was that she was not in a good mood. She looked to be in her late twenties, with a crew cut, large beaded hoop earrings dangling from pierced ears, and clothing that had most likely been purchased from the local Army Navy surplus store.

The loft itself was the total opposite of Roz's studied elegance. Most of the objects in the place looked used, recycled. Old rugs. Mismatched kitchen chairs. Painted crockery. Junk culled from all corners of the city—but tasteful junk. Lots of bright primary colors. Here and there a new and obviously expensive item was thrown in. Six hand-blown goblets adorned the top of a curio cabinet. Jane had seen them at Dayton's and knew the price. On the kitchen counter, a state-of-the-art food processor rested next to several bottles of Warre's Warrior Port. It was a curious mix, as if Kelly wanted to tell the world she had little money, but she still had rich-kid tastes, and she indulged those tastes whenever possible.

The far end of the room was empty. Kelly had affixed a basketball hoop to the wall and, by the looks of the scuffed floor, tossed a few every now and then. She had to be given credit. The way the haphazard garage-sale furnishings all blended together was nothing short of delightful. Sort of an inner-city third-world village.

As Kelly continued to paw through her folders, Jane's eyes fell to a glass-topped coffee table in front of her. Underneath a jumble of poetry books were several clippings from local newspapers. Jane picked one up. The subject was the death of a gay man in Loring Park. John Merchant had been a lawyer who was gunned down last summer by an unknown assailant as he walked through the park. The police seemed baffled as to a motive.

"It was a hate crime," said Kelly, sitting down cross-legged on the floor next to them.

Jane looked up.

"John Merchant. Somebody blew him away because he was gay."

"Do they know that for sure?" asked Roz. "I think WTWN did a feature on it. Nothing's really known about the motivation." She shivered. "You know, I'd really grown to like him."

Jane was surprised. "You knew him?"

"Yeah. He came to lots of the potlucks Arno had in his apartment."

"Really? Did he live here?"

"No," said Kelly. "I invited him. He was one of my best friends growing up, and we stayed close." She gave Roz a contemptuous look. "And come on. Everyone knows what it means when a gay man is attacked in Loring Park. In the last five years, hate crimes have skyrocketed."

Jane knew what Kelly said was true, and it sickened her. There was so much hate out there, some of it masquerading as political expediency, some even as Christian love.

"Anyway," Kelly grunted, grabbing the pen above her ear, "we should get this signed." She handed it to Jane. "It's fairly standard. You're only committed to one month. In fairness, I have to tell you that I'm going to continue to try to rent the space. The sooner you're able to give me your decision, the better."

Jane took out her wire-rimmed glasses, put them on, and read it over, scribbling her signature at the bottom.

"Here are the keys," said Kelly, flipping them across the table. "If you don't mind, I'll let you check the place out by yourself. It's one floor above us. I'm having kind of a hard time going in there right now. My dad—" Her voice cracked.

Jane watched as Kelly drew her legs up close to her body, her arms hugging her knees. She pressed her lips together tightly, struggling to regain control.

"I was sorry to hear about your father's death," said Jane after several uncomfortable seconds.

"Yeah. Thanks." Her pain turned almost instantly to anger. "But it wasn't a suicide."

Roz blinked. "What?"

With her fists, Kelly rubbed her eyes. Her face had become flushed. "Oh, just drop it."

Roz waited, but when Kelly didn't continue she said, "What an absolutely incredible thing to say. If it wasn't suicide, what was it?"

Kelly's expression grew defiant. "It was murder, Roz."

Roz was clearly stunned. "But he *jumped* from the Foshay Tower. He wasn't pushed."

"That's your opinion."

"It's not an opinion. It's a fact."

With an indignant twist of her head, Kelly said, "Just drop it, okay?"

"But—"

Kelly gave her a hard look.

After a moment of thought, Roz asked, "How did the reading of the will go yesterday morning?"

"Absolutely fabulous."

"You sound upset."

"I am."

"Do you want to talk about it?"

"No."

Roz shot Jane a perplexed glance.

Kelly saw the exchange and became even angrier. "All you wonderful, concerned friends of my father think you know the truth. Well you don't. You're all wrong. Why don't you just come out and say it!"

"Say *what?* What do you mean?" demanded Roz. She was losing patience.

Kelly folded her arms over her chest and glowered.

"Look," said Roz, "if you think someone murdered your dad, you have to go to the police."

"Oh, right. And get my butt kicked out of here? Not on your life."

Jane wondered how she could get kicked out if she owned the building.

"I'll take care of this in my own time and in my own way," said Kelly. Her words were meant to sound ominous, and they did. She ran a hand over her prickly head. "I don't want to talk about it any more. It was a mistake to bring it up."

After a pause during which Kelly got up and walked to the door, Jane and Roz also stood.

Kelly turned to Jane and in her best down-to-business voice, said, "Just a couple of points before you go. Feel free to use any of dad's sheets and towels. Most of his furniture is still up there. You wanted to rent it furnished, right?"

Jane nodded.

"I'll see that she's given the full tour," said Roz.

"It's pretty exciting," said Kelly, "if you like freight elevators. We should probably have a tenants meeting one of these days, but right now, I just can't think about it."

"I understand," said Roz. She made a move to touch Kelly's arm, but pulled back at the last second.

"Say, did you ever find out who that mug belonged to?" asked Kelly, stuffing her hands deep into the pockets of her fatigues. "The one you found in your apartment?"

Roz's expression soured. "No."

"But you haven't had any more problems since you changed the locks, right?"

"Well, actually, I have. I think someone was in my apartment several nights ago—while I was sleeping."

"You're kidding."

"My journal had been moved from the right side of my desk to the left. And," she added, clearing her throat somewhat self-consciously, "it was crooked."

Kelly shook her head. "How any human being could possibly know something like that is beyond me."

"She's extremely neat," offered Jane, pleasantly.

"That's putting it mildly. Does anyone else have a set of the new keys?"

Roz seemed to grow uneasy. "Yeah. A friend."

"Thurman?"

She nodded. "But it's not him. He'd never come into my apartment uninvited."

"Yeah, well, if I were you, I'd get my keys back."

"I already have."

"Good. Then you shouldn't have any more problems. That is, unless he made himself an extra set. If that's the case, I'll tell you right now, I'm not paying for the locks to be changed again. That's your problem. You need to be more careful who you give your keys to."

Roz's mouth set angrily.

"Anyway," said Kelly, turning to Jane without a smile, "Welcome to Linden Lofts. I hope you like it here."

6

"Can you believe what Kelly just said about her father?" Roz trudged up the iron steps to the top floor. She needed to work off some steam.

"Is is possible she's right?" asked Jane.

Roz shook her head. "I can't even begin to imagine what she's thinking of. Arno's death was a suicide. He even left a note behind. What more proof does she need?"

"What about that comment she made about being kicked out of the building," asked Jane. "How can she be kicked out of a building she owns?"

Roz stopped and turned around. "She did say that, didn't she? I don't have a clue. Who else would Arno leave Linden Lofts to but his daughter?"

"What about that woman you mentioned? The one he moved in with?"

Roz considered the issue. "I suppose it's possible. Before the will was read yesterday morning, Kelly talked as if the building was already hers. I guess I assumed Arno had told her he'd left it to her in his will." She gave a perplexed shrug and then continued.

The sixth floor hallway looked just like the others had. Long, lit by bare bulbs attached to the ceiling, a scuffed plank floor underfoot. When Arno Heywood had renovated the top three floors of the Linden Building, he obviously hadn't spent much money or effort on the interior corridors. At the far end of the hall, Jane could see a partially open door. "What's the room down there?" she asked as Roz slid the key into the lock.

Roz looked up. "Oh. That's the laundry. You share it with Peg. You'll like her, Jane, I guarantee it."

Jane saw a shadow fall across the laundry room door. She was pretty sure someone was eavesdropping on their conversation.

Roz moved hesitantly into the loft and flipped the light switch on the wall. When nothing happened, she flipped it again and again, muttering to herself.

Jane stepped in behind her, her eyes drawn to the huge skylight above their heads. The glass-enclosed dome covered at least a third of the ceiling expanse. Cold December moonlight filtered in through the darkness, making the loft seem like a dreamscape, strangely devoid of life. As her vision adjusted to the darkness, her attention was drawn to a glistening spot on the hardwood floor. She bent down to take a closer look.

"There," said Roz, snapping on a lamp next to the couch. "Someone must have been fiddling with the lights in here." She turned around and smiled. "Is this a great space or what?"

Jane stood up. "I feel kind of funny being in here."

"You mean because of Arno. Yeah, me too. But he would have wanted a tenant who could appreciate it."

Jane was almost positive she heard the floor creak just outside in the hallway. Moving soundlessly back to the door, she pulled it open, ready to catch whoever was outside. Much to her relief, the hall was empty and quiet, except for the faintly metallic thud of retreating footsteps on the stairs.

"What are you doing?" asked Roz, switching on the track lighting in the kitchen.

"Nothing. I just thought I heard a noise."

"It might have been Peg. She sometimes goes down to Athena's Garden for dinner. She likes their specials."

Jane sat down in one of the living room chairs, stretching her legs to relieve some of her tension. "I suppose she's pretty upset about Arno's death."

"Yeah. Very. I've hardly seen her since the funeral on Sunday. But I suppose if anyone's equipped to deal with grief, she would be."

"Why do you say that?"

"She's a psychologist. A very sharp woman. She and Arno first met years ago when he was a patient of hers. It was right after his divorce, a pretty terrible time. They hadn't seen each other for almost ten years when they bumped into one another at a grocery store several years ago. I guess Peg mentioned something about being dissatisfied with where she was living. Arno had just purchased the Linden Building, so he suggested she come by and take a look at one of the lofts. One thing led to another, and she moved in. It wasn't long after that that they began dating." Roz perched on the edge of the couch. "You know, I should probably invite Peg down for a drink. I just . . . haven't known what to say."

Jane thought of all the friends who'd left her alone after Christine's death. Later, like Roz, they'd insisted they simply didn't know what to say. Yet to Jane, it hadn't felt like reticence. It felt like abandonment.

"Well," said Roz, changing the subject, "what do you think?" She let her eyes sweep over the room.

Jane liked the eclectic furnishings. Of all the lofts she'd been in, this one felt the most homey. Over-stuffed chairs. Quilts scattered here and there. A state-of-the-art music system. A great library and study that dominated the center of the room. A kitchen appointed with copper pots, well-used pans and intelligent accessories suggesting the person who owned them actually knew how to cook, not just how to shop.

Taken as a piece, Arno had successfully mixed the modern with the old. Each loft said something different about its owner. Jane found herself wondering what kind of man Arno Heywood had been. She knew the public persona, the image he projected on TV, but the private person might be an entirely different matter.

"How come he left so much of his stuff in here?" asked Jane. "I'd think he would have moved it across the hall."

"Peg's place is fully stocked. Even so, if this loft had been rented while he was alive, I'm sure he would have removed a good deal of it."

"He sure liked antiques," said Jane, her eyes drawn to a Chippendale tea table. On top of it sat a gothic-looking shelf clock.

Roz laughed. "His nephew, Eric, is an antique dealer. He lives down-stairs—across from Kelly. If you think this place is something else, wait till you see Eric's loft."

"Arno's daughter lives here. *And* his nephew?"

"Right."

"*And* Arno's girlfriend."

"An inadequate word. Peg's hardly a girl. But since they weren't mar-ried, perhaps it's partially accurate."

"And then you."

"We were good friends. We even co-anchored the six o'clock news for a while."

"Who's the seventh member of the group?"

"Oh, you mean Teddy. Another friend. He's a writer—or a biographer to be more exact. A few years back he published a biography of M.F.K. Fisher. I'm sure it would interest you. He's about the same age as Arno. Early sixties."

"Interesting," said Jane under her breath. "Which one of them do you think was in your apartment? Unless it was Thurman."

Roz's expression sank. "God, I wish I knew. Maybe I'm making too much of this. Do you think I'm overreacting?"

Jane's eyes dropped to the bit of melted slush she'd discovered near the front door. "No. You're not overreacting. I promise you, I'll do my best to get to the bottom of what's happening here." As she said the words, she wondered what she was getting herself into.

Roz nodded. "Thanks. Not being alone helps a lot."

"Well," said Jane, rising and switching off the light next to the couch, "why don't you go back downstairs. I'll be along in a minute. I need to make a brief phone call. That is, if the phone hasn't been disconnected."

"It hasn't," said Roz. "Arno still used his office in here occasionally. And I understand, you want some privacy." She crossed to the door and with a wave over her shoulder, made a quick exit.

Jane shut and bolted the door behind her. She wasn't taking any chances. Walking into the kitchen, she picked up the phone and punched in Cordelia's number.

After a few rings, Cordelia answered, "After the beep, state your message. I may or may not respond, depending on my level of interest. Beep."

"Cordelia, it's me."

"Janey! Hi. What's up?"

"I understand you talked to Roz Barrie this morning. She told you about the problems at her loft."

"She sure did. You're moving in tomorrow, right?"

"That's right."

"And you need a mule to help you with your steamer trunks. I'm flattered, Janey, I truly am. But try United Van Lines. I do not *haul*."

"Actually, I'm just going to bring over a suitcase. I don't need that much."

"I forget how you like to camp out. You're *such* a pioneer."

Jane looked around the stunningly beautiful room. "I'd hardly call this camping out."

35

"Look, it's a *warehouse*, right? Give me some credit. It does have running water, doesn't it?"

"Yes, Cordelia."

"Where are you now?"

"In Arno's loft. The one I'm going to rent for a month."

"When do you want me to come over? Between the two of us, I'm sure we can clean it somehow. You bring the blow torch. I'll bring the sledge-hammer and the Ajax."

"Actually, that's what I called to talk to you about."

"Okay, here's my schedule tomorrow. Mugs is leaving for a conference in New Orleans. I'm taking her to the airport in the morning. I have to be over to the theatre by noon. I should be finished by three. So, any-time after that."

"Great. Meet me here at five. I'll cook you dinner."

"Over a roaring can of Sterno?"

"Cordelia, there's a kitchen."

"Do tell. And for a refrigerator, I bet we have a cute little plastic cooler."

"Do you want to eat or not?"

"Don't get huffy."

"One more thing. Don't take this the wrong way, but . . . bring your gun."

A long pause.

"Cordelia?"

More silence. "Why should I bring my gun? Do we have to *shoot* this dinner before we eat it?"

"No, nothing like that."

"A rodent problem then?"

"The truth is, the longer I'm here, the more certain I am that Roz's loft isn't the only one being cased."

"*Cased!*"

"Or whatever. Someone else has a key to Arno's apartment too, and that someone was in here shortly before Roz and I arrived."

"And how do we know this?" She sounded like an impatient grade-school teacher.

"I found some slush near the front door. When we first walked in it was still melting, but I could make out the grid of a boot."

"Big boot or little boot?"

"I couldn't tell."

"Great. That narrows the field. It could be Thumbelina or Orson Welles."

"I may be wrong, but I'll bet someone's been in every one of these lofts. The only reason Roz knew about her intruder was because she's so neat."

"Hum. Her mother would be proud. But what's the motive? What's this intruder *doing?*"

"I have a feeling we're not going to like the answer to that."

"Maybe it's time to call the police."

"I'm not sure what they could do. At any rate, I'm committed to staying here for one month. And, if only for Roz's peace of mind, I'm going to keep that promise."

"You be careful."

"I will."

A pause. "Janey?"

"What?"

"You know, I haven't wanted to say too much, but you've been kind of . . . down lately."

"Thanks for the vote of confidence."

"But you know what?"

"What?"

"You don't sound down anymore."

"Goodnight, Cordelia. Give Mugs a big kiss from me."

"Not on your life!"

7

"Beryl? Are you dressed?" hollered Jane as she hopped around her bedroom floor pulling on her thick wool socks. "Someone's at the front door."

"I'll get it, dear," called her aunt from downstairs.

Jane opened her dresser drawer and selected her favorite ragg wool sweater, pulling it over her head. It was another cold morning. Temperatures in the teens. Four inches of snow had fallen overnight. Jane decided to do the shoveling before breakfast. Afterward, she'd have to get over to the Lyme House, but not before she and Beryl had shared a cup of tea. One of the perks of being the owner of her own business was that she'd recently been able to hire an assistant manager.

As she bounded down the steps, her dogs trotted out of the kitchen to greet her. She gave them each a good scratch and then went to the closet to get her coat. The sound of laughter drew her attention to the living room.

"Jane, dear," called Beryl, still giggling, "Edgar's brought us a box of lovely cheese Danish."

Edgar Anderson, sporting his usual colorful bow tie and red suspenders over a crisp white shirt, emerged from the room holding a paper sack. "Morning, Jane. Looks like we got buried again last night." He nodded to the pine tree. Its bottom boughs were bent to the ground under the heavy load of snow.

"I'll start the tea," said Beryl moving up beside him and slipping her arm through his.

Jane stared at them, realizing for the very first time that more than mere friendship might be brewing here. Sometimes her thick-headedness appalled her. They were a great-looking couple, both white-haired, plump and hardy. They even shared many of the same interests. Gardening. Bridge. A love of old movies. But perhaps a more telling point was a certain shared loneliness after the death of their mates.

Edgar grinned at Beryl. "I'll help."

"I'm going to shovel first," said Jane, yanking on her jacket. "It won't take me long."

"Take the dogs out with you," suggested Beryl as she strolled into the kitchen. "You know how much they like to play in the fresh snow."

Edgar gave her his best confidential wink.

After finishing the front walk, Jane leaned on her shovel, gazing back at the house. The dogs were leaping about in the deep snow near the sun room, poking their snouts into the fluffy top layer and yipping at each other. A loft might be a nice place to visit, but it would take a lot to make her want to give this up.

As Jane breathed deeply, taking in the barren elms and the bleak, almost white, winter sky, her thoughts turned to another building, Linden Lofts, and to all she'd learned last night. What bothered her most were the comments Kelly Heywood had made about her father. What if she was right? What if he had been murdered? But since there was a suicide note found at the scene, how was that possible? Had someone pushed him from the window? From what she'd read, he'd been alone in the room before he jumped. It didn't make sense. Then again, what if Kelly had been implying that someone had forced him to jump from the Tower in some other way? But how could one person *compel* another to commit suicide? And what, if anything, did Roz's prowler have to do with any of this? Jane couldn't help but wonder if there wasn't some connection. Standing in the bitter cold, it was that thought which made her shiver.

"Janey?" called Beryl from the front door. "You've got a phone call. It sounds urgent."

Jane stuck the shovel into a snow pile and dashed back up the walk. Once inside, she took off her jacket and mittens, stamping the snow off her boots. The dogs trotted in behind her, shaking wet snow all over the Oriental carpet. She herded them into the kitchen where they could snuggle together on their favorite braided rug until they dried off.

Edgar was sitting at the round oak table reading the morning paper. He looked up, smiling pleasantly as she entered. From the bowl on the counter, Jane could see Beryl was about to make scrambled eggs.

She picked up the receiver. "Hi. This is Jane."

"Jane!" came the breathless response. "You've got to come right away."

It was Roz. "What's going on?"

"It's awful. It happened about an hour ago."

"Slow down. What happened?" A voice was speaking loudly in the background. Jane could tell she didn't have Roz's full attention.

"One of the tenants was attacked!"

Jane waited for more details. When none were forthcoming she said, "Roz, talk to me."

"Can you come right now? I have to get off the phone. One of the policemen needs to use it."

"Are you okay?"

"Yes, I'm fine." A pause. "No, I'm not. I'm scared to death."

"I'll be right over."

"You've got keys now so I don't need to buzz you in."

"Right. Just sit tight." She hung up, turning around and finding both her aunt and Edgar staring at her.

"Trouble at Linden Lofts?" asked Beryl.

Jane was glad she'd had a chance to fill her aunt in on some of the details last night. "Yeah. I'm not sure exactly what."

"Why don't you have some tea before you go. You look cold." Without waiting for a response, Beryl poured her a cup.

Jane wrapped her hands gratefully around the steaming mug. "Thanks. Maybe I will."

"Is your friend all right?" asked Edgar, pulling out a chair for her.

Jane sat down. "Yes, I think so, but she sounded pretty shook up. One of the residents was attacked."

Edgar scowled, but said nothing.

Beryl had no such reticence. "Do you think you should be going over there, Jane? I don't like the sound of this."

"My friend Roz just needs some moral support."

Beryl didn't look convinced. She was about to pour another cup of tea when she sagged suddenly against the counter, a hand shooting to her chest.

"Something wrong?" asked Edgar. In a flash, he was by her side.

"I don't know. I just felt weak."

"Come and sit down," he insisted, helping her to a chair.

Jane was a bit shaken by the loss of color in her aunt's face. She took her hand very gently. "Are you sick?"

Beryl shook her head, but closed her eyes. "Don't mind me."

"Of course I mind!" said Jane. "If something's wrong—" She caught Edgar's eye. "Has this happened before?" she asked, sensing from his worried look that it had.

He gave a guarded nod.

"It's just old age," said Beryl, waving off the question.

Jane wasn't going to be put off so easily. "Look, you have to see your doctor. Right away."

"Oh Janey, don't make more of it than it is. I'm fine. Really." The conviction in her voice wasn't overwhelming. "Drink your tea now. You need some warmth inside you before you go out on such a cold day."

Jane wasn't about to let the subject drop. "I want you to call him first thing Monday morning and make an appointment. No arguments."

Beryl's chin raised slightly in protest. But she didn't say no.

Jane found that even more disconcerting. She finished her tea in several quick gulps and then pushed away from the table. "You take good care of her," she said to Edgar, glad for his steady, concerned presence.

"Don't worry. I'll see to it that she rests."

"But we're still attending the mum show at the Como Park Conservatory, Edgar. I insist."

Jane's hands rose to her hips. She knew how much her aunt loved gardening. The only flower or shrub growing in the dead of winter was in a greenhouse. Or a place like the conservatory. "You're incorrigible, you know that?"

"Like my niece?" Beryl looked at her defiantly.

"She has a point," said Edgar with a cautionary nod.

"You're ganging up on me now," said Jane.

Beryl gave her an amused smile and then rose and returned to the counter. She began whipping the eggs in the bowl.

Jane was feeling more conflicted by the minute. "This isn't a good time for me to be away at night. Maybe I should—"

Beryl held up her hand. "I'll be fine, dear. You mustn't change your plans because of me."

"But—"

"It's settled. If I need anything, Edgar's just down the lane."

"Well, I suppose I won't be that far away," added Jane, more for her own peace of mind than Beryl's. "If you start feeling sick —"

"I am not *sick*. And I am not an invalid to be fawned over."

Maybe not now, thought Jane. Yet less than two years ago her aunt had been terribly ill with hepatitis. Jane knew that Beryl would be giving her a much harder time about staying at Linden Lofts if her own ability to remain independent wasn't at issue. This need for independence was a quality Jane admired, and probably shared. But was it possible her aunt's recovery hadn't been as complete as everyone thought? "I'll be back later to pack my suitcase."

"Fine," said Beryl, her back to her niece as she stood at the stove. "We won't be here. We'll be out having fun."

8

When Jane arrived at Linden Lofts, she found a note taped on Roz's front door telling her to come across the hall to Teddy's apartment. Even without the instructions, she couldn't have missed the two policemen standing a few feet away. The door to his loft was wide open and she could hear voices coming from inside.

As she approached, she saw Roz perched stiffly on the arm of an old, dark blue mohair couch. Another officer was sitting next to a man, undoubtedly Teddy, finishing up his statement.

Jane wondered if the police in the hall would try to stop her from entering, but as she passed in front of them, they merely nodded, then resumed their conversation.

Roz jumped to her feet when she saw her. "You made it," she exclaimed. "Thanks for coming."

Both the officer and Teddy looked up.

"This is my friend, Jane Lawless," said Roz. "The one I told you about. She's renting Arno's loft on the sixth floor. I asked her to come—I hope you don't mind." She was talking too fast, obviously nervous.

Teddy touched the top of his head, wincing in pain. "Why not? The more the merrier." His tone oozed sarcasm.

Under the circumstances Jane figured sarcasm was a reasonable response. She could see traces of dried blood just under his hairline. She knew that even minor head wounds bled a lot.

Physically, Teddy was thin, almost frail, with an intellectual bearing heightened by a somewhat sardonic set to his mouth. A small mustache adorned his upper lip. Except for his curly brown hair which was combed straight back and sprinkled liberally with gray, he could have come straight out of a college yearbook, circa 1920.

The furnishings in the loft were sparse, and the way everything was spread around almost haphazardly suggested Teddy might view his living arrangement as merely temporary. The furniture was old, but well cared for. Less than ten feet from the living room couch sat the bed. It faced the windows, giving its occupant maximum view of the river. The apartment's dominant feature was a series of ten tall mahogany bookcases placed back to back, separating the dining room from the study/ living room. Each was stuffed with folders, papers, and of course, books.

"We'll do our best to find out who did this to you, Mr. Anderson," said the officer, rising and placing his hand over his gun.

Anderson? thought Jane. The same as Beryl's new friend. Not that it wasn't a common name in Minnesota. Shake a tree and four of the five people who fell out would be called Johnson, Nelson, Olson or Anderson. If this Teddy was related to Edgar, there wasn't much of a family resemblance.

Teddy coughed deeply several times. "Shouldn't you be looking for the guy? He could be anywhere in the building!"

"Two of my men have already completed a search. We found nothing."

"Nothing!" He covered his face with his hands. It was not the answer he wanted.

Roz rummaged in her purse for a small bottle. "Here," she said, handing him a couple of pills. "These are stronger than the aspirin you were going to take. It should help your headache." She went into the kitchen and returned a second later with a glass of water.

He took them gratefully.

"You might want to have yourself checked out by a doctor," offered the policeman. "You could have a concussion."

"I'll think about it," grunted Teddy.

As Teddy and the officer continued to talk, Roz moved restlessly around the room, her eyes darting in every direction. Pausing behind the couch, she leaned over. When she straightened up, she held a man's leather glove in her right hand.

"What's that?" asked Jane.

Teddy squinted. "Just throw it on my desk. I'll try and find the mate later."

Roz continued to examine it.

She seemed so absorbed, the policeman asked, "Is there something wrong?"

A guilty look crossed her face. "Actually, it, ah . . . belongs to a friend. He's an ex-boyfriend," she said hesitantly.

"How do you know that?" asked the officer.

"I gave it to him. Several months ago. I had his initials stamped at the top." She held it up. "See?"

"What's his name?"

"Mark Thurman."

The policeman eyed Teddy. "I assume you know Mr. Thurman."

He nodded.

"Has he been in your apartment recently?"

"He's *never* been in my apartment," he said indignantly.

"Then how did his glove get in here?"

Good question, thought Jane.

"I have no idea," said Teddy. "Perhaps you should ask him."

"I take it you don't like him," said the officer.

"Look," said Teddy, shifting uncomfortably in his seat, "it's none of my business, but I didn't care for the way he treated Roz on several occasions. End of story."

Roz looked stricken, but was apparently not up for defending either her ex-boyfriend or her questionable taste in men.

"Which occasions would those be?" asked the officer.

"Several potlucks held in one of the other lofts. All the tenants were there. So was Mr. Thurman and a few others."

The patrolman turned to Roz. "Can you tell me where we can locate Mr. Thurman?"

"He, uh . . . he works for WTWN-TV. He co-anchors the ten o'clock news."

The officer screwed up his face in thought, the light of recognition dawning. "Him?"

She gave a resigned shrug.

"Ed," he yelled, "get in here and bag and tag this glove." He waited while one of the other policemen entered. "You can take it out to the squad car when you're done. I'll be along in a sec."

Roz raised a finger. "I've got something I wanted to say before you go."

"What is it?" asked the officer, turning to look at her.

She glanced at Jane for support, then continued, "Whoever attacked Teddy obviously had a key. The door wasn't damaged and the lock wasn't tampered with, at least not that I can tell."

"That's correct," said the officer. He turned to Teddy. "Have you given your key to anyone, Mr. Anderson?"

"Absolutely not," he snapped.

"I'd like to point out," continued Roz, "that my loft was illegally entered recently. You'll find the police report if you care to look. Just like this morning, it was no break-in. The individual *must've* had a key."

The officer adjusted his cap over his sandy hair. "Well then, offhand I'd say you folks got a problem. You might want to call a tenants meeting. Change the locks on all the doors."

Teddy seemed to have lost all patience with him. "Thank you for your professional advice," he said dismissively.

"Before I leave, let me ask one more question." The officer paused. "Do you have any enemies, Mr. Anderson? Or, since it doesn't appear that anything was stolen, can you think of any reason why someone might want to break in here?"

The question seemed to startle Teddy. "I'll give it some thought," he replied evenly. "Now, if you don't mind, I'd like to lie down. I have a splitting headache."

"Sure. If we learn anything new, we'll let you know." Giving Jane and Roz a parting nod, the policeman made a quick exit.

Teddy leaned back in his chair and closed his eyes. He let out a defeated sigh.

Jane was about to suggest that she and Roz should leave too when she heard footsteps in the hall.

"Eric!" said Roz, seeing a blond man appear in the doorway. "Come in. Something terrible has happened."

Eric seemed ill at ease, looking over his shoulder several times before actually stepping into the room. "What are the police doing here?"

"Someone attacked Teddy," said Roz. "He'd just come back from breakfast. I found him out in the hall as I was leaving."

Eric's eyes dropped to the blood on Teddy's white shirt.

Pinching his nose, Teddy sat up a bit. "I ate downstairs as usual. My daily stab at death by ptomaine poisoning. I usually drive over to visit my wife when I'm done, and then go on to work. Today I came back upstairs. I'd forgotten some papers on my desk."

Eric continued to stare. "Did you get a good look at him?" He stood next to the dining room table, slightly behind Teddy, his right hand clasped formally around the wrist of his left.

Jane thought he seemed awfully jumpy. She wondered why? Unless he was the nervous type by nature, there had to be an explanation.

"I'm afraid not," sighed Teddy. "It all happened way too quickly. All I saw was a blur. The next thing I knew I was on the floor."

Eric seemed to mull this over. "That's terrible," he said finally, looking up. His eyes came to rest on Jane.

Roz quickly introduced them, adding, "She's moving into Arno's loft later today."

"Really?" said Eric, somewhat at a loss for words. "I didn't realize Kelly had rented it."

"Eric is Arno's nephew," said Roz. "Kelly's cousin."

"We're just one tight, happy little family around here," agreed Teddy, touching the top of his head gingerly.

"Are you going to be all right?" asked Eric, his wary expression turning to one of concern.

"Fine. I just need to rest."

Eric glanced at Roz and motioned to the door with his eyes.

She got the message. "I guess we'll leave you in peace then. If you need anything, I'll be at work."

"Me too," said Eric.

"And I'll check in on you later," said Roz, patting him on the arm.

As Jane followed them to the door, she turned, taking the opportunity to ask Teddy one last question. "I'm just curious," she said. "Are you any relation to Edgar Anderson?"

Teddy's face stirred with interest. Up until now, he'd barely looked at her. "How do you know Edgar?"

"He's a friend of my aunt's."

"Is that right? Well, it's a small world." He pushed himself out of his chair, swaying as he put a cautious hand to his forehead. "If we're talking about the same man, he's my brother," he said offhandedly. "We aren't close."

That seemed an understatement. If Edgar didn't know his brother lived at Linden Lofts, they couldn't even be in contact.

"Edgar's almost ten years older than me." As he started for his bed, the sardonic expression returned. "I guess you could say I was the baby, the contraceptive failure. Now, if you don't mind, close the door on your way out."

"Sure," she replied. "I hope you feel better soon."

Even before she said the words, she could tell he'd tuned her out. Standing with her hand on the door knob, she watched him remove his suit coat, set his glasses carefully on the nightstand and then sit down on the bed and take off his shoes and socks, balling up the socks and stuffing them inside the toe of the shoes. Next, picking up a can of air freshener, he sprayed the air around his head, and then adjusted his tie and tie tack, making sure everything was perfectly smooth and straight. Finally, he leaned back against several plump pillows and flipped a quilt over himself, pulling it up over his head. Skinny, stick-like feet stuck out from the bottom.

At that moment, Jane knew she was in the presence of a truly eccentric man.

9

It was nearly five-thirty when Cordelia finally knocked on the door to Arno's loft. Jane was already inside preparing dinner. Before she answered it, she turned down the volume on the stereo. She'd been listening to a series of Renaissance motets, some of the most sublime choral music ever written. Somehow, it seemed a perfect match in this cavernous, almost cathedral-like space.

"I know I'm late," muttered Cordelia, bustling into the room carrying a huge pot of yellow mums. "I wanted to stop by the florist first to find something to brighten your —" She stopped dead in her tracks, her eyes transfixed by the loft's interior.

Jane watched, an amused smile on her face.

Reverently, Cordelia took a few steps further inside. "I believe I've died and gone to—" Her eyes rose to the skylight. "—Arno Heywood's loft."

"Pretty great place, huh?" said Jane, taking the pot from her friend's limp arms.

Cordelia was speechless. At least momentarily.

"It's eighty feet long, with fourteen-foot-high ceilings."

"This . . . is theatre!" she announced, still moving hesitantly around the room. "It's utterly grand. Wagnerian. The home for a diva!"

"Meaning you?"

"Of course *me*," she snapped testily. "How many divas do you know?"

Jane walked over and set the mums on a china cupboard, then returned to the kitchen. Cordelia could emote while she finished chopping the eggplant.

"I've finally found home!" gushed Cordelia, twirling around the room in her fake-fur Cossack hat and red cape.

"Mount Olympus?"

"Yes!"

"You forget, you have a home," said Jane, switching on the flame under a saute pan. "It's the top half of a duplex near Powderhorn Park."

"Don't be tedious. You can't *live large* in a duplex." Cordelia leveled her gaze. "How much does this rent for?"

"You'll have to ask Roz. She's paying."

"Well, whatever it is, it's a steal." She ran her hand along the top of a particularly lovely Queen Anne lowboy, spying the stereo. "Why the Catholic mood music?"

"It's Gabrieli."

"Whatever."

"It helps me think."

"You already spend too much time in your head, dearheart. You need to spend more time in your body."

"Like you?"

"You could do worse. I try to use every ounce of sensuality and intellect the great Goddess gave me."

"Good for you."

Cordelia dumped her coat on the arm of a chair and flopped backwards onto the couch, draping her Reubenesque form dramatically over the cushions. "I forget. You're musically challenged."

"Speak English."

"You entirely miss the point of a space like this, Janey. This room positively shrieks for rock & roll. In my next life I'm going to *be* Melissa Etheridge."

"Your next life?"

"The contract says I get nine."

Jane ignored her. "Are you serious about wanting to rent it?" She began dredging several chicken breasts in flour.

Cordelia leapt up and crossed to the dining room table which had already been set with candles, wine glasses and a basket of crusty French bread. "I think I am. Yes."

"You better talk to Kelly, then. She's the manager here. Arno Heywood was her father."

"Ah. I suppose she owns the place now that papa is kaput."

"Show a little respect. And no, I'm not so sure she does." Jane turned the flame on under another saute pan. In the first she added a bit of olive oil. In the second, she tossed in several pats of butter.

"Was Arno married?" asked Cordelia.

"No, divorced. And Kelly is an only child."

Pulling up a stool, Cordelia sat down to watch Jane work her culinary magic. "Not to change the subject, but what are we having?"

Jane began sautéing the chicken breasts in butter. Into the first pan she dumped a handful of sweet red pepper as well as the chopped eggplant. "It's something new I've been working on."

"It's starting to smell awfully good."

After the chicken was nicely browned, Jane removed it to a waiting platter. She deglazed the pan with a splash of brandy, and then added several chopped scallions and a small bowl of dried currents she'd plumped in white wine. She turned up the heat and began reducing the liquid. To the vegetables in the first pan she added a hefty teaspoon of curry powder, some salt and fresh ground pepper, a pinch of sugar, and a fresh tomato she'd seeded and chopped. Once the wine mixture in the second pan had reduced by half, she added heavy cream, several teaspoons of ground coriander seed, and then returned the chicken to the sauce, simmering it until it was reduced to the proper consistency. Finally, she tasted it all for seasoning.

"You're amazing," said Cordelia, pouring herself a glass of the spicy Gewürztraminer Jane had chilling in an ice bucket on the counter.

"Just something simple," she smiled, placing a piece of chicken on each plate, napping it with sauce, and then spooning some of the curried vegetable next to it. She finished off the arrangement with orange slices that had been marinating in Triple Sec.

Cordelia helped carry everything over to the table. Once seated, she asked, "So, since we last talked, have you found out anything new about our neighborhood friend, the Linden Lofts' Prowler?"

Jane adjusted her glasses and took a bite of the curried vegetables. Perfect. "Not really. Except that someone got into another one of the apartments this morning."

"That's a good sign. How did it happen?"

"Well, a man who lives on third floor, his name is Teddy Anderson, had gone out for breakfast and when he got back, someone clobbered him. He must have surprised the guy."

"Anderson? Any relation to Beryl's new beau?"

"Yes," said Jane. "His brother."

Cordelia whistled. "No kidding. Small world."

"Teddy made the same observation. He's a strange man. Sort of from another century."

Cordelia tasted the chicken. "This is fabulous! You've outdone your-self." She waved her fork around for a moment until she'd swallowed and then said, "I think I'll wait until you solve this little conundrum before I make my move to rent the place."

They ate in silence for a few minutes, listening to Gabrieli.

"I don't suppose you've ever met Arno Heywood?" asked Jane finally.

"As part of the true artistic *glitterati* in the Minneapolis-St. Paul scene I know everyone."

"When did you meet?"

Cordelia chewed thoughtfully. "Well, he interviewed me a couple of years ago for his evening show, 'Eye On Minnesota.'"

"And what did you think of him?"

"Actually, we really hit it off. He had a great sense of humor, and quite a flair for the dramatic. You could tell by the kind of questions he asked. Nothing tried and true. Nothing safe. He liked to mix it up."

"I never caught the show," said Jane.

"No, that's because you're too elitist to watch TV."

"I watch lots of TV."

"Like what? The weather report? *Everyone* in Minnesota watches *that* nightly ritual so they can torture each other with freezing drizzle predic-tions and wind chill factors."

Jane took a sip of wine, savoring the flavor. "Did you ever see him in drag?"

"Now, that was a new one." She broke off a chunk of bread and then offered the basket to Jane. "After I read the article on him in the newspa-per, I guess I figured he must be a cross-dresser. He always did like costumes. You remember that show he did back in the early sixties, 'Arno's Fun House'? He played all sorts of parts—both male and female—Johnny Haystack the Farmer, Lori Lee the Milkmaid."

"These were timely characterizations designed to help kids deal with the stresses of the sixties?"

"Exactly. And of course, Arno the Clown. That clown act was what made him famous, at least in Minnesota. It was on Saturday mornings. I'm pretty sure that's how he first broke into television. I can still remem-ber the poem he recited at the end. You want to hear it?"

"No."

"It's about bunnies." She grinned, poking Jane in the ribs.

Cordelia was probably right. She didn't watch much TV.

"And it was *very* educational. Every week Arno the Clown took a new subject and explored it. One time it might be giraffes. You can never learn too much about giraffes, Janey. That kind of information always makes a huge hit at dinner parties. The next week it would be clouds or bugs or whatever."

"'Arno's Fun House.'"

"Catchy, huh?"

"And he was a clown."

"He was a *stitch*. I think the program even won him a Grammy, or an Edsel, or some such thing." She poured more wine.

"You know, maybe this sounds crazy, but Kelly thinks her father's death wasn't a suicide."

Cordelia stopped chewing. "I beg your pardon?"

"I can't explain it. It's just what she said."

A knock on the door interrupted their conversation. Before Jane could get up to answer it, she heard a key slip into the lock. An instant later a woman burst into the room. "What are you doing in here?" she demanded, her eyes blinking furiously. She was wearing a tan full-length coat and holding a leather briefcase.

Slowly, Jane stood. "Who are you?"

"Who are *you!*"

"I'm the new tenant."

"Tenant?" repeated the woman. She regarded Jane from a chilly distance.

"I signed the lease last night."

"Did Kelly do this?"

Jane nodded.

Her anger seemed to deflate, but only slightly. "She didn't say anything to me."

"And you are?" asked Cordelia, standing and rising to her full six-foot height.

Jane could tell her friend had moved into a theatrical persona, most likely the loud and bitchy Martha from *Who's Afraid of Virginia Woolf.* It was a particular favorite.

"I'm Peg Martinsen. I live across the hall. Arno and I were—"

"Of course," said Jane, elated at her good luck. Peg was just the woman she wanted to meet. "Would you like to come in? We're just finishing dinner, but perhaps you'd join us for a glass of wine."

Peg seemed uncertain.

Cordelia seemed positively dumbfounded. She glared at Jane as if she'd lost her mind.

"Please," said Jane. "We'd enjoy the company. My friend here is kind of . . . boring."

Cordelia's eyes opened wide. "I'm . . . *what?*"

Peg cracked a smile. "You two seem like pretty good friends."

"We *were*," said Cordelia, wiping her mouth on a napkin and tossing it over her empty plate.

"Please," said Jane, pulling out a chair. She got out another wine glass.

"Well," said Peg, hesitating. "Sure. Why not. It's been a long day." She took off her coat and made herself comfortable. Underneath, she was wearing floral print from head to toe, a walking advertisement for Laura Ashley. "Wednesdays are always the worst. I have clients all day long."

"I understand you're a psychotherapist," said Jane, studying her new neighbor. Peg Martinsen appeared to be in her late fifties. She had straight dark gold hair which curved gracefully to her jaw line, minimal lipstick covering full lips, and a determined expression.

Peg nodded. "I am. My work is the only thing keeping me sane right now." She adjusted the collar of her dress, looking around the room. "You'll have to forgive me for bursting in like that. I just didn't expect—"

"It's all right," said Jane. "We startled you too."

"You're very kind," said Peg.

"Isn't she *just*," said Cordelia, holding out her glass for more wine.

"It seems strange being in here like this again," continued Peg. "After Arno's death I couldn't bring myself. . . ." She let the sentence trail off. Brightening a bit she asked, "How did you find out about the loft? It's been on the market for quite a while without attracting much interest."

"Roz Barrie down on third floor is an old friend," explained Jane.

"Ah, I see. And so, you're both renting the space?" She looked at Cordelia who was now playing with a piece of bread, turning it into a cartoon character.

Cordelia smiled, holding up her creation. "I'm working on becoming age-appropriate. I'm up to six, maybe seven on a good day."

Jane kicked her under the table. "No. It's just me. I live in south Minneapolis and I'm thinking of moving."

"She's being evicted," said Cordelia with perfect sincerity.

Peg began to laugh. "I'm sorry, but if you told me, I don't remember your names."

"Jane Lawless. I own the Lyme House Restaurant on Lake Harriet."

"No kidding. It's one of my favorites. No wonder it smells so good in here."

"And this is Cordelia Thorn."

With great delicacy, Cordelia set her cartoon creation in the center of her plate and gave a small bow.

"That name is familiar."

Cordelia gave Jane a nasty look. "I'm the *boring* artistic director for the Allen Grimby Repertory Theatre in St. Paul."

"Of course," said Peg. "Arno and I got tickets to a play there just last month." An awkward pause followed as she took out a tissue and wiped her eyes.

"I was very sorry to hear about his death," said Jane.

"Thanks," she sniffed. "It was just so . . . sudden. Nothing I ever expected."

"Roz said the two of you were dating."

"Actually, we'd moved in together. Arno didn't want another marriage, and that was fine with me. But we both felt strongly about commitment."

Jane knew she had no right to interrogate her, but she couldn't help asking the next question. "The first time I talked to Roz, she was sure Kelly would inherit Linden Lofts."

A pained look crossed Peg's face. "I know Kelly thought that."

"But she didn't?"

"Kelly's angry with me, Jane. And with good reason. She was kept in the dark about Arno's new will."

"She didn't inherit, then?"

"No," said Peg. "I'm the new owner."

"I suppose you could still give it to her?" offered Cordelia, only too happy to be helpful.

Once again, Jane kicked her under the table.

"Hey," scowled Cordelia, "I need these legs for a few more years."

"No, she has a point," said Peg, looking down into her glass of wine. "I did consider it, but several days ago I was given some rather upsetting information. Once I have the actual proof, Kelly and I will need to sit down and talk. She's not going to like what I have to say."

"Sounds serious," said Cordelia.

"It is." She didn't elaborate.

Jane decided to see what kind of reaction her next comment would get. "When I talked to Kelly yesterday, she said she was almost certain her father's death wasn't a suicide."

Peg's head snapped up. "What?"

"She thinks he was murdered."

A look of horror crossed her face. "*Murdered?*"

Jane nodded. "Do you think there's anything to it?"

When Peg didn't respond, Cordelia asked, "How could someone be forced to commit suicide?"

"I don't know what she could be thinking." Her brow furrowed in thought. Tentatively she asked, "Who does Kelly think murdered him?"

"She wouldn't say." Jane watched her. "You seem . . . uncertain."

Again, Peg was silent. After a moment she said, "I . . . I'm sorry. This is the last straw in a day filled with last straws. I'm afraid I'm going to have to excuse myself." She rose, picking up her briefcase and coat.

"Of course," said Jane. She accompanied her to the door, surprised and a bit perplexed by Peg's need for such a quick exit.

At the last minute, Peg turned around. "It was nice meeting both of you. I'm sure we'll run into each other again."

"I hope so," said Jane.

"Toodles," chirped Cordelia with a small wave.

After she was gone, Jane closed the door and then leaned against it, shaking her head.

"*Boring*, huh?"

"Oh, come on. I just said that to get her to stay."

"Do tell."

"Knock it off, will you? I wanted to meet her. Get a chance to ask a few questions. *You* certainly didn't have much to say."

"That's because every time I opened my mouth my lower extremities were attacked."

"Oh please."

"And besides, according to you, I would have put everyone to sleep."

Jane took a deep breath, exhaling slowly. "Look, you're the least boring person I know, okay? Surely you know that?"

"May I take that as an apology?"

"You may." She trudged back to the table and sat down, picking up her glass of wine and taking a last sip.

"That woman did it," announced Cordelia.

Jane nearly choked.

"She murdered him."

"Really. And what's the motive?"

"She wanted to own the building."

"Don't you think that's a little too pat?"

"No. Read the newspapers. Greed's still a prime motivator, dearheart, last I checked." Cordelia tapped her temple. "I have a trained eye and I don't miss a trick. Mark my words, that woman's hiding something."

"Where's your empathy? She's obviously in pain."

"Where's yours?" Cordelia rubbed her sore shins.

"I didn't kick you that hard. I just needed to get your attention."

"Yeah? Next time try waving."

"I'll bet I can redeem myself. How about . . . a strong cup of French roast and a raspberry trifle for dessert. Compliments of the Lyme House."

Cordelia harumphed. "You think my forgiveness is that easily bought?"

"Maybe."

She propped her head on her hands and turned a pair of lazy eyes on Jane. "Make the coffee."

10

Teddy Anderson stood in front of a window in his loft and gazed at the downtown Minneapolis skyline. In the distance he could see specks of light glitter along the huge expanse of the new Hennepin Avenue suspension bridge. Beyond were the lights of St. Anthony, where it all began; the stirrings of a small community soon to become one of the largest milling and lumbering towns in the country. Teddy's sense of history was at a pitch right now. So was his rather ironic view of human destiny. He took a drag from his cigarette, exhaling smoke high into the air.

His research on the new book was taking longer than he'd expected. That, coupled with a miserable cough he couldn't seem to shake had left him feeling weak, and at the same time, strangely agitated. He should be working tonight, yet the events of the morning, indeed of the last few years had left him feeling weighed down. Depressed. His life was out of control, and nothing he did to manage the chaos seemed to help. After his son had been sent to prison, his wife had suffered a stroke. There was nothing he could do but watch, dying a little more every day inside. And now, having to keep secrets from her, something he'd never done, was exhausting all his reserves. Even so, he had no other choice. In this matter, for good or ill, he was alone.

A knock broke his concentration. Stubbing out his cigarette on the way through the living room, he stepped up to the door and opened it. "Kelly," he said, unable to hide his dismay. She was the last person he wanted to see.

She stood rigidly outside, fists clenched. "We need to talk."

"Why . . . of course. Would you like to come in?" He said the words with a fake pleasantness he hoped she could read.

"Stuff the niceties."

"I beg your pardon?"

"Oh come on, Teddy. You got what you wanted." She bumped past him into the room and then whirled around. "Why did you do it?"

"Do what?" Where was his lighter? He needed another smoke.

She fixed her fierce eyes on him and said, "You murdered my father."

"I what!" He stared at her, dumbfounded.

"And now you're trying to ruin *my* life. Get me kicked out of here."

Of course, he knew what she meant. But, just as always, she had it upside down. "You left me no choice."

"We had a deal, Teddy!"

"I don't make *deals*."

Her head snapped back as if she'd been slapped. "Then you're not only a murderer," she whispered, "you're a liar."

"Stop it." This was too much.

"Don't order me around."

The hatred he saw reflected in her eyes truly shocked him. He knew he had to calm her down. Get her to understand. "I care about you, Kelly."

"Right. *Uncle* Teddy. Isn't that what Dad always insisted I call you? You know what? You never loved him *or* me. He couldn't see your envy, but I could. You're a bitter old man, but you made a mistake this time. You messed with *me*."

He reached for her hand but she darted around him and retreated back into the hall. Still, he persisted. "I'm not going to allow you to turn this around. You know why I had to talk to your father."

"You only *think* you know. But you don't know shit. You couldn't!"

"Are you calling my bluff?"

Her scowl deepened. "That's right. You're bluffing. You're full of hot air, just like always. But for the love of God, why did you have to go and tell everyone? John! My father! Couldn't you have left it alone? And now you've fed your lies to Peg. Do you hate me that much?"

"Kelly, listen to me." He was pleading now. He knew that when she was like this she was almost beyond reason. He'd seen her destructiveness before. And it scared him.

"I don't need your help. I just need to be left alone! I'm warning you, Teddy. Stay out of my business!" She turned and steamed off down the hall.

"Kelly, stay and talk to me," he shouted, but she'd already disappeared into the stairwell.

He listened to the echoing sound of her shoes slapping against the iron steps. "Damn," he said into the empty hallway. He shut the door behind him, knowing she wouldn't listen to reason tonight anymore than she had weeks ago. As he stood wondering what he should do next, he heard another knock. Preparing himself for Round Two, he opened the door.

This time, instead of an angry young woman, it was Eric Lind, a pair of reading glasses dangling from a silver cord around his neck, who stood before him. "What a relief," he said, releasing his breath.

"You look worse than you did this morning," said Eric in his resonant bass voice. "Can I come in?" He entered and dumped his tall frame into a chair in the living room. He held up a bottle of brandy. "Consider me the Saint Bernard with the keg."

Before sitting down himself, Teddy grabbed two clean glasses from the kitchen counter and handed them over.

Eric lived one flight up. Teddy found him to be good-natured, shy—especially around women—and dull. Then again, Teddy found most people dull. He wished this particular young man would spend a little less time blow-drying his perfect blond hair and more time on his wardrobe. He was nearly always dressed in faded, threadbare jeans and a flannel shirt. Tonight was no exception.

As Eric poured the brandy, Teddy noticed that darkness had finally descended on the city. The only light in the loft, a mellow glow from downtown Minneapolis, streamed in through the vast expanse of windows. The feeling it created was a lot like sitting in a movie theatre. The colors in the room were flattened, washed out. But it seemed like the perfect place to hide. And hiding, right now, was what Teddy wanted.

"So, how are you feeling?" asked Eric, pushing a partially filled glass across the table.

"I'll live."

"Did you ever figure out if anything was stolen?"

"Actually, nothing was missing, at least that I could tell."

"Huh. Weird." He peered over the rim of his glass. "It's too bad you didn't get a good look at the guy."

"I agree. The police thought I might remember something after I had a chance to calm down, but no such luck." He retrieved a pack of cigarettes from his pocket and offered Eric one.

The young man shook his head.

"I don't hold out much hope that they'll figure it out," he continued, lighting up. "They didn't seem all that interested to me. Probably hadn't had their morning donuts yet."

"Don't you think that's kind of a cliche?"

"No." Teddy loathed being accused of lazy, stereotypic thinking, even when it was true. He sipped his brandy. It felt good, the first time he'd relaxed all day. Again, his gaze drifted out the window. His mind wandered so easily these days.

"So," said Eric, stretching his long legs. "How's the book coming?"

Teddy grunted. He knew it was Eric's thin attempt at conversation. "Slow."

"What was the architect's name again? I keep forgetting."

"August Boline."

"Oh, right. I read about him in high school history."

Teddy doubted that. He doubted Eric had read much of anything. Still, he didn't want the young man to leave just yet—or, to be more precise, he didn't want the bottle of brandy to disappear before he'd had another. It was his turn to introduce a subject. "And how's your mother?"

Teddy had known Mabel Lind almost as long as he'd known Arno. As far as he was concerned, they were a brother and sister with little in common. Arno was charming, full of life and humor, and Mabel was, to put it simply, a drudge. Also, Teddy was convinced she saw herself as the family martyr, the kind that made everyone around them pay for their martyrdom services every chance they got. And now, with Eric, she was collecting in spades. Teddy could almost see the tragic Mabel in his mind's eye, sitting in her La-Z-Boy, grieving for her dead husband, and now for her dead brother. A noble soul, she was the embodiment of that insufferably tedious sentimentality Teddy found so utterly repugnant in the American character.

Eric shook his head. "She's not so good."

"No, she wouldn't be."

"Pardon me?"

"Does she still work over at the antique store?"

"Once in a great while. We're having some money problems right now," he said, raking a hand through his hair. "She's been thinking about selling her house, but I told her to wait. You never know. Business could pick up."

"Especially around the holidays."

61

"Yeah."

Teddy took a drag off his cigarette. "I suppose she could get a job."

"No, she's not well enough. Besides, the business belongs to her. If it hadn't been for the car accident, Dad would still be running it."

"And you'd be a free man."

"Well, that's one way to look at it. And now with uncle Arno dead, Mom's in kind of a bad way. She talks about him a lot. Says he always understood. Always cared about people."

Teddy had had about as much crap as he could stand for one day. "Right."

"You okay?" asked Eric, a concerned look on his face. "You seem kind of distant tonight." He pushed the brandy bottle across the table.

Teddy took the opportunity to pour himself several more inches. "I'm fine," he said, taking out his handkerchief. He felt a coughing spasm coming on.

"Have you seen a doctor about that? It doesn't seem to be getting any better."

"It'll pass. It's just stress."

Eric waited a second and then said, "You know, I saw Kelly on the stairs as I was coming down. She didn't look too happy."

Teddy shook his head. "She's not."

"Some problem?"

"It's a long story."

"I got time."

Teddy took a deep drag from his cigarette, considering how much he should say. He was surprised by how upset he felt.

"Come on," said Eric. "What's up? Kelly and I are getting closer all the time. I'm her cousin, for Pete's sake. We *should* be friends. I'd like to think I could help if there's something wrong."

Teddy eyed him wearily and then picked up his drink. "I'm afraid she's making some rather wild accusations."

"About what?"

"Me. If she starts in on it, Eric, do me a favor, take it all with a large grain of salt."

"Can't you be more specific?"

Teddy took off his rimless glasses and rubbed his sore eyes. "Well, I know this sounds crazy, but she's saying I had something to do with

Arno's death."

"Huh? But . . . I mean, did you?"

Teddy held his gaze. "Maybe."

"Teddy!"

He could feel himself losing control. He'd never broken down in front of another human being before, and he wasn't about to now. "I can't tell you any more."

"But—"

"Look, Kelly's entitled to her opinion. I did what I had to do and now I have to live with the consequences." Seeing that this wasn't going to satisfy him, he added, "In case you never noticed, I'm not a nice person."

"Where's all this coming from? I don't understand."

"Kelly called me bitter a few minutes ago. Maybe she's right."

Eric shook his head. "You know, my mother calls bitterness soul poison."

"More platitudes from Mother Mabel?" Even so, the words stung. Teddy batted a tear away from his eye, but the tears wouldn't stop. Why was it that he, the same man who prided himself on his unflappable self-possession, was having so much trouble controlling his emotions tonight? He could blame it on the brandy, but he knew better. It was all getting mixed up in his mind. Arno. Kelly. His son. The book he was working on. And his wife. Always, his wife. Once more, he took out his handkerchief and began to cough, feeling his entire body shake. Oh god, no! thought Teddy. Eric was getting up. He was coming to comfort him. This was too much. "I'm fine," he said, leaping to his feet. "I just need a good night's sleep."

"Are you sure?" asked Eric. He looked stricken, almost guilty.

Teddy wondered what on earth Eric could feel guilty about. Unless, in true liberal fashion, he felt guilty about everything. "I'm fine. Really."

"Should I leave the brandy? Would that help?"

Teddy took hold of his arm firmly and walked him to the door. "Yes. It would."

"You call me if you need anything."

"I will."

They stood for a second, each staring at the other. For the first time, Teddy noticed how sad the young man was tonight. It was so completely out of character, it startled him.

"Arno was your best friend," said Eric, finally, clasping his hand over Teddy's shoulder. "You have a right to be upset."

Teddy clenched his teeth. He hated displays of emotion. "Goodnight, Eric. Don't give me another thought. I'll be right as rain in the morning."

11

"What time does Roz get home?" asked Cordelia as she breezed down the stairs from the raised bedroom loft in Arno's apartment. She was wearing her new black and gold striped satin pajamas and drying her thick auburn curls with a bath towel.

Jane had been finishing up in the kitchen. Before answering, she switched on the dishwasher and dimmed the track lighting. "Around ten. She had a dinner date with some friends."

"But she's going to stay up here tonight, right?"

"That's the plan."

"Splendid," beamed Cordelia, eyeing the accommodations. "I'll take the couch in the living room. Since I'm here first, I think it's only fair I get first dibs. It also has the best view of the stars." Her eyes rose worshipfully to the skylight.

Jane wasn't particularly up for Roz's idea of a slumber party tonight, even though she knew Cordelia was. "You know, there's really no need for you to stay the night. I'm perfectly fine by myself."

"Famous last words. Besides, this will give me a chance to see what loft living is all about. And," she added, her tone pregnant with meaning, "I've brought all the goodies. The popcorn. The gin and tonic. I'm essential, dearheart. You can't toss me out."

"Speaking of what you brought, where'd you put the gun?"

"It's upstairs in the bedroom—in the bottom drawer of the nightstand."

"Good." Jane walked into Arno's study and sat down behind his desk, taking in the antique ambience. Cordelia ambled in a minute later and sat down casually on the edge of the desk, glancing up at the painting behind them on the wall. "Hey, there's Arno the Clown." She pointed.

Jane turned to look. It was an oil portrait of a man wearing a conservative, double-breasted business suit, but the face was done up with white, orange and black greasepaint. No doubt the image was meant to be jarring. And it was. The hair was a snarly yellow mop. And the figure was grinning—almost leering. Jane shook her head. "How long did he play this TV character?"

"Five or six years, I think. I don't remember exactly. Isn't he grotesque?" She said the words as if they were high praise. Moving in a bit closer she added, "You know, this is too weird."

"What do you mean?"

"It's the face."

It seemed like a standard clown face to Jane.

"I don't mean to wax philosophical before my first G&T, but don't you think it's interesting that the only picture of Arno Heywood in this entire loft is one where his real face is obscured? Is he hiding something with that greasepaint, or illuminating it?" She cocked her head and stared. "Hey, I think the frame's crooked." She got up to straighten the painting. As she took hold of the edge, it moved away from the wall revealing a safe. "My stars and garters, will you look at that."

Jane swiveled all the way around and then stood, running her hand along the safe's metal door, feeling as well as seeing the result of someone's attempt to break it open. "See those jimmy marks?"

"Of course I see them!" said Cordelia. "And since I feel confident Arno knew the combination to his own safe, there's only one explanation. Whoever was in here last night before you and Roz arrived, had to be involved in a bit of safe cracking." She glanced suspiciously around the room. "I doubt they were trying to steal Arno's record collection. Unless they were heavily into musical comedy."

Jane gave her a sickly smile. "It only proves my theory. Roz's apartment was not being singled out. This intruder, whoever he or she is, has been in all the lofts."

"Roz will be so comforted."

Jane pushed the portrait back against the wall. As she resumed her position behind the desk, she saw that Cordelia's normal relaxed posture had become ramrod straight. She looked like a soldier about to receive a military honor.

"Turn out the light," ordered Cordelia through clenched teeth.

"What?"

Pushing Jane aside, Cordelia reached over and snapped it off.

"Hey!"

"We're being watched."

"Cordelia, we're six stories above the ground. How—"

Cordelia's eyes shot upward. "The skylight," she hissed, pulling her robe protectively over her cleavage.

Jane looked up.

"Don't!" She grabbed Jane's arm and pulled her out of the chair. Without moving her lips she asked, "What are we going to do?"

"Could you see who it was?"

She gave her head a stiff shake.

Jane had to think fast. "Put your arms around me."

"I beg your pardon?"

Jane moved in close. "Just do it. Touch my hair. Pretend you like me."

Cordelia closed her eyes. "This is the first time in my entire life I've been asked to close my eyes and think of England."

Using Cordelia's body as a shield, Jane kept her head down but allowed her eyes to travel upward. Sure enough, at the very edge of the skylight she could make out a dark form.

"Now what?" said Cordelia, yanking on Jane's hair.

"Jeez, you certainly have a subtle touch."

"So sue me."

"Okay, listen." She put her mouth next to Cordelia's ear and whispered, "I'm going to walk calmly to the other end of the room. There's another door down there. I can get out of the apartment without being seen. Thankfully, that skylight doesn't run the entire length of the room."

"Lucky us. It sits right over the bedroom, you know."

"I'm sure Arno planned it that way."

"Really? He liked the pigeons to watch him snore? Sounds kind of kinky, if you ask me."

"Just zip it. Now, walk over to the stereo and choose some music."

"You're kidding."

"You're not in any danger. Just do it."

Cordelia stood very still. "I think we should both leave."

"You can leave later, if you want. But right now I need your help. You have to keep him entertained."

She narrowed one eye. "Define entertained."

"Nothing sordid. Just distract him. Make him keep his eyes on you while I sneak out."

"And where would you be sneaking out *to*? This isn't smart, Janey. It's time to call the Mounties."

"He'd be gone by the time they got here."

"Good."

"Look, we can analyze this later."

She let out an exasperated squeak. "But what do you want me to *do*?"

"I don't know. Dance around. Pretend you're Ginger Rogers."

"In a bathrobe with wet hair?"

"Mary Martin, then. Just cooperate, will you? You only need to be entertaining for a few minutes."

Cordelia seemed to consider the issue. After a moment she said, "Cole Porter okay?"

Jane backed away from her. "Perfect."

Striking a pose, she swirled in circles through the living room until she reached the record collection. Selecting an album at random, she dropped it on the turntable. "Be careful, *darling*," she cooed, blowing kisses all around.

As Jane slipped out the far door, she could hear the opening strains of *The Music Man*. Not exactly what she'd expected, but not to worry. Cole Porter and Meredith Willson were completely interchangeable. Weren't they? And anyway, she had confidence Cordelia could emote to anything.

Once in the hall, she crossed quietly to the stairs. She had no interest in coming face to face with the voyeur, she just wanted to get a better look. Even though she'd never been on the roof before, it seemed logical, given the floor plan of the building, that this was the only way up. Sure enough, as she approached the top of the steps she could see that the door leading outside had been left ajar. This had to have been his route. She also noticed that there was no padlock. Anyone who gained entrance to the top three floors was free to explore the roof.

Jane decided then and there to go buy a padlock before turning in for the night. There was an all-night superette not far away. At least until Kelly noticed it, she'd be the only one with a key.

Cracking the door just enough to see out, she quickly got her bearings. The beginning of the skylight was a good thirty feet away. The other end, where the figure was standing, was protected from view by a low concrete wall. The base of the roof was covered by several inches of new snow which reflected the minimal light better than Jane would have liked.

Still, she decided to chance it.

Crouching down, she crept to the edge of the glass. As she hid behind a vent, she could see Cordelia downstairs in the living room, leaping from chair to chair, lip-synching with such verve she would have made Ethel Merman proud. The whole scene was really pretty funny. Cordelia had outgrown her size eighteen jeans by the time she was a junior in high school. Still, by anyone's standards, she was a knockout. She had a certain presence, a kind of radiant vitality her height and size only accentuated. The black and gold striped pajamas lent a theatrical quality to the performance. It was perfect.

A tiny creak brought Jane instantly back to the moment. She had to be careful. Like the voyeur, she didn't want to get caught, she only wanted to observe. Inching further into the darkness of the vent, she waited. Sooner or later he was going to get tired of Cordelia's one-woman show and decide to take a hike. That's when she'd get her look at him. She pulled the sleeves of her sweater down over her hands, praying it wouldn't take too long.

A few minutes later, she heard boots creak toward her in the snow. Barely breathing, she watched as a man emerged into view. He was small, dirty, wearing stained white overalls and a red and black plaid hunter's jacket. But it was his face that made her blood run cold. If Charles Manson had a twin, this guy was it. Long curly brown hair fell over a narrow face with a pathetically thin, scraggly beard. As he flipped his hair behind his back, Jane could see he had cold eyes and a nervous, almost twitchy manner. He held a smoke in his right hand. From the sweet, acrid smell, she knew it wasn't a cigarette.

How on earth had this sleaze gained entrance to the loft area? Roz had assured her that security was tight. Yet here was living proof it wasn't.

Knowing she'd gotten what she'd come for, she waited until she could no longer hear his footsteps on the metal stairs, and then, still being cautious, she made her own way back downstairs.

"Did you see him?" demanded Cordelia, removing a lamp shade from her head as Jane reentered the apartment.

"Turn that off," she said as she sat down on the couch in the living room. Right now, Robert Preston was more than she could take.

Cordelia snapped off the sound and then looked up at the skylight.

"He's gone," said Jane.

"I can see that."

She massaged her cold hands.

"Well?"

"Well what?"

Cordelia crossed her arms over her chest and glared down at her. "Look, I've been busting my buns for the last fifteen minutes trying to save the precious youth of River City from a bloody pool table. Don't make me drag it out of you. It won't be pretty."

Jane sniffed. She hoped she wasn't going to come down with a cold. "There's no padlock on the door to the roof. I want to go buy one before Roz gets back from dinner."

"All right. But you're not leaving me here alone."

"Fine. Get dressed."

"First things first, Janey. Did you recognize him?"

"No, but I will next time."

"What do you mean, *next time?*"

"I just have a feeling I'm going to see him again."

"And what do you think he was doing up there?"

"Just what it looked like. Sneaking around to see what he could see. Smoking a little weed."

"Do you think he's our intruder?"

"I don't know."

Cordelia unbuttoned the top button of her pajamas. "All right, I am now going upstairs to get dressed. It will take me, oh, five minutes. Here," she said, grabbing a quilt from one of the chairs and tossing it to Jane. "Your job, should you choose to accept it, is to warm up. You look chilled to the bone." Without another word, she turned and flew up the steps.

Jane was only too glad to oblige. After dinner she'd planned to make a thorough examination of the loft, but now wasn't the time. She didn't have the kind of concentration needed to make the effort. After tonight, every unexplained sound was going to make her jumpy. She'd have to get a grip on her nerves if she was going to be of use to anyone.

It wasn't simply that somebody might be watching her, or the creepy sensation she got when she walked in the halls, the bare light bulbs casting their macabre shadows against the brick and mortar walls. It was less tangible than any of that, though every bit as real. Some presence was moving quietly around this huge old monster of a building looking for— what? An incriminating piece of paper? Money? It could be anything. Was Arno Heywood's suicide tied to this dangerous interior expedition? Was the man on the roof part of it? And was Kelly right? Had her father's death been a murder? Perhaps Arno was privy to some secret. But would he have known what was being sought in every apartment in the building?

As a child, Jane had been intrigued by the deep closets and locked cupboards in her grandparents' home in Dorchester. It was funny, but just recently she'd remembered a tree-covered footpath in Lyme Regis, the town on the southwestern coast of England where she'd grown up. Beside the path ran a high stone wall covered in thick vines. Late one afternoon, while she was playing with a friend, she'd discovered a small wooden door behind some of the vines. She'd become almost obsessed by where it might lead, yet she'd never found out. Even now, she could see it vividly in her mind's eye. Low to the ground. A rounded arch at the top. A child's door, catching and holding fast a child's imagination.

Years later, she'd asked friends and family, but no one knew what she was talking about. It was strange, but for the past few nights, that door, and the secret which lay behind it, had found its way into her dreams. In a way, that image had never left her consciousness. Even though Jane couldn't explain it, she felt this youthful remembrance had formed the basis for all of her adult curiosity. One day, if she ever went back to England, she might find the answer to that childhood secret. But whatever the case, at forty, she felt she was right back where she'd been at age seven.

Tantalized by the unknown.

12

The following Tuesday, Roz stepped out of the WTWN building, tucked her head into the hood of her wool coat, and headed north along Nicollet Avenue. As far as she was concerned, this fifteen minute walk to her loft was one of the perks of living downtown.

A cold blast of night air slashed at her face, ruffling the short hairs sticking out from under her hat. Still, for December in Minneapolis, it wasn't a bad evening. The Christmas lights and decorated shop windows, always a sight to behold this time of year, would light her way to the edge of downtown. Pausing briefly in front of her favorite display—Rudolph and the other reindeer sitting down to supper inside a cozy English country house—she noticed a reflection in the window move up next to her and stop. As a reflex she spun around, finding Thurman standing mere inches away.

"I thought I saw you dash out a few minutes ago," he said. He wasn't smiling, but his voice was friendly.

Roz could feel her shoulders tighten. She hadn't spent the entire day avoiding him just to be nailed this easily outside Daytons. He'd left several messages with her secretary, but she'd tossed them in the trash.

"Come on, Roz. Have a drink with me." He touched her arm.

She pulled it away. "I don't see any point."

"Okay. Then, for auld lang syne."

"Aren't you jumping the seasons?"

"Just give me ten minutes. Let's walk over to Mick's." He nodded, and then gently slipped his arm through hers.

In the festive glow of the decorated street lights, he looked so handsome, and so miserable. Unfortunately, Roz had always been a sucker for handsome and miserable. And his cologne. It pulled her in. Made her remember all the good times. She could feel her resolve crumbling. And what was even worse, she knew he could read her like a book.

"Come on, sweetheart. Just ten minutes."

Mutely, she accompanied him down the street and allowed him to lead her to a table in the bar. It was a large room, made slightly more boisterous tonight by a Christmas happy hour. The waiter arrived and took their drinks order. As Roz glanced around, paying particular attention to the hustling going on at various points in the room, she could feel his eyes on her. It made her skin burn. Why couldn't life be simple? You make an intellectual decision, one you know is for the best, and all your emotions blithely follow suit.

"What are you thinking?" asked Thurman. He leaned away, removing his body to a neutral corner. His gaze, however, was no less direct and probing.

Roz knew he was good at sexual psychology. Better than she was. "Just that a lot of effort goes into . . . finding that certain someone."

He flicked his eyes to the bar and then back again, shifting toward her in his seat. "That's true."

Time out. Their drinks arrived. Roz was glad for the momentary change in mood that it brought. Thurman took out his wallet and dropped some cash on the small round tray. The waiter seemed pleased with his tip as he walked off.

"Should we toast?" asked Thurman.

Roz decided to take the initiative. "Sure. How about . . . to a great Christmas."

"All right." He seemed disappointed. "I had something else in mind, but that'll do."

They clinked glasses, each taking a sip of their Scotch and water.

Thurman stared at her for a moment longer and then said, "I got a call from Fred Unger this morning. Everything's ready for the new show. Even the set's been changed. It will be a lot more upbeat than before. 'Eye On Minnesota' is going to target a much younger audience, which makes our advertisers happy. And since Unger's in charge, management is ecstatic." He took another sip of his drink, a frown forming. "Arno Heywood was a dinosaur in this town. He was too big to touch, but he'd long ago ceased to understand what was relevant."

Roz could feel her stomach sour. She hadn't expected him to talk shop. Perhaps he was more nervous than she'd suspected. "Arno wasn't like *you*, you mean."

"I know you don't believe this, but yes, I think I've got a great deal more to offer the station and this community." His voice held no room for doubt.

She looked down into her drink. "How'd you do it, Thurman? How'd you get Arno to resign?"

"Me? If the old man hadn't resigned, he would have been fired."

"How could you possibly know something like that?"

He started to laugh. "After he showed up dressed like a dowager empress for the last taping, it didn't take a genius to figure he was cracking up."

"He did what?" Surely she'd heard him wrong.

"Sure. He came dressed to the nines. Gray silk blouse. Tasteful navy blue skirt. Pearls. Oh, and let's not forget the nylons and spike heels."

Roz was stunned. "This is a joke, right?"

He held up an innocent hand. "I'm telling the truth."

"But someone would have said something to me."

"No they wouldn't. You were one of his close buddies. People were really embarrassed. But if you'd been standing around the water cooler with the rest of the hired help, you'd have gotten an earful. The guy was a cross-dresser, Roz. A complete weirdo."

Now she was furious. "God, but you're quick to judge. To condemn what you don't understand."

He leveled his gaze. "All I am is a reflection. I'm Middle America incarnate. I know what plays in Peoria and what doesn't."

"You don't have any values of your own?"

"Oh, cut the crap. Of course I do. I think what he did was ridiculous. Dressing up like a woman. It's pathetic."

"That's the crux of it, isn't it, Thurman? Why would a man want to be like a woman—*in any way*."

"Well, I don't want to dress like one."

"But women dress like men all the time. Since men have more power it's reasonable, even logical, for women to want to emulate them. But a man should never try to look or act like a woman. That's going *down* the power ladder—and that's unthinkable. Pathetic, to use your term."

"You're such a card-carrying feminist."

"I never thought you had anything against that."

"I don't," he protested. "You're just . . . missing my point."

"Am I?"

He gave her a disgusted look. "Look, you can intellectualize all you

74

want. All I'm telling you is that Arno Heywood was finished at WTWN."

"You saw to that."

His face went blank. "Excuse me?"

"Ever since you started as anchor, I've felt you were gunning for him. For his job."

"I'm ambitious. Most people don't consider that a liability."

"He was my friend, Thurman!"

"I know that."

"He opened his home to you. You spent many evenings getting to know him, eating his food and swilling his whiskey, all the while plotting his demise. I feel like a traitor, do you know that? Like I'm partially responsible for what happened to him."

"Don't be ridiculous. I never did any such thing."

Suddenly, a thought occurred to her. Under normal circumstances she would have dismissed such an absurd idea, but tonight, she couldn't. "Did you know Arno was a cross-dresser before he appeared at the station dressed as a woman?"

He cracked his knuckles. "What's the difference?"

"You did know! How did you find out?"

A smirk formed. "A little birdy told me."

"Was it something you saw when you were in his loft? Am *I* really responsible for that poor man's demise?"

"You mean his suicide? Come on Roz, he did that all by himself. Nobody pushed."

"Maybe you pushed, Thurman. Maybe we both had a hand in pushing him right out of a job. If what you're telling me is true, his career was finished. No wonder he was depressed. Even suicidal."

"He brought it all on himself."

"But why did he come down to the station in drag? I've worked with him for over fifteen years. He'd never done it before."

Thurman played with his napkin. "I don't know. And to be honest, watching him destroy his career wasn't much fun for me either."

She didn't move. She just sat there, trying to figure out what had happened. "Are you telling me you're completely innocent? You had nothing to do with getting him sacked?"

"No one's completely innocent, Roz. Haven't you ever read your Bible."

He was *so* infuriating. "Answer my question."

"All right. It was a complete surprise to me when they named me his replacement. Cross my heart and hope to die." He finished his drink in one gulp.

"You used me."

His face grew stony. "I never used you. Never. You may not believe me, but I love you, Roz. I want you back. And I'm not going to take no for an answer. We're good together. We make a great team."

"Right. I set 'em up, and you mow 'em down."

"That's not true."

"No?"

His eyes narrowed in anger. "You don't think I saw how it amused you to parade me in front of your female colleagues down at the station? You're almost forty, Roz. I'm twenty-nine. You got a charge out of showing me off." He reached for her hand, his expression softening. "I never minded that. I thought it was kind of cool. You're a sexy woman. I don't give a damn what our birth dates are. We both want it all, Roz, and I'm not ashamed to admit it. That power ladder you're so quick to dismiss— we both want to climb it. I can help you and you can help me."

She pulled her hand away. She knew part of what he was saying was true, and for the first time in her adult life, it sickened her. Had she been kidding herself? Was that what had attracted her to him in the first place?

"I forgive you, Roz." The sadness had returned to his face. "Really. And I even forgive you for planting that glove in Teddy's apartment."

His words stopped her. "What?"

"The police came to see me yesterday. They said Teddy was attacked in his apartment when he came back from breakfast last Wednesday morning. My glove was found at the scene. I guess it was lucky for me I was already at work. I have an air-tight alibi, as they say on TV." He winked, then folded his arms casually over his chest. "You didn't need to do it. There are lots of other ways to get back at me if you're still angry about the fight we had on Thanksgiving."

She was almost speechless. "I never planted that glove."

"Of course you did. How else did it get into his apartment?" His tone was restrained. Patient.

"But I didn't! All I did was identify it." What kind of game was he playing?

"I left my gloves at your apartment the night I gave you back your key."

As she thought about it, she did dimly remember tossing them into the trash in a fit of anger. "But you never said anything."

He crumpled up the napkin and dropped it into his empty glass. "I have more than one pair of gloves, Roz. It slipped my mind."

This was too much. She needed some fresh air. Time to think. "I've got to get home."

"I'll walk you."

She stood, pulling on her coat. "No thanks."

"It's not wise for a woman to walk alone at night." He didn't get up. "If you'd spend a few minutes watching the ten o'clock news, you'd know that. I've never liked the idea of you walking home alone. Those dark streets in the warehouse district aren't safe."

Was this some kind of veiled threat? "It's safer than sitting here with you."

"You're being unreasonable."

"And you're a bastard. My guess is, it's a permanent condition."

Without so much as a backward glance, she snaked her way through the tables and burst through the front door into the cold December night.

13

Peg sat on the couch in her apartment and dictated comments from the day's patient sessions into a small tape recorder. Her secretary would type everything up tomorrow.

Earlier, just after arriving home from her office, Peg had stood at the window in her kitchen, coffee cup in hand, and watched the night redefine the city. She felt completely sapped, but much to her dismay, unable to relax. All she could think to do was more work. Now, several hours later, her eyes wandered aimlessly around the gloomy loft. A Christmas CD droned softly from the stereo. Outside it was beginning to snow.

As she looked down, Arno's white cat, Sebastian, jumped up next to her, crossing his paws and snuggling his nose under her arm. He seemed so confused and upset these last few days, almost as if he knew Arno was gone for good, not just on one of his many vacations. Strange that an animal could know something like that. She'd never had a pet before, so perhaps she was reading too much into his behavior, but he seemed to understand, and to share her grief.

Even though it had been a long day and she knew she should make herself some dinner, she didn't have any appetite. She felt no pleasure in cooking or eating without Arno there to share the meal. And wasn't that what she dreaded most? The loneliness. One towel in the bathroom. One toothbrush. And the silence. After her divorce, she'd lived by herself for many years. But then she'd met Arno. Long after he was no longer a patient, they'd begun dating. He was so much fun, so playful. She was glad she'd been able to help him with his problems.

When they'd first met, Arno had been a mess. After many years of listening to his first wife tell him he was sick and crazy, he desperately needed a non-judgemental ear. Peg had helped him to explore that part of his nature which compelled him to cross dress. They talked about his feelings. His sexuality. His needs as a man. She helped him understand that he wasn't sick, and that simple answers weren't always the best. In philosophy as well as in life, simplicity and brutality were often synonymous. She even went so far as to accompany him to bars when he was dressed as Sharon, his female persona. Before he'd ended his therapy, they'd formed a friendship built on trust and mutual respect. The romantic feelings that bloomed many years later were a natural outgrowth.

Peg's thoughts turned to the nights when she'd come home to find him standing at the stove, cooking a pot of chili, or making his favorite lamb stew. Those had been the best of times. Just doing everyday things together. Having a glass of wine. Laughing. Talking about their day. If only she could've seen what was really happening before it reached critical mass. For God's sake, she was a psychologist! How could she have dismissed the signs?

A soft knock drew her attention to the door. She felt immediately edgy. She dreaded the thought that it might be Kelly. Peg had left a message on her answering machine earlier in the day. She'd asked her to call or come up. They had to talk. But it was nearly ten now and she was tired, not interested in an angry confrontation.

Wearily, she stood and walked to the door. Before opening it, she peeked through the peephole, immensely relieved to see Jane Lawless standing outside. "What a nice surprise," she said, smiling as she pulled the door open.

"Hi," said Jane. "I hope it's not too late."

"Not at all." Peg stood for a moment studying her new neighbor. Jane's appearance was less formal this evening than it had been the other night. Gone was the French braid, blue blazer and gray wool slacks. Instead, her long chestnut hair hung loosely around her shoulders. She was wearing jeans, white high-topped tennis shoes, a ratty red sweatshirt, and holding a laundry basket filled with clothes. Even in the garish corridor light, she was a strikingly handsome woman.

"I'm sorry to bother you," said Jane, resting the wicker basket against her hip, "but can you tell me if there's a key to the laundry room? The door seems to be locked."

"It's not locked," said Peg. "It's just stuck. Give it a good shove and it'll open."

Jane blew a lock of hair away from her forehead. "Thanks."

"A hard day?"

"I'm afraid so. Running a restaurant has its moments."

"I don't doubt it. Would you like to come in for a glass of wine? Let me pay you back for the other evening?"

Jane glanced at the dirty laundry. "Just let me run this down to the washing machine and then I'd love to join you."

"Great. I'll find us something nice." She watched her sprint down the hall. When she was sure Jane had successfully negotiated the laundry room door, she went to the kitchen, took down a bottle of Bardolino, uncorked it, and then selected two wine glasses from the cupboard. She resumed her spot on the couch just as Jane reappeared at her door. "Come in and make yourself comfortable," she called.

"This is really nice of you," said Jane, closing the door behind her and then taking a chair on the other side of a white wicker coffee table. "I'd brought some work home with me and I needed an excuse to ignore it."

Peg laughed. She could tell she was going to like her new neighbor. As she poured the wine, she noticed Jane's scrutinizing gaze, which took in the loft's interior. Peg doubted those bright, blue-violet eyes missed very much. "So," she said, handing her the glass and then leaning back into the couch cushions, "how do you like Linden Lofts?"

"I think what everyone has done with their space is incredible."

"Have you seen all the apartments?"

"All but one."

"Well, they're cold and drafty. You'll notice that eventually, after the arty-ness of it all wears off."

"You don't like it here?" Jane twisted the wine bottle around so she could look at the label.

"Teddy and I are the only dissenters. He can't stand the tricky plumbing. And neither of us like that awful old freight elevator. Oh, and the floors may be strong as steel, but wait till you get a dusting of ceiling plaster in your morning oatmeal. I think we're too old to find it *cool*. You've met Teddy, haven't you?"

"Not under very happy circumstances. It was the morning he was attacked."

Peg couldn't keep the chill out of her voice. "Thank God he's all right."

"Did you know other apartments in the building had been entered as well?"

"Yes, Roz told me, though I find it hard to believe."

"You never noticed anything out of place in here?"

"In *here*? No, of course not." She found the idea ridiculous.

Jane fingered a book on the end table next to her. "I can't help but wonder how safe it is to live at Linden Lofts. You have to admit that having a prowler on the loose is pretty scary."

"If it's true, I agree with you. But you have to admit, Roz is a little high strung. And Teddy, well, that was awful, but I don't think it's proof that someone's been in all the apartments."

"Maybe," said Jane.

"Does that hesitation in your voice mean you won't be staying?"

"I guess it depends on what happens." She set her glass down on the coffee table and then picked up the book, opening it to the title page. "Hey, this is by Teddy Anderson. It's dedicated to his wife."

"Yes, I found it on my bookshelf just last night. I thought I might read it again. It's his only published novel. Other than a few well-received biographies, he's made most of his money as a ghost writer. You're welcome to borrow it."

Jane leafed through the first few pages. "Are you two good friends?"

"Yes, we are. Since I moved here two years ago, he and Arno and I have had a standing date the first and third Friday of every month. We all love the theatre, so we usually took in a play and then we'd go out to dinner."

"He and Arno were pretty close?"

"Good friends. They met in college. Arno was the best man at Teddy's wedding."

The cat jumped down off the couch and padded over to Jane, rubbing up against her legs. "Beautiful cat," she said.

"His name's Sebastian. He was Arno's pride and joy. I guess he's mine now." She sighed. "Really, he should go to Eric, his nephew. He and Teddy took turns coming upstairs to feed and play with him when Arno and I were away on vacation. But Eric is the one who really loves him."

Jane turned and looked over her shoulder. "You have a lot of art work in here."

"The sculpture, you mean." Peg tipped her head back so she could get a better view of the entire room. "It was all done by a young man who rents studio space in the basement."

"I didn't know there was a basement."

"Oh, you'll have to make your way down there eventually. There's a music cabaret on weekends. Kelly takes care of all that. Anyway, since most of his work is so large, he needed a place to store it. And since I admire his talent almost as much as he does, it was a perfect fit."

"Do you mind if I look at them?"

"Not at all." Peg watched as her new neighbor got up and stepped over to an I-beam suspended from the ceiling by ropes. "That's called *Waterfall*. When it moves you hear the tiny rocks in that plexiglass box on top roll over each other. It's very soothing. Like a rippling brook. Kinetic, you know."

"What about this?" asked Jane, standing in the center of a circle of huge boulders. Each had a different symbol carved on the top.

"That's my favorite. It's entitled *Dreamscape*."

After bending down to get a better look at the carvings, Jane turned her attention to several smaller welded-metal pieces.

"He's going to move a new sculpture up here in the next day or so. It's fine with me—I've got lots of room."

"Did Arno like them too?"

She shook her head. "Not as much. I think the main problem was, he didn't like the artist."

"What's his name?" Jane returned to her chair.

"Brandon Vachel."

"I'm not familiar with him. Does he ever show his work at galleries around town?"

"So far, no. It's a disappointment to him. The rejections hurt. It's pretty hard putting your heart and soul into a piece and then having people make condescending remarks like, 'gee, what a cute thing to do with an I-Beam.'"

Jane nearly choked on her wine. "That *is* hard. There's nothing more deadly than faint praise."

"I suspect most creative people live with a good bit of it. It's exactly the same for Kelly."

"She's an artist?" asked Jane.

"No, a poet. Or I should say, an aspiring poet. She's taken a lot of classes. Arno was happy to pay for them, although I think he was always a bit worried she'd spend her whole life dabbling, never really getting anywhere. He often said that being a poet was a good front."

"Ouch."

"Yes, I know. In most cases I would disagree, but Kelly's never really been interested in hard work. She barely made it through school. I think

Arno had reason to be concerned."

"And what about Eric? Are you pretty close to him too?"

She nodded. "He's a fine young man. His father died in a car crash two years ago. Eric was driving. Amazingly, he walked away with nothing but a few scratches. I know he feels intensely guilty that he lived and his father didn't. Under the circumstances, it's not an unusual reaction. I think he'd do anything to make it up to his mother. Sometimes I worry about that, Jane. He's always had a strong desire to please his parents, but when you add a huge load of guilt into the mix, it's potentially very unhealthy. Sometimes he must feel pretty trapped."

"Feeling trapped can make a person desperate."

Peg cocked her head. What did she mean by that?

Jane continued to sip her wine. "And how's everything going with you?"

"You know, I really must apologize for leaving so abruptly the other night. But what you said about Arno being murdered—"

"I didn't mean to upset you. Really." Jane sat forward, a concerned look on her face.

"No, of course not. But while we were talking it hit me how badly I'd hurt Kelly. I simply couldn't stay. You see, it wasn't just that I'd inherited Linden Lofts. It was—" Her voice weakened. She straightened her back and began again. "I was the one Kelly was talking about. She thinks I murdered Arno."

Jane looked shocked. "I don't understand."

"No, I don't suppose you do." Again, her voice weakened.

"Did Kelly tell you she thinks you murdered her father?"

"No, she didn't have to. She blames me because . . . I should have seen it coming."

"Because you're a psychologist?"

Peg closed her eyes and looked down. As Arno's one-time therapist and now his lover, she had no right breaking a confidence. "In a manner of speaking, yes. I should have acted to prevent it."

"But you didn't realize."

Peg gave a sad smile. "You're a kind woman. No. I didn't. I was so caught up in my own happiness, I didn't fully grasp his pain. I thought it was simply stress from his job."

"I think you're being too hard on yourself."

"Maybe." She said the word with little conviction.

"I was wondering about something," said Jane. Her voice was a bit hesitant. "Just tell me to back off if it's none of my business, but . . . was Kelly cut out of Arno's will completely?"

"No. It's kind of a long story. You see, when Arno and I moved in together, neither of us wanted another marriage. So, to show me this wasn't just an affair—that I was truly the woman he wanted to spend the rest of his life with—Arno willed Linden Lofts to me and made me the executor of the rest of his estate. What it means in real terms is that the rather substantial sum of money Kelly will inherit is going to be administered through me. Arno left specific instructions that in the event of his death, she should not be given any part of her inheritance until she turned thirty-five, and then it would be available only under certain circumstances. I insisted all this wasn't necessary, but he wouldn't listen. He said Kelly would understand. I wasn't so sure, though I thought we'd have time to sort it out."

"But you didn't."

"No," said Peg softly. "I wanted to tell her about the change in the will right away, but Arno kept putting it off. To be honest, he'd been having some problems at work before his suicide. A man named Mark Thurman had replaced him several times on his TV show. I think he felt Mark was gunning for his job. I have no proof, but I believe the station's inaction led directly to his death. At the reading of the will last week, Kelly was furious. I tried to get her to talk to me afterward, but she refused. Needless to say, she made some rather unpleasant comments." Holding up the wine bottle she asked, "Would you like some more?"

"Sure." Jane steadied her glass while Peg poured.

This new neighbor was an easy person to talk to, thought Peg. She hoped they would become friends. "You know, Kelly has always been a difficult kid. When Arno and his wife split, Kelly pretty much sided with him. She hasn't spoken to her mother in years. Arno's been her only parental figure since she was in her early teens. He had one major rule when it came to his daughter. One and only one, but it was inviolate. Kelly knew if she ever broke it, she'd be out of here instantly."

"And?"

Peg took a sip from her glass. "She broke it."

"Did Arno know?"

She nodded. "And now, so do I."

"That sounds ominous."

"It all depends on Kelly."

Jane bent down and retied one of her tennis shoes. As she straightened up she said, "You know, Peg, I was thinking about something else. The newspaper article I read about Arno's suicide said he'd left a note behind."

"That's true." She opened a drawer in the end table next to her and drew out an envelope. "This is it."

"Was it addressed to you?" she asked.

"It wasn't addressed to anyone. The police found it in his purse, the one he had with him that last day." Sensing Jane's interest, she asked, "Would you like to hear it?"

"Oh, it's probably too personal."

"Actually, it isn't. And it's not very informative either. Still, it's exactly what I'd expect of him." She unfolded the note and read,

> *Little bunnies everywhere,*
> *Playing hard without a care,*
> *Hush now and close your eyes,*
> *And dream of green woods in the sky.*
>
> *Until next time, this is Arno the Clown*
> *saying goodbye, God bless, and be the*
> *best little girls and boys you can be.*

As she finished reading, she looked up. "It's how he ended that TV program he did back in the early sixties—'Arno's Fun House.' Every week he'd read the same poem and then sign off with the exact same words. You know," she said, her expression turning pensive, "once in a while he'd refer to Linden Lofts as Arno's Fun House. I hate to say it, but it always struck me as grotesque."

"What do you think the note meant?" asked Jane.

"The only conclusion I can come to is that it was the most comfortable way he knew to say goodbye." As she said the words, she started to cry. She reached over and pulled a tissue out of a box on the end table.

"I'm sorry," said Jane. "This is too painful for you to talk about."

"No, I'm fine," she insisted, dabbing at her eyes.

Jane watched her for a moment and then picked up a framed photo resting next to Teddy's novel.

"That was taken at one of our potlucks," sniffed Peg, wiping her nose.

"I recognize everyone except this guy," said Jane, pointing to a dark haired man with a heavy five o'clock shadow. He was standing on the other side of Eric. The only one wearing a suit and tie.

"That's John Merchant. The lawyer who died last July."

"Did you know him well?" asked Jane.

"Not really, but I liked him." Peg was a bit surprised by Jane's interest in John and the residents of Linden Lofts. It had been her experience that most people liked to talk about themselves, given any chance at all. But since Jane was thinking of moving in, perhaps it was natural curiosity. "You know, this is going to sound totally off the wall, but a few days after John died, Arno told me he thought he knew who'd killed him."

A look of intense interest crossed Jane's face. "Did he give you a name?"

"He made me promise never to tell." She glanced down at the tape recorder on the coffee table. It was voice activated, and from the red light blinking on the side she could see it was still on. She picked it up and turned it off. Placing it on top of her written notes, she took another sip of wine.

"You know, Peg," said Jane very slowly, "A lot of us thought John Merchant's death was a gay-related hate crime."

"Yes, I'd heard that too."

"But Arno didn't agree?"

"No, I don't think he did. Then again, when it came right down to actually telling me who he suspected, he couldn't do it. He said until he had actual proof, he couldn't say more." Peg let her eyes wash over the gloomy apartment. She hated this drafty old tomb. Maybe she should think about moving.

"You look tired," said Jane, setting her empty wine glass on the table. "I think I'd better get going."

It was true. Peg knew she had to get some rest. She had clients all day tomorrow. "It was nice you stopped by. I hope we can do it again sometime soon."

"It's a date."

Peg followed Jane to the door. "It's a good feeling having a neighbor across the hall. One I can count on."

"You can," said Jane. She fished in her pocket for her apartment key and then turned to go.

Peg was surprised when, after a moment, Jane turned back and gave her a hug.

14

The next morning, Jane took time off from her restaurant duties and drove over to the Allen Grimby Repertory Theatre in St. Paul to talk to Cordelia. She hadn't been able to get last night's conversation with Peg out of her mind.

After checking Cordelia's office and finding it empty, Jane took the elevator back down to the main floor and entered the darkened theatre. A single spotlight illuminated center stage. Two softly glowing chandeliers loomed high overhead as she moved quietly down the central aisle, crossing in front of the orchestra pit and trotting up the side steps. There, lying flat on her back on the stage floor, arms and legs outstretched, eyes wide open, was Cordelia.

"You look like a human mandala," said Jane, sitting down on one of the furniture props, a copy of an eighteenth century French settee. It was lumpy and hard and smelled strongly of shellac.

"I'm meditating," came the prickly response.

"I thought maybe you were contemplating the catwalks."

Still recumbent, Cordelia lifted her hand and pointed to the nearest exit. "Run along, now. I'm busy."

"We need to talk."

She let out a long, tortured breath.

"I thought meditation was supposed to put you in a more pleasant mood."

Rigidly, Cordelia raised the upper half of her body to a sitting position. "All morning it's been nothing but phone calls, problems with this, whining about that. I'm an artistic director, for chrissake, not Mother Teresa. I do not do domestic counseling, drug rehabilitation, apartment searches, re-plumb bathrooms, or give household cleaning tips."

"Poor thing. And all you wanted was a little time alone."

"Exactly."

"And I've ruined it."

"Well . . . not entirely," she sniffed, fluffing her hair. "I was getting kind of sick of my mantra so I started reciting Keats. Then I moved on to 'Ash Wednesday.' T.S. Eliot can be pretty depressing, that is, if you can understand him—which I don't always, you know what I mean. So that got me thinking about Anne Sexton. I recited a couple of her poems. But then, when I got to Sylvia Plath, I knew I was moving into a full blown depressive episode. What I did next was going to be of critical importance—the fulcrum, one might say, on which the rest of my day would turn. So—"

"Yes?" prompted Jane.

"I may break into 'Green Eggs and Ham' at any moment. Whatever you've come to say, you better make it quick."

"I can't take this kind of pressure."

"Then let me guess." She leaned back, supporting herself on her arms. "Your visit has something to do with that bastion of historic architecture and human warmth, Linden Lofts. You know, I was perusing a book on loft living just last night."

"Do tell."

"Yup. Some of the decorating was way too artsy fartsy for my taste. I mean, come on. All one guy had in his apartment was a black table and a red tulip."

"Not very comfortable."

"No, but easy to organize. One day, the tulip could be on one end of the table, the next day, the other. Once in a great while, you might grit your teeth and put it in the center, but that would probably be too formal for everyday living."

Jane shook her head.

"I suppose if he was having a really terrible day, he could put the tulip *under* the table." Cordelia's nose wrinkled at the idea.

"I think you gave the world a great gift by not becoming an interior decorator."

"I couldn't agree more. So, what's up?"

Jane stretched her legs. "I got lucky last night."

Cordelia's eyes nearly popped out of her head. "No kidding! Tell me *everything*," she said, rubbing her hands together. "Auntie Cordelia wants to know all the details. Who was she? Do I know her?"

"No, no," said Jane waving her arms in the air for time out. "I didn't mean *that* kind of lucky. I had a long talk with Peg Martinsen."

"Oh. The woman who, thanks to you, believes I'm a complete bore."

"That's the one. Anyway, she gave me some information. The more I think about it, the more important it seems."

"Like what?"

"Well, she said before Arno died, he told her he thought he knew who'd killed John Merchant."

Cordelia scowled. "Do you believe her?"

"I have no reason not to."

"But I thought it was a more or less random hate crime."

"The police haven't established a motive. But just think about it, Cordelia. If Arno knew who the murderer was, then perhaps *he* was murdered too."

"To ensure his silence."

"Exactly."

With some difficulty, Cordelia assumed the lotus position, palms up, posture erect. "All right. Let's say that's true. And you're fairly confident it was a suicide, right? No one pushed him out that window?"

"As much as I can be, yes."

"Then we're still stuck with the same question. How do you *make* a man commit suicide?"

Jane's shoulders sank. "I don't know."

"Think!"

"Well, Peg said Kelly blamed *her* for Arno's death. In other words, she was the murderer Kelly was talking about."

"See, I was right!"

"I don't think so. Even though Peg feels intensely guilty she didn't see it coming, I have a gut instinct that's *not* what Kelly meant the other night. I think she was referring to something far more tangible." Jane sat forward, resting her arms on her knees. "You know, Roz called me this morning. She said that Mark Thurman, her ex-boyfriend, found out—she's not sure how—that Arno was a cross-dresser before he died."

"So?"

"To some people it's a big deal."

Cordelia rolled her eyes. "I think it's time for a deep, cleansing breath."

"No, really, Cordelia. You have to see it from Thurman's point of view. It was a juicy bit of gossip. One he could have used against Arno. Roz was pretty sure the station wouldn't take kindly to that kind of personal information becoming public knowledge."

"Well, for Pete's sake, what was Thurman going to do with his juicy little dish? Slip it into the ten o'clock news as a special bulletin?"

"Maybe."

Inhaling deeply, Cordelia held her breath for a few seconds, and then let it out slowly. "Pish."

"Excuse me?"

"Unless Thurman had some pretty graphic photos—and if he did *I*, by the way, would *love* to see them—all Arno needed to do was deny it. The gossip might generate a few minor headlines, but nobody gets too excited about issues like that any more."

"I think you're wrong."

"Nah. And besides, what's the point? What could Thurman possibly want from Arno?"

"'Eye on Minnesota.' He wanted to be the new host."

"Oh. I suppose that does put a different light on it."

"Roz said Arno was deeply depressed about his job before he died."

"For what reason?"

Jane shrugged. "Thurman. Arno thought he was after his job."

"Lord in heaven, will nothing save us from that man's smarmy heartland banter? It gives me heartburn just thinking about it. And that fake John Boy Walton vulnerability." She shuddered. "If I weren't at one with the universe right now, I'd puke." She re-straightened her back and closed her eyes.

"Thurman also mentioned that Arno showed up on the set for the last taping dressed like a woman."

"Ha!" Cordelia hooted. "What *fabulous* melodrama!"

"He was shown the door."

"Bigots."

"I simply can't fathom why he'd do something like that. And then two days later jump from the Foshay Tower. Roz thinks it's all related. I'm inclined to agree."

"What about John Merchant?"

"What do you mean?"

"Do you think Thurman was the man Arno suspected of murdering John Merchant?"

Jane rubbed the back of her neck. "I don't know."

"What about the Linden Lofts' prowler? Where does he fit in?"

"Well, I've been thinking about that. See, I think whoever's been getting into the apartments has been conducting a search. Since nothing has been stolen, that means something very specific is being sought."

"Evidence having to do with John Merchant's death?"

"I can't prove it, but it seems logical. If Arno knew the truth, he might have left some evidence behind. Some clue."

"A diary?"

"It's possible. Only problem is, I don't think the prowler has been able to find it. After the incident in Teddy Anderson's apartment, I think he's lying low. But he'll be back."

"You keep saying *he*. Do you have someone in mind?"

Jane shook her head. "Not really. But remember all those potlucks Arno had at his place? Roz said he kept his keys on a hook near the front door. Anyone could have lifted them, run over to the hardware store to make a quick copy, and then replaced them without Arno being any the wiser."

"Not great security."

"But everyone in the building was either a relative or his friend. There wasn't any need."

"True."

"And, if I'm right, it means one of four people was responsible."

Cordelia counted the names on the fingers of her right hand. "Arno's daughter Kelly. His nephew, Eric. His best friend, Teddy. His lover, Peg, and then Mark Thurman. That's five, Jane. You can't count. Oh, and what about that sleazeball up on the roof the other night."

Jane shrugged. "I forgot about him. I suppose he is a possibility. But I think we can exclude Peg."

"Hey, don't be so hasty. I told you, that woman is hiding something."

Jane had no doubt that she was hiding a great many things. Taking off her wire-rimmed glasses, she rubbed her forehead. She hadn't slept well since she'd moved to Linden Lofts. "Well, time will tell. Let's move on. Putting aside how someone could be *forced* to commit suicide, we need to deal with a couple of motives here. First, the motive for Arno's death."

"He knew who killed John Merchant."

"For the sake of argument, let's say he did, and that he was right. Therefore, it could easily follow that someone wanted to silence him before he went to the police with his suspicions."

"Okay, but what about Merchant? If it wasn't a bias crime, what's the motive for his death?"

"*That's* the key, Cordelia. Who might have wanted to murder this young, gay lawyer? Who had motive and opportunity? If we find the answer to that, we may have found the Linden Lofts' prowler *and* Arno's killer."

"*You* make it sound simple."

"Hardly."

Cordelia shook out her hands to relax her arms, rested her palms on her knees and touched thumbs to middle fingers. "I'll work on it."

"Good, you do that. In the meantime, I've got to do some digging into John Merchant's life. Find out what he was working on. See if I can shake loose any details about his personal relationships. I called my father before I drove over. I wanted to know if he had any contacts in the law firm where Merchant worked."

"And?"

"He does. A guy named Paul Krause. A senior partner. I thought maybe you and I might just drop in. See what we can find out."

"We?" An eyebrow arched upward.

"That is, if you can tear yourself away from the lotus position long enough for some exploring and a leisurely lunch."

"Are you buying?"

"Of course. You like hot dogs, don't you?"

"I won't even dignify that with a response."

"We'll discuss it in the car."

"I have a meeting at three. And a rehearsal at four."

"Plenty of time."

Cordelia thought it over. "All right, but on one other condition."

"Name it."

She cleared her throat. "Help me get up before my spine becomes permanently fused in this ridiculous position."

"It's true. You're not exactly Siddhartha."

"Don't be cute. I can feel my knees cracking even as we speak."

Jane grinned, slapped her thighs and stood. "I'll call downstairs and get them to send up the fork lift."

15

"This *feels* like a law office," said Cordelia, stepping out of the plush wood-paneled elevator that had just whisked them up to the third floor, the floor on which Paul Krause had his office. Her voice took on a confidential tone. "I can smell the testosterone."

"I think what you're smelling is money," said Jane, walking up to the reception desk. "But don't be too hard on yourself. It's easy to confuse." She cleared her throat, waiting for the woman behind the desk to notice them.

"May I help you?" asked the receptionist.

"I was wondering if Paul Krause was in?"

"Do you have an appointment?"

Jane knew that would be the first hurdle. "No, but he's a good friend of my father's. If he's not terribly busy, I'm sure he'll see me." Her eyes took in the large area behind the receptionist. Private offices flanked the room, but most of the space was open and contained desks and computers, with men and women sitting behind them. It was probably some sort of secretarial pool.

"And your father's name is?"

"Raymond Lawless."

"The defense attorney?" The woman seemed impressed.

"Perry Mason incarnate," smirked Cordelia.

Jane gave her a withering stare.

"Well I'm terribly sorry, Ms.—"

"Lawless," said Jane. "Jane Lawless."

"Of course. But Mr. Krause is in Spokane right now for the holidays. He won't be back until after New Year's. I'd be happy to make an appointment for you when he returns."

"No. That won't be necessary." Bad timing. She'd have to figure some other way of getting the information she needed.

"Is there anyone else who can assist you?" asked the woman, attempting to be helpful.

"Well," said Jane, not sure how she should approach this, "I was interested in talking to anyone who worked with John Merchant."

"I see," said the receptionist, her voice dropping to a more confidential tone. "Is this part of the official police investigation?" For the first time, she really looked at the two women standing before her.

"No. A private inquiry."

"I understand. You work for your father."

Jane and Cordelia exchanged glances.

"Well, let me think. You might want to speak with his secretary. She's been reassigned, but I'm sure she'd be willing to talk to you. Wait just a second and I'll ask her to come out." She pressed several buttons on the intercom. Less than a minute later, a plump red-haired woman approached the desk. She had a pencil stuck over her ear, and was wearing hot pink slacks and a matching hot pink sweater.

Cordelia moved up next to Jane, elbowed her in the ribs and whispered, "Grab your beach blanket, sweetie."

The receptionist rose. "Amy McGee, I'd like you to meet Jane Lawless. She's working on the John Merchant case for her father, Raymond Lawless. You may have heard of him." She gave Amy a knowing nod. "She'd like to speak to you for a few minutes."

Jane could feel her face burn as the young woman's eyes rose to hers. Amy McGee, the strange, somewhat pathetic woman she'd met at Cordelia's *Richard the Third* party, her erstwhile Thanksgiving Day "date," the person she had failed to call and ask for another date, *and* the same individual she had no intention of ever calling or seeing again, stood before her, a bemused look on her face. Amy, of course, knew Jane didn't work for her father. One word and the receptionist's cheerful cooperation would come to a screeching halt.

"Ms. McGee," said Cordelia, picking up the conversational slack before the silence became too obvious, "My name is Cordelia Thorn . . . berg. Thornberg."

"Thorn . . . *berg?*" Amy's eyebrow arched ever so slightly.

"Yeah. You got a problem with that?"

"None," she smiled, looking like the a cat who was about to eat a very large canary. She extended her hand.

Cordelia gritted her teeth, shook it and then wiped it surreptitiously on the back of her cape.

Jane eyed all this with growing dread. "You know, since it's so close to lunch, perhaps you'd like to join us." Surely Amy must know she was in a panic and wanted to get her out of there before she blew their cover.

"You both look awfully familiar," said Amy, peering over her reading glasses. She fingered the top button of her sweater and blinked innocently.

She's enjoying this, thought Jane. She attempted a friendly smile, knowing it wasn't completely convincing. "What do you say? There's a cafeteria on first floor. Lunch is on me."

Cordelia tapped Jane on the shoulder. "I thought we were going to the—"

"Cafeteria downstairs," said Jane through clenched teeth. "The perfect spot for a quick bite."

"All right," said Amy. She slipped her hands casually into the pockets of her slacks. "I suppose I could do that."

Jane felt like a kindergarten teacher. She thanked the receptionist and then crossed to the elevator with Amy following directly behind, Cordelia's morose and snarling form bringing up the reluctant rear.

Once downstairs, they moved speedily through the line, selecting their lunches. They ended up at a table next to a large window on the Fourth Avenue side. Frost ringed the glass, placing a wintery picture frame around the downtown street scene.

"I never thought I'd see you two at my office," said Amy, digging into her macaroni and cheese. "So give. What's the caper?"

Again, Jane and Cordelia exchanged glances.

"It's not a caper," replied Cordelia, peppering her meat loaf. "It's a heist." She leaned closer and whispered, "The water cooler. We figure it's worth millions. You want in?"

Amy blinked.

"Really, it's no big deal," said Jane, picking at her salad. "We just need a little information." Of all the people in the world, Amy was the last person she wanted to run into. Or ask a favor of.

An awkward silence followed while Amy slowly chewed her food. After swallowing she said, "Information, huh?"

"Hey, before we talk shop," said Cordelia, her voice full of fake heartiness, "tell us how've you been. I haven't seen you since Thanksgiving."

Jane realized it was a question she should have asked. She looked down into her coffee, feeling even more ill at ease.

"Okay, I guess," said Amy. "A little lonely, like always. But then, I'm used to that."

Jane couldn't stand the badly-veiled guilt trip. She decided to forego the niceties and forge on. "I understand you were John Merchant's secretary."

"That's me. Amy McGee." She took a sip of milk. "Why are you so interested in him? I know you aren't working for your father, like Iris said." She gave them a wink, suggesting they were all part of some intimate conspiracy.

"No, I'm not," continued Jane. "But I am trying to help out a friend. It's kind of a long story."

"And you don't want to tell me about it because it's none of my bee's wax."

Jane cringed. "Well, I wouldn't put it that way—"

"Absolutely not," agreed Cordelia.

"But it's true," said Amy, wiping her mouth on a paper napkin. Her voice had taken on a certain martyred resignation. "I understand."

"It's nothing personal," said Cordelia, trying to be helpful.

Jane knew that was the whole point. It *wasn't* personal, and Amy wanted it to be. "I do have a few questions," said Jane, crossing her fingers under the table and hoping Amy wouldn't slam the proverbial door in their very real faces.

Amy took another sip of her milk. "I suppose."

"Great. I really appreciate this."

Her smile was all sweetness and light. "Let's just say, you owe me, okay?"

"Sure. Now, how long did you and John work together?"

"About three years."

"Did you know him personally as well as professionally?"

"We talked some, but I never went to his apartment or anything like that. He lived in one of those *Riverplace* condos. I guess you could say we were just work friends."

"I'm curious," said Jane, stabbing a tomato wedge with her fork, "Was he out at work? Did others know he was gay?"

"Well," said Amy, chewing her macaroni thoughtfully, "he didn't wear it on his sleeve, if that's what you mean. But sure, people knew. At last year's Christmas party he brought a guy he was dating." She glanced at Cordelia who was devouring her meat loaf and mashed potatoes. "You have to understand, he was a really good lawyer. Almost everyone liked him. He was given lots of responsibility."

Jane took a photograph out of her pocket. It was a picture taken at one of the potlucks in Arno's loft. She'd removed it from a frame on Arno's desk before she'd left for work. She handed it to Amy. "Do you recognize any of these people?"

Amy put her reading glasses on and examined it. "There's Kelly Heywood. She was one of John's best friends. I think they'd known each other since high school. You know, it's kind of funny, but one afternoon right before he died, we were riding down in the elevator together. Kelly had been to see him earlier in the day. He had this really pained look on his face, so I asked him if anything was wrong. He said, no. Then about a minute later he said he was worried about a friend who was into something illegal. I couldn't help but think he meant Kelly."

"Did he say what it was?" asked Cordelia. She nibbled at the edges of a dinner roll.

"He didn't elaborate."

"Did Kelly come to see him often?" asked Jane.

She shrugged. "No. Not often."

"What about the others in the photo?"

"Well, there's John. He's sitting on a couch next to Mr. Anderson."

Jane was surprised. "How do you know Teddy Anderson?"

"Our law firm is handling the Boline estate."

"What's that?" asked Cordelia, her eyebrow raised, her fork poised in mid-air. "It sounds like a 1940s B movie."

"You've never heard of August Boline?"

"The architect?" replied Cordelia.

"He's only one of the most famous builders in Minnesota history."

"But what does that have to do with Teddy Anderson?" asked Jane.

"He's been commissioned to write the biography. Montgomery, Carlson and Krause are the executors of the estate. They hired him. Before his death, John was the liaison between Mr. Montgomery and Mr. Anderson."

Fascinating, thought Jane. "Did Mr. Anderson come to John's office very often?"

"No. Mostly, John went to where Mr. Anderson was working."

"And where was that?" asked Cordelia.

"The old Boline Mansion on Nicollet Island. It was close to where John lived."

"Sounds suitably atmospheric."

"I beg your pardon?"

"Why does he work there?" asked Jane, ignoring Cordelia.

"Well, as I understand it, when August Boline's grandson died last winter, the house became part of the estate."

"What was his name? The grandson, I mean."

"Richard Crawford. He was in his late sixties. His son, Dick Junior, is his only heir. He's living in Arizona right now, but I hear he intends to move back to Minnesota. Anyway, the son called Mr. Montgomery and asked him to send an appraiser over to the mansion to get an idea of its current value. While the guy was looking around, he discovered tons of Boline's personal papers and business records scattered all over the house. Mostly up in the attic and down in the basement."

"Fascinating," said Jane. "That's when they hired Teddy Anderson."

"Right. After some lengthy consultation with Mr. Montgomery, Dick Junior asked the firm to find someone to do a biography of his great grandfather. He also insisted the papers be left on the premises. I guess he didn't want anything to get lost, or to upset whatever filing system Boline had maintained. So an office was set up in the house. The place is really incredible. I drove by it once because I was so curious. It looks like a castle complete with a turret and a formal garden in the back."

"Have you ever talked to Mr. Anderson?" asked Jane.

"Yes, once."

"What did you think of him?"

"Well?" She twisted her napkin around her index finger. "I guess you could say he's kind of eccentric. Very serious. Even a little pompous. But he came highly recommended."

"Did he and John get along well?" asked Jane. She'd given up on her salad. She wasn't hungry.

Amy scrunched up her face in thought. "I think so. John was always going over to the Boline Mansion to check on his progress."

"You never went with him?"

"I wish." She chewed her macaroni resentfully.

Jane decided to change the subject. "What about the others in the photo. Do you recognize any of them?"

Amy picked it up again. "Sure. I recognize this man. The one with the platinum blond hair." She pointed.

It was Arno's nephew.

"His name is Eric. He came to the office once. I'll never forget it. I thought he and John were going to get into a fist fight. Even though the door was shut and they were trying to keep their voices down, you could tell they were arguing. After Eric had gone, I went into John's office. He was standing next to the desk, wiping off his suit coat and pants. Evidently, Eric had tossed a cup of coffee at him. John was furious. I'm sure, since his clothes were light tan that the coffee stains ruined them." She looked at the picture again. "The only other person I recognize is this guy here." She pointed to Mark Thurman.

Cordelia snorted. "Because he's a TV personality, right?"

Amy looked confused.

"He's the professional Ken doll on the WTWN nightly news."

"Ken doll?"

"Oh, come on, sweetie. You look like you've played with a few Barbie dolls in your day."

"So what if I have?" she countered indignantly. "What's that got to do with the price of tea in China?"

Jane winced. She didn't like being critical, but it was such a nerdy thing to say.

Very patiently, Cordelia explained, "He reads the news for the ten o'clock report on Channel 7. Then G.I. Joe comes on and does the sports."

"Huh?"

"How do you know him?" asked Jane, shaking her head at Cordelia.

Amy finished her macaroni and cheese and then pushed the plate away, drawing her glass of milk in front of her. "I don't know. He just looks familiar." She checked her watch. "Hey, kids, duty calls. I've got to get back upstairs."

Jane tried unsuccessfully to hide her relief. Bottom line was, Amy made her uneasy. It wasn't just that she knew this woman wanted more from their limited relationship than she did. The way she hinted and guilt-tripped drove Jane nuts.

"Maybe you'll call sometime," said Amy, a slight pout forming on her heart-shaped face.

"Sure," said Jane. After she said it, she felt like a complete shit. She had no intention of calling.

"Great," said Amy, her expression brightening. "Maybe we could go to a movie. Or rent one. I could cook you dinner. Just name the night." With an excited look on her face, she got up.

Jane rose too. "Thanks for all your help."

"And it was great seeing you again too, Cordelia."

Cordelia remained seated but gave Amy a little wave. "Likewise, I'm sure."

Jane couldn't help feeling annoyed that Cordelia was so damned amused by the whole situation. The least she could do was keep it to herself.

"And I promise," said Amy, holding a finger to her lips. "I won't tell Iris that you misrepresented yourselves. It might get you in trouble."

Jane didn't have a clue how it could, but she felt it was a reference to the newfound power Amy felt she possessed. It was all so indirect. So icky.

"Later kids," said Amy. She nearly skipped off down the hall, giving them a wink and a grin as she got on the elevator.

"Boy," said Cordelia, after she'd gone. "Have you got yourself a problem."

"Meaning what?"

"Meaning her."

Dejectedly, Jane sat back down. "I know."

"Well, look on the bright side."

"What bright side?"

"It's a new experience. An adventure. Being adored can't be all that bad."

Jane groaned. "It feels awful if it's not what you want . . . if it's not mutual."

"Well, look at it this way. All the women you've ever dated have been pretty normal, healthy adults. This could be interesting."

"I'm not dating her."

"In *her* mind, you are." She paused. "Are you going to call?"

"No."

"I didn't think so."

Jane massaged her temples. "I don't know what possessed me to say I would."

"You're too kind-hearted."

"It wasn't *kind* to lie."

"No, you're probably right."

She sighed deeply, her eyes sinking to Amy's empty milk glass. "If I'm lucky, I won't run into her again."

Cordelia laughed, and then stopped herself. Her expression turned a bit more serious as she said, "I wouldn't bet on it, dearheart. I'm always amazed at what a small town this big city is. And Amy seems like the tenacious type to me."

16

After dropping Cordelia back at the theatre, Jane used her car phone to call the restaurant for messages. As she drove along Minnehaha Parkway, she tapped in her private number and then the security code. A man's voice came on the line.

"Jane, hi. It's Edgar Anderson and it's Friday, about noon. There's a problem. Beryl had another one of her spells this morning. We'd gone out to brunch and then shopping at Southdale. When we got home she nearly collapsed. I don't know why she didn't tell me, but she's had a fever for the last couple of days. So I took her over to Northwestern Hospital. That's where I'm calling from now. I've also left a message at your father's office, and one at your brother's house." A pause. "She's in the emergency room, Jane. They haven't admitted her yet. Her temperature is almost a hundred and four." A longer pause this time. "Can you come over? She wants to see you. I'm going to stay, so I guess we can talk more when you get here." The line clicked.

Jane was momentarily disoriented. How could this have happened? She'd spoken with her aunt just this morning and she'd said she was fine. She also said that she'd made an appointment with her doctor for next week. It was the first open time he had. But if she was feeling ill, why hadn't she said something about it? Jane felt immensely guilty that she hadn't been following her aunt's health more closely. But then, it was so true to form. Beryl had always resisted going to doctors. She waited until the very last minute, when she was too sick or in too much pain to do anything else. This time was no different.

Jane checked her watch. It was nearly two. Making a sharp turn onto Chicago Avenue, she headed straight for the hospital.

When she arrived a few minutes later, she found Edgar and her father sitting together in the waiting room.

"What's happening?" she called as she rushed toward them.

Her father stood. "The doctor's in with her right now." His silver gray mane and strong features were a reassuring presence. He put his arms

103

around her and held her close. "We'll know soon."

"Does she still have the fever?"

Edgar nodded. "And . . . well—"

"And what?" demanded Jane.

Edgar scratched the back of his neck. "In the last couple of days she's turned a funny color. Kind of yellowish. I noticed it first in her eyes. But you know Beryl. She said it was my imagination."

Raymond shook his head. "She's not taking care of herself like she should." He punctuated his statement by sitting down.

Jane gazed around the empty waiting area, feeling powerless and impatient. Her partner of ten years, Christine, had died many years ago in a bed just three floors up. Yet this felt more reminiscent of an earlier time. She remembered vividly the hours spent in a room very much like this one, playing cards with her younger brother, Peter. They were waiting for her father to come and give them word of their mother's condition. Jane recalled looking around, straining to wake herself up. She was positive she was having a bad dream and if she concentrated hard enough, it would all go away. But it hadn't. She was thirteen then, and overnight her world crumbled. It was ironic that in many ways, Beryl had become the mother she'd lost. She cleared her throat, feeling her body tighten in a kind of irrational anger. How could Beryl have let this happen?

A short, dark-haired man in a business suit walked down the hall toward them. Jane recognized him as Dr. Pagliaro, her aunt's internist. He spoke to a nurse briefly and then approached. The look on his face didn't inspire confidence.

"How is she?" asked Edgar, shooting to his feet.

Jane had been thinking so hard about her own feelings, it hadn't even registered how upset Edgar was. She saw now that his face was flushed and his eyes blinked rapidly as he waited for the doctor's response.

Dr. Pagliaro spoke slowly, deliberately, as if to a child. "It's a reoccurrence of the hepatitis."

"How serious is it?" asked Jane's father, also rising.

"We're going to have to do a biopsy of her liver to get a better idea of what's happening. For now, I've ordered some blood work." At their questioning looks he added, "Mainly, I'm interested in the liver function tests. But it's not enough. I'm calling in a liver specialist, Dr. Victoria Ries. She's excellent."

"What does the biopsy entail?" asked Jane.

"It's done with a needle," said the doctor. "It shouldn't take very long. We need to get a piece of liver tissue to examine. In the meantime, I've started her on prednisone again. We've got to get her fever down. The blood tests should tell us more. I'll get the results later tonight, but right now, I'm having her admitted. She should be in her room shortly."

"When will you do the biopsy?" asked Edgar.

"Dr. Ries will do it. And it will be tomorrow morning."

Jane waited for her father or Edgar to ask more questions, but both seem silenced by the information.

"But ... will she be all right?" asked Jane, feeling stupid, but needing the reassurance.

"We'll do everything we can for her," said the doctor kindly, sounding for all the world like Mr. Rogers.

Not the answer she wanted. "But, I mean, it's not so serious that she might . . . die, is it?" She could feel her father's arm slip around her shoulders.

"We'll know more in a few hours. Right now what she needs is rest. I know you all may want to stay and see that she gets settled into her room, but after that, my advice to you is to go home and let her sleep." He looked at Raymond. "I'll call you when I know anything more. I'll be up to see her again this evening."

"I'm staying," said Edgar, his voice firm. "I won't interrupt her rest, I'll just sit by the bed and read. If she needs anything, I'll be there." As if he felt a further explanation was necessary, he added, "I'm retired. I've got lots of time."

Jane knew it was more than that, but said nothing. She also had no intention of leaving.

"Thank you, doctor," said Raymond, extending his hand.

The doctor shook it and then left.

Jane sank into a chair. "I can't believe this is happening. I thought the hepatitis was cured."

"Apparently not," said her father. "I'm sorry, Janey. I know how close the two of you are. We've all come to count on her."

Edgar sat down next to Jane. "I guess all we can do is wait. And pray."

Raymond pulled out his pocket watch. "I know this is terrible timing, but I've got to duck out for a while. I've got a meeting I can't reschedule.

Will you two be okay until I get back?"

Jane nodded. "You go. We'll be fine."

"Peter should be here soon. He was out on assignment when I called the station, but they said he'd be back around three." He hesitated. "And I'll be back up later."

"It's fine, Dad. Really. I'll leave a message with Norman at your office if we hear anything new."

Raymond grabbed his briefcase and top coat. "You give that old windbag my love. Tell her she's too ornery to be sick."

Jane knew her father's gruffness was just a cover, a way of interacting that sounded like the old days—when he and Beryl truly hated each other. Now, it was a mere remnant, a habitual way of speaking that had become infused with great affection.

"Here," said Raymond, handing Edgar a package of peppermint Lifesavers. "I can't get through a day without them. They might help."

Edgar nodded. "Thanks, Ray. See you later."

"Right. Well." Again, he hesitated.

Jane knew he was stalling because he felt guilty for having to leave. She took his hand. "Maybe Peter and Sigrid will be here when you get back."

He held her eyes. "She's going to be fine."

"I know."

"You call me if you need anything."

"I will."

After he was gone, Jane collapsed against the back of her chair, resting her head in her hands. She knew hearty reassurances meant nothing. So did her father.

From the other end of the hall, Jane could hear voices as they approached the waiting area. Two women in heavy winter coats swept past, briefcases in hand. One was Peg Martinsen.

Glancing into the room and seeing Jane, Peg stopped, said a few parting words to the other woman, and then walked over. "What a coincidence," she said, a big smile on her face. "I just left a message for you at your restaurant."

Jane stood to greet her. "You did?"

"I know this makes me sound hopelessly disorganized, but do you remember what I did with my tape recorder last night? Before you came by, I was recording comments from yesterday's patient sessions. I think I left it on while we were talking because, at one point, I remember turning it off. But then what did I do with it?"

Jane shrugged. She did recall seeing a recorder, but beyond that, her memory was a blank. "I'm sorry."

"I'm not usually this forgetful. I came home at lunch just to get it, but for the life of me, I can't think where I put it." She shook her head. "Well, I'm sure it'll turn up eventually."

"I'm sure it will."

Peg unbuttoned her coat. "I wanted you to know that I really enjoyed our talk last night."

"Me too."

"I hope we can do it again soon."

Jane was just about to introduce Edgar when she saw Peg's eyes dart to the clock on the wall.

"Good lord," she exclaimed. "Will you look at the time? I've got to get going. I donate several hours a week at a walk-in crisis center here and I'm already late." She hesitated, then gave Jane a concerned look. "Say, is everything all right with you?"

"It's my aunt. I think it may be a reoccurrence of her hepatitis."

Peg laid a reassuring hand on Jane's arm. "I am sorry. But when you're sick, there's no better place than Northwestern."

"Thanks." Her voice held little conviction.

"If you have a minute, stop by tonight. Let me know how she's doing."

"I will."

After she'd bustled out, Jane saw that Edgar had unwrapped the Lifesavers.

"Would you like one?" he asked, holding them up.

She shook her head.

"Not quite the pill we need to make us feel better, but it was a nice gesture on your father's part."

"Dad's a pretty great guy."

Edgar nodded. "If you ask me, Beryl's got herself a pretty terrific family." He popped one into his mouth. "I wonder how long before they take her up to her room?"

Beryl's newfound friend seemed determined to carry on a conversation. Oh, well, thought Jane. It might get her mind off the boring institutional wallpaper—and the gloom. "I don't know. Sometimes it takes a while." She settled down next to him.

"That doctor seems like a nice enough fella."

"Pagliaro? Yeah, I like him. He's a good doctor."

He sucked on the candy. "Say, while we're on the subject of occupations, how do you feel about mailmen? Retired mailmen, that is."

She turned, catching his drift as well as the twinkle in his eye. "Even more positively."

"Good." He cracked a smile.

"You know," said Jane, "not to change the subject, but I met your brother the other day."

Both eyebrows arched upwards. "Is that right." His good humor seemed to evaporate. "I haven't talked to him for ages."

"He's living in the Linden Building."

"The place you moved to for a few weeks?"

She nodded. "Actually, he was the reason I had to race over there last Saturday morning. Someone attacked him in his apartment."

Edgar looked stricken. "Is he all right?"

"I think so. But he took a bad knock on the head."

"I'm sorry to hear that." He seemed to reflect as he folded an ankle over his knee. "Teddy and I never really got along very well. He was the youngest. I'm nine years older. I guess I'd like to blame the age gap for our distance, but it's more than that. The last time I saw him was the day he asked me to be the best man at his wedding."

Since Peg had already said Arno Heywood had been the best man, Jane felt a *but* coming on.

"But," sighed Edgar, "it didn't work out." He scratched his chin, his face turning wistful. "That was a long time ago. I see his name in the newspaper every now and then. And I have tried to follow his career." He paused, turning to look at her. "You religious, Jane?"

"Not really."

"I'm what they call a lapsed Catholic. So's Teddy, from what I remember."

"Will you get together with him now that you know where he's living."

Edgar sucked on the Lifesaver. "I'd really like that. But I'm not sure he'd even speak to me."

This brotherly rift was sounding worse by the minute. "From what I hear," she continued, "Teddy's pretty busy right now. He's been commissioned to write a biography of August Boline."

Edgar's head popped up, a startled look on his face.

"Something wrong?"

"You mean the architect?"

She nodded. "You seem surprised."

"I am."

"Why?"

"Oh—" He face took on a faraway look. After a long moment he said, "Well, I guess Teddy always did like architecture."

For the first time since she'd known Edgar, she felt he wasn't being entirely open.

Catching Jane's eye, he added, "It's a long story. Sometime maybe I'll tell you about it."

Jane wasn't sure what to make of his reticence.

"Excuse me," said a nurse, popping her head around the corner. "If you're waiting for Beryl Cornelius, she's up in the room now."

Jane was instantly jolted back to the moment. "Great," she said getting up. "Do you know the room number?"

"4215. Take the north elevators just outside the door here."

"How's she doing?" asked Edgar, leaning forward in his chair.

"She's resting."

"Thanks," said Jane. "We're on our way."

17

By the time Jane got home from the hospital that night, it was almost ten. Beryl was resting comfortably after an endless stream of early evening visitors. Cordelia had come. So had the rest of the family. And Beryl's best friend, Evelyn Bratrude had arrived bearing a huge red poinsettia and a promise to take good care of the dogs until either Jane or Beryl returned home. By the end of the evening, the private hospital room looked like a florist's shop.

Through it all, Beryl had remained alert and amused. Her good humor and quiet English charm appeared to have completely won over the nursing staff. Nevertheless, Jane couldn't miss the tension in her aunt's face. Edgar had been right. Her skin had taken on a yellowish cast. Beryl was putting up a brave front, but she was worried, no doubt about that. Edgar had sat by Beryl's side all evening, holding her hand. They spoke to each other now in a kind of shorthand, as if they'd known each other for years. As Jane said goodnight, she assured her aunt she'd be back first thing in the morning, before the biopsy.

Tossing her coat over the couch in Arno's loft, Jane trudged into the kitchen and opened the refrigerator door. Except for several gallons of coffee, she hadn't eaten a thing since the rabbit food she'd pretty much rejected at lunch. Unfortunately, the pickings were slim. Unless she was in the mood for capers, wilted lettuce and skim milk, she was out of luck. On the way to the elevator, Jane had passed through the Greek restaurant downstairs. The smell of garlic and lemon made her realize just how empty and in need of nourishment she really was. Yet she didn't want to eat alone. Not tonight. Cordelia had gone back to the theatre. She wanted to catch the second act of the evening's performance. And Roz was working late at the station. What potential company did that leave close at hand? Jane's thoughts turned immediately to Peg Martinsen. Sure. She'd even said to stop by.

Returning to the hall, she knocked on Peg's door.

No answer.

She waited a few seconds and then knocked a bit harder.

This time, the door creaked inward several inches. It obviously hadn't been shut all the way. That was odd.

She called Peg's name, but when she still got no response, she kicked the door in and stood back. The interior was quiet and dark. It didn't take a rocket scientist to figure something was wrong. She doubted Peg had forgotten to lock her door, so what was up? Jane stood there a moment longer, trying to decide whether to go in herself, or wait and let the police do it. Waiting was the safest bet, but what if Peg was hurt? She might be jumping to a rather wild conclusion, but the intruder, if that's who was behind this, had already attacked one person in the building. If Peg had surprised someone in her apartment when she got home from work, and if she'd managed to get a good look at him, there was no telling what might have happened. That thought alone was enough to galvanize Jane into action.

She stepped resolutely into the darkness and felt along the side wall until she found the light switch. Flipping it on, she gasped as her eyes took in the carnage. It looked as if a bomb had gone off. Drawers were pulled out and dumped on the floor. Couch cushions were ripped apart, revealing the white foam interior. In the kitchen, dishes were smashed on the tile floor, the cupboards swept bare. The oriental screens which separated the bedroom from the living room were knocked flat, the yellow silk covering torn away from the wood. Nothing was where it should be. Nothing, that is, except for Brandon Vachel's sculptures. They remained completely intact and in place, eerily untouched in a room turned upside down and inside out. The track lighting shining down on them set them apart, infused them with a kind of electric presence that made Jane's blood run cold.

For what seemed like an eternity she stood staring at the destruction, unable to exorcise an almost palpable feeling of death floating through the room. The thought finally penetrated that Peg was nowhere in sight. Maybe she'd gotten lucky. She was safe somewhere, having a quiet dinner with friends, or out doing some Christmas shopping. Jane hoped beyond hope that her inner sense was wrong. Wading slowly into the mess, she began her search.

After an examination of the living room, Jane stepped over to the huge I-beam sculpture, the one attached by heavy ropes to the ceiling. On top was a plexiglass box filled with stones. Just last night Peg had said that when the beam moved back and forth, the rocks made a soothing sound. Tonight, however, its use had been anything but peaceful.

Jane bent down and touched the collar of Peg's flowered dress. Her head had been horribly battered in by the end of the beam. It wasn't the kind of wound a human being could recover from. Blood, sticky and dark, was everywhere. If Jane had to guess, she would have said Peg must have been standing with her back to the intruder, looking out the window. Did that mean she knew him? Surely she wouldn't turn her back on someone she didn't trust. And the floors squeaked entirely too much for anyone to sneak up on her. Whatever the case, a huge steel girder had been sent crashing into the back of her head. Her forehead had also been crushed. Jane looked up and saw a crack much like a spider web in the thick window glass. She checked the side of Peg's neck for a pulse, but it was useless. Whoever she'd invited into her apartment, whoever she'd made the mistake of trusting as she gazed down on the night skyline, had brutally murdered her.

As Jane stood up, she slumped heavily against the window, feeling utterly sick and hollow. If only she could have prevented this. That kind of empty wish had little meaning to Peg now.

As she was about to head back to her apartment to call 911, a tiny noise startled her. Why hadn't she considered that the murderer might still be in the loft!

Adrenaline fired through her system as her eyes darted furiously in every direction. But before she could react, she heard a scratching sound coming from several pillows next to the bed. Suddenly, a cat leapt acrobatically up on the I-Beam.

"Sebastian," she whispered, releasing the breath she hadn't realized she was holding. He arched his back and hissed as she approached.

She spoke softly, reassuringly. "You poor baby. You must have been here when it happened." She held her hand next to his face and allowed him to touch her fingers with his nose. As he butted her arm playfully, she picked him up, running her hand gently over his fur to make sure he was all right.

He mewed his high, frightened response.

"Don't worry, you're going to be fine. I'll take you back to Arno's loft. You'll like that." She stroked his fur and cuddled him next to her as she beat a hasty retreat. She couldn't be sure the murderer wasn't still around somewhere.

As she entered her own apartment, Sebastian seemed to recognize the place and immediately took off for points unknown. Locking and bolting the door behind her, Jane switched on Arno's desk lamp and sat down, punching in 911.

A woman's voice answered. "State your name and your location."

Jane gave the information. Then she said, "There's been an accident." That was wrong. She quickly amended her statement. "No, I mean . . . a murder. Peg Martinsen. Apartment 6B. I'm the next door neighbor. I just went in and found her."

"You say it was a murder?"

"Yes."

A pause. "We're sending a team of paramedics and a squad car right away. Are you sure this woman is dead? Did you check for vital signs?"

"I'm sure," said Jane.

"How do you know it was a murder?"

Jane couldn't bring herself to describe the scene. "When the police get here, they can decide for themselves."

"Are you in any danger?"

She looked up at the door. "I don't know."

"Just sit tight," said the woman. "We'll have an officer there shortly. Are you all right? Have you been hurt in any way?"

"No, I'm not hurt." She had nothing more to say.

She dropped the phone back on the hook and then leaned forward, head resting on her hands, her face wet and knotted with tears.

18

An hour later, after giving a full account to the police, Jane sat in a dark corner of the Greek restaurant downstairs staring into her third glass of retsina.

"Don't take this personally, Jane, but you look like road kill." Roz approached the table, her cheeks flushed from the cold night air. "I really mean it. You look terrible."

"Thanks."

Unbuttoning her coat, she said, "Drinking alone, are we? I've never seen you do that, not even in college."

"That's because I was alone, Roz. Get it?" She didn't smile. It took too much effort.

"Are you going to bite if I join you?"

Jane pulled out an empty chair.

Roz hesitated, but then sat down. "Bad day?"

"You could say that."

"Couldn't have been worse than mine. Thurman followed me around most of the morning. He just doesn't know when to give up." She glanced back over her shoulder as two policeman entered. "Say, what's going on anyway? How come all those squad cars are outside?"

Even though she wasn't up for another lengthy explanation, Roz needed to be told. Better to hear it from a friend. "It's Peg."

Roz's expression turned serious. "What happened?"

"She was attacked in her apartment earlier this evening."

Roz nearly jumped out of her chair. "Is she all right?"

"I'm afraid not."

"What are you saying?"

There was no easy way to say it, thought Jane. "She's dead, Roz. I'm sorry."

"But—" Her eyes bounced around the room. "I just talked to her a few hours ago. She'd rented a movie and was going to stay in and have a quiet evening."

"Alone?"

"How should I know!"

Once again, Jane's eyes fell to her wine glass. The semi-mellow state she'd achieved before Roz's arrival was beginning to wear thin. "She didn't say anything about inviting someone to watch it with her?"

"God, I don't think so." Roz wiped tears away from her eyes with the back of her hand. "This is . . . insane."

"I know."

She stared straight ahead, unwilling or unable to move. After a long pause she said, "You know, the doorbell rang while we were talking. That's when she said she had to go. We made a date for brunch on Sunday and then she said goodbye."

They looked at each other, both realizing the implications.

"Do you think—" Roz let the end of her sentence trail off. "Tell me everything you know about tonight, Jane. I need to hear it. Don't leave anything out." She grabbed several tissues from her purse, readying herself for the ordeal.

Jane took another sip of wine to fortify herself, and then repeated what she'd just told the police.

When she was done, Roz blew her nose, leaned forward in her chair and said, "This is a nightmare."

"I agree."

Neither said anything for several minutes.

Finally Roz asked, "Do you think it's all connected? The apartments being cased? Arno's death? Teddy being attacked?"

"Without a doubt."

"So what are we going to do?"

"Maybe we won't have to *do* anything. The police will figure it out for us."

Hesitantly, she asked, "Are you going to move out now?"

"I don't know."

"You're probably too scared to stay. I don't blame you. It sure makes me wonder what the hell I'm doing."

Jane felt immensely weary. She dropped her head in her hands and said, "I really liked Peg. I feel . . . responsible for her death."

"Why?"

She pushed the wine glass away. "If I'd had a better sense of what was going on, maybe I could have prevented it."

"I'm sorry I got you into this, Jane. I really am."

"Don't be." She motioned to the waitress for another glass of retsina. It was a mistake having four drinks after eating virtually nothing all day, but she consoled herself by remembering it wouldn't be the last mistake she'd ever make. "You know, I could be wrong, but I think I know the key that ties everything together."

"What's that?" asked Roz, making little circles on the oil cloth with her finger.

"The murder of John Merchant."

She fixed Jane with a hard stare. "Meaning?"

"Arno thought he knew who murdered Merchant. I had a long talk with Peg last night. He told her that a couple of months before he committed suicide."

The waitress arrived with Jane's drink, placing it in front of her. Before she left, she turned to Roz. "Would you like something?"

"No thanks." Roz waved her away. "Who did he suspect?"

"He wouldn't say because he didn't have any proof."

"I can't believe he wouldn't confide in Peg."

"She says he didn't."

"And you think *that's* the motivation behind Arno and Peg's deaths!"

"I do. Someone wanted to silence them. You know, I ran into Peg this afternoon. She asked if I remembered what she'd done with her tape recorder last night. Apparently she'd come back home to to get it this morning and it was nowhere in sight. It accidentally recorded most of our conversation. As I thought about it, I realized she'd switched it off just as she was telling me about Arno's suspicions. And now today, it's missing."

Roz tapped a finger against her chin. "What do you think it means?"

"I wouldn't be at all surprised to find that our prowler entered her apartment shortly after she left for work this morning, listened to the tape, and thought she knew more than she really did."

"How awful! Did you mention any of this to the police?"

Jane shrugged. "Sure. Everything."

Roz sat back and crossed her arms over her chest. "Do they think your ideas have any merit?"

"I don't know," she said, looking up as Kelly Heywood entered through the front door. She was accompanied by two skinny, bald young men, both carrying guitar cases. Jane watched as they made their way to the elevator.

Roz glanced around to see what Jane was staring at. "They must be on their way down to the cabaret in the basement."

"Right. I knew there was a music stage down there. What's the name?" she asked, sipping her wine.

"TownDown Jam. It's really popular. Live acts perform from ten to one. It's usually only on weekends, but before Christmas, Kelly has scheduled Wednesday and Thursday night performances as well."

"Funny, but Peg did say I should take a look at it."

"The cabaret was Kelly's idea. I can't believe you haven't been down there yet."

"Haven't had time. But I have a strange premonition you're going to take me."

"Tonight?"

Jane finished her wine in two quick gulps. She was beginning to feel a major buzz, more than she was used to. "Consider it our first date." She waved for the bill.

Roz reluctantly led the way down a long, dingy corridor. "Back in the late eighteen hundreds, this part of the basement was used to house the horses for the livery business upstairs."

"It's dank."

"Yeah. I guess they thought horses didn't need much ambience."

"And it smells like an amusement park. Bubble gum. Popcorn." She looked down and saw several Bazooka wrappers on the floor.

Roz laughed. "You're right. They sell popcorn, cookies, and coffee in the cabaret."

Jane could easily imagine it. Between the exposed limestone pillars there were boarded-up sections which probably held the stalls. The basement had been cleaned a couple of times since the eighteen hundreds— or at least it had been swept. New dry wall had been thrown up to separate the space into rooms. Most of the panels were covered with graffiti. Long black arrows over bold red signs pointed the way to TownDown Jam. Every now and then they passed a door with a name on it.

"Who uses these rooms?" asked Jane, stopping in front of one that said, Neatherland Productions.

Roz turned around. "They're artists studios. It's pretty cheap. Kelly keeps it that way so they're always rented. Oh, and a few rock bands practice down here during the week."

"What's that?" Jane pointed to a double door set back deep into the limestone. It looked like the entrance to a low-rent fortress. "I suppose that's where Kelly stores her anti-tank weapons and intercontinental ballistic missiles." She giggled. She had to watch it. She was dead tired, depressed, and slightly drunk. Not a great combination.

Roz gave her a disgusted look. "Have you eaten today?"

"Bits and pieces. Mostly bits."

"It's obvious. It's not good to drink on an empty stomach."

"I'll write that down in my book of rules. Answer my question."

Roz walked over and pulled back one of the doors. "Kind of neat, huh? It's a tunnel."

Jane was intrigued. She stood at the edge, peering into the darkness. "Where does it lead?"

"The stable hands took the horses through here to water them. The Mississippi is only a few blocks away. You can still see the hooks on the walls where they hung lanterns. Teddy told me a number of the old warehouses had these tunnels. Some of the basements were even accessible by boat."

"Is it open on the other end? I mean, if we found a horse wandering around down here, could we still get out to water it?"

Roz rolled her eyes. "I think so. The city has renovated a lot of the river front area, but so far, they've left the tunnels alone."

Fascinating, thought Jane. "What's that on the floor?" She noticed lots of cigarette butts littering the dirt.

Before Roz could comment, four men carrying a coffin came clattering down the hall.

One of them nodded grimly to Jane as he moved past. Matching his seriousness, she nodded back. She turned back to Roz. "There's a funeral parlor down here too, right?"

"Cute, but no prize. No, those guys call themselves Death Trip. A popular group."

"Heavy metal?" she asked with little interest.

"Well, actually, the music is sort of a cross between Frank Sinatra, Guns N' Roses and a barbershop quartet. But in this case, it's five guys. The lead singer's inside the coffin."

"And are they playing tonight?"

"Probably."

"Let's go take a look."

"You're really up for it? I mean, after everything that's happened?"

"Listen, Roz. If I go back upstairs, all I'm going to do is obsess over Peg, or . . . worry about my aunt Beryl."

"What's wrong with your aunt?"

"Don't ask. It's another long story." Jane desperately wanted to get her mind on something else, if only for a little while. "What do you say?" She chucked Roz under the chin.

"I say you need some coffee."

From the other end of the hall they could hear clapping and loud cheers.

"Not an answer," said Jane.

Roz looked around, considering her options. "All right, sure. What can we lose?"

19

"What a dump," muttered Jane under her breath as she gazed at the makeshift stage. A group of women were setting up their equipment.

"*All About Eve*, 1954," said Roz. "Or was it *Beyond the Forest?*"

"What did you say?" She stopped and stared.

"*You* said, 'what a dump.' That's a Bette Davis line."

One thing Jane disliked about Roz was her tendency to view all life as a game of Trivial Pursuit. "No, I mean it. It's kind of crummy, don't you think?"

"Yeah, it's great. Rough, tacky and glitzy all rolled into one." She pushed through a crowd next to the espresso bar and grabbed an empty table near the front. "But you know, after what's happened, I feel awfully guilty being here tonight."

"I do too," said Jane. "But we can't change anything."

"I know."

"Let's just try to relax. Reality will intrude soon enough." She sat down on a rickety wood chair. "By the way, who did all the neon?" It was beautiful work. Tall green and yellow palm trees. Pastel pink and blue storks. Even a generic red and orange skyscraper.

"One of the artists Kelly rents studio space to. I can't remember her name. She studied at the College of Art and Design."

As Jane continued to admire the work, she noticed two police officers emerge from behind the stage area and walk toward the back. "What did I tell you?" she said, watching them speak to one of the women standing by the entrance. She was stamping hands and taking money. "Reality revisited."

Roz had seen them too. "They must still be searching the building."

"So it would appear."

"I wonder if they're looking for someone specific? Well, we'll find out sooner or later."

After a few more minutes spent mostly moving slowly through the crowd and observing, the officers left.

"You want a cappuccino?" asked Roz. She wasn't in the best of moods. "Don't bother answering. You need some coffee and you're going to drink it."

"Even if it kills me."

"Right. And if they have cookies, you're eating some of those too." She found some change in her purse and marched off.

Jane leaned back and continued to survey the room. It was another cavernous interior, and to give Roz credit, it did have a definite sleazy underground appeal. Sort of a modern *Phantom of the Opera* setting. None of the tables and chairs matched, obviously Kelly's handiwork. And from the cover charge and the apparent lack of overhead, Jane guessed she was doing a banner business. Tiny specks of colored glitter were scattered everywhere on the floor. It did make the dirty concrete look a little less bare.

"Here we go," said Roz returning a few minutes later. She set the oversized paper cup in front of Jane. "I got you a double. And one of Maggie's Famous Gorilla Bars."

Jane stared suspiciously at the huge brownie studded with M&M's and nuts. "Young or old gorilla?"

"Don't worry. Your teeth can handle it."

She took a bite. It was remarkably good. Even fresh. "Thanks."

Roz made herself comfortable, lifting her own cup to her lips and blowing on it as her eyes flitted about the room. "The next set should start in a few minutes. Hey. There's Eric." She waved. He had just entered. "Over here," she called, turning to Jane. "You don't mind, do you?"

She didn't mind at all. As a matter of fact, she was glad for the opportunity to talk to him again.

Eric walked up and pulled an unused chair away from another table. "I assume you know what's happened upstairs."

Roz nodded and then looked away.

"The police stopped me as I got off the elevator. I saw the squads outside as I was coming in. Jeez! I can't believe this. I feel like someone's hit me over the head! I think I can even see stars."

"I feel kind of dazed myself," said Roz. "I know the real meaning hasn't sunk in yet."

She seemed so upset, he bent down and put his arms around her. "It'll be all right."

"Not for Peg it won't," she sniffed.

Eric's body was a study in dejection as he sat down. He was quiet for several seconds before nodding hello to Jane. "You picked a terrible time to move in here," he said, rubbing his hands nervously against the sides of his jeans. "Kelly tells me you and Roz are pretty good friends. How'd you two meet?"

It was a stab at normal conversation. Jane was grateful. "We were in the same sorority back in college."

"Jane Lawless, right?"

She nodded.

"Your name's familiar."

Eric was an attractive man, with a complexion so ruddy, and hair and eyebrows so light, he almost looked like a photo negative.

"Do you work downtown?" he asked.

"No, I own a restaurant. The Lyme House."

"*You* own that?"

By the faraway look in his eyes, Jane assumed he was putting something together in his mind.

"I've read about you in the newspaper," he said. "You've helped solve a bunch of crimes in Minneapolis."

"I'm afraid that's me." She felt ill at ease under his scrutinizing gaze. Opting for a change in subject she asked, "What do you do for a living?"

"I manage an antique store."

"Oh, that's right. Peg told me."

At the mention of Peg's name, his eyes fixed on a crack in the center of the table and he grew silent.

After several uncomfortable seconds, Jane asked, "Do you like working with antiques?"

"It's a living." He slouched against the back of his chair, glancing up at the stage.

Before a new subject could be introduced, the house lights were shut off and a single spotlight hit center stage. So much for high tech electronics. The glow from the neon sculptures cast a watery, pastel light over the audience. Jane guessed there were at least seventy-five people waiting for the music to begin. Some were still standing by the espresso bar in the back.

Even though she would've liked to talk longer, she knew the decibel level of the music would make it impossible. She might as well sit back, sip her cappuccino and nibble on her Gorilla Bar. Besides, no one was in the mood for a conversation anyway.

Applause and cheers followed the first number. Jane liked the group. She'd have to find out when this band was on the bill again and bring Cordelia and Mugs down here.

Stifling a yawn as the next song began, she glanced absently over her shoulder to see if any more police had arrived. It was just about twelve-thirty. The tables were almost full. A group of a dozen or so had moved to the front, sitting down on the cold, concrete floor. As Jane's eyes moved over the nervous knot of caffeine addicts near the bar, she spied a familiar face. The narrow features and long curly hair were part of a countenance she never wanted to see again, but there he was, standing alone just inside the door. It was the Charles Manson look-alike. The man who'd been up on the roof of the building, peering down into Arno's loft.

Reacting quickly, she touched Roz on the arm. "I'll be right back," she whispered.

"This song is their best number," pleaded Roz. "Just wait."

"I can't." She pushed back from the table and snaked her way through the room, knowing the four glasses of wine she'd had earlier had probably affected her otherwise perfect judgement. No matter. She was determined to find out who this guy was. They weren't alone on a dark rooftop tonight.

Passing by a table of eight, she accidentally bumped into a young man's arm, which in turn knocked his coffee cup over. Liquid spilled onto the table top.

"Shit," said the man, pulling back from the table.

"Hey!" said a woman sitting next to him as coffee poured onto her lap. She quickly grabbed everyone's napkins and began mopping it up.

"I'm sorry," said Jane weakly. "Let me buy you another cup."

"Forget it," said the guy, wiping off his jeans. "Just get out of my way. You're blocking my view."

Jane continued to the rear of the room, but by the time she reached the spot where Charlie Manson had been standing, he was gone.

"Did you see a man here a minute ago?" she asked of a couple who'd just come in. "Short. Thin. Long, curly dark hair. Kind of a scary face."

The man shook his head.

The woman said, "Yeah, I think he just left."

"Which way?" asked Jane, bumping past her.

"Back toward the elevator."

She shouted her thanks as she bolted out the door and steamed off down the hall. When she got to the elevator and found it open and empty, she knew she'd lost him. The hall was quiet. No police anywhere. But where could he have gone? He was only a few seconds ahead of her and there was only one route from the cabaret to the elevator. Unless he'd evaporated into thin air, he still had to be around.

That's when she remembered the stairs. Problem was, she didn't have a clue where they were.

Down the other end of the hall came three guys in their late teens, all with shaved heads, and all dressed in army fatigues. They were laughing hysterically.

"Do you know where the stairway is?" she asked as they swept past.

One of them twirled around and pointed behind him. "That a-way, lady. Just came down 'em."

"Thanks."

"My ass!" shrieked one of the others.

The other two began to knock him on the shoulder and snort.

"The way to San Jose, man," said the second one.

"Retro," shrieked the third. "Truly fine, man. Truly fine." He waited a second and then screamed NOT in the first guy's ear.

They walked off, shoving each other against the walls.

Jane had nothing to lose. She called after them, "Did you see a long-haired man on the stairs when you were coming down?"

"We ain't seen nothin'" shouted the first guy, falling on one of his friends for support.

The last one turned and called, "Just us chickens!"

"Chickens!" gushed the first guy, wiping a hand across his mouth. "Great, man. Rare."

They continued to poke and shove each other as they rounded the corner.

Jane savored the relative silence which descended after they were gone. She doubted these mental weenies would have noticed if the entire Viking offense had been rushing up the stairs as they were slithering down.

As she saw it, there were two remaining possibilities left to be checked out. First, this Manson look-alike might have disappeared into one of the several studios Kelly rented to artists. If that was the case, as far as Jane was concerned, the search was over. She didn't intend to bang on doors this late at night.

The second possibility was that he'd gone into the tunnel Roz had shown her earlier. And as luck would have it, the tunnel entrance was only a few feet away.

Jane stepped quietly over to the doors and bent her head down, listening. All appeared to be quiet. She took hold of the handle and pulled it back several feet, poking her head inside. It only took a moment for her eyes to adjust to the dimness. When they did, she could make out the burning tip of a cigarette about ten feet away. A second more and the smell reached her. It wasn't a cigarette at all, but a joint.

A man crouched against the right side wall. The light from the doorway created a wedge of brightness, enough for Jane to make out his face.

It was him.

The temperature inside the tunnel wasn't as bitter as outside, but it was cold.

"Either come in or get out," said a thin, reedy voice. Jane was repelled by the sound. She also wasn't very happy with the two choices he'd given her. Hesitantly, she shut the door behind her.

"You want something from me?" he asked. The only light in the tunnel now came from the burning tip of his joint.

"I don't know," she said, her voice something less than assertive. Suddenly, a bright beam of light struck her face. She held up her hand, shielding her eyes from the intensity. "Turn off the flashlight," she demanded, taking several steps backwards.

"Why? I like to see who I'm talking to."

The brightness was disorienting. She struggled to get away from the beam, but he kept it on her. She felt he'd gotten up, but she couldn't tell for sure. She thrashed around in her mind for something to say. She didn't want to confront him here any more than she had up on the roof, yet she wanted to get him to talk to her. "I heard this was a tunnel," she said conversationally.

"The tour left an hour ago." The voice was closer now.

"But where does this lead?" She backed up until she could feel the door hard against her back.

"It leads nowhere, lady. Just like everything else in this fucking life."

As he pointed the flashlight at the ground, she could see his body tremble, hear him sniff and resist the urge to cry. Perhaps because she found him so scary, his emotion surprised her. Backing out of the door she said, "Sorry, I didn't mean to bother you."

It took a moment for her eyes to readjust to the bright light in the hall. In an odd way, she felt sorry for him. He was pathetic, really. Smoking his dope. Crouching in a dank cave. But an inner voice told her she was right to be careful. He might be a passive voyeur, or, he might be something far more frightening.

20

Eric was awakened by the sound of banging on his door. He'd been dozing, but not really asleep. For what seemed like hours, he'd tossed and turned, unable to shut off his thoughts. The light leaking in through the bedroom blinds informed him another day had begun, though the sun would do little to lighten his mood.

The bottom line was his life totally sucked. Everyone had a few personal demons, but his seemed to be growing angrier with each passing day. And today would be worse than usual. As soon as he showered and dressed, he had to drive over to his mother's home and give her the news about Peg. He usually tried to keep his conversations with his mother brief, but this morning it would be impossible.

He knew how it would go. He'd sit her down at the kitchen table and tell her what had happened. She would, of course, be devastated. It would be another blow, in a long series of blows, which proved conclusively that the world was a dangerous and sinful place. Next, she'd move on to how everyone was a either a liar or just plain evil, or both, and consequently, families must stick together. Meaning, of course, that he had to knuckle under and do what she wanted him to do. The message was clear, not that she would ever put it so directly. In fact, she rarely asked outright for anything. Instead, she just stated her opinions with the force of the Almighty. For instance, there was this edict: Children were put on earth to help their parents. Never would she simply ask for help from her son. Citing moral principles was a much safer approach. Some people didn't see the distinction, but to Eric, it was the difference between a kindly request and a thug's demand.

"Go away!" he shouted, as the banging on his door got louder. "No one's home!"

And finally, after all the tears were done, she would descend into blame. Blame was where she felt most comfortable. And that's where the conversation, as always, would dead end. Amazing as it seemed to him now, somewhere in all of this he was certain Peg herself would not be held blameless. The very thought nauseated him.

The worst part was that Eric knew, deep in his soul, that he was just like his mother. She'd taught him well. Just like her, he wielded blame with the force of a weapon. He believed in its efficacy, had faith that once blame was assigned, the world would regain its moral order. Blame wasn't just an act, it was a solution. Yet there was a flaw in this thinking which he'd discovered early on. Not only was there crime, but there was punishment. Blame was just one side of the coin—naming the crime, and who had perpetrated it. But it was the need for punishment—in his case, the act of atonement—that his mother had never prepared him for. She'd never explained to him where to draw the line. When enough was enough.

The banging continued. "Just a minute!" he shouted, angry at his visitor's tenacity. He'd hoped that if he didn't answer, whoever it was would go away. "I'm coming," he grumbled, as he tugged on his flannel bathrobe. Padding through the living room in his bedroom slippers he threw open the front door. He intended to get rid of whoever it was as quickly as possible.

Kelly stood outside, her face a tight knot of frustration. "I've been standing here for hours!" she declared, pushing past him without being invited.

"Jeez, cut me some slack," he said, raking a hand through his uncombed hair. "I just woke up."

She glared at him, flopping down onto the couch.

"What's up?" He could tell by the look on her face it wasn't good.

"You heard about Peg?"

He nodded, sitting down across from her.

She squeezed the back of her neck. "What's happening around here, Eric? Who's doing this?"

"I don't know," he said softly. He felt ashamed of himself for feeling annoyed. Kelly needed him right now, and he had to be there. He'd always wanted to be her friend, ever since they were kids. Since he was an only child, he'd thought of her as an older sister. In fact, getting to know her better was one of the reasons he'd moved to Linden Lofts. Not that Kelly was easy to get close to. But, little by little it was happening. She'd come to him this morning, hadn't she? Peg's death must have hit her hard. He had to be patient and sensitive. Let her pour out her feelings, but at her own pace. "I'm here for you, Kelly."

She stared at him blankly, and then, without missing a beat, said, "To top it off, this morning I get a call from a guy named Barber. Says he's a reporter for 'Inside Affair.'"

Eric wasn't sure he was hearing her correctly. "You mean that gossip TV program?" This wasn't exactly what he'd expected to pour from her soul.

She got up and drifted over to the windows which overlooked the river. "They want to do a feature on my dad. You and I both know what it will be like." She made her voice go nasal and snotty. "Local TV celeb a closet drag queen, details at ten. Arno Heywood's classic wardrobe tips. Or how about, ex-clown commits suicide, but tastefully."

"Kelly, stop."

"They want to interview me on camera! Get *my* perspective—the tear-ful daughter." Again, she assumed the interviewer persona. "Outside of his silk and pearls, Miss Heywood, was your daddy a *manly* man, or would you say he was more like a mom to you? Did you ever swap make-up secrets? Ever discuss with him how to keep a girlish figure?" She whirled around. "In other words, was your dad a fag, Kelly dear, or just a complete weirdo!"

Eric couldn't help but cringe. "That's so cruel."

"And he *wasn't?*" She turned back to the window and rested her head against the glass. "The question remains, am I going to do that inter-view?" She seemed to be considering her options. After a long pause, she said, "Yes, I think I am."

"But why, Kelly! Those programs are freak shows."

Her face hardened. "They offered me money."

"Oh, please. You can't need money that badly."

Her eyes locked on his. "I don't even know if I'm going to have a place to *live* next week."

"You're exaggerating."

"Really? According to the will that was read several weeks ago, this building went to Peg when dad died."

"Why didn't you tell me immediately!"

"What good would it do? We'll all just have to wait and see how everything shakes out. Anyway, the reason I raced over here in such a state was that, for the life of me, I can't find one of my photo albums."

"Huh?" She was changing subjects way too quickly.

"Photos," said Kelly slowly, as if he were as thick as a brick. "This Barber guy asked for pictures of me with my dad when I was a kid, and anything I have that's more recent. Peg had given me a whole bunch of them taken the night we all went to the Guthrie for her birthday celebration. She probably gave you some too, right?"

"I . . . think so," he replied.

"Well, when I looked through my albums, I couldn't find the most recent one. I've got nothing from the entire last year."

"Where could you have put it?" he asked, his face suggesting an interest he didn't feel.

She slumped into a chair. "Beats me. But no big deal. It'll show up sooner or later. In the meantime, I have to ask you a favor."

He knew what was coming. "You want my photographs."

"Just the most recent ones."

"I've got some from Thanksgiving."

"Ah . . . sure. That would be great. But I'm specifically interested in one of my father and I that Peg took. It's . . . you know. Flattering." She waited. When Eric didn't respond, she asked, "So? Have you got them?"

"I'll have to look."

Again, she waited. "So look!" she said finally, erupting out of her chair.

Eric got up and walked over to a lacquered Chinese box resting on a table next to the sofa.

"What's that?" she asked curiously.

"It's where I keep them. I don't have many. I've never gotten them organized into an album, or anything like that." He flipped through half the stack, then thought better of it and handed them over. "You might as well look through them yourself. You know which ones you want."

She grabbed the box and began her search.

"I've got to tell you," he continued, standing next to her and watching her rifle through the pile, "that I'm not thrilled to be helping you with this cheesy interview. I wish you wouldn't do it. I think you'll regret it later."

She ignored him. After paging through the entire stack several times, she looked up. "They're not here."

"They're not?"

"You got ear problems?" she said impatiently. "They're not here! You said Peg had given some to you."

"I thought she had."

"Well then, where are they?" She dropped the box back on the table, her eyes rising to his.

Both jumped at the sound of a loud rap on the door.

"Now who?" said Eric. All he wanted was a nice, hot shower. A few moments alone to collect his thoughts before the day began. Re-tying his robe, he marched to the door and opened it. "Teddy," he said, trying to sound pleased. It was a struggle.

"Sorry to bother you," said Teddy, apologetically. He looked worse than usual this morning. His brown wool topcoat appeared dusty and rumpled, his eyes sunk in dark circles. "I think your van's parked me in. I'm sure none of us feels much like working this morning, but in my case, I've got a meeting I can't put off. You heard about Peg, didn't you?"

The flat way he asked the question struck Eric as grotesque. "Yes."

Catching sight of Kelly over Eric's shoulder Teddy called, "Morning."

"Morning," she echoed. Her tone held little warmth.

"Would you like to come in while I get dressed?" asked Eric. "Sorry about my van. I guess I had a lot on my mind when I got home last night."

Teddy stepped inside. "No problem."

"I'll only be a minute," said Eric, dashing off to his bedroom.

Kelly made a move toward the door saying, "I guess I'd better get going."

Teddy blocked her exit. "Why don't you keep me company?"

"Why? So we can have a nice uncle to niece chat?"

"You know, Kelly, your cynicism is getting kind of tiresome."

"Oh, that's a good start. I like being insulted."

Teddy shook his head. "You're so busy posturing, I don't even know who you are any more." He took off his hat and stood awkwardly, pulling on the brim. "Let's start over, okay? I called Peg's daughter in Maryland this morning. I didn't know if anyone else would think to do it. But of course, the police had already informed her about . . . you know, what happened. She's going to make all the funeral arrangements when she gets into town later today."

Kelly nodded.

"Are you all right?" he asked, his voice almost a whisper.

"Funny you should ask."

"Don't be like that. Talk to me. Tell me what you're thinking."

"Oh, right. First insults, and now concern. How *should* I think? Should I smile? Act like nothing's happened? Maybe you want gratitude."

"You know I only did what I had to do."

"You're so full of it, Teddy. You lied to John, and you lied to my father. And then you turn around and offer that same load of crap to Peg."

"You know it's not crap."

"The hell I do! What are you, psychic? You got a crystal ball or something? Because if you do, what's it tell you about Peg, Teddy? Who murdered her?"

He grabbed her by her shoulders. "Stop it!"

"Let me go," she snapped, breaking free of his grasp.

"Just tell me what I can do to help you," he pleaded. "I'm getting old. The world is so much more complex then it used to be. I . . . well, I will admit that I may have handled this badly. Is that what you want? An apology?"

Her eyes fell to the small lacquered box.

"What? What is it?"

For the first time, she seemed to warm to the conversation. "Let me borrow your photos of my father."

"Why?" He was clearly taken aback by the abrupt change of subject and mood.

"I need some recent photos of my dad. Specifically, I'm looking for one Peg took of us the night we all went to the Guthrie for her birthday. Do you remember? I assume Peg gave a bunch to everyone. Can I get yours now?"

"Kelly, I don't have any photographs."

"What do you mean?"

He walked over and dropped his hat and gloves on the coffee table, unbuttoning his coat and then turning back to her. "I can't be bothered with that sort of detritus. Except for a few old family photos, and a couple of my wife, I don't keep them around." He looked at her pointedly. "Why are you so interested?"

"I just am," she said nonchalantly.

"I don't believe you."

"Nothing new in that," she muttered. "Oh, well . . . if you must know, it's for an interview. 'Inside Affair' wants to interview me about my father."

He looked away thoughtfully, his eyes scanning the huge expanse of windows. After a moment, he began to laugh. "This is a joke, right?"

"No joke, Teddy."

The smile faded. "You'd even consider it?"

"Why not? Maybe it's *my* fifteen minutes." She ignored his stern look.

"I'm all set," called Eric, emerging from the bedroom. "Let me just get my coat and keys and I'll be right with you."

"Catch you later, Eric," said Kelly making a quick exit.

"Will I see you later?" he called, picking up his watch and keys from a bowl on the dining room table.

Instead of an answer, he heard her door slam shut. What had gotten into her? Turning to Teddy, he asked, "Everything all right with you two?"

Teddy picked up his hat and placed it carefully on top of his head. "I'm hardly the person to ask," he replied, smoothing the brim and then giving it a frustrated yank.

21

"I'm sure glad that's over," said Cordelia, dropping a copy of *Family Circle* back on the waiting room table. She watched as the doctor was swallowed by a flurry of activity near the nurses station. "You know, from the content of these magazines, you'd think the only people who frequent hospitals are jocks and housewives. Then again, I suppose those *are* two of the most hazardous professions."

Jane was immensely relieved that her aunt had made it through the biopsy, and was now resting comfortably in her room. "All we have to do is wait for the results."

Jane and Cordelia had arrived at the hospital shortly after seven. Both wanted a chance to talk to Beryl and Edgar before the procedure began. Beryl had spent a restful night and was feeling a bit more confident today, though not strong. Her hands had been uncharacteristically shaky as she combed her hair. The fever was down too, also a good sign, though her temperature was far from normal and her color still showed signs of jaundice, especially in the whites of her eyes.

Jane picked up her book and stuffed it into her backpack. It was a volume she'd found yesterday morning at a local used bookstore. Retrieving her coat from the next chair, she said, "Come on, let's get out of here."

"Do you think Edgar's going to stay?" asked Cordelia, accompanying her to the main lobby.

"I think the doctor was pretty clear that Beryl needed complete rest for several hours. No visitors."

"Meaning?"

"I have no idea what Edgar will do."

"Her illness has certainly brought them closer," smiled Cordelia, slipping into the red and black plaid hunting jacket she referred to as her lumberjack frock. It belonged to an ex-girlfriend. Cordelia usually wore it, as she liked to point out, when she wanted to feel both virile and fashionably Minnesotan. Black jeans, black cowboy hat, and a pair of tiger-rimmed shades completed the morning's ensemble. "Hey, where's the fire?" she scowled, puffing to a stop just as they'd pushed through the main doors out into the cold morning sunlight.

"I want to drive over to the Boline Mansion."

"Why?"

"Remember Amy McGee said that John Merchant was the liaison between his law firm and Teddy Anderson over at the mansion?"

"So?"

"I want to see it. And if we're lucky, maybe Teddy will be there and will show us around. I'd also like to ask him a couple of questions."

Cordelia's hands rose to her hips. "You know, dearheart, sometimes you bear a striking resemblance to the Spanish Inquisition—always running around, asking leading questions."

Jane gave her a dirty look.

"Not that I'd agree with that characterization, of course."

They resumed their half-block trek to the parking garage.

"But, I mean," continued Cordelia, "don't you suppose the police have already interviewed Teddy?"

"I'm sure they have. But I haven't."

Without warning, Cordelia came to another dead stop, whipping off her sunglasses. She clamped a firm hand over Jane's arm and spun her around.

"Hey!"

"You know, Jane dear, after what happened last night, I'm not sure we should be going anywhere. Maybe you should stop all this—go home and live a safe, boring life with occasional visits from your *boring* friend, Cordelia."

Jane was afraid Cordelia was going to have that reaction. Nevertheless, in the wee hours of the morning, she'd come to an important decision. She would keep her promise to Roz and stay in Arno's loft until the end of the month. She owed her—and Peg—that much. "I can't do that."

"And why not?"

"Two reasons. First of all, I gave Roz my word I'd stay through the end of December."

"And you'd never break your word."

"Not willingly."

"How middle-America of you. What's the second part?"

135

"I just don't think the police believed me when I said I thought there was a connection between Peg's murder and John Merchant's death. I think I'm on to something, Cordelia. I'd feel like a coward if I didn't do everything in my power to catch Peg's murderer. Besides, I'm being careful."

"Right. You'll know exactly what speed you're traveling when your car careens off the cliff."

"Oh, come on. Come with me. It's a beautiful day. We can stop for coffee and a muffin when we're done."

"Oh, no you don't. You're not bribing me with food this time, sweetie." She adjusted her cowboy hat. "Especially some puny muffin."

"You can tell me about the new play you're working on. I'd love to hear how you're going to stage it."

"Hah! Now it's an appeal to my ego," she sniffed, though she seemed to mull it over. Finally, she said, "I suppose *someone* should keep an eye on you. There's no telling *what* you might get yourself mixed up in without my calm, steady presence. But I must be at the theatre by two. And I want to check in on Beryl before that."

"We're in complete sync."

With a regal twist of her head Cordelia muttered, "I doubt that, dearheart. I doubt that very much." As she stomped away, she looked over her shoulder and called, "Chop chop, Jane! No dawdling."

After a short drive through downtown, Jane turned onto the Hennepin Avenue Bridge and headed for Nicollet Island. She adjusted her rear view mirror, catching sight of a blue car about two cars back. "Guess what?"

Cordelia was examining the whites of her eyes in the passenger's side mirror. "Do I look yellow to you, Janey? Tell me the truth."

"I think we're being followed."

She blinked and then swiveled her head around and looked out the back window. "You're kidding."

"The same car has been two cars behind us ever since we left the hospital parking lot." Several streets past the end of the bridge Jane made a hard right onto University Avenue. She didn't signal first, thinking that if the car behind them also turned, she'd proved her point.

"Are they still there?" whispered Cordelia, hunching down.

"Afraid so."

"Cool! I've never been followed before. This is so . . . so 'Rockford Files'!" She peeked over the back of the seat. "You mean the Escort?"

"One car looks just like another to me. If it's blue, and it's two cars behind, that's the one." Jane swung over to the right hand curb and waited as the car sped on past.

"Could you see inside?" asked Cordelia, scrunching in next to her and shoving her own head over the steering wheel for a better view.

Jane got a mouthful of cowboy hat. She spit out some fuzz and then said, "It had tinted windows."

"Well, of course it did! An Escort with *tinted* windows!" She shrieked with laughter. "Only in Minnesota."

"I wonder who it was," mused Jane.

"Who do we know with such Budget Rent A Car taste?"

"Oh, don't be such a snob."

"That from a woman who drives a vehicle not even Rent-A-Wreck would touch?"

"Don't start on my car."

She smiled innocently as she fished a five dollar bill out of her pocket. "Listen, I need a bubble gum fix. Just sit tight, I'll be right back." She unstuck herself from the front seat and dashed into the small superette across the street.

Jane drummed her fingers impatiently on the steering wheel. Maybe she'd been wrong about the tail. There was always the chance that the car was just going in the same direction. Perhaps she was just feeling jumpy after what had happened last night.

When Cordelia finally returned, she offered Jane the gum. "It's sugarless."

"Kind of takes the element of danger out of it, doesn't it?" Glancing over her shoulder, she pulled back into traffic. "All right. The house is on Fairmont. I got the address before I left for the hospital this morning."

Cordelia chewed and bubbled away contentedly.

"We have to turn around and head back the other way," said Jane, glancing up at the rear view mirror again. "Oh, great," she groaned.

"Hum? You know what, dearheart? Surely it's close enough to the

holidays for us to find some insipid Christmas music to lighten our mood."
She reached for the radio dial. "I always look forward to hearing 'The
Little Drummer Boy' four or five hundred times."

"Look behind you."

"First I have to—"

"Cordelia, look behind you!"

"Don't get nasty." She turned around.

"I'm right, aren't I? It's the same car. I'm talking about the one that's
half a block behind us."

"This is too . . . too 'Dragnet'!"

It was also a clear indication that Jane's first instinct had been right.

"Can't you lose them?" said Cordelia, popping a second lump of gum
into her mouth.

"I don't think they realize we're on to them."

"So?" said Cordelia.

"So, hold on to your black hat." Jane braked, skidded into the far left
lane and then, without signaling, made a hard left directly after the 35 W
exit onto Tenth. She burned rubber through the stop light at the next
corner and headed into sorority row. It was familiar territory. If she
could lose a tail anywhere, it was here.

Making a hard right at Fifth, she sped down the street and turned into
the Kappa Alpha Sigma parking lot. Here the traction was poor. Taking
it a bit more slowly, she pulled into a empty space, threw the car into
reverse and backed up. Threading through a maze of parked cars, some
covered in snow, many parked with no rhyme nor reason, she came to a
stop behind a delivery truck next to the building. She positioned herself
so that she could see the street. At the same time, her own car would be
almost impossible to pick out. If the blue car was following, she'd know
in very short order.

Sure enough, the Escort rumbled down the street less than a minute
later. It moved slowly, the driver obviously looking to see where Jane's
car might have gone. Waiting another minute, Jane backed out of her
space and inched the car forward. She could see the Escort had continued on down as far as Dinkytown. It had on its blinker and was about to
turn left. Skidding out of the lot, she made a quick right on Eleventh
and headed for University. Another hard right and they were on their
way back to Nicollet Island.

"That should do it," said Jane, looking over her shoulder.

Cordelia's hands had grasped the sides of her cowboy hat, pulling it down as far as it would go.

As Jane turned to look, she could see her friend's eyes were completely covered. But she was still madly chewing her gum. "You can come out now," she whispered.

"I feel . . . sick," mumbled Cordelia.

"I think we lost them."

She lifted the hat. "You're amazing, Janey."

"Thank you."

"Oh, don't take that as a compliment. I meant amazing as in *crazy*." She placed a hand over her stomach. "Are you sure we lost them?"

"No."

"I need a barf bag."

"Use your hat." Jane stopped at the red light. An idea had just occurred to her.

"What do we do next?"

"Why, we're going to go see a house, Cordelia. And we're going to *love* it, right? But first, in case Lady Luck shines on us and Teddy actually happens to be there, I need to talk to you about a small part I want you to play."

Cordelia didn't turn her head, but instead, glared at Jane out of the corner of her eye. "You forget, Jane dear, I'm a director, not an actor."

"It pains me to to see you sell yourself so short."

"Cut the crap."

"Fine. Here's what I want you to do."

22

Jane and Cordelia stood on the sidewalk outside the Boline Mansion and gazed up at the graceful redstone building. It was three stories high, with deep pointed gables and two-story bay windows on the north side. A tower sat off to the right, the scrollwork underneath badly in need of repair. Jane counted seventeen windows on the front facade alone.

"Are we gawking?" asked Cordelia, unable to take her eyes off of it. "This must be what King Kong felt like when he got his first glimpse of the Empire State Building." Her eyes rose to the top of the tower. "Look at that tiny window way up there. I bet you can barely see out of it."

"It's bigger than you think. We're pretty far down."

"Must be twenty rooms in that place," said Cordelia, her tone reverent.

"There are twenty-*six*," said Teddy Anderson, walking up behind them. He stopped just a few feet from the main gate.

By the rosiness of his cheeks, Jane figured he'd walked a fair distance.

"What brings you here this morning?" he asked, his gaze coming to rest on Jane. "Say, you're that friend of Roz Barrie's, aren't you?"

"That's right."

"I'm sorry. I don't recall the name."

"Jane Lawless."

"Of course." He nodded pleasantly.

"And this is Cordelia Thorn," said Jane.

"Nice to meet you." He extended his hand.

Jane was thrilled at her good luck. This sure beat knocking on the front door with some lame excuse to get inside. "Roz was telling us about the biography you're working on. And about the mansion."

"Right," beamed Cordelia. "We're just *fascinated* by conspicuous consumption."

"Me too," said Teddy, giving her an amused smile.

"I guess we wanted to see it for ourselves," continued Jane, "before the city fathers decide to tear it down and replace it with a parking ramp."

She hoped this small hook would draw him into the conversation.

"Oh, that won't happen," he said, his expression growing serious. "The Boline estate is in the process of restoring the entire building. They're working on the exterior and some of the interior plumbing right now." He nodded to a scaffolding along the north wall. Workmen were coming and going from the rear.

"When was it built?" asked Cordelia.

"1884," he replied. "Would you like to see inside?"

"We thought you'd never ask," she exclaimed.

Jane felt she was piling it on a bit thick, but it seemed to be working. They walked up the wide front walk and stood by the front door while he unlocked it.

"There are more renovations scheduled for the house in the next few months," he said, taking off his coat and hat and placing them carefully on an upholstered bench in the foyer. He smoothed back his hair and then strolled casually into the living room. He seemed to be enjoying his stint as tour guide.

Jane found the interior to be quite grand, with beautiful wood panels covering the walls. Yet the the water-stained ceilings and soiled carpeting spoke more of neglect and disrepair than it did of riches and old-fashioned opulence. Most of the furniture was covered by white sheets.

"I can't tell you much about the furnishings," he said, his voice echoing in the silent hall. "Boline's grandson lived here until he died early last winter. He was known for being something of a miser. I can't imagine why. The estate is worth many millions."

"You must freeze to death working here," said Cordelia, rubbing her hands together.

"My office is on the third floor. I keep a small heater by my desk and it seems to do the trick." He crossed into the dining room and then led them into the kitchen. "Of course, the appliances have all been updated, but by the looks of them, I'd say nothing is newer than 1965." He turned to Cordelia. "Would you like to see the basement?"

She wrinkled her nose. "Not a lot."

"All right," he said. "Let's go upstairs then." He led them back into the foyer and up the main staircase. "Eventually, after all the restoration is done, the Minnesota Historical Society will take it over."

They poked their heads into a couple of the bedrooms, oohing and ahhing at the antiquity of it all. Teddy ended the tour near the servants stairway in the back, resting his hand one of the painted balustrades. "I think this is about all there is to see."

"Really?" said Cordelia, her eyes slowly rising.

"The third floor's off limits to visitors."

"What's up there?" asked Jane, attempting to keep her tone light.

"It's mostly storage now. Boline's personal papers, files and business records. If I do say so myself, a small army couldn't get through it all in the time the estate managers have given me."

"Yeah, administrators can be real buttheads," agreed Cordelia.

He looked down his nose at her, a smile pulling at the corners of his mouth. "So true."

Jane decided to take a chance. "I understand that you and John Merchant were working together on the Boline biography."

He seemed a bit startled. "Yes, since you bring it up, we were. Why do you ask? Was he a friend?"

"No, but we had mutual friends. I was terribly sorry to hear about his death."

Teddy nodded. "I was too." He leaned away and coughed deeply several times, covering his mouth with his hand. "As a matter of fact, I was shocked. We used to meet here every couple of weeks so he could get a feel for the progress I was making. The night he died, I was his last appointment of the day." He took out a handkerchief and began cleaning his rimless spectacles.

Jane was surprised.

"I'm not telling you anything I haven't already told the police."

"How long did he stay?"

"Well, he arrived around four, and then left shortly after five. As I think about it, one of the workmen outside saw him drive away. I believe he verified the time as five fifteen. If I do say so myself, John was fascinated by my research. He was concerned that I make the biography positive, though he wanted it accurate as well." He turned, fixing his eyes on Cordelia. "Everyone has warts, you know."

Her hand rose to her hip. "Excuse me?"

"Did he say where he was headed when he left?" asked Jane. She couldn't believe her good fortune. This was exactly the kind of hard information she needed.

"He said he wanted to stop in and see Eric Lind over at his antique store. It's only a few blocks away. Peg Martinsen's birthday was that night. Apparently, John hadn't gotten her a present yet. He said he hoped he could find just the right gift over at the shop. It was on his way home."

"Did he often shop there?" asked Jane.

"I wouldn't know," said Teddy, his tone growing decidedly more cool.

Jane felt she'd crossed the line. She was appearing too nosy.

"I must say, I don't quite understand all your interest."

"Oh, you know," said Cordelia, giving him a knowing nod. "She's kind of a crime freak. I think it's sick, myself, but I try to humor her."

"I see," he said, eyeing Jane with distaste.

Jane thought it was a good time to pull out the book. She took off her backpack and reached inside. "I wonder if you'd mind doing me a favor." She handed him a copy of his first and only novel.

"Where did you get this!" he exclaimed. He flipped eagerly through the first few pages.

"A used bookstore downtown. I started reading it this morning. I like it very much."

He held it lovingly in his hand. "This has been out of print for twenty years."

"I noticed it was dedicated to your wife."

"Yes," he said, running his hand over the cover. "She's always been my inspiration."

Jane thought she saw tears come into his eyes.

"Here," he said, taking out his pen with a flourish. "I'll inscribe this to . . . Jane Lawless." He wrote quickly.

"I look forward to finishing it."

"Thank you. You must let me know what you think when you're done."

"I will, I promise. Oh, and before we go, I wanted to tell you that I told your brother, Edgar, that I'd met you."

At the mention of his name, all the pleasure drained from Teddy's face. "So he tells me."

"You've talked to him then?"

"Yesterday. Very briefly."

"He and my aunt have become quite close."

"Women have always been attracted to Edgar."

Jane wondered what he meant by that.

He replaced his glasses, lifting the rounded bows over his ears, and then headed for the main staircase. "I'm sorry to end our tour so abruptly, but I'm afraid I've got a mountain of work to do. I don't feel much like being here today, not after what happened . . ." He stopped and turned around. "Say, Roz told me you were the one who found Peg. That must have been awful for you."

"It was."

"Then again," he sighed, "these last few months have been an awful time for everyone. Do you still plan on making Linden Lofts your home?"

"For the time being," she answered.

"Well," he said, continuing on down the hall, "matters will get sorted out, I'm convinced of that. We have to believe in the future, not dwell on the past. That's what my wife always says, and I, for one, believe her."

As they reached the bottom of the stairs, Jane touched Cordelia on her arm, giving her the high sign.

Taking her cue, Cordelia sagged against the balustrade, raising the back of her hand to her forehead. "Ohhhh," she groaned, attempting to get Teddy's attention.

"What's wrong?" he asked, coming to her aid. He held her arm, steadying her.

"It's . . . my heart. I have to sit down."

"Of course." He led her into the living room. "Just a second while I uncover one of the couches."

Cordelia winked at Jane.

"Here," he said, helping her lie down. "Can I get you a glass of water?"

"No," she said, sighing and flapping her eyelashes. "Jane has my medication. But she'll need to prepare it."

"Can I use your bathroom?" asked Jane. "It should only take a couple of minutes."

"Well," he said, eyeing Cordelia a little suspiciously, "the one on this floor isn't working right now."

Cordelia groaned even louder. "Oh . . . the vapors. I'm fading, dearhearts. The room is spinning. I can see my grandmother walking toward me in the mist."

"Vapors?" he repeated.

"I'm a sick . . . sick woman," she mumbled.

"But I thought it was your heart."

"It is," she snapped. "Now tell Jane where she can go fix my medication." She picked up an old *Look* magazine and began fanning herself.

"There's a working bathroom on the second floor," said Teddy quickly. "I'll show you."

"No!" protested Cordelia, "I can't be left alone to die like a dog."

Teddy raised a hand to calm her. Then, motioning Jane over to the stairs, he whispered, "Is she always this melodramatic?"

"I'm afraid so. She's kind of a hypochondriac too. But she does have heart problems. If you wouldn't mind staying with her—"

"No, of course I wouldn't mind. There's a bathroom right off the front bedroom. You may have seen it when we passed through there earlier."

"Thanks," said Jane. "I'll be back in a flash."

Several *long* minutes later, Jane returned carrying a glass of pink liquid. "Now, I want you to drink this up like a good girl."

Cordelia was lying on the couch with Teddy massaging her feet.

How on earth she'd gotten him to do *that* was completely beyond Jane. "Drink up," she urged, sitting down next to her.

Placing a pathetic hand over her chest, Cordelia sat up, coughed, and then slurped several mouthfuls. "There," she said, dropping back down, "I should feel better soon. Special thanks go to you, Mr. Anderson." She gave Teddy a coy little smile.

"Let me help you up," said Jane, a bit nauseated by the interaction.

"Deary me," said Cordelia, draping a lazy arm over Jane's shoulder, "but I'm dizzy." She wobbled to her feet.

"You certainly are," said Jane turning to Teddy. "Thanks for showing us the house."

As he walked them to the door, he said, "It was my pleasure. I hope you found your visit . . . enlightening."

Jane wondered what he meant by that. "I'm sure I'll be seeing you around Linden Lofts."

"I'll look forward to it. I wish you both a pleasant afternoon."

Once back in Jane's car, Cordelia said, "So? Was that not an Oscar-winning performance by a leading lady in a short docudrama?"

"It was a supporting role, Cordelia, but yes, you did wonderfully."

She snorted. "Supporting, my ass. Did you get a good look at his office?"

Jane rested her hands on top of the steering wheel, looking out at the street. "Yes. But it just looked like a lot of research to me. Tons of photographs. Letters. A diary. Oh, and lots of baseball paraphernalia. Also some rather ancient looking contracts, and a legal pad with numbers all over it. The wastebasket was filled with page after page of addition and subtraction problems."

"Well, before you insist that he's a cold-blooded killer, I just want to point out that I liked him. He's a curious mixture of snotty condescension and occasional bursts of sweetness."

Jane started the motor. "All right. I have no problem with that. But tell me, how did you get him to rub your feet?"

Cordelia gave Jane her most indulgent smirk. "*Leading* ladies have their ways."

23

After stopping off to see Beryl and finding there were still no results from the biopsy, Jane spent the rest of the day at her restaurant. Catering requests for holiday parties were beginning to pile up, and she was concerned that they wouldn't have enough staff to take care of the demand. She spent part of the afternoon meeting with her executive and banquet chefs, trying to nail down the numbers.

She finally left the restaurant around seven and drove home to spend a few minutes playing with her dogs. Their presence, always a given in her life, was sorely missed when she had to be away. She got down on the floor and scratched and cuddled them, tossing an old tennis ball around the living room until they were completely worn out. The meat scraps she plunked into their bowls were of some passing interest as well.

After kissing them goodbye and giving them each a Milkbone and an admonition to stay out of her bedroom closet, she took the stack of cards and letters addressed to her aunt and headed back to the hospital for another brief visit.

Edgar and Beryl were playing poker when she arrived. They explained that the liver specialist had been in earlier and would have the final results of the biopsy in the morning. Jane was disappointed she'd missed the conversation, but hoped she'd catch her tomorrow.

She stayed until around eight-thirty, losing three hands of gin rummy and a big fifteen cents, and then drove back to Linden Lofts for the night. On the way, she was almost positive she'd caught sight of that same blue Escort following about three cars behind, but when she pulled into the small lot in back of the building, the street was deserted.

Trudging at last up the loading dock stairs, she glanced into a short, dark alley that was used to house the restaurant's garbage dumpster. Even in the frigid night air, the smell of rotting food wafted from the open top. She unlocked the back door and slipped into the welcome warmth of the building.

Riding up in the elevator, she decided to make a stop on the fifth floor.

Kelly Heywood had left a message on her answering machine earlier in the day, asking her to return the call as soon as possible. Since she hadn't had time, she figured it was just as easy to talk to her now in person.

Shutting the heavy metal doors behind her, she breezed down the empty hallway, stopping outside Kelly's loft and knocking several times. It only took a moment for the door to swing back, revealing a far different Kelly Heywood from the one Jane had met several weeks ago. Tonight, she was dressed in a gauzy cotton granny dress, reminiscent of the sixties. She was barefoot, with a print scarf worn pirate-like around her head. And she had on large, dangly gold earrings, bright crimson lipstick and eye make-up—*lots* of eye make-up. But what struck Jane most was the overpowering smell of pot mixed with incense.

With a joint dangling casually from one hand, Kelly motioned her into the room. "I'm glad you're here," she said, sitting down cross-legged in front of her glass-topped coffee table. A square brass plate containing the remnants of several joints rested next to a book on the Sistine Chapel. Another small brass bowl held at least a dozen roach clips. "You want a smoke?" she asked, lifting the top off a wicker basket and pushing it across to Jane.

"No thanks."

"Suit yourself," she shrugged, leaning back against the edge of the couch.

"I'm sorry I didn't get a chance to call you earlier. It's been kind of a hectic day."

"For me too," said Kelly. "Sit down, will you? You're making me nervous." She stretched out, taking a toke. "The police were around most of the afternoon. I told them, if they wanted me for anything else, I wouldn't be available until tomorrow morning."

By then, thought Jane, she could fumigate the place and make it presentable again. "So, what did you want to talk to me about?"

"It's that padlock on the door to the roof. Do you know anything about it?"

Jane had known that it would be only a matter of time before it was discovered. "Yes, I do. I put it there."

"No shit. Care to tell me why?"

"I don't like voyeurs."

"Huh?"

"There was a guy up there one night last week peering down at me through the skylight. I guess you could say I value my privacy. There was no lock on the door, so I put one on."

Kelly seemed genuinely surprised. "Did you get a good look at him?"

"He was small, with shoulder-length black hair, a long thin face, a scrubby sort of pathetic beard, and he was dirty."

"Jesus, you saw all that from down in my father's loft?"

"I have good eyesight. Do you know him?"

Again, Kelly shrugged. "Maybe."

"I'd be interested in hearing a name."

"I'll have to check it out first."

"Fine. But until you do, I want the lock to remain where it is."

Kelly took another toke, considering the issue. "I suppose that's reasonable. As long as you give me the key."

"I don't have it with me." The last thing Jane intended to do was hand it over.

"That's all right. You can drop it by later."

"Sure. Oh, by the way, I should tell you I'll be moving out at the end of December."

"Don't like it here, huh?"

"Not as much as I thought I would."

A faint smile touched her lips, then faded. "Well, you know best." Another toke.

Jane waved smoke out of her face. She'd used marijuana some back in college, but she'd never really liked taking smoke into her lungs. "I assume the police were here this morning because of Peg."

"Yeah."

"You've certainly had a lot of loss recently. First your friend, John Merchant, then your father, and now, Peg. It must seem pretty hard to cope sometimes."

"It does. That's why a friend suggested. . . ." She nodded to the rolled joints.

"Not much of a solution."

"No, but it helps."

"You smoked much dope before?"

"When I was a kid, but not for years. Actually this is the first time I've used since I was sixteen. I remember now why I liked it so much. It takes the edge off."

"Did John smoke much dope?"

"John? Nah, he was way too straight." She laughed at the irony of her words.

"I heard that on the night he died everyone at the loft was supposed to meet at the Guthrie to see a play."

"That's true."

"And you were all going out to dinner afterwards."

"Yeah, but John never made it." She wiped a hand across her eyes.

"I'm curious. Did everyone get there on time?"

She lit another joint, took a deep drag and then held her breath. "Yeah. I mean, well, no, I take that back. Eric was late. He didn't get there until well into the first act." She exhaled.

"I wonder why?"

"Oh, he's always late."

"Yeah, I have a friend like that too." She studied Kelly for a moment. "You know, I hear you're an aspiring poet."

"I'm not *aspiring*. I *am* a poet. If you write poetry, you're a poet."

"Kind of like, if you cook, you're a chef?"

She bit the nail on her index finger. "You sound just like my dad. Me, I don't go in for all that hierarchy crap. Dad was always wanting me to do something productive with my life. But see, to him productive meant putting on a suit and going to work for The Man. I'd sleep in my car and work at Burger King before I'd sell out like that."

"But if it weren't for his money, you wouldn't be living here."

Her laugh was harsh. "Yeah, The Bank of Dad. All I can say is, if the money's there, why not take it? The path toward personal wholeness doesn't always come well-greased with cash. But even so, I'd still rather be emotionally, spiritually, and intellectually satisfied than have a big bank account."

"Are you emotionally, spiritually, and intellectually satisfied?" asked Jane.

She took another toke. "I'm working on it. Oh, don't get me wrong. I know you need money to live. I'm just not willing to sell my soul to get it."

She seemed to space out. Her head tilted back and she stared expressionlessly at the pipes running across the ceiling.

"Well, I've got to get going," said Jane, feeling any further conversation would be pointless.

"Right," mumbled Kelly. She got up and shambled over to the door. "Bring that key down when you get a chance."

Jane was simply never going to get the chance. As she stepped into the corridor, she nearly dropped her briefcase as she bumped into a man who was about to knock on Kelly's door. She stared in wonder as she realized it was the voyeur.

He looked her up and down. "Evening," he said with a formal nod. The formality was completely out of character with the way he was dressed—jeans and a ratty Dr. John sweatshirt.

Up close, he seemed a bit older than he had the first night, but he was still every bit as dirty. Jane glanced down at his hands and saw that they were blotched with red paint, and his fingernails were so black that he looked like he'd been digging in the dirt all day.

By Kelly's nervous expression, Jane could tell she knew this was the man Jane had spoken of earlier.

"Hey, babe," he said, pecking Kelly on the cheek.

Kelly made her own stab at civility by saying, "Brandon, I'd like you to meet Jane Lawless. She's living upstairs in dad's loft."

"Brandon?" repeated Jane. "Are you the sculptor who did that artwork in Peg Martinsen's apartment?"

He squared his shoulders. "Yeah."

"He rents studio space downstairs," said Kelly. "He's really talented. He studied in New York for years. Spent some time in Amsterdam. And he's had shows all over, just none so far in the Twin Cities. He thinks we're kind of provincial." She was speaking too fast. Explaining too much. Jane wondered why.

"Hey, babe, you look great," he said seductively, kissing Kelly smack on her lips. After lingering a moment, he turned back to Jane and said, "Nice meeting you." Then, herding Kelly into the apartment with the force of his body, he swiveled around and took hold of the door knob. "Later, babe," he said with a dismissive glance.

Jane watched as the door was slammed in her face.

24

"Jane! Hi," exclaimed Roz, jumping up from her spot on the couch. She fussed nervously with her gold earrings. "I didn't expect you home so . . . early." As an afterthought, she asked, "How was your day?"

Jane saw immediately why Roz looked as if she'd been caught with her hand in the proverbial cookie jar. Mark Thurman sat casually on Arno's leather sofa, sipping from a red and green holiday glass. Roz had obviously been sitting next to him, and by the looks on both their faces, they hadn't been swapping camp stories.

"Want a Tom and Jerry?" she chirped, her eyes moving from Jane to Thurman, and then back again. She was guilt incarnate. "I suppose you're wondering . . . I mean, well . . . he stopped by."

Jane could see that. She set her briefcase down next to Arno's desk and unbuttoned her coat.

"So, what do you say?" asked Roz, attempting a cheerful smile.

"About what?"

"The Tom and Jerry."

"Oh, sure. That would be great."

"I'll just be a minute." She rushed off into the kitchen.

Jane sat down on the edge of the desk. Thurman hadn't said a word yet. She thought she'd wait and let him fire the opening shot.

After a leisurely sip from his glass, during which he looked her up and down, he smiled his benign network smile and observed, "You haven't got any Christmas trimmings in here yet. Kind of missing out, aren't you?"

Jane felt her skin crawl. She was completely unable to understand what Roz saw in this turkey. She refused to believe it was simply because Roz was heterosexual and she wasn't. Jane found lots of men both attractive and great company. To her mind, Thurman was neither. "We've hardly been in a festive mood around here lately."

"Oh, right. I suppose not." He shifted in his seat. "Jane, I want you to know how truly shocked I was to hear about Peg. That's actually why I'm here tonight. Roz was a basket case all day at work. I did my best to comfort her."

"I'm sure you did, Mark."

His jaw set angrily. "I finally managed to convince her to have dinner with me. And then I brought her home. We had a long talk over dinner. And I think we managed to resolve some of our differences."

Roz returned with the drink. She handed it to Jane and then said, "So, you two've had a chance to talk. What did I miss?" Again, she seemed tense.

"Well," said Thurman, "I was just telling your friend here about our dinner conversation." He held out his hand, motioning for her to sit down next to him.

She didn't move. "What did you say?"

"Just that we'd managed to mend some fences."

She fixed Jane with another less than convincing smile. "We'll talk about all this later, okay?"

Not only was Jane nauseated by Roz's choice in men, which was nothing new and was also none of her business, but she was also genuinely worried that Roz might be in real danger by continuing to see him. "If I could just speak to you for a second—"

Thurman erupted. "I don't see that Roz needs any advice about the men she dates, especially from . . . from someone like you."

"Oh, *please*, Thurman," said Roz.

He sat up straight. "Roz, she's—"

Here it comes, thought Jane. "I'm a dyke, right?"

"Well . . . I wouldn't have put it quite that way—"

"Sure you would have, Mark."

He glared at her, yanking on his French cuffs. "But, yes. That's it exactly. You hate men."

"Thurman!" snapped Roz, hands rising to her hips. "You're making a fool of yourself."

"Am I? Have you ever slept with a man, Jane? Have you?"

"Are you telling me that's the only way I can prove I don't hate them?" Jane had heard the same, moronic nonsense a thousand times.

"You're twisting my meaning."

"Thurman, *stop*," said Roz. She sat down next to him and clamped a hand over his mouth. "This isn't helping."

He threw it off. "Look at the way she treats me. Utter contempt."

That about covers it, thought Jane.

"That's the way you treat *her*," said Roz.

Jane knew debating a buffoon was pointless. She shook her head silently, knowing Roz would simply have to make her own decisions. She wasn't stupid. She had to be aware of the potential danger.

"Well, I've had about as much of this little drama as I can stand for one evening," he muttered, rising and lifting his coat off a chair.

Roz stood too. "Jane, I think Thurman and I need to talk a while longer. Maybe we'll go downstairs to my loft." She looked at him for a response.

"Fine," he grunted, sweeping out of the room without a parting glance.

Roz walked over and squeezed Jane's hand. "Don't be upset with me."

"Listen, kiddo. What you do with your love life is your own business, but I can't help being concerned. I'm just not sure it's smart to trust him, or to spend time alone with him, at least until everything here is cleared up."

Roz gave her hand another reassuring squeeze. "Every now and then he may be a complete jerk, but I'm convinced he'd never hurt anyone. You don't know him the way I do, Jane. He had an awful time growing up, bounced from home to home. Not much love in his life. He may not always behave the way I'd like him to, but when things quiet down, he's a very special, very sweet man to be with. I thought I could walk away, but I can't."

Since there was nothing more Jane could say, she figured it was best to let the subject drop—for now. "Fine. You just be careful, okay?"

"I will."

"Hey, before you go, answer one question for me. Do you know anyone who drives a light blue Escort?"

Roz put a finger to her lips. "No," she said slowly. "Nobody around here. I think my cousin in Bloomington drives an Escort, but it's red. Why do you ask?"

"Oh, it's nothing really. Just curious."

"By the way, I took the cat down to Eric's loft. I know Eric really loves him. And at least down there he'll get some attention. Anyway, we can talk more later. Right now, I've got to run." As she got to the door, she called, "Oh, and don't wait up for me. I may be . . . late."

. . .

Around eleven, Jane laid down Teddy Anderson's novel and went into the kitchen where she put on the tea kettle. It had been a hectic day, but even so, she didn't feel much like hitting the sack. Visiting her house earlier had made her restless. She realized how much she missed the familiar surroundings—and the company of her aunt. She simply wanted everything to get back to normal. Tomorrow, no matter what, she was going to corner that doctor and find out what was going on with her aunt's health. Not knowing was driving her crazy.

After brewing the tea, Jane poured herself a cup and strolled back into the living room, imagining what it might be like to live permanently in a place like this. She wasn't as taken by the size as Cordelia was, and yet she had to admit the openness and the eighty-foot expanse of windows was pretty incredible.

She stood for a moment and looked out at the night skyline. The world was a different place in the dark. Easy definition was gone. In the distance, the Foshay Tower was dwarfed by the larger, flashier, more modern skyscrapers. When Jane was a kid, the tower had been one of the tallest buildings in Minneapolis. The new replacing the old, she though to herself. Just the normal ebb and flow of life. But change was never easy.

Standing alone now in Arno's loft, she couldn't help but wonder if, on the day he jumped to his death, Arno Heywood had looked west toward the Linden Building. What had been his last thoughts? Had he found the courage to say goodbye to the people he loved? Or, because of anger or pain, or some emotion she couldn't even fathom, had he merely turned his back?

On that depressing note, she moved away from the windows and drifted over to the front door. As she opened it, she was surprised to find the strains of a familiar aria wafting softly from Peg's apartment. The yellow police tape was still intact, though there was a gap at hip level wide enough for someone to climb through. The door was open wide. She couldn't imagine who might be inside, since she was pretty sure no one was allowed in, at least not legally.

As usual, her curiosity got the better of her. She crept across the hall and peeked inside. There, a good forty feet from where she was standing, a woman sat quietly in the semi-darkness. She'd placed a chair upright in the midst of the chaos and was leaning forward, arms resting on her knees. Even in the dim light, Jane could see she had golden hair, thick and swept back from her face. Her expression wasn't exactly sad. It was more remote.

Seeing movement near the door, the woman called, "Who's there?"

Jane moved into the center of the doorway, holding her mug of tea in front of her. The tape prevented her from going any further. "Evening," she said a bit awkwardly. "I . . . live across the hall. My name's Jane."

The woman rose, slipping her hands into the pockets of her dark pleated pants. She was wearing a striped vest over a white shirt and wide silk tie. All the elegant pleats and tucks accentuated her slim figure. "You're the neighbor," the woman replied. "The one who found my mother." Her voice was controlled. Yet after a moment, she raised a hand to her mouth, holding it like a fist against her lips.

Jane knew she had no business interrupting this woman's privacy. She backed away. "I'll just let you—"

"No," said the woman, taking a few steps toward her. "Don't go." She raked a hand through her hair. "I, ah . . . I don't really want to be here, but I had to come. The police told me not to touch anything until tomorrow." Her eyes fell to the stereo. "I didn't think they'd mind if I switched on some music. I don't know what came over me. I just had to know what she'd been listening to. It was the CD I sent her for her birthday last summer. *The Magic Flute.* She loved opera. I . . . I guess I've always thought it was kind of tedious, myself." Her voice faltered. "I'm sorry," she said, looking away and rubbing her forehead. "You must think—" She swallowed back her tears.

Jane felt terribly sorry for her. "I think . . . maybe you'd like some tea?" she said softly.

She pressed her fingers hard against her temple. "Yeah. I would."

"Come across the hall, then. I just made some."

"Have a seat anywhere," said Jane, ducking into the kitchen. She began preparing a tray with the tea pot, another mug, cream and sugar, and some crackers she'd found sitting out on the counter. Thinking that perhaps Peg's daughter might not have eaten much, she checked in the refrigerator to see what else might be available. To her delight, she found several wedges of imported cheese resting next to a bottle of Merlot. She wondered idly if Roz had been planning a little late night snack with her on-again, off-again, and now on-again boyfriend. Well, too late now, she thought, selecting one of the wedges, shutting the door, rearranging the tray and then returning to the living room.

The woman had made herself comfortable on the couch. When she saw Jane approach with the tray, she quickly cleared the newspaper off the coffee table to make room. "I didn't expect all this," she said, her gaze rising to Jane's face.

"Are you hungry?"

"Well, I wasn't. But I think maybe I am now." For the first time, she smiled. It wasn't much of a smile, but it made her face come alive.

Only a pillar of salt, thought Jane, could fail to notice that it was a great face. She poured the tea, then sat back and picked up her own mug.

"I didn't realize I was so hungry," she said, chewing on a cracker. She cut a thick slice of the Jarlsberg. "I don't think I've eaten all day. I flew in around noon, and spent most of the afternoon making the arrangements for my mother's funeral." She stared at the cheese in her hand for a few seconds before adding, "I think it was probably the worst day of my life."

"What's your name?" asked Jane.

"Oh, I'm sorry. It's Julia. Julia Martinsen."

"Did . . . your husband come too?"

"I'm not married." She took a sip of the tea. "This is so good. Thanks. No, no husband and no children. My work has always come first. And now that's . . . well, let's just say my whole life seems to be in a state of flux."

"Peg never mentioned having a daughter. Then again, I've only known her for a few days."

"Yeah, Mom was a wonderful woman, but very private. I admired her probably more than she'll ever know. That's why being here doesn't even seem real. I mean, how could she just be gone? It's too fast. I didn't even get a chance. . . ." She closed her eyes and looked away. After several seconds she said, "Besides, this is Minneapolis, not New York or Chicago. I grew up here. It's a safe place."

"Not always," said Jane. "Where do you live now?"

"Bethesda. I was thinking about moving back to the Twin Cities. Now, I'm not sure I've got anything to come back to." She clenched her jaw, fighting back the tears that were just under the surface.

"Do you still have friends in town?"

"No," she sniffed. "Nobody close. I haven't been home in years. Mom's come out to Maryland a couple of times. The last visit she brought Arno Heywood. I assume you knew him?"

"We'd never met, but I knew who he was."

"He was such fun. And he and Mom were so much in love. Now they're both gone." She wiped the back of her hand over her eyes. "God, I can't talk about anything tonight without crying."

"It's all right," said Jane gently. She waited until Julia seemed more comfortable and then said, "My mother died when I was thirteen. In some ways, I think I'm still mourning her. The older I get, the more I realize what I missed. And—" She hesitated, but only for a second. "I was in a relationship for almost ten years. Christine, my partner, died of cancer six years ago."

Julia looked up. She held Jane's eyes for several long seconds before saying, "I'm sorry."

"No sorrier than I am about your mother."

"Thanks." She took another cracker, but made no attempt to eat it. "I guess life goes on. But . . . I mean, how can we sit here eating and drinking when. . . ." She pulled one of the couch pillows in front of her, hugging it close to her body. After taking a deep breath she said, "I have to talk about something else for awhile."

"Sure."

"So . . . what do you do? For a living, I mean."

"I own a restaurant on Lake Harriet."

"No kidding. That's a beautiful spot. Have you owned it long?"

"Since the early eighties. It's called the Lyme House. I named it after Lyme Regis, the place where I grew up."

"And where's that?"

"The southwestern coast of England. My mother was English. She and my dad met just after he'd graduated from law school. We lived in England until I was nine, then we moved back to St. Paul. That's where Dad was from."

"You know, in most ways, you sound like everyone else, but yet, there's something about your voice. I don't know how to describe it. Maybe it's that you sound more . . . cultured. It's a funny word to use in the nineties, but it fits. You certainly don't have any Scandinavian twang."

Jane grinned. "I'm not Scandinavian."

"Don't say that too loudly around here. You'll anger the natives."

"How about you?"

"You have to ask?" She pointed to her blond hair. "So," she continued, her tone a bit more relaxed, "do you like living in a loft?" Her eyes took in the room, eventually rising to the skylight. "This used to be Arno's place, right?"

Jane nodded. She wasn't sure just how much to explain. "Actually, I'm only staying until the end of December. It's kind of a favor for a friend."

"Apartment sitting?"

"Not exactly. My friend—she lives down on the fourth floor—asked me to stay here for a month and see if I could help her get to the bottom of some rather strange occurrences. She thinks her apartment was entered illegally several times—while she was out."

"Meaning what? A thief?"

"It's a rather convoluted story. I don't want to bore you."

She gazed at Jane over the rim of her mug. "I doubt that's possible." After several more seconds she said, "Have you done this kind of . . . private investigation before?"

"A couple of times."

"With some success?"

"I guess you could say that."

"Do you ever get paid?"

"Yeah. Not all that much."

"So in a sense, you're a professional."

Jane shook her head. "Nothing that serious."

"*And* you run a restaurant." Julia studied her as she sipped her tea. "You know, don't take this the wrong way, but you seem like an unusual person, Jane."

"I think you'd better smile when you say that."

They stared at each other for a long moment, and then Julia did smile. This time, it was a real one.

"Hey, look what time it is," said Julia, checking her watch. "I've got to make a call. Would you mind if I used your phone?"

"Not at all," said Jane. "There's one on the desk in the study."

"Thanks." She got up and walked over to it. Easing into Arno's desk chair, she punched in some numbers, waited, and then punched in several more.

Jane assumed it was a long distance call and she was using her credit card.

"Hi, it's me," she said finally, her head bent down, her voice low. She listened, then swiveled her chair around until she was facing the wall. Her eyes rose to the portrait of Arno the Clown. "How is he?" She listened. "That's good. It's exactly what I'd hoped for. Listen, Leo, I apologize for leaving so abruptly. I never would have if it hadn't been an emergency." Another pause. "Thanks. The funeral is the day after tomorrow. Yeah, I'll check it out. I've got a couple of leads. It may work here, it may not. In the meantime, let me give you my number at the hotel." She took out a slip of paper and repeated it slowly. Then said, "Yeah, I miss you too. And I'll call tomorrow night. Don't forget to give him my love."

Jane couldn't help but overhear the conversation. And of course, she had her questions about what it all meant. But she couldn't stand any more mysteries right now.

Julia didn't return to the couch. Instead, she stood next to it, gazing down at Jane, an unreadable expression on her face. "I'm afraid I've got to get going. I wish I could stay, but I have an early appointment in the morning."

Jane walked her over to the door. "Will you be all right?" she asked.

Julia's smile was almost tender. "Yes. Thanks to you."

"I didn't do anything."

"Sure you did. You were a friend. In a town where I'm beginning to realize I'm virtually friendless. I hope I can return the favor sometime."

Jane found herself hoping she could too. She didn't want this to be the last time they'd meet. If nothing else, she'd see her at Peg's funeral, but for Julia, that would be a day of acute sadness. It would take all her energy just to get through it.

After a few parting words, they said goodnight. Once Julia had stepped onto the elevator and the heavy doors had clanged shut in front of her, Jane leaned back against her door and listened to the silence. Strange that the building could seem so empty now, as if this woman she'd just met had taken all the life and warmth with her.

25

"This is the third time you've moved her in less than a month!" declared Teddy Anderson, standing before the head administrator at the Mary Ogden Hathaway Nursing Home in north Minneapolis. It was Friday morning, just after nine. "And as far as I can see, she's getting *no* physical therapy."

"Just calm down, Mr." . . . the administrator checked the file in front of him . . . "Anderson. You have to understand, we're understaffed and underfunded. I can only assume you placed your wife in our care because of financial considerations of your own. Please understand that we have them as well."

In other words, thought Teddy, you're getting exactly what you and the government are willing to pay for. He clenched and unclenched his fists. "That's all you've got to say?"

Again, he glanced down at his notes. "Your wife is on the fourth floor. Room 418. She should be done with her morning bath by now, so I'm sure she'll be happy to see you."

Morning bath my ass, thought Teddy, stomping out of the room and making straight for the elevators. As far as he could tell, baths were a rare occurrence around this place, and that included the staff. What good were any of these people? No one gave a damn about the patients. They were all sick and old. Not much clout in that. Control only came if you had money, and Teddy, unfortunately, was just about out. Over the last few years he'd spent virtually every penny he had, first on his son's legal defense, and then on his wife's care. This dump, the government's so-called safety net, represented his last hope. It stunk of unwashed bodies, urine, and hopelessness. So much for the glad-handing politicians and their empty promises. Without money, this was where his wife would live, and eventually die.

Entering her room, he passed by two unmade beds and finally found her sitting next to the window in a cracked Naugahyde chair. She was bent over, her hair uncombed, her night clothes still on. She appeared to be asleep.

He sat down next to her, taking her hand in his. The ten years difference in their age had never really been that apparent before. Now it was. Mainly, it was due to the stroke. She'd been making progress with her speech, even beginning to feed herself again. But in the months since she'd come here, she'd failed terribly. It was hard for him to watch, but still he visited her every morning. Just like clockwork. He liked to read to her. On her good days they might even have a conversation of sorts. She was still lucid, at least that's what he saw, no matter what the doctors said. She was just trapped inside a body that didn't work anymore. And that was the worst tragedy of all.

She seemed to rouse when he stroked her skin.

"Ella, it's me," he smiled, smoothing back her hair. "How are you?"

She nodded, her face brightening. "Fine," she tried to say, though it came out more as, "Fuh."

He understood. He smiled back, gazing into her eyes. They were still so clear. And young.

"Ba-hee?" she asked almost immediately. It was how she said the name of their son, Bobbie.

"No, I haven't heard from him yet this week. Maybe we'll get a letter today. If we do, I'll bring it up tomorrow." Since his first days in prison, Bob had written to them four or five times a month. Teddy knew his wife lived for those letters. It was all she had left of him.

"Ouh soon?" she asked.

She never seemed to remember that, according to the judge's ruling, Bob still had another year to serve before he would be eligible for parole. Teddy didn't correct her anymore. There was no use. Sometimes he'd catch her looking over at the door. He knew she was waiting for their son to walk through it. How could he take that away from her? "Yes, he'll be out soon."

She licked her lips. "Uhm."

"But listen now, I do have something to tell you. Can you sit up?" He helped her get situated in the chair a bit more comfortably. "Are you cold?"

She motioned to the bed. "Blanket," she said, clear as a bell.

That's how it was sometimes. He didn't understand it. Some words she could say perfectly. Others she wouldn't even attempt. He placed it softly around her shoulders and then sat back down. "You'll never guess who called me a couple of days ago."

She blinked, waiting.

"Edgar." He wanted to see what her response would be.

"Edgar," she repeated, her eyes reflecting surprise, though her expression didn't change. "Wha . . ."

"What did he want?"

"Uh."

"Well, I'm not sure exactly. He said he wanted to get together and talk. Someone must have told him I was working on Boline's biography. I wasn't sure how much I should say."

She made a small nod.

Teddy hadn't wanted to tell her until now. He didn't want to upset her. Yet in mulling it over, he realized it wasn't Ella who'd never forgiven Edgar, it was he. "Do you think I should see him?"

"Uhm," she said immediately, her eyes twinkling.

"I think he's got a new girlfriend. Some English woman. Her name's Beryl. I knew he wanted to tell me all about her, but I cut him off. I thought that was a lot of nerve."

She closed her eyes.

"I'm sorry. I wish I had your ability to forgive sometimes, Ella. But the truth is, he treated us both like dirt and I haven't forgotten. Kelly called me bitter the other day and she's right. I've spent the last thirty years trying to achieve the good life for us, and look where we are? You deserve so much better than this place. I feel like a failure." The old acid in his stomach began to churn.

"No," she said, pushing her hand against his. Her eyebrows knit together.

God, he'd upset her. He'd never meant to do that. Quickly, he took her hand again. "I just don't think sometimes. Isn't that what you always say? I'm a thoughtless old man."

She gave a half nod, one side of her mouth curling in a slight smile.

"But I'm getting close. It's only a matter of time now. And we still have each other. Promise me you'll hold on to that, Ella."

Again, her head moved forward in a small nod. "La'you," she whispered.

His voice trembled as he repeated, "I love you too."

26

Jane had just stepped out of the shower when the phone rang. She threw on her robe and then crawled across the unmade bed, grabbing the receiver before the answering machine could pick it up down in Arno's study. "Hello?" she said, flopping onto her back.

For a moment, the line was silent. Then, "Jane, is that you?"

"Yes?"

"It's Amy McGee."

She groaned inwardly. Amy had left a couple messages on her answering machine at home, which she'd failed to return. But how could Amy have found out she was staying at Linden Lofts? She cleared her throat. "Hi. How are you?"

"Oh, you know. So so. How come you didn't return my calls?"

"Well," she said, propping herself up against the pillows, "I didn't get them until last night. I've been staying at a downtown loft since the beginning of December."

"I know."

"Ah, right. That's interesting, Amy. *How* did you know?"

"I think it was Cordelia who told me." Her voice was glum.

"Really." Jane obviously needed to have a brief chat with Cordelia.

"Why are you staying there?"

"Well, it's kind of a long story."

"Some woman?"

Jane laughed. "No. Nothing like that."

"Yeah, well, so are we on? I could fix you dinner tonight. I make a great tuna casserole. I use crushed potato chips on the top. Some people think those hard Oriental noodles are better, but they're not."

Clearly, Amy had no interest in trendy cuisine. Or clothing. "Well, you see I—"

"You're busy, right?"

"No, it's not that." Jane was was beginning to think she was not only gutless, but mean. Not a particularly flattering constellation of personality traits.

"You're never going to believe what happened at the office yesterday."

"The office?" she echoed, realizing her voice was a little too high and too bright. She was a complete jerk, that's all there was to it.

"Yeah, the police came by. They had a picture of Eric Lind with them. They showed it to everyone on the twelfth floor and asked if we'd ever seen him with John Merchant."

"And?"

"A couple of people recognized him, but that was all. So I told them my story. You know, what I explained to you and Cordelia at lunch."

"Why were they asking questions in the first place?"

"Well, from what I could gather, this Eric was spotted at John's apartment the night he was murdered. Some neighbor reported seeing a man with his description come out of John's front door shortly after seven-thirty."

"Alone?"

"Far as I know."

Fascinating, thought Jane. She wondered if the police had already talked to Eric, and more to the point, why had he been there in the first place?

"So, are we on?" asked Amy.

"On?" repeated Jane.

"For tonight. You haven't already forgotten?"

"Oh, right. Tonight." The truth was, she had. "Well. . ." She made a gun out of her hand and pulled the trigger. "Sure. That would be fine." Then she added, hoping Amy would get the point, "I'm going to have to make it an early evening."

After a long pause, Amy said, "Okay."

"What time?"

"How does seven-thirty strike you?"

"Fine."

"Oh, and Jane?"

"Yes?"

"You bring the wine, all right? You know about that kind of stuff."

Stuff? thought Jane. "Sure."

"See you later," she said, adding a giggling "*alligator*" to the end of the sentence.

165

Jane cringed. The line clicked, leaving her with one of life's most pressing questions. What wine did one serve with tuna casserole?

27

"Ripple," said Cordelia without missing a beat.

Jane did see a certain culinary symmetry in the suggestion.

"Leave it in the brown paper sack. That's the only way to drink it and stay completely in character."

"I think you've hit on a nearly perfect suggestion."

"Of course I have."

"Only problem is," said Jane, tapping her fingers on Cordelia's mantel, "you'd have to drink it."

Jane had arrived at Cordelia's house less than an hour after her conversation with Amy. Cordelia was draped over an overstuffed chair in her living room, her right leg propped up on a footstool. Another woman, someone Jane had never met before, sat on the floor in front of her, examining the bottom of Cordelia's naked foot.

"We're just about done," announced Cordelia, watching the woman take one last look at her big toe and then make a few notations on a note pad.

"I'll call you on Monday," said the woman. She stood, stuffing her charts and a large feathered gizmo Cordelia seemed particularly fond of into her purse.

"Splendid. You know your way out."

After she was gone, Cordelia sat forward and rubbed her toes, then put her red and yellow striped sock back on.

"What was all that about?" asked Jane walking around the crowded room. Cordelia liked to collect old theatre props. She always had some recent acquisition lying about. Today, however, the new acquisition was bigger than normal. As a matter of fact, it looked like half of a Roman wall, complete with fake ivy and chiseled Latin lettering.

"Pompeii," said Cordelia, waving away Jane's question before it was asked.

"But what about your foot?"

"It's beautifully formed, don't you think? Especially the little toe."

"No, I mean is something wrong with it?"

"Of course not."

"Then why was that doctor examining you? Not that I have the slightest idea what that feathered contraption was."

Cordelia made a bridge out of her fingers, giving Jane her most patient expression. "She wasn't a doctor, dearheart, she was a *reader*. She does foot readings. It's like palm readings, only better." After taking a sip from a glass of chocolate milk resting next to her she added, "I need to get a sense of where my love life is headed."

"What do you mean?" Jane sat down on a fake Egyptian bench. "What about Mugs?"

Cordelia's head sank down on her chest. "She's not coming home for Christmas."

"She's not?"

"She's taking a cruise with a bunch of friends. She asked me to come along, but what could she be thinking? I can't leave here now. Other than Halloween, Christmas is my favorite time of year! I can't leave everyone I love just to go off and ride around on some refurbished battleship. I mean, what could a trip like that offer . . . well, other than warm weather, crystal blue water, and time to frolic in various stages of undress on the beach. No, it's not for me."

Jane was pretty sure she wasn't getting the entire story. "What's wrong?" she asked gently.

Cordelia threw her shoe at the wall. "It's not working with the two of us."

"Why?"

She sighed deeply and then said, "Mugs wants me to move to Dallas."

Jane's mouth nearly dropped open.

Cordelia got up and hustled over to where her shoe had landed. "She's got a job offer down there that sounds great. But I can't leave here," she said, picking it up and heaving it against another wall. "I can't!"

"I'm really sorry."

"Yeah. Me too. It makes me wonder if I'm cut out for any kind of long term relationship. I mean, I'm not like you. You and Christine were like Ozzie and Harriet. Stable. Loving. Totally together."

"Not always."

"Yeah, but most of the time."

"I haven't had much luck recently."

"Well," said Cordelia, scooping up her shoe and dropping it into Jane's lap with an evil grin. "There's always Amy McGee. It's your turn to throw it now. Just don't hit the cats."

Jane shook her head. "Don't remind me. Say, speaking of Amy, I've got a bone to pick with you."

"What a disgusting cliché."

"Why did you tell her I was staying at Linden Lofts?"

Cordelia cocked her head. "*Moi?*"

"Yes, you."

"But I beg to differ. I haven't said a word to her since the day we shared that truly marvelous luncheon experience. It was, as they say, a Maalox moment."

"But she said—"

"She's pulling your leg, dearheart. Another cliche, I grant you, but one with far more visual appeal. And anyway, I don't know how she found out, but it wasn't from me."

Jane mulled it over. "Well, I guess she did say she *thought* it was you. I don't think she was sure."

"An aging beach bunny with memory loss," smirked Cordelia. "This gets better every minute. Throw the shoe, Janey. It will make you feel better." She scurried back to her overstuffed chair and dropped down on it like a sack of flour. "Say, what brings you here this morning? Other than the force of my magnetic presence."

"Well," said Jane, opening her briefcase and pulling out a file folder. "I asked my dad's paralegal to see if he could get me a copy of the police report on John Merchant's death."

"You mean, Norm the stress junkie?"

She nodded.

"And, of course, Norm always does everything you tell him to do."

"Well, most of the time, yes."

Cordelia closed her eyes. "Go on."

"Okay, listen to this. The initial report is short. Around 4:00 A.M. on the morning of July tenth, three guys found the body in the park under a low-hanging pine near the corner of West Fifteenth and Willow. One of them called the police and a squad car arrived within two minutes. Next, a detective showed up. And then someone from the Medical

Examiner's office. Merchant was pronounced dead at the scene at exactly 4:14 A.M. That's the official time of death, not when he actually died. Now, the cause of death was listed as non-penetrating head trauma, in other words, someone hit him over the head with enough force to kill him, but not enough force to break the skin and cause him to bleed."

"Unlike Peg."

Jane swallowed hard. "Right." She continued. "No weapon was found at the scene. Merchant's car was discovered parked on the street about half a block away. At first the police thought he must have been walking through the park on his way to the Guthrie when the attack occurred."

"I feel a *but* coming."

"In a supplemental report, the police now think he was murdered somewhere else, and his body was transported to the park."

Cordelia whistled. "Gruesome."

"I know."

"So that people would think it was a gay-related murder?"

"Maybe. And who knows, that might be accurate."

"But what time did he actually die?"

Jane looked back down at the report. She flipped through a couple of pages. "Anywhere between six and ten the night before."

"Not very specific."

"It's hard to be much more accurate than that without an eyewitness." She continued to read. "It started raining pretty hard that night around seven. That no doubt cleared the park of people. The spot where they found him was covered with muddy footprints, but there was nothing they could really use to identify the murderer. The three guys who found him pretty much destroyed the scene by tramping all over it."

"What about fingerprints? Clothing fibers?"

"Nothing about that here, but they found some items at or near the spot where the body had been dumped. A couple of muddy ticket stubs, a generic brown button, a small gold earring— and, about five feet away, a partially smoked joint."

"Standard park garbage."

"Maybe."

Cordelia shook her head. "So what do you think?"

"Well, first, you've got to hear what Amy told me earlier." Jane quickly explained about the police coming to her office with a picture of Eric

Lind.

"Doesn't look very good for Brother Eric."

"When I picked up the police report from Norm a while ago, he said he'd had an interesting conversation with one of the cops on the case. It seems Eric came down to the station yesterday afternoon and explained that he was at Merchant's house that night because he'd just delivered an antique cedar chest to him. Merchant had bought it several weeks before. Eric even produced a bill of sale."

"Was Merchant home when he got there?"

"Eric said he'd been given a key so he could let himself in. His instructions were to bring it inside and return the key to Merchant later that night, when they all met over at the Guthrie."

"And?" said Cordelia, motioning Jane on with her hand.

"Well, the police checked the photographs taken of his apartment the day after he died. There *was* a chest inside, but the cop said it didn't look as if it had just been delivered. A bunch of crystal decanters were sitting on one side of it, with glasses and an ice chest on the other."

"Maybe Eric does instant interior decorating along with his deliveries."

Jane got up and began pacing. "What I don't get is his motive. If he *was* the one who murdered Merchant, why?"

Cordelia raised a finger and said, "'Why, may not that be the skull of a lawyer? Where be his quiddities now, his quillets, his cases, his tenures, and his tricks.'"

"What's that?"

"*Hamlet.* Act five, I think. It's the first lawyer verse that came to mind. If it wasn't helpful, Janey . . . sue me." She fluttered her eyelashes cheerfully.

"I just don't have enough information," snapped Jane.

"Well, let's use our imagination then, shall we? Suppose Eric was a closet case. Sure. He and Merchant were lovers. That's why he had the key. Maybe the good lawyer threatened to out him and he got hysterical."

As much as Jane resisted such a simple solution, it could explain a lot. "You may have something there, Cordelia."

"Ask Roz if she's ever seen him date a woman."

"Not that it would prove anything one way or the other."

"No, but just ask." She stifled a yawn.

"Speaking of Roz. I think she and Thurman are back together."

Cordelia eyebrows floated upward.

Jane figured that would wake her up. "I came home last night and found them together in Arno's loft."

"Together as in—"

"Sitting on the couch."

"Oh."

"A few minutes later they went down to Roz's loft to talk."

"And?"

"She never came back."

"Dearie me."

"She called about midnight to say she was spending the night down in her own loft. I called her at work this morning just to make sure she was okay. I mean, she's an adult. I can't go around monitoring her personal affairs."

"Heavens no."

"So I guess, when it comes to Thurman, she's on her own. She has to make her own decisions. I just feel uneasy because I'm not sure what his involvement in all this is."

"Look, if the police are right about Eric, then Roz's only problem is that she's dating a fatuous, though somewhat decorative, gasbag."

Jane gave a serious nod. "Well put."

"Thank you."

"Well, I suppose I'd better shove off."

"So soon?" said Cordelia, lifting her feet up onto the footstool and stretching out. "Close the door on your way out."

"Not so fast."

"Hmm?"

"I thought I'd take a run over to Eric's antique shop before I go to work. You like antiques, don't you?"

"Never touch the stuff. I prefer new antiques." She drew her arms wide, taking in the entire room.

"But you'd love a little fresh air."

"No I wouldn't. It's five above zero out there, Janey. And I don't have to be at the theatre until one."

"Coward." Jane put the police file back into her briefcase and picked up her coat.

"Call me what you will, dearheart, but when it comes to Eric, delivery boy extraordinaire, you're on your own."

28

Flour Island Antiques was located in a brightly painted wood frame building about four blocks from August Boline's home. Even though it wasn't in the mansion category, it was still a fairly large two-story Victorian, with deep front gables, an open, wrap-around porch, and lots of gingerbread. In other words, thought Jane, as she walked up the front steps, what it lacked in size, it more than made up for in charm.

As she entered the front foyer, a middle-aged woman in the living room caught her eye. She was running a soft cloth over an antique sideboard.

"Kind of an icy morning out there," called the woman, bending down to get the legs. "Is it going to snow?"

Typical Minnesota small talk, thought Jane. "I haven't heard," she said, stopping near a display of blue and white china. "But the sky looks like snow."

"Yeah, we're due for it. 'Course, it's December. What do we expect?"

Weather small talk could go on forever. In the land of *Minnesota Nice*, where everyone was supposed to be pleasant at all times, it was an inherently safe topic.

"You have some beautiful pieces in here," said Jane, touching the top of a mahogany pie crust table.

"Best antique store in town, if I do say so myself. But my son always forgets to dust. I only come in once in a while and when I do, I usually spend most of the day cleaning." She raised a hand to her brow. "Are you looking for something specific?"

So, this was Eric's mother. Jane hadn't expected to find her here. "I just met your son. I'm renting one of the lofts in the Linden Building."

"Is that right?" Her interest wasn't overwhelming. "Well, there's only one vacant loft that I know of. My brother Arno's."

Jane had failed to make the connection. "Of course. You're Arno Heywood's sister."

"Since you didn't recognize me, I guess that means you didn't catch 'Inside Affair' last night." She finished dusting the sideboard and then lowered herself onto a Queen Anne bench near the front window. She was a stocky woman, with steel gray, beauty shop hair, nylons sagging around swollen ankles and a passing resemblance to Margaret Thatcher. "A crew came out and interviewed me just last week. It seems my brother is big news these days. They wanted me to reminisce about what he was like growing up. The inside scoop, so to speak."

The manner of Arno Heywood's suicide was a perfect 'Inside Affair' story. Jane would have been surprised if they hadn't shown interest.

"A man named Barber contacted me right after he died. Asked if I'd be willing to talk on camera about the kind of a brother he was. I said, sure. Why not? I mean, *I've* got nothing to hide. Besides, he was a decent man, although I can't say I approved of everything he did." She said the last words with distaste.

Jane got the point. Since they were on the topic, she asked, "Did you know about his cross-dressing?"

"Not firsthand, you understand, but his ex-wife and I were pretty close at one time. She alluded to a few problems in their marriage. She wasn't all that specific, but I got the point."

Jane was amazed that this woman would discuss such personal matters so openly, especially with a complete stranger. But then, after last night's televised revelations, she was probably in the mood. "Tell me, did you ever talk to your brother about his cross-dressing? Ever ask him why?"

"Oh, I'd never pry."

No, you'd just judge, thought Jane. *That* came through loud and clear.

"Besides, I wouldn't have known what to say. If you ask me, he would have been just fine if he'd thrown away all those pills and concentrated on his diet. I know people don't believe it, but we are what we eat." It wasn't an opinion, it was a pronouncement. She punctuated the statement by folding one leg over the other and tugging her skirt down over her knees. "If you're sick, you've broken a natural law. But would Arno listen to me?"

Jane assumed it was a rhetorical question.

"I even bought him an electric juicer—told him to forget what his doctors were telling him and go buy some carrots. But it just sat there on his kitchen counter, unused. He'd be alive today if he'd taken better care of his health. All that coffee and sugar—and city water."

"So," said Jane, attempting to steer her away from her rant, "What was the interview like?"

"Well, I talked for quite a while, though very little of it got onto the show. I can't say I liked those bright lights much. They damage the eyes. I hear they want to interview Kelly next. You know my niece, don't you?"

"We've met."

"Beautiful young woman, even with that awful haircut."

Jane wasn't going to touch that. "Was Eric close to her growing up?"

"No, not really. We lived in St. Cloud until my son was in junior high school. Kelly is five years older. And, if you don't mind my saying so, she was a wild kid. My husband and I discouraged any contact between them, at least until she went through drug treatment."

Jane was stunned. "Kelly has a problem with drugs?"

"*Had.* She's been drug free for years, my brother saw to that. Arno had one rule with her, and it was absolute. No drugs. I think he felt sorry for her, since she did so poorly in high school. She barely graduated. He wanted her to manage the Linden Building just to prove to her that she could do it—and do it well. Not that there haven't been problems. But Arno was always trying to build her up. Tell her what a good job she was doing. You know what they say, a little praise goes a long way. Then again, if she'd ever gone back to her old ways, he'd have thrown her out and cut her off without a penny." She lifted her chin and gave Jane a between-you-and-me nod. "Of course, I blame the crowd she was running with back in high school. You can't be too careful about who your friends are. They're to blame for so many of our kids' problems. We always made sure Eric associated only with other young people of quality. Homes with good family values."

"He seems like a fine young man."

"Oh, he is. He's my rock. Right now, with all the financial problems we're having, I suppose I've been leaning on him a bit hard. But I've had to. My health isn't good. His father died two years ago and he's taken over the business."

Jane wanted to ask if *her* electric juicer had broken down, but thought better of it. "Does he date much?"

"Date?" She gave Jane the once over. "He's a quiet boy. Always has been. I don't mean to insult you, but aren't you a little old for him?"

Jane laughed. "No," she said, shaking her head. "That's not what I meant."

As they were talking, the front door opened and in walked Eric, holding several large gilded frames in his arms. "It was a pretty fair-sized estate," he shouted to his mother, not seeing Jane until he'd come into the living room. "Oh, hi," he said, smiling his surprise.

"I thought I'd stop by to see your shop."

He glanced over at his mother. "Great. I see you two've already met."

"Not really," said Mrs. Lind. "I don't believe I got your name."

Before Jane could respond, Eric said, "It's Jane Lawless. You remember, mom. She's the one I told you about."

Jane wondered what that meant. "Well," she said, her eyes giving the room one last sweep, "I'd better shove off." She didn't feel much like talking to Eric with his mother around.

"Oh, do you have to?" he asked, clearly disappointed. "I'd be happy to show you around. We've got a terrific selection of old kitchen accessories in the back room. I know you'd like them." His eyes strayed to his mother. "Jane owns a restaurant on Lake Harriet."

At that bit of news, Mrs. Lind's expression brightened considerably.

"Well—" said Jane, beginning to waffle. She did enjoy rummaging through antique kitchen equipment. She had quite a collection at home.

"Please," he said, his tone implying that it would mean a great deal to him if she'd stay.

"Well, all right. Sure. I don't have to be at the hospital for another half hour."

"Hospital?" he said, a concerned look on his face.

"Oh, it's my aunt. She's not feeling well. I want to stop by and see her before I head off to work."

"Those doctors don't know a *thing*," muttered Eric's mother. "They're *ignorant*."

"Not now, Mother," said Eric, setting the frames down next to a cedar chest. "Come on back," he said to Jane. "I'll only keep you for a few minutes."

29

Teddy was down on his hands and knees searching through the contents of a trunk when he heard a voice call, "Teddy, are you there?"

He straightened up and listened, thinking that perhaps his ears were playing tricks on him. He'd been digging into the past for so many months now that the present and the past were becoming all mixed together.

"Teddy?"

But no, there it was again, that same familiar voice. It was his father calling him down to dinner. He was eleven years old, sprawled across the bed in the room he shared with his brother, reading a comic book.

"If you're there, I'd like to come up. It's Edgar."

Teddy couldn't help but laugh at the errant perceptions of a silly old man. How on earth he could have confused his brother's voice with that of his father he'd never know. He scrambled to his feet and crossed to the door. "I'm here," he called, hearing footsteps on the stairs.

Edgar's head appeared over the balustrade.

"My God," he gasped, "You're an old man too!"

The brothers stood staring at each other, each one's face filled not only with amazement at the obvious change in their appearances, but also with a kind of hesitant wonder.

Finally, Edgar said, "What has it been? Thirty years? I'm not even sure I'd have recognized you, except that you look so much like Grampa."

They examined each other for several more seconds, neither moving any closer, neither speaking. Then, as if on cue, they each broke into laughter.

"Come and sit down," said Teddy eagerly, motioning for Edgar to follow him into his office. He was amazed at how pleasurable it was to see his brother again. His feelings weren't what he'd expected.

Edgar took a seat on an ancient, somewhat dilapidated leather chair and Teddy settled down behind his makeshift desk. It was only a hollow core door placed across two filing cabinets, but it served its purpose.

"How did you get in?" asked Teddy.

"One of the workmen. I told him I was your brother and he said your office was on the third floor and to just go on up. The back door wasn't locked."

"Ah." He rearranged the papers on his desk, not sure how to begin.

"Well . . . so," said Edgar, still smiling. "Merry Christmas."

"Same to you."

"This is . . . hard, but then I knew it would be. I don't know where to start." He took off his hat and smoothed back his white hair. "Gracie died about ten years ago. Did you know?"

Teddy shook his head.

"Well, it was a short illness. Unexpected. I miss her every day."

"But you've found someone new."

Edgar appeared to be momentarily thrown by his brother's directness. "Yes, I have. I'd love for you to meet her. She's English." His eyes grew soft. "A very special woman."

"How lucky for you," said Teddy, unable to keep the coldness out of his voice. He could tell Edgar had caught it. At that instant he saw with absolute clarity that this conversation was going to proceed with the inevitability of a runaway locomotive. No matter how glad he'd been to see his brother, there was too much between them.

"And, so . . . how's Ella?" asked Edgar kindly. "You mentioned her on the phone when I called. I'm glad she's still with you."

"She had a stroke two years ago."

Edgar was silenced by the news.

"Since you never wanted me to marry her in the first place, I hardly believe you'd care all that much."

"Are you still carrying a grudge? After all these years, you're still angry with me?" He sounded incredulous.

Teddy wanted to bang his fists on the table and scream, yes! Instead, for Ella's sake, he said, his voice flat, almost indifferent, "You did everything in your power to prevent our marriage. You said she was wrong for me. I believe *crude* was your term."

"She was more than ten years older than you. You were thirty and she was almost forty-one. She worked in a dive downtown and she'd already been married twice and had a six-year-old son. You turned a blind eye to the kind of woman she was, but I couldn't. I was your older brother. I had to protect you, had to tell you I thought you were making a mistake."

"I admit she was irreverent. She broke all the rules. But she was good for me, Edgar, and that's what you never saw. She and Bobby have been the best part of my miserable life!" He knew his face had turned beet red, and he could hear Ella's voice in the back of his mind telling him to calm down. Slipping off his glasses, he took out his handkerchief. It was what he always did when he felt stressed.

"Teddy, listen to me."

"No! This time, you listen to me." He began polishing the right lens, his eyes cast down. "I told you the day you refused to be my best man that if you persisted with your self-righteous pomposity, you'd never be welcome in my home. And you never have been. And you never will be."

Edgar sat forward in his chair, not speaking for several seconds. Finally, he said, "Don't you ever feel the need to forgive?"

"When I die, dear brother, I will not be forgiven for my sins. I can tell you that with complete certainty."

"I assume that means you don't go to confession any longer."

Teddy shuddered inwardly. "I haven't been to mass since the day I was married. The church did a great deal more than frown upon our union, Edgar. In case you'd forgotten."

"But . . ." He hesitated. "I'm not the church. I'm your family. And I'm truly, truly sorry. We're all that's left of the old group. Can't we at least decide to go on from here? Maybe you're right. Maybe we can't ever really forgive, but . . ." His voice faltered. "Won't you give me a chance?"

Teddy concentrated on polishing each lense to a perfect shine. He hated disorder.

"Please," pleaded Edgar.

The word echoed in the cold room.

After holding his glasses up to the light and pronouncing them spotless, he put them back on and stuffed his handkerchief back into his pocket. Coughing slightly, he said, "All right. I promised Ella . . . I'd try. And for her sake, I will."

Edgar didn't move. Then, seeming to understand that this was the best he was going to get, he relaxed back into his chair he said, "I thank you for that. And if you'll give me the chance, I'll thank Ella too."

This isn't going to be easy, thought Teddy. He wasn't even sure it was worth it. What did he need a brother for at his age? "So," he said, eyeing Edgar thoughtfully. "I see you still wear those ridiculous bow ties and red suspenders."

Edgar's smile was slow. "I guess I do."

"Still smoke a pipe too?"

"When no one objects."

"Well, don't take that filthy thing out in here."

Edgar's smile broadened. "You sound just like Mom."

"I know."

"And how about you? How's the writing coming?"

"Oh, I've got a couple of novels in the pipeline. The market's always tight."

"But your first book did well. I loved it, you know. And the reviews were great."

Teddy tapped his fingers impatiently on the table. "In the thirty-five years I've been writing," he said, his voice a mixture of weariness and resentment, "I've never received anything but benign condescension."

"You've got to watch it," said Edgar, shaking his head. "Bitterness can eat you alive."

You arrogant ass, thought Teddy. You walk in here after not seeing me for decades and think after five minutes of chit chat you can define my problems for me? "You still see yourself as the older, wiser brother, don't you? Always there to give advice. Well, tell me your life has been a total success, brother dear. I'd like to hear all about it."

Edgar shifted around in his seat. "But . . . aren't you working on something else?"

"You mean the Boline biography?"

"Right."

Teddy grinned. "Now that may just turn out to be a horse of a different color."

"Meaning what?"

"Wait and see."

Edgar scratched the back of his neck. "You know, I followed your son's trial in the newspaper a couple of years ago. Wasn't Boline's grandson an eyewitness to the robbery?"

Angrily, Teddy responded, "He was."

"It was a convenience store hold-up, right? Two men. And the owner was shot and badly wounded. He died a few weeks later."

"Bob had nothing to do with it! He was home in bed at the time."

"Alone?"

"Yes, *alone*," he repeated, shaking his head and looking down. "He would never have done anything like that! He had a good job, a woman he wanted to marry. He didn't even know the other man, the one who was accused of pulling the trigger. If it hadn't been for Richard Crawford and his absolute certainty on the witness stand, he would never have gone to jail."

Edgar hesitated, but only for a moment. "How on earth did the Boline estate ever hire you to do August Boline's biography?"

A smile formed on Teddy's lips. "Bad homework, I guess you could say. To give the lawyers some credit, Bob and I don't have the same last name. Ella's first husband wouldn't let me adopt him legally, so his name was never changed. And the trial was three years ago. Ancient history. How many murders have we had in Minneapolis since then? And besides, I wasn't hired to do the book until last spring. It never even came up."

Edgar eyed his brother. "So this biography is a vendetta."

"Edgar," said Teddy, holding up his hand, "you wound me. Do you think I'd do something unethical?"

"Well, I—"

"Boline was a crook, plain and simple. Even though he's a revered figure in this country, an architectural visionary, a man who helped the poor, and one of the most famous and beloved entrepreneurs in Minnesota history, he was also a thief. Don't get me wrong, what I write will be entirely factual. But you must enjoy the irony, Edgar. This project was dropped right in my lap—the Boline estate came to me. And the best part," he added, his eyes gleaming, "is that, with the publication of this book, I will finally receive the critical success I've always wanted."

"You seem very sure of that."

"I am."

Edgar shook his head. Pushing himself up out of the chair, he began to wander around the room.

Teddy assumed it was his way of changing the subject.

"My God," said Edgar, "somebody in Boline's family sure was a baseball fanatic. Look at all the mementos." He stopped next to a rack of baseball mitts.

"Crawford was a collector. Take your pick," he said, aware of his brother's own enthusiasm for the game. "It won't be missed."

"Oh, I couldn't," said Edgar. "But it sure is fun to see it all. I hope this will be donated to some museum so everyone can enjoy it." His eyes took in the clothing, bats, balls, shoes, and club photos. "Say, who's this guy?" he asked, walking up to a framed photo on the wall.

Teddy shrugged. "Probably some coach."

Edgar tapped a finger against the side of his cheek. "You know, he reminds me of that friend of yours. Arno Heywood." He continued to walk around the room, picking up an object here and there. "I was really surprised to hear he'd committed suicide. I suppose you saw his sister being interviewed on TV last night."

Teddy's head snapped up. "What did you say?"

"Sure. She was interviewed on one of those gossip shows. I don't usually watch them, but I was visiting Beryl at the hospital and you can only play cards for so long."

Teddy was appalled. "I can't believe she'd be that tasteless."

"Sounds like your friend had a hard life. And to think he tried to commit suicide once before. It's too bad they can't help people like him. But then, I suppose that's what the depression medication was for."

Teddy leaned forward, looking Edgar straight in the eye. "Say that again."

"Say what again?"

"About the suicide."

"Didn't you know? Apparently his daughter found him. That's when he started using all those depression medications. Teddy . . . are you all right? You've gone as white as a sheet." Edgar moved toward him.

Teddy could hardly bring himself to speak. So that's what Kelly had meant when she'd accused him of murdering her father. She knew his mental health was far worse than anyone ever suspected. Even though she was privy to only a small part of what had happened between them, she must have thought the knowledge of her drug use had driven him over the edge. "Poor kid," he whispered, his eyes fixed on his computer monitor.

"What did you say?" asked Edgar.

Teddy's gaze sank to the keyboard in front of him. "You know, I'm sorry, but I've got to make an important phone call."

"Of course. I've taken up enough of your time. How about if we talk later? Maybe we can get together for dinner some time next week."

"Fine."

Edgar picked up his his hat. As he was about to leave, he stopped near the door and said, "I'm glad we had this chance to talk, Teddy. I think we've cleared the air. Perhaps that's the first step back to each other. It's ironic isn't it that Beryl's niece should've moved into the loft where you live? If she hadn't, this reunion would never have happened."

Irony seemed to be the order of the day, thought Teddy. He waited until his brother had left before he picked up the phone.

30

"More presents?" exclaimed Beryl, taking the small package Jane handed her and removing the bow. "I'm going to be so spoiled when I leave here, you won't even want me around."

"Not likely," grinned Jane, sitting down on the edge of the hospital bed. "Open it."

Beryl tore back the delicate yellow paper revealing a beautiful blooming violet. "Oh, this *is* lovely. Do you remember your second cousin Camilla's east window? It was violets from top to bottom."

Jane was glad to see her aunt in such good spirits today. "I'm surprised to find you alone."

"Oh, I've had lots of company. Evelyn Bratrude stopped by after breakfast. And then that friend of yours left just a few minutes ago."

Jane had no idea who she meant. "What friend?"

"You know, that nice young woman you invited to join us for Thanksgiving dinner."

"Amy McGee?"

"Why, of course, dear. She brought me those lovely buns over there." Beryl pointed. "This is the second time she's been by."

"When was the first time?"

"Yesterday afternoon."

Jane got up and walked over to the window ledge, removing the foil cover from a plate of Rice Krispie bars.

"Wasn't that sweet?"

She couldn't help but wonder if this culinary masterpiece was what Amy was preparing for dessert tonight. Face it, she thought. When it comes to food, you *are* a snob. "But how did she know you were here?"

"Oh, she said she talked to your father the other afternoon, and he mentioned I was ill."

Jane was confused. "She talked with *Dad* too?"

"So she said. This is only a guess, you understand, but I think she wanted some advice from him on what to buy you for Christmas."

Jane felt sick.

"Something wrong, dear?"

"What could be wrong?" She tried not to sound defensive. Replacing the cover on the bars, she made a decision. Tonight, no matter what, she was going to end this relationship, such as it was, and that's all there was to it. She'd only dug herself in deeper by agreeing to have dinner in the first place.

Beryl plucked a dead leaf from the plant. "Amy led me to believe the two of you were—"

"We're not."

"No. I didn't think so. She hardly seems your type."

Jane wasn't sure what her type was, but she had to agree. Amy wasn't it. "Beryl, think for a minute. Did you happen to mention to Amy that I was staying at a loft downtown?"

"Yes, I think the subject did come up."

So, here was the leak. She could hardly expect her aunt to keep her whereabouts a secret. "Where's Edgar?" she asked, leaning back against the ledge. The room still looked and smelled like a florist's shop.

"Oh, he went to see his brother, Teddy. I expect him back any time now." She set the violet down next to the phone, feeling the dirt to see if it needed water.

"You two have certainly become close."

"Yes," said Beryl, patting her hair. "We have. He's a dear man, don't you think?"

Jane could see the expectant look on her aunt's face. It was obvious she wanted a positive response. "I like him a lot."

"Oh, that does make me happy," she smiled. "I think we shall be seeing him a great deal when I get home." She looked up. "Here's the doctor now."

A tall woman entered the room. She was wearing street clothes and carrying a chart.

"Finally, you have a chance to meet my niece," said Beryl.

"Good afternoon," said the woman, offering Jane her hand. "I'm Dr. Ries." Her eyes dropped to the chart as she made a notation on the front page. "And how are you feeling today?" she asked, her gaze moving to Beryl.

"Better, I think. My appetite seems to be returning."

The doctor bent over and looked carefully into her eyes. "You're right. That's a good sign. Now, I've only got a couple of minutes, but I wanted to tell you that the results from all your tests are back, and it's pretty much what I expected. It's a reoccurrence of the hepatitis. We've already started you on prednisone. According to your records, you were given that several years ago."

Beryl nodded.

"This time I'd like to use it in conjunction with another drug called Imuran. It's normally given to transplant patients. In your case, we've found that Imuran helps us to lower the prednisone dosage to a more manageable level. Steroids, like prednisone, are important drugs, but they have some inherent dangers."

"Why do you give it to transplant patients?" asked Jane.

"It suppresses the immune system and thereby lessens the chances of organ rejection."

"But a drug like that," said Jane, standing up very straight, "I mean, it sounds pretty scary."

Dr. Ries took off her glasses. "I'm not going to sugarcoat this. Your aunt is seriously ill. If we can't reduce the inflammation in her liver, the prognosis isn't good. I really feel this is the best, and safest, protocol. Right now, your aunt is on seventy milligrams of prednisone a day. That is a large dose, especially for a woman of her age. I'd like to bring that down to twenty, less in time. But we can only do that with the addition of the second drug."

"How much of this Imuran would she need to take?" Jane hated all this talk about drugs and side effects. She was always impatient with anything she didn't understand.

"Approximately fifty milligrams. It's a very small dosage. Using the two together, I think we can achieve the best results." The doctor slipped the chart under her arm. "I should tell you that it's not a universally applied therapy. But in my practice, I've had a great deal of success using the two drugs together. Now, I've got some other patients I need to see so I'll let you two talk it over. You need to decide how you want to proceed. If you want to get a second opinion, I'd be glad to suggest another liver specialist, or you can find your own."

"Thank you, doctor," said Beryl. She glanced up at Jane, the look on her face suggesting that she didn't want to anger the good doctor by suggesting her method of treatment was anything less than perfection itself.

Dr. Ries squeezed Beryl's hand and smiled. "Your color really does look much better today."

"I thought so too," said Beryl, returning the smile.

"When can she go home?" asked Jane, faintly annoyed by the entire interaction.

"Soon, I hope," replied Dr. Ries. "I'll know more in a couple of days." With that, she nodded to them both and left.

"I think I'll do what she says," said Beryl after she was gone. She leaned back against her pillow. "What do you think? You have to remember, she's the expert. We know nothing about any of these drugs, Jane."

"But your immune system. That frightens me."

"It frightens me too. This body has served me well all my life, and now it's failing . . . at the very moment when I have so much to live for."

Jane sat down on the bed and put her arms around her aunt, giving her a reassuring hug. It surprised her to find that Beryl was shivering.

"I mean, I have you," she sniffed. "My darling, Jane. And our family. And . . . well—"

And Edgar, thought Jane, silently finishing her aunt's sentence. You have Edgar now, too.

31

After a hectic afternoon at the restaurant, Jane drove back to the Linden Building to spend a few minutes relaxing before she headed over to Amy's apartment. Needless to say, she was dreading the evening.

She spent some time lingering quietly over a double latte in Athena's Garden and then, as she was about to leave, she spotted Brandon Vachel steaming toward the stairway in the back. Since she wanted to talk to him about Kelly, she dropped some change on the table and followed him—at a suitable distance—downstairs to his studio. As he pulled out his key and put it into the lock, she called his name.

He turned, not recognizing her at first. Then, the light dawning, he said, "Hey, babe," using his typical greeting.

Jane assumed he knew it was annoying, and that's why he did it. She let it pass. "Hey," she said, echoing his words.

"What's up?"

"I thought maybe we could talk for a second."

He thought it over. "Sure. Why not?" He pushed through the door and switched on the overhead light.

The acrid smell of turpentine mixed with the basement's amusement park ambience assaulted her nose as her eyes swept quickly over the interior. Like other artist's studios she'd seen, the place was a mess. Welding equipment, scraps of metal, paint cans, tubes of oil paint, old pizza cartons, bubble gum wrappers, crushed cans of pop, filled ashtrays, filthy rags and mounds of junk were everywhere. Several plywood boards had been placed across wooden sawhorses, providing ample work space. In the center of the room sat the welded metal sculpture he was currently working on. It looked like a metal cow, at least six feet high, stuffed with rags and straw. Bright green yarn was wrapped around several of the protruding metal ribs.

"Make yourself at home," he announced somewhat grandly, hopping up on a stool. Today his hair was pulled back into a pony tail.

Since there was no place to sit, Jane just stood by the door.

"So, Kelly tells me you were the one who padlocked the roof." He lit up a cigarette, picking a bit of leaf out of his teeth.

"Did she tell you why?"

He laughed. "Sure did. You wanted to pull the plug on my home movies." He took a deep drag. "Believe it or not, I started going up there for the fresh air."

"Ever tried the front door?"

He took another drag and then blew smoke out of his nose. "In case you haven't noticed, this isn't a particularly safe part of town. You'd be smart to be careful when you're out late at night."

"Thanks for the warning."

"Don't mention it." He crossed his arms over his narrow chest, holding the cigarette casually to his lips. "Somehow, I don't think you believe me."

She shrugged. "Does it matter?"

"No, but I'm not lying. I got fresh air up there and lots of peace and quiet. Not to mention the great view." His smile was almost a leer.

"Of the stars?"

"At first, yeah."

"But then you noticed the skylight."

"It had a certain X-rated appeal. I had a ringside seat right above old man Heywood's queen-sized bed. I guess you could say I'll watch anything."

God, but he was disgusting. "Did Arno or Peg ever catch you?"

"I wouldn't be standing here today if they had. But then when Arno moved across the hall, I thought my X-rated days were over. That's when the blond appeared."

"What blond?"

"Just a guy I know."

"Eric Lind?"

"Yeah, that's the one. When he figured Heywood and his girlfriend were out of town—which they were a lot—he'd use the place for a little recreation."

"You mean he brought women up there?"

Brandon wiggled his eyebrows. "Wouldn't you like to know."

Maybe coming down here had been a mistake. This guy was about as sleazy as they came.

"See, it's titillating, isn't it? Look at you. You're just as curious as the next asshole." He took another drag, flicking ash onto the floor. "But, for the record, it wasn't women. It was men. One man in particular. But then I'm not fussy. As I said, I'll watch anything."

Jane couldn't believe her luck. Here was proof dropped right in her lap that openly or not, Eric *was* gay. "Can you describe the man Eric brought upstairs with him."

"In vivid detail."

It nauseated her that he was enjoying this so much. "Just the basics."

"Sure, babe. But why all the interest?"

"Like you said, I'm fascinated."

"Why do I doubt that?" He let the cigarette dangle from his lips as he continued, "Well, he was about five-nine. Dark hair. Heavy beard. Good looking, but not as good looking as the Swede. Most often he was wearing a fancy suit. Not the entire time, you understand." He raised a suggestive eyebrow.

"I understand."

"I thought you would."

"Do you know his name?"

He took another drag. "It was John."

"Kelly's friend?"

"Yeah. Say, how come you know so much?"

"I keep my eyes open. Just like you."

He bit the edge of his lip, thinking that over. "Well, whatever," he said, stubbing out the cigarette, "that's the end of my story. The balcony's closed now, thanks to you. My evenings are free."

"What a shame."

"Is it? You smoke dope, Jane?"

She was startled that he knew her name. "I have."

"I can give you a great deal. We could have a party."

"Like you and Kelly?" It had been quite some time since she'd had a conversation with a man who maintained eye contact with her breasts instead of her face.

"Yeah, since you bring it up, just like me and Kelly."

"You don't think she has a problem with drugs?"

"Oh, Jeez." His amused expression vanished. He got down off the stool and moved over to his sculpture, examining part of the cow's head.

"You're going to give me shit now, right? You and I both know there's not an ounce of difference between smoking dope and having a drink."

She had no intention of discussing the morality of American drug use with this bozo. "Offhand, I can think of one rather large difference."

"Name it."

"It's illegal."

"That's just political bullshit. Some bigshot tells you one drug is fine and the other drug isn't. I'm supposed to buy that crap? Give me *some* credit. Besides, if you're worried about Kelly, she handles her use about as well as anyone I know."

Not a glowing testimonial. "Okay, for the sake of argument, let's say I agree with you. It's still kind of an expensive habit. How can you afford it?" Brandon didn't look all that flush to her.

"I manage."

"With a little help from Kelly?"

"Hey, she doesn't give me a dime!" he snapped.

Obviously a sore subject.

He threw his lighter on the table and stomped over to the other side of the room, picked up a roll of heavy plastic and set it next to a door.

Jane saw that it was padlocked. "What's behind there?" she asked. It was a nosy question, not that Brandon was much concerned with boundary issues.

"It's a storage room, not that it's any of your goddamned business," he said, shoving his fists into the pockets of his white painter pants. "Now get out of here. This is my space and I don't want *you* in it."

She'd found more than she came for so she wasn't about to argue.

An hour later, after taking her second shower of the day—she needed one after her delightful conversation with Brandon—Jane headed out the rear door of the Linden Building. By the looks of her car, several inches of new snow had fallen. Big fluffy flakes floated down from the night sky. She stopped for a moment and looked up, amazed. Every year she had the exact same reaction. She adored winter. She loved the cold and the snow. On nights like this, the world really did feel like a wonderland.

As she passed the restaurant's alley, she heard someone call her name.

As she turned, she felt a hand like a vise seize her shoulder and spin her around, slamming her against the dumpster. She struggled to regain her balance but her boots slipped on the wet snow and she hit the ground. She screamed as she felt herself being dragged back into the darkness.

"Shut up!" demanded a raspy voice, slapping her across the face. Strong hands flipped her over onto her stomach.

As she tried to get up, she felt a weight land on her back. "Stop it!" she yelled, flailing her arms.

"Did you hear me? Shut up!" He slammed her face into the concrete.

With every ounce of strength she possessed, she struggled to get away, somehow managing to crawl out from under him. As she scrambled to her feet he lunged at her, catching her around her knees, sending her sprawling once again. She looked around wildly, trying to get her bearings. This couldn't be happening.

"You stupid bitch," said the voice. It was deep and nasty.

She felt him land on her stomach, knocking the wind out of her as he pinned her to the ground.

"If you're not going to shut up, I'm going to shut you up!" he snarled.

He pulled her head back and forced a huge handful of snow into her mouth.

She gagged, thrashing her head from side to side to get away from his fingers.

Grunting angrily, he pinned her arms under his knees and then ripped open her coat. Her flannel shirt came next. Before she knew what was happening, his hands had found her skin.

She'd never felt this close to hysteria before in her entire life.

He reached behind her and fumbled in her back pocket.

She was completely helpless, watching him mutely as he rifled through her wallet. Where his face should have been there was a ski mask, ominous and ugly. He held her captive, his left hand at her throat as he tried to read the driver's licence, moving it back and forth to catch what little light was available. "Yeah, you're the bitch." He threw it against the wall, but not before removing all the money.

"Now," he said, stuffing the cash into his coat pocket. He grabbed her roughly around the waist with both hands, his thumbs digging into her flesh. "You got the picture? This would be easy as shit. But I got instructions. Not that I always follow them."

She was paralyzed. The snow in her mouth stung. She wanted to cry out, but she was too terrified to move. He was like a giant, his strength immense.

"Now listen up. Stop asking so many goddamned questions. You got no business poking your nose in around here. Got it?" When she didn't respond, he whispered almost sweetly, "Got it?"

She nodded.

For a second he just looked at her. "I don't think you do," he said finally, his voice hard and sullen. He yanked her to her feet and slammed her against the dumpster again. She would have fallen to the ground except that he held her upright, one hand at her throat, the other grasping the top of her jeans. "You like this?"

She shook her head.

He slapped her. "Do you?"

She choked on the snow trying to answer. If she could just hold on.

Seizing her arm, he threw her against the opposite brick wall. This time she felt her head hit with a sickening thud. She slid to the ground, disoriented and dazed.

"Don't say you weren't warned," he said, kicking her in the side.

She closed her eyes as his silhouette faded out of view.

32

"Take her upstairs!"

Jane felt herself being lifted. She opened her eyes but the lights were so vivid and intense, she closed them again. The air felt heavy and hot against her skin.

"Put her down on the bed," said the same voice. "Jane? Stay with us. You're in your loft, and you're safe." She felt her coat being removed. "I'm going to take off your boots because they're wet. We have to get you dry and warm."

"What do you want me to do?" asked another voice.

"Go downstairs and make some coffee—or tea. Anything hot. Bring it back up right away."

Jane felt disoriented, and very, very drowsy. All she wanted to do was lie back and sleep.

"Jane, look at me!" the voice commanded.

Her eyes opened. Peg's daughter, Julia, bent over her, her expression full of urgency. "Can you tell me how long you've been outside?"

Outside, thought Jane. "I—" The words wouldn't form.

"You were attacked. I need to examine you, make sure you're okay. But right now I'm most concerned about hypothermia."

Her mind felt thick and slow, and it was hard to focus. "Yeah," she nodded. "But—" She blinked several times, gazing at Julia in confusion.

"I'm a doctor," said Julia, helping her off with her wet shirt. "I'm afraid the pants have to go too."

Jane felt Julia yank them off. "Where are your socks?" she asked as she helped Jane into a warm robe.

"I'm . . . cold."

"I know. We're going to fix that." She smoothed back Jane's hair, examining a cut near her eye.

Jane relaxed back against the pillows as Julia covered her with an electric blanket, several more wool blankets, and then a down quilt. Finally, heavy socks were found and put on.

"I need to examine you," said Julia, easing back part of the covers. "You've got some bad bruises, and a couple of cuts on your face. Also I noticed a fairly nasty mark just above your waist."

"He . . . kicked me," said Jane slowly. Some of it was coming back to her now.

"Who kicked you? Can you describe him?"

She closed her eyes against the memory.

"That's fine," said Julia quickly. "You just rest. I'm concerned about a rib fracture. Do you feel any tenderness here?" She untied the robe and drew it back, touching the bruise.

Jane shook her head.

"You may later."

As Julia completed her examination, Roz returned with the mug of hot tea. She sat down on the bed next to Jane and held the cup to her lips. "Here you go," she whispered. "You drink up now."

Jane could see the terrible strain on Roz's face, and it frightened her.

"Should I bring up some brandy?" asked Roz, turning around to look at Julia. "That might help warm her."

"No. That's the worst thing we could give her. Listen, go across the hall to my mother's apartment. There's a portable heater in the front closet. Bring it up here right away."

"I'll ask Thurman to get it," said Roz, rising quickly and disappearing down the stairs.

"Thurman?" repeated Jane. She touched her face, feeling a bruise near her mouth.

"He found you," said Julia, wrapping Jane's head with a towel. "He called Roz from the restaurant downstairs, and then she called me. She knew I was up in mom's apartment trying to clean the place. And she also knew I was a doctor."

"What . . . time is it?"

"It's almost nine. Funny, but I came by around seven to see if you were home. I knocked, but there was no answer. Can you tell me how long you were outside?"

"I left about . . . six-thirty. I had to go buy some Ripple."

Julia cocked her head. "Ripple? As in the wine, Ripple?"

Jane nodded.

"You drink Ripple?"

"Not willingly."

"Sounds like there's a story in there. Well, you can tell me later. Anyway, so you left about six-thirty. That's when the guy must have jumped you."

Her jaw tightened.

"It's all right," said Julia, her voice very gentle. "You're safe now."

Safe, thought Jane. She turned her head away.

"When Thurman found you, you were covered by an inch of snow. You were groaning or he'd never have noticed you. If you'd stayed out there much longer—" She abandoned the end of the sentence.

Jane was beginning to shiver. The numbness she'd felt a few minutes ago was disappearing. Every part of her body hurt.

"Here, drink some more of this," said Julia, sitting down next to her and lifting the mug to her lips.

Jane took several gulps. It was hard to hold her head still because she was shaking so violently.

"Shivering is good," said Julia. "It's nothing to be afraid of. I know you're in pain. I'll give you something for it, but not until I'm sure we're totally out of the woods with the hypothermia. Right now, your temperature is several degrees below normal. You have a bruise on the back of your head, but I see no evidence of concussion. We'll want to watch it though." She tucked the covers around Jane's shoulders.

"I've never felt this cold," she said, trembling uncontrollably.

"Drink some more tea."

It did feel good going down.

"You're going to be fine," said Julia, her voice reassuring. She touched Jane's cheek with the back of her hand. "I provide only the best medical care for my friends."

Friends, thought Jane. "Am I your friend?"

She smoothed back the covers. "I have to go downstairs and talk to the police. Roz called 911 just after we got you up here. I need to file a report on this. From the looks of your wallet, I'd say the guy was after your money. But you got lucky. He didn't take any of the credit cards. I don't suppose you got a good look at him."

Jane closed her eyes. "No."

"Too bad. Well anyway, you rest now. I'll be back up in a few minutes."

. . .

Jane drifted in and out of consciousness. But mainly she shook. Not just from the cold. Pieces of the attack flashed through her mind with a sickening vividness. Again and again she felt the snow being forced into her mouth, and the man's hands as they ripped open her shirt. If she'd fought harder, could she have gotten away?

When Julia finally returned, she was carrying a heater with her. She plugged it into a wall outlet and then set it on a chair right next to the bed. "This should help," she said, taking out a thermometer from her bag and slipping it into Jane's mouth.

Jane's head was clearer now. As the fan cranked up, she could feel the added warmth. Her eyes rose to the skylight, but it was dark, covered by snow.

"Are you feeling any warmer?" asked Julia, removing the thermometer and checking the temperature.

"Not much."

"It's come up. I think you'll live."

"You'd never know it from the way I feel."

"Pretty sore, huh?" She studied the bruises on Jane's face. "Well, I think I can help with that." She dug through her bag and found a bottle of pills. "I want you to take three of these. It'll not only take some of the edge off the pain, it will also help you sleep." She lifted the mug and with the last bit of tea, Jane swallowed the pills.

"Where's Roz," asked Jane through chattering teeth.

"I sent her back down to her loft. Thurman too. I want you to have complete quiet. You need to rest. Doctor's orders."

"What did the police say?"

"They took my statement, as well as Thurman's. When they left, I think they were going to check out the alley. See what evidence they could find. They'll want to talk to you too as soon as you feel up to it."

Jane held her hands together under the covers. "Thanks."

"I'm just sorry this happened to you."

The phone on the nightstand began to ring.

"Kind of late for a call," said Julia. "I'll get it down in the study." She got up and dashed downstairs. "You rest," she called after her.

After a few seconds, Jane could hear a low conversation. It didn't take long for her to grow impatient. She wanted Julia to come back. She couldn't stand the idea of being alone right now. Finally, after what seemed like an eternity, she heard footsteps on the stairs

"Are you asleep?" whispered Julia, stepping over to the bed.

"No," said Jane, her voice thick and low.

She sat down. "That was a friend of yours."

"Cordelia?"

"No, Amy McGee."

"Oh," she groaned.

"Seems you were supposed to have dinner at her apartment tonight."

"Was she furious?"

"I think that's a fair description. She said she'd left four messages on your answering machine."

"Four?"

"Maybe it was five. Whatever, I told her you'd had an accident. I didn't elaborate."

"And?"

"She wanted to know who the hell I was."

Jane started to laugh. "Agh," she said, her hand flying to her face.

"Does it hurt?"

"Only when I laugh." She grimaced.

"You're much more lucid than you were an hour ago. You had me pretty worried." She held her hand to the side of Jane's face. "Has the medication helped at all?"

"A little, I think."

Julia reached up and snapped off the light. "You've got to try and sleep." She took hold of Jane's hand. "You poor kid. You're still chilled to the bone."

"What are you going to do?"

"What do you mean?"

"You won't leave me, will you?" Jane tried to keep the panic out of her voice, but it was useless. It was all there for Julia to read, if she cared to.

"Of course I won't leave. You close your eyes now. I'm just going to sit here a while."

Jane looked up at her gratefully.

"Try to sleep. The medication should help, if you don't fight it."

"I don't have much fight left in me," she said. "I'm . . . glad you're here."

Julia hesitated, and then held Jane's hand to her lips. "I'm glad I am too."

As soon as Jane shut her eyes, she noticed a pleasant floating sensation. Her body felt light, almost weightless. In a strange drug-induced sort of way, she was beginning to relax. A few minutes later, she felt Julia get up. In the dreamlike semi-darkness, she watched Julia lift up the covers and climb in beside her.

As she slipped her arm ever so gently around Jane's body and drew her close, she whispered, "I'm here. Just sleep now."

This felt so right, thought Jane. She drifted to the rhythm of Julia's breathing. Drifted and floated, and finally, slept.

33

Jane didn't rise the next morning until after eleven. Every muscle in her body hurt as she got up from her bed and shambled into the bathroom, examining herself warily in the mirror. Last night felt like a remote and impossible nightmare, and yet the cuts and bruises on her face were clear proof it had all happened.

As she touched a tender spot just under her left eye, the sound of a radio being turned on downstairs caused her to jump. Who was down there? When she'd awakened, she'd been so sure she was alone. Julia had left earlier, saying she had an early appointment. But there was no mistaking it. Someone else was in the loft. She began to panic. Her eyes searched the room frantically for a weapon. Suddenly remembering the gun Cordelia had brought over the first night, she crawled across the bed and threw open the nightstand's bottom drawer.

"Jane," called a soft voice from the stairs. "Are you awake?" Julia breezed up the steps, a glass of orange juice in her hand. "Oh, God, I'm so sorry," she said, stopping dead in her tracks when she saw Jane poised on the bed, a gun pointed directly at her chest. "I didn't mean to frighten you! I thought I heard the floor creak so I figured I'd bring you some breakfast."

Jane's eyes fell to the gun in her hand. She dropped it on the quilt as if it were a hot coal.

"Are you all right?" asked Julia, stepping toward her.

"I think so. I just . . . I don't know. I panicked." She felt dazed, and frightened by what she'd just done.

"You're going to have to take it easy for a few days. I mean it. An attack like that takes more than just a physical toll."

"Doctor's orders?" Her smile was faint.

"No, Julia's orders."

Jane ran a hand through her hair. "I thought you'd left."

"I had. But my meeting was canceled so I picked up some groceries and came back. How's that bruise on your side?" She handed Jane the juice.

"It hurts."

"A sharp pain?"

She was so thirsty, she downed it in one try. "No."

"That's good. That heavy coat you were wearing probably saved you from a broken rib."

Jane eased herself back against the pillows, giving Julia the once over. "How come you're so dressed up?" She looked great. Better than great.

"It's my mother's funeral today."

"Oh!" Jane was mortified that she'd forgotten. "I . . . forgot."

"Small wonder."

"No, really. I'd planned on coming."

"I know you had."

Jane could read the sadness in her eyes. "I should be the one asking you if you're all right."

Julia looked down at her dress. "We're kind of a sorry pair, aren't we?" Somewhat hesitantly, she sat down on the edge of the bed. "I'm just glad you're feeling better. I don't think I could handle another tragedy in my life right now."

"I'm fine. Really. But thanks."

"I didn't do that much."

"You stayed with me last night."

Julia made no reply. Instead, her eyes strayed to the windows.

"So, what time is the funeral?"

"In less than an hour. I've really got to run." As she stood she said, "I didn't know how you'd feel about being alone, so Roz offered to stay with you while I'm gone. She should be here any minute."

Jane wasn't quite sure what to say. She didn't much care for the idea of a baby sitter, and yet spending the afternoon all by herself wasn't that appealing either.

"You're going to be all right now, aren't you?" asked Julia. "No other medical problems I should know about?"

"No, doctor."

She smiled. "Then I'll see you tonight."

The thought of spending the evening with Julia lightened her mood more than she dared admit, even to herself. "I think I'll take a shower."

"Good idea." She held Jane's eyes for a long second.

Jane sensed that she was about to say something more, but instead she just turned and left.

Jane spent the next half hour showering and dressing. Even though she was sore from head to foot, she refused to treat herself like an invalid. If she thought about the beating, her stomach knotted in a kind of cold terror. Yet, by far and away the most predominant emotion she felt this morning was anger. She was furious at whoever had engineered last night's attack. If it took the rest of her life, she was going to find out who murdered John Merchant, and who'd set her up. She had no doubt it was one and the same person.

Sitting back down on the unmade bed, Jane picked up the phone and punched in Cordelia's private number at the Allen Grimby. It only took two rings for her to answer.

"You've reached Cordelia *M.* Thorn. Wonderland is in crisis, consequently, this had better be good. You have five seconds."

"Jeez, what a grump," said Jane.

"Hey, Janey! I've been on pins and needles all morning waiting for your call. How'd the dinner with Amy McGee go last night? Don't leave out a single cheap, tawdry detail."

"It didn't go at all," said Jane.

A pause. "Then, can I assume you're still a virgin?"

"Cut me some slack, will you? I'm not having so great a day myself."

"Really? Did she give you a D- in wine procurement and refuse to let you sample the tuna?"

"I never got there. As I was leaving the Linden Building, I was jumped."

"Jumped?" Her voice was no longer amused.

"As in attacked. Mugged."

"That's awful! Did you get a look at the guy. I assume it *was* a guy."

"He had on a ski mask."

"Creepy. Are you all right?"

"I'm alive."

"It was that bad?"

"It was a *message*, Cordelia. From John Merchant's murderer direct to me. I'm to stop asking so many questions."

"Sounds like good advice," said Cordelia. "You're going to take it, right?"

"What do you think?"

A muffled shriek. "I'm going to call your father and demand that he lock you in his attic!"

"Look, I didn't call to get a lecture. I want you to promise that you'll keep what I just told you a secret. Everyone here thinks it was a robbery. The guy who jumped me took all my money."

"Oh, how splendid. Credit cards too? You'll be completely insolvent in a matter of days."

"I'm not going to back off, Cordelia. I'm simply going to be more discreet. I must be getting close or this wouldn't have happened. I want you to help me think it all through."

"Right," she snorted. "I should have my head examined if I even consider—"

"Cordelia?'

"What?"

"Do you have any bubble gum?"

Silence. "Who are you, the tooth police?"

"Listen, just lean back in your chair, put your feet up on the desk, blow some bubbles and give me five minutes." Jane could hear Cordelia tapping her fingernails on the desk top. "Look at it this way. It's either me or back to Wonderland."

"Well, when you put it that way—"

"Good. Now, here's a rundown on the leading suspects. First, Teddy Anderson. Since he was attacked himself a couple of weeks ago, he seems a less likely candidate than some of the others."

"But what about that book he's working on? Maybe that's the motive."

"A good point, and one I've considered. Something he said the other day sparked a thought. What if some of the information he wanted to include in the Boline biography wasn't all that flattering."

"He said as much," said Cordelia.

"I know. And I can't help but think that the Boline estate might not take it too kindly if too much emphasis was put on, shall we say, the *less* morally upright aspects of Boline's life. What if Merchant discovered that Teddy had crossed the line from biography to exposé, and wanted to put a stop to it?"

"So, Teddy murders him just to keep him quiet?"

"Right."

"Kind of a stretch, if you ask me. Murdering someone just to get a book published hardly seems like a strong enough motive."

Reluctantly, Jane had to agree. "The other problem with that scenario is that I'm sure Teddy would never have let Merchant see anything he didn't want him to see. They scheduled regular meetings. It would have been simple enough to feed him only the information he chose. No, you're right. There has to be more or Teddy isn't our man."

Cordelia chewed her gum with unusual stealth. She obviously didn't want to let Jane know she'd followed orders. "And, from what I know of the publishing world, I'm not sure how much power the Boline estate would have to stop a book, even if they did disagree with the content. Consequently, it may have been immaterial whether Merchant liked what he saw or not."

"All right," said Jane. "When it comes to Teddy Anderson, let's just say I need to do more checking."

"Fine. As long as it's *discreet*," said Cordelia. "Next suspect."

"Kelly Heywood. Her motive is much clearer. If her father had found out about her drug use, her rather easy berth as manager of Linden Lofts would be history. Again, according to Amy McGee, Merchant knew Kelly was in some kind of trouble—most likely drugs. Maybe Kelly wanted to silence him before he went to her father with his juicy news flash. After all, she did have the easiest access to the apartment keys, and thus to all the apartments."

"So she could be our prowler. Not that the security over there is much to brag about."

Jane stretched out on the bed. "But to my mind at least, it's not a strong enough motive for murder—especially if the victim was someone she considered a close friend. The night I first met her, Kelly insisted his death was a gay-related hate crime."

"A logical position for the guilty party to take."

Jane knew that was true. "Yes, but I'm not convinced. There had to be more at stake. *So what* if Arno found out? *So what* if Kelly got kicked out of Linden Lofts? Would that be the end of the world?"

"For a ne'er-do-well who doesn't much care for real work and thinks the world owes her a living, it might be. Besides, you're assuming a motivation beyond shallow self-preservation."

"I guess I am."

"Well, what about her inheritance? If Arno knew she was back doing drugs, he might have changed his will."

"He *did* change it," said Jane, "but Kelly didn't know about it until after his death. Even so, I don't think that's enough of a motive. Arno was healthy. There was no reason to think he'd die soon."

"Well, I think you'd better train your dazzling brain cells on that a little longer, too. Who's next?"

"Eric Lind, for one. A young, closeted gay man."

"Hey, aren't you jumping to a rather broad conclusion there, sweetie? I merely suggested it. I have no proof."

Jane realized she hadn't had a chance to tell Cordelia about her conversation with Brandon Vachel late yesterday afternoon. She relayed the information quickly and then asked, "So what do you think?"

"I think, since Brandon is the worst possible man on the premises, that Roz is missing a good bet by not dating him."

"Ouch," said Jane.

"Well am I wrong?"

"No, but I wish you were." She fluffed a pillow behind her head. "Let's get back to Eric."

"Not so fast there, tootsie. You're glossing over Brandon way too quickly. What if *he* killed Merchant?"

"What's his motive?"

"To protect Kelly."

Jane laughed out loud. "You've never talked to him, Cordelia. Brandon takes care of Brandon. Period, end of sentence."

"But maybe he had something at stake as well as Kelly."

"Like what?"

"How should I know! Do I need to solve everything for you?"

"I wasn't aware that you'd solved *anything*."

More fingernail tapping. "I am unwrapping my last piece of bubble gum here, Jane, so talk fast."

"All right. Back to Eric."

"We did Eric. He and Merchant were lovers. He was closeted, and seen coming out of Merchant's apartment the night he died. Does that exhaust your list of suspects?"

Jane could tell Cordelia was losing patience. "No, I've got one more. Mark Thurman."

"Ah, yes. John Boy Walton, riding a TV set and spreading Republican warmth and open-mindedness across the fruited plain—and I do mean *fruited.*"

"He does seem to me to be the least likely suspect. He had only minimal contact with Merchant—at Arno Heywood's potlucks—and no motivation for wanting to see him dead. On the other hand, Arno Heywood was a different matter. It seems clear to me that Thurman wanted Heywood's job. I can't help but wonder what lengths he'd go to to get it."

Jane heard the door downstairs open and then shut. "Roz is that you?" she called. "I'll be down in a sec."

"So what's your next move?" asked Cordelia, snapping her gum.

"I'm going to hang up and make the bed."

"Ah, it's good to know you have an aggressive agenda."

"I'll call you later, okay?"

"Alas, I suppose Wonderland *is* beckoning. I've got a rehearsal in ten minutes."

"Give my regards to the Queen of Hearts."

"Well, I'm afraid I can't do that, Janey. You see, that was the crisis in Wonderland this morning."

"What do you mean?"

"The Queen of Hearts. I fired her."

34

"Roz," called Jane again, wondering why she hadn't responded. She brushed quickly through her long, chestnut hair. Normally, she put it up in a French braid, but today she just let it fall naturally around her shoulders. As she stood at the head of the stairs feeling that same nagging fear tighten her shoulders, she turned, gazing back at the gun still lying on the bed. No, she thought to herself, that wasn't the answer. She'd been a hair's breath away from hurting Julia just a few minutes ago. She wasn't going to chance that again. Screwing up her courage, she headed down into the living room.

As she got to the bottom of the steps, she looked around, but Roz was nowhere in sight. She had to be here somewhere, thought Jane, rounding the corner into Arno's study. She came to a dead stop when she saw Eric sitting casually behind the desk. He was holding a gun.

He looked up as she entered, a smile forming. "Jane. You look better than I thought you would."

Her mind raced. Where was Roz? How had he gotten in? She started to back away.

"Where are you going?" he asked, his tone suggesting nothing more than curiosity.

"I . . . just remembered. I'm supposed to meet a friend."

"Really? Can I give you a lift somewhere?"

"No." She said the word way too fast. "Ah . . . where's Roz?"

He set the gun down and then rose calmly from his chair. "She had an emergency at the station."

"I see. And, ah . . . how did you get in here?" She tried to keep her voice steady.

"Roz gave me the key, of course. I just got through talking to her. See, she was getting ready to go to Peg's funeral when Peg's daughter called and asked if she'd be willing to change her plans and come up here instead. She fully intended to do that, Jane, but then she got a call from her boss. She rushed up to my apartment and asked me if I'd mind missing the funeral to stay with you in her place. I said, sure, so she gave me the key so I could come in without waking you. She said you might be sleeping." He took several steps toward her. "You do have some nasty bruises on your face."

"I'm fine." She looked behind her, wondering if she could beat him to the door.

"Sure you are," he said, his voice reassuring. He glanced down at the gun. "I don't mean to upset you, but I thought you might like to have this. Just keep it under your pillow at night. I have one myself. It makes me feel safer. Then again, if you've got a problem with hand guns, I'd understand. They're not for everyone. This particular gun is antique, but it works fine. I've cleaned it. And it's loaded." He picked it up, admiring the mother-of-pearl handle.

"Why don't you give it to me?" said Jane, trying to match his casualness.

"Sure." He handed it over, then rubbed his hands against the sides of his jeans. "I suppose you want me to leave now, huh? I get the feeling I'm making you nervous. That wasn't my intention."

Her eyes had been bouncing so frenetically around the room, she realized she'd barely looked at him. Taken at face value, what he said was not only plausible, but not the least bit threatening. And his manner seemed entirely open and honest. She took a deep breath, holding the gun down at her side, and said, "Yeah, I really don't need a baby sitter."

"And you've got to go meet that friend."

"Right."

"So you want me to go?" he said, hesitating. "Because, see I was kind of hoping . . . I mean, I've been hoping all week that I could speak to you alone. I tried yesterday at the store, but with mom there and all, it just wasn't the right time."

"What did you want to talk to me about?"

"Oh, I had a couple of questions."

She knew that was all she was going to get unless she agreed to let him stay. Even though she might be placing herself in a vulnerable position by allowing it, she couldn't help herself. She was intrigued. She also felt more confident now that the gun was in her hand, not his. "You feel like a cup of coffee?"

"Great," he said eagerly, following her into the kitchen.

After placing the gun in one of the kitchen drawers—the one closest to the coffee maker—she retrieved the beans from the refrigerator.

Eric made himself comfortable on a stool next to a butcher block table.

"So," said Jane, getting down the small hand grinder. "What can I do for you?"

As he watched her preparing the coffee, he seemed to grow uncomfortable. He fidgeted with his watch for a few seconds before getting to the point. "You're gay, aren't you, Jane?"

It wasn't quite the opening she'd expected, but it didn't surprise her either. "Yes, I am."

"I thought so. I've read about you in the papers. You've helped your father on some of his cases."

It had become a common misconception around the Twin Cities that Jane's sleuthing successes had come as a result of assisting her father in his law practice. Generally, she just let it slide, since it was easier than the real explanation.

"I don't mean to pry," he continued, "but . . . have you known for a long time that you were gay?"

"Pretty long. Since I was about fifteen."

He traced a line in the wood with his hand. "Does your family know?"

"I told my dad when I was a senior in high school. My brother and I were close growing up, so he already knew."

"And your mother?"

"She died when I was thirteen."

He nodded. "Was your dad pretty mad when you told him?"

Jane gave the coffee beans several good grinds before answering. "No, not mad, exactly. See, my parents were always pretty liberal, politically and socially. When I was growing up, one of dad's best friends, his name was Arthur Ames, was gay. He was at the house quite regularly, sometimes he'd bring along a friend. I never talked to him much, but my parents were very clear with me about what it meant to be gay. That's why, when I decided to tell my dad, I thought it wouldn't be a big deal."

"But it was?"

"I think his reaction even surprised him. He was *very* unhappy about it. Apparently it was one thing to have a gay friend, and another matter entirely to have a gay daughter. But in time, he worked it through. My dad and I have struggled over lots of issues through the years. We're closer than ever now, but it's been hard won."

Eric said nothing.

Jane dumped the coffee grounds into the filter. "I will say that I think telling him was the right decision. It was awful having to live a lie, having to pretend I was someone I wasn't."

He placed his hands flat on the table, his eyes cast down. "I don't know many gay people."

Jane poured water into the coffee maker, switched it on and then turned back to him. "People like you, you mean?"

His eyes rose to hers. "Yeah," he said softly.

"What about you and John Merchant?" Jane felt it would be incredibly revolting to tell him she already knew some of the details, specifically because she'd have to tell him *how* she knew. It was better to simply let the story unfold.

"Did Kelly figure it out? Was she the one who told you?"

"I just guessed."

"I see." He ran a hand over his mouth. "I really cared about him, Jane. But—"

"But what?" she coaxed.

"I don't know if you can understand, but he had this rigid idea of what gay men should be. They had to support all the right causes, have all the right political ideas. And they had to dress in expensive suits and be trim and perfectly groomed. He was forever taking me downtown so I could try on Armani this, Donna Karan or Ralph Lauren that. Shoes. Belts. Ties. Cologne. You'd think he was Rex Harrison and I was Audrey Hepburn!" He gave a rather silly laugh. "I mean, I don't exactly see myself as the Eliza Doolittle type." He flexed the muscles in his neck.

Jane had to agree.

"It was the running argument between us. I needed to dress differently. I needed to join this group. He wanted me to get my hair styled. And worst of all, he thought I should stop managing my parent's antique shop and look around for some stupid junior executive job! I mean, tell me the truth, Jane. Do all gay men have to project such a one note image?"

"No, of course not."

"But then why do I feel so out of it. When I was with him, I never felt good enough."

"Is that why you tossed coffee all over his suit the day you visited him at his office?"

"Oh, you heard about that, did you? Yeah, that's exactly what I did. And I didn't give a damn what anybody thought. He pushed too hard sometimes."

"You're a very attractive man, Eric. Somewhere along the line I hope he mentioned that."

"Yeah, but with the wrong look and all the wrong aspirations."

She shook her head. "I think you just found the wrong man."

He nodded, and then kept nodding. "Thank you. I needed to hear that."

Jane got down two mugs from the cupboard and poured the coffee. "Do you take cream or sugar?"

"Black is fine," he said.

She set the mug in front of him and then picked up her own. "You just have to keep looking. I will tell you that I think it'll be a lot easier if you're more open about your sexuality. The closet is a coffin, Eric. It's no place for living, breathing human beings."

"Yeah, I know."

She took a sip, thinking his situation over. "Your mother has no idea?"

His expression was full of defeat. "I've wanted to tell her. A million times. She won't take it well, I can guarantee that. The problem is, I don't know how I can lay this on her when I've already hurt her so much."

"Hurt her in what way?"

Passing a hand over his eyes he said, "My father died two years ago in a car accident. We were both in the car, but I was driving. I had a green light and never even saw the guy who broadsided us. Dad never had a chance, but I walked away with nothing more than a few cuts." He shook his head and looked down into his cup. "My mother's never said anything to me directly, but I know she blames me for his death."

"Oh, I'm sure that's not true."

"That's because you don't know her. She blames me for the financial problems the store is having. If Dad were around, he'd fix them. She seems to forget that this is the same man who wouldn't take out life insurance because he was too *young*. Mom even blames me for the health problems she's had since the accident. And there are moments, Jane, when I think she's right."

She could sense his depression, even his agony. Trying to come to terms with his sexuality was just one part of it. She felt terribly sorry for him, having to live with such an unnecessary emotional burden. "I wish you could talk to someone," she said, trying to sound encouraging. "A counselor, perhaps."

His only response was, "Yeah. I'll think about it." He pushed the coffee mug away as if it contained something foul.

Jane didn't want the conversation to end just yet, especially since they were talking so confidentially. "Eric, I hope you don't think I'm prying, but I was wondering. Did John ever threaten to tell your mother about you?"

"Nah, although he didn't like the fact that I was so secretive. It might have become an issue if—"

"If he hadn't died."

His head sank to his chest. "And now the police think I had something to do with it."

"Did you?"

"No!"

"Then why did you lie to them?"

"You mean about delivering the chest? I had to! That nosy neighbor had me dead to rights coming out of John's apartment. I'd delivered the chest weeks before, but since I had a bill of sale, I thought I could use it as an excuse. After all, if they knew we were lovers, I'd become their prime suspect."

He had a point. So did the police. "Why were you there, then?"

"I was waiting for him," said Eric. "We'd had another fight earlier that day. He came by the antique shop after work, but I was out. I knew I had to talk to him before we all got together over at the Guthrie that night. We wouldn't have had a minute to ourselves."

"But you didn't see him?"

He shook his head. "I waited around until I couldn't wait any longer. As it was, I didn't get to the theatre until about fifteen minutes into the first act."

"You had a key to his place?"

"Of course. Just like he had one to mine."

She might be a complete fool, and maybe she'd live to regret it, but she believed him. "Look, if you don't mind talking about this a moment more—"

"Sure," he said, giving her a go ahead nod.

"Did John know Kelly Heywood had begun smoking pot again?"

The question made him uneasy. "Yeah, he was pretty worried about her, although I don't think it's as big a deal as everyone else seems to think. Teddy Anderson was the one who told him about it in the first place. He wanted John to intercede, try to get her to see what she was doing to herself."

"But didn't she have an addiction problem back in high school?"

"Yeah, I guess so. She doesn't talk about it much."

"Did John talk to her?"

"Sure. But Kelly wouldn't listen. That's when John threatened to go to her father."

"How did she take that?"

"She was pissed as hell. Told him if he did, she'd never speak to him again. And she wouldn't have, either. When it comes right down to it, Kelly knows how to hold a grudge."

Jane wondered if that's all she threatened. "Did John go to Arno with the information?"

"I'm not sure. I think so." Eric wiped a hand across his eyes. "It was a lot of bullshit, if you ask me. I tried to talk John out of going to Arno, too. Nothing's wrong with Kelly. John should have let well enough alone."

Jane could see this was hard on him. "I'm sorry."

"It's all right. It's good for me to talk about this to someone, instead of keeping it all inside."

Jane waited a moment and then asked, "Did John ever talk much about Teddy and the book he was working on?"

Eric pulled his coffee mug back in front of him and took a sip. "Oh, he thought Anderson was a curmudgeonly old fart, but they basically got along. Now and then he'd say something about Teddy being a bit too interested in the more lurid aspects of August Boline's life. Teddy is kind of a weird guy, isn't he?"

"I don't know him very well."

"That's just it. I don't either. And I talk to him several times a week. Then again, I think the fact that his son was sent to prison a few years ago hit him pretty hard."

"I didn't know he had a son. Why is he in prison?"

"He helped some guy rob a small grocery store, although Teddy maintains he was innocent. The owner of the store was shot and later died."

"Did his son do it?"

"No, the other guy did. Bob, Teddy's son, should be out in a year or two. Even so, it's been a long haul."

It was interesting information, thought Jane, she just wasn't sure it had any relevance to John Merchant's murder. "One other question. Did John ever mention anything about Mark Thurman?"

"The guy Roz is dating?"

She nodded.

"No. Not that I recall."

She finished her coffee and then set the mug down on the counter. "Would you like some more?" she asked, holding up the pot.

He shook his head. "I'm afraid I'm not much of a coffee drinker. And anyway, you look kind of tired. I should probably leave you alone so you can get some rest." He pushed back from the table and got up.

"That was my doctor's prescription."

"Well, then, you'd better follow it."

She nodded, a smile forming. "Except, I foresee a small problem. Since I fully intend to drink every last drop of that coffee, I'll never fall asleep."

He returned the smile. "I see your point. So, what are you going to do?"

She thought for a minute. "Do you play chess?"

"Not as well as Bobby Fischer."

"Just the answer I was looking for. I challenge you to a game." She saw his hesitation. "Please," she said. "I'd like the company."

"Well, if you insist—"

"I do."

He grinned. "Where's the chess board?"

35

"My God, what happened to you!" Edgar stood outside Jane's door, a horrified look on his face.

"A guy jumped me outside the building last night. I'm afraid he took my money." She added quickly, before he could respond, "But you have to promise not to tell Beryl. I don't want her to know, at least not just yet. It will only upset her."

Shaking his head, he moved resolutely into the loft and tossed his coat over a chair. "You're right about that. I won't say a word. But are you okay?" he asked, his white eyebrows knit together in concern.

"A little banged up, but basically fine."

Jane had spent most of the early afternoon playing chess at the dining room table with Eric. He'd left about an hour ago.

"I can't believe this happened to you," said Edgar. Without even a second's hesitation, he put his arms around her and gave her a comforting hug.

Jane was more than surprised by his show of affection, not that it wasn't appreciated.

"Come and sit down," he said, taking her arm and helping her over to the couch. After she was safely ensconced under a blanket, he asked, "Can I get you anything? Anything at all. I could pop downstairs and bring back a meal. I'm not much of a cook, myself, although I make a pretty mean omelet."

She smiled at him, understanding a little better why Beryl had grown to care about him so much. "No," she said, touched by his concern. "Nothing, really. Except, I'd enjoy your company, if you've got a few minutes."

"I sure do. I was downstairs visiting my brother, Teddy, when I thought to myself, why not run upstairs and see if Jane is home." He dragged a chair over and sat down next to her.

"Would you like some coffee? I just made a second pot, so it's fresh."

He shook his head. "I've been drinking way too much at the hospital."

"That's not coffee, Edgar, it's motor oil."

"Boy, are you right about that."

"So, how are you and Teddy getting along?" she asked, noticing that he had on a new bow tie this afternoon. It was red with green holly leaves. Very festive.

"Oh," he sighed, "you know, it's always been a struggle between us. I suppose it's because we're so different. But we're both working at it. The problem is, every time we seem to connect, some unresolved issue from our past gets in the way. But since we're both older now—and maybe lonelier—having a brother around is a far more appealing idea than it was when we were thirty."

"I hope it works out for you," said Jane.

"Thanks." He sat back, folding his arms over his chest. "I guess you could say most of our conversation today centered on two rather pressing issues in his life."

"Which are?"

"Well, that biography he's writing, for one. Just between you and me, I think he's riding for a fall there. He thinks it's going to be the jewel in an otherwise mediocre career."

"You don't agree?"

He shook his head. "I'm afraid the book is going to include some pretty damaging information. Teddy said Boline was a crook, plain and simple, and that he's not going to bury the evidence now that it's been unearthed."

"I figured he might do something like that."

"But you don't know the whole story. You see, his son was convicted of a felony a few years back. About six months after the boy went to prison, his wife had a stroke."

"I'm sorry," said Jane. "I didn't know."

"It gets worse. The man whose testimony put Teddy's son in jail was none other than Richard Crawford, the grandson of August Boline."

Jane's eyes opened wide in surprise. It took her a moment to put it together. "You mean this biography is going to be his revenge?"

"Exactly."

As she thought about it, she realized that here was a potentially strong connection to John Merchant's murder. If John had somehow found out about the planned exposé, maybe he tried to stop it. Teddy had resorted

217

to violence to prevent him from blowing the whistle. Perhaps Teddy saw it as his one and only chance to pay the family back for a perceived wrong. But, as Eric had mentioned just a few hours ago, Teddy's son would be out fairly soon. Even if it had been hard on everyone, was it worth committing a murder over? Somehow, she couldn't see it. Teddy might be eccentric, but he hadn't lost touch with reality and he wasn't stupid. Still, she tucked it away in her mind for further thought. "Wouldn't the Boline estate refuse to let a book like that be published?"

"You know," said Edgar, straightening his tie, "I asked him the same question. He said he was doing an *authorized* biography, meaning, the estate was officially allowing him to use Boline's private papers—and interview family members. Teddy's convinced that he's working with one of the best editors in the business. The contract sounds airtight—in favor of the publisher, of course. I don't think the estate would have a prayer of stopping the publication, even if they wanted to. But that's not my problem with all this. See, even though Teddy is certain the book is going to be a blockbuster, I'm not sure the world cares much about August Boline any more. I mean, even if the guy danced naked down Hennepin Avenue, so what?"

He had a point.

"Now, if we were talking about someone famous like, say, Elizabeth Taylor, people might be interested. But August Boline? Come on. Other than a few historians, who'd care?"

"Did you say that to him?"

Edgar snorted. "Hardly. I didn't want to get into a fist fight." He eyed her thoughtfully. "You know, not to change the subject, but it really surprised me to hear that you feel Teddy had something to do with that gay lawyer's death—the one who died in Loring Park last summer."

"Did he say that?"

Edgar nodded. "He said you came over to the mansion the other day to snoop. Is that right?"

"Well I—"

"Because if you did, I've got something I need to get off my chest. I know at times my brother can be a hothead. This vendetta he has against the Boline family, however misplaced, is still understandable. Even though you might not realize it to look at him, he's a passionate man, Jane— passionate about his work, and the people he loves. But he'd never physically harm another human being. I believe that with all my heart. Deep down, Teddy is an honorable man."

"I'm sure he'd be gratified to hear you say that."

"He'd be surprised as hell. But it's the truth." His smile was kind.

"What was the other pressing issue you two talked about?"

"Oh, well, he's very worried about Arno Heywood's daughter."

"Kelly? Did he say why?"

"It seems that when she was in high school, she got mixed up with the wrong crowd and got pretty heavily addicted to a couple of different drugs. Apparently, Arno insisted she go into treatment, and she did. She's been drug free for years, but now Teddy says he's got proof that she's smoking marijuana again. Some guy she's dating smokes it rather openly, although I don't think Kelly does." He bent forward, resting his arms on his thighs. "Teddy has always felt close to her. She even called him Uncle Teddy when she was younger."

"Did he say what the proof was?"

He shrugged. "It's right there in her apartment for anyone to see. I don't know how much more proof you'd need."

Good point, thought Jane. She'd seen it too.

"And now, he just found out that the money Arno left to her via his will is going to be administered by her mother. It was supposed to be handled by Peg Martinsen, the woman who died here the other day. The problem is, it turns out Kelly hasn't even talked to her mother in years. Teddy referred to her as a *loathsome* human being. And now he's afraid that by the time Kelly is allowed to inherit, the money will be gone. He's furious that Arno didn't make better provisions."

"I'm sorry to hear all that."

"When I stopped by to see him, he'd just come back from this Peg Martinsen's funeral. He was already feeling pretty down. When he started talking about Kelly, he got even worse. I thought to myself, if there was only something I could do to cheer him up. That's when I got an idea."

"And what's that?" she asked.

He folded his hands together and fixed her with a serious look. "I want you to know that I've grown to care about your aunt very much. We've become . . . quite close."

"I know that," she said, curious what his relationship with Beryl had to do with Teddy.

"You do?" he said, his head twisting with interest. "Has she said anything specific to you about me?"

"About the same as what you've said about her."

"Oh."

Jane could tell that didn't satisfy him. "Well, also that I should expect to see you around the house when she gets home from the hospital." She watched him digest this information. "Look, Edgar, if you want to know how my aunt feels about you, I think you'd better ask her. That being said, I'm not giving away any secrets by telling you that she lights up like a Christmas tree every time your name is mentioned."

"Really? You think so!" His smile was positively brilliant. "Jane, I haven't felt like this since I was a schoolboy. I even . . . well, I was walking past my neighborhood jewelry store the other day and I noticed a very delicate diamond engagement ring in the window. I couldn't help but think how beautiful it would look on Beryl's finger."

Jane had no idea it had gone this far.

"You're surprised?"

"I guess I am."

"You know her better than anyone. Do you think she'd be upset if I brought the subject of . . . well, you know—"

"Marriage?"

"Right."

"I don't have a clue, Edgar."

He sat back and sighed. "I guess there's nothing else to do but take the bull by the horns and ask. Maybe Christmas Eve, that's what I was thinking. She'll be home by then. She's feeling so much better today, Jane. That doctor of hers started her on a new medication this morning."

At that bit of news, Jane felt her stomach go hollow.

"Well, I'm glad we had this talk." He slapped his knees. "Beryl probably loves you more than any other person in the world, Jane. She's always talking about you. I know we haven't had much of a chance to get to know each other, but . . . I hope we can be friends."

"That would mean a lot to me too," said Jane.

"You wouldn't object to my becoming part of your family?"

"Not if you're good to Beryl and make her happy."

"Oh, you have my word on that!" His eyes gleamed. "But back to that point about my brother. When I was talking to him earlier, he seemed so depressed that I asked him what he was doing for Christmas. His wife is in a nursing home, you know. He'll probably spend the morning with her, but the rest of the day he'll be alone. I was wondering. . . ." He paused. "Since your father and brother didn't mind that I tagged along on Thanksgiving, I was hoping. . . ."

"Christmas is going to be at my house this year," said Jane. "By all means, invite him."

"Oh, that's great! That's really kind of you."

A soft knock drew their attention to the door.

"I'll get that," said Edgar, bouncing out of his chair.

Jane turned just in time to see Julia enter. She smiled a greeting, noticing that Julia was carrying a cloth briefcase in one hand, the strap of a large sack purse was slung over the other shoulder. But it was the suitcase in the hall behind her that caught and held Jane's attention. In an instant she was on her feet. "What's going on? You aren't leaving, are you?"

"I'm afraid I am," said Julia, her smile uncertain. "I said I'd come by after the funeral. I wanted to make sure you're doing okay, and to say goodbye." She nodded to Edgar. "I'm Julia Martinsen."

"Nice to meet you," he said, shaking her hand.

Jane felt a sinking feeling in the pit of her stomach. She *couldn't* be leaving. This wasn't the plan at all.

"I thought I'd call a cab from here. My flight leaves at six."

"Say," said Edgar, "I'd be happy to run you out to the airport. It's not that far."

"Oh, I couldn't possibly bother—"

"It's no bother. You're a friend of Jane's, and any friend of Jane's is a friend of mine." He gave her his best grandfatherly smile.

"Well," she said, still hesitating, "I feel kind of funny—"

"Don't," he insisted. "The matter is closed. I'll just take your bag and meet you downstairs by the front door. My car is right across the street."

"I really appreciate it," she said.

Edgar scurried back into the living room and gave Jane a kiss on her cheek and then said, "I'll just leave you two to say goodbye." He picked up the bag and headed for the waiting elevator. In a moment, he was gone.

Since they were completely alone on the sixth floor, Julia didn't bother to shut the door. She turned to Jane with a half-hearted smile and said.

"I'm sorry I have to leave so suddenly. It's a patient of mine. I'd planned to stay until tomorrow, but—"

"You can't."

She nodded.

Jane couldn't help herself. She was hurt, and frustrated, and had no business being either. "Well, have a good flight."

"You're angry with me."

"Why should I be angry? You have a job. Responsibilities. Although I thought you said you were leaving Bethesda."

"I might be. But my plans aren't firm yet."

"No, of course not."

"You *are* angry."

Jane took a deep breath. "What right do I have to be angry?"

For a moment, Julia looked out the window. A deep winter twilight had fallen over the city. "I think we need to talk. But it can't be now."

"Right."

She set her briefcase down next to the door, took off her purse, and walked up to Jane.

A flush climbed Jane's cheeks. She was glad the lights in the loft were not only few, but dim. "So was Edgar right?"

"What do you mean?" asked Julia.

"He called us friends. Are we? You never answered me last night."

"Of course we are."

Jane ran a hand through her hair, giving herself a minute. "Look, this is my fault. I'm just being stupid. I don't usually . . . I mean, it's a rule with me. I don't make assumptions. I don't know you. You don't know me. We just met a couple of days ago."

Julia said nothing.

"I realize it's dumb to think—" She abandoned the end of the sentence. All she knew for sure was that a minute from now Julia would be out the door and they might never see each other again. She couldn't let that happen without making some attempt at clarity. "Am I wrong? Or more likely, am I crazy? I feel this incredible crackle of electricity between us every time we're together. If you tell me to back off, I will. I'll never mention it again. We'll say goodbye, we'll wish each other well, and that will be the end of it."

Julia didn't respond for several more seconds. Finally, slipping her hand through Jane's, she said, "I think we'd better just say goodbye."

Jane felt as if she'd been slapped. Even though she hadn't allowed herself to dwell on it, she'd been so sure of what was happening between them. "All right," she said. "I apologize for getting my signals crossed."

"There's nothing to apologize for." Very gently, she touched Jane's hair. "You didn't get your signals crossed. I just don't know what to do with them. Do you understand what I'm saying?"

Before she had a chance to speak, Julia kissed her. And then, taking her into her arms, she kissed her again.

As they stepped back from their embrace, Jane steadied herself on one of the dining room chairs. "So let me get this straight. You're just going to leave now, right?"

"I have to."

"And I'm never going to see you again."

Julia picked up her purse and hooked it over her shoulder. "I've got to come back in late June. My mother's estate should be settled by then, and so should my own plans."

"You mean, you might be moving back here?"

"I don't know."

"Will you write?"

"Probably not. I'm not much of a letter writer. But, I'll call."

"Promise?"

Julia put her hand into the pocket of her leather jacket and pulled out a card. "Here's my office address and phone number in Bethesda. I've written my home phone on the back. If I don't call you, you can call me." She dropped it on a table near the door, and then looked up pointedly at Jane. "Listen to me for a minute. I feel I owe you some kind of explanation, though this isn't easy for me. I've been in two relationships in my life, Jane. Both with men, and neither terribly successful. I guess I thought when the right man came along, it would be different. In the meantime, I had my work. I've wondered sometimes about women, even found myself attracted to a few. But I've never found a woman who I cared about, who returned my feelings." She hesitated. "Now I have, and I don't know what to do about it."

Jane's head was spinning, almost literally. "You care about me?"

Julia's eyes grew soft. "Very much."

"But," said Jane, knowing she had only moments left, "when will we

223

talk again?"

Julia placed her hand lightly on the doorknob. "I have a feeling I'll want to talk to you as soon as I get home tonight. And probably tomorrow morning too. But I won't call, Jane. Don't expect it. At least, not right away. I have a lot to sort out. And there are some important parts of my life you know nothing about. I'm not sure what my future holds, but I'll promise you this. We will see each other again. Don't doubt that for a minute."

36

"Hey, babe. How was the funeral?" Brandon was lying on his stomach on Kelly's bed, reading. He didn't look up as she entered.

"Oh, just peachy keen," she said, throwing her bag on the coffee table with such force that it scattered the contents of an ashtray all over the floor.

He put down the magazine. "Good shot."

"Oh, shut up."

"Hey, come on. What's wrong?"

"What could be wrong, Brandon? My life totally sucks and you sit there reading a porno magazine."

"See," he said, sitting up and drawing his legs underneath him. "You're a prime example of why I don't go to funerals. It fucks up your whole day."

"Spare me," she muttered as she kicked off her wet boots and dumped herself into a chair.

"Look, I cared about Peg as much as anyone else in this dump. She was a good friend." He studied her. "What are you so edgy about? I can tell this isn't just your usual bad humor. Didn't you get to read your poem at the service?"

"You make it sound like I'm in kindergarten."

"Did you or didn't you?"

She shrugged. "Sure. I read it."

"The one about the crow?"

Placing a hand on her forehead she said, "It was the only poem of mine my dad or Peg really ever liked."

"You're breakin' my heart."

She tossed a pillow at him. "Just fuck off."

"No problem, babe." He picked up the magazine and continued to page through it.

Kelly watched him. After a moment she announced, "We're in deep shit, Brandon."

"We've been in deep shit since the day we were born. So what's new?" He turned a page.

"Do you realize how trite that sounds? All this pathetic angst, this studied world weariness."

He laughed. "This from the angst princess of North America?"

She gave him a nasty look. "I should never have listened to you. Look what you've got me involved in."

Very coldly he replied, "We do what we have to do to survive. You've benefited as much as I have, Kelly. Even more. Besides, I've got all our bases covered. Except for old man Anderson's hallucinations—"

"You and I both know he wasn't hallucinating."

"Whatever. We're clean. Nobody will listen to him anyway."

"John did."

"John was a busybody. So's Anderson. Busybodies I can handle."

"Don't call John that!"

He got up and walked over to her chair, standing over her, his fists resting on his hips. "What's the difference now? He's dead."

She turned her head away, pushing her face into a cushion. "How can you be so cold?"

"Like I should miss him or something?"

"I do," she said softly.

"Yeah, like you'd miss a sinus infection." He flopped down onto a chair opposite her. "Look, Kelly," he said, lighting up a joint, "we're going to be just fine. All along the way, I've taken care of everything."

Woodenly, she replied, "If you only had."

"Meaning what?"

"Oh, just leave me alone."

Tossing his lighter onto the coffee table, he said, "What's eating you?"

She didn't move.

"Answer me."

She sniffed. "In the last few months I've lost John and my father. Teddy and I are barely speaking, and I haven't seen most of my friends in so long they probably wouldn't recognize me. And what do I have in return?" She twisted her head around and looked at him. "*You.* There's something wrong with that equation."

"Look, I care about you, babe. You're my woman now."

"Lucky me."

"You know I'm going places. I don't give a shit if these morons around here can't see my talent."

"But that's work stuff, Brandon. What about all the *people* in our lives? You have a daughter. Don't you ever miss her?"

"Sure I do. I helped raise her."

"Until the woman you impregnated tossed you out."

"Oh . . . don't be such an old sourpuss." He smirked, holding the smoke in his lungs for several seconds before releasing it.

"*Sourpuss?*"

"Sure, that's what my mom used to call my dad. Lighten up, Kel. We're fine."

She regarded him from a chilly distance. "You only say that because you don't know what happened today."

"Enlighten me." He took another toke.

"At the funeral," she said, getting up and moving restlessly around the room, "Peg's daughter came up to me and said that according to her mother's will, she would be inheriting the Linden Building."

"Fuck!"

"Yeah, I know. On the advice of her attorney, she gave me notice that as of the end of next month, I will no longer be needed as manager here. She's bringing in a professional management company to take care of it. You know what that means?"

He pressed his lips together tightly. "We're screwed."

"Yeah. Totally. What are you going to do to take care of *that*, Brandon? I mean, I can't even afford the rent in this place if I have to pay full price, let alone—"

"Just shut up. Let me think."

"Well you better think fast, *babe*. Or we're dead meat."

37

"Ain't she a beaut!" exclaimed Cordelia, holding the door open as Roz and Thurman carried a nearly seven foot high Norway Pine into the loft. "This is just what the doctor ordered to cheer you up." She turned around and fixed Jane with a scrutinizing stare. Raising one eyebrow, she whispered, "You look worse than I expected."

"Thank you." Jane felt as if her peaceful evening had just been invaded by storm troopers.

"We need to talk," said Cordelia quietly, out of the corner of her mouth.

"About what?"

She bent close and whispered, "Later."

Jane wasn't in the mood for games. "What are you waiting for? A heavenly sign?"

"All I can say for now is underestimate Cordelia Thorn at your own peril." Pressing a finger to her lips, she sauntered away.

Roz and Thurman had already positioned the Christmas tree in its stand. Thurman was down on all fours, making sure it was straight.

"What do you think?" asked Roz, standing back to admire their purchase.

"Did you check it for squirrels?" asked Jane, her tone betraying her lack of enthusiasm.

"Oh, don't be such a spoilsport," replied Cordelia. She dumped her sacks on the dining room table and then bounded into the kitchen and began rummaging through the cupboards. "I've got eggnog," she called, "ten strings of colored lights, and a sack of the most tasteless, glitzy decorations this side of Kmart. And," she said, pausing dramatically as she returned to the room. She set four glasses down on the dining room table, whipped a CD out of her pocket and said, "To set the musical mood—" She held it up, pointing to the title.

Jane knew what was coming.

"Lawrence Welk!" she declared, her face beaming.

Thurman got up from the floor, brushing off his pant legs. "You've *got* to be kidding."

"I always decorate my Christmas trees to Lawrence Welk," she said, ignoring his peeved expression. She swept over to the stereo and put it on. As the opening strains of the Lawrence Welk theme song burst forth from the speakers, she grabbed him by the hand, slipped her arm around his waist and danced him through the room.

Roz touched Jane's arm and asked, "How are you feeling tonight?"

"Better."

"You certainly look better than last night. You've got some color back in your cheeks." She watched Cordelia tip Thurman backwards in true tango fashion, right him, and then twirl him around. "You know, you and Cordelia are providing him with a rather liberal education."

"He seems to be enjoying himself."

"Who wouldn't enjoy dancing with that crazy woman?" She continued to watch. "Is Julia around?"

"She caught a flight back home a couple of hours ago."

"I'm sorry I didn't get a chance to say goodbye." She moved closer to Jane, placing her back to the dancing duo and said, "Thurman wants to talk to you."

"Why? Has he been working on some new insults?"

Roz gave her a pained look. "He came clean last night about what happened between him and Arno. I think finding you outside in the alley like that shook him more than he would ever admit. I'd tell you what he said, but he said he wants to do it himself."

Over the din, Jane heard a knock on the door. "Just a sec," she said to Roz, walking over to answer it.

Kelly and Brandon stood outside. Their sullen faces told her this wasn't a neighborly visit.

Brandon's expression turned into an amused sneer when he saw the bruises on Jane's face. "Run into a wall?" he asked.

Jane had no time for his usual crap tonight. "What do you want?" she asked curtly.

"Is Julia here?" asked Kelly.

"She flew back to Maryland."

"Oh." Her eyes darted to Brandon and then away.

"Something I can help you with?" asked Jane.

Brandon curled a thumb around his belt. "You got her address?"

"I can get it for you."

"That would be great," said Kelly. Her manner was decidedly less hostile than Brandon's. "You may not have heard, but she served me notice this afternoon."

"About what?" asked Jane.

"As of the end of January, I'm no longer going to be the manager here. Julia's inherited the building."

Jane found that surprising news, especially since Julia hadn't said a word about it. Not that they'd had much chance to talk. "I'm sorry. I didn't know."

"Yeah," said Brandon. "The rich just get richer."

Kelly put her hand on his arm to silence him. "Brandon's going to be moving in with me. I was just wondering if the rent on my loft was going to stay the same or go up. Dad and Peg were giving me a break because I was the manager."

"And I want to know about my studio downstairs," grunted Brandon. "Kelly was giving me a deal too."

So that was it, thought Jane. She understood their anxiety. She'd had some pretty lean years herself. "Well, I'll drop the address by in the morning."

"Fine," said Kelly, checking her watch. "Come on, Brandon, we better get going or we'll be late."

"Where are you headed?" asked Jane.

"We've got some friends with a farm in Cannon Falls," said Kelly. "This great heavy metal band practices there every other Saturday evening. Sometimes we go out, spend the night, and . . . you know. Have a party."

"You driving?" asked Jane.

"What's it to you?" muttered Brandon.

"I hear the highways are pretty bad."

"We'll be fine," said Kelly. "I don't have a car. We're taking Brandon's."

"Really? What kind is it?" she asked, keeping her tone conversational.

"It's pretty new," said Kelly, pushing Brandon down the hall. As she got to the elevator she called over her shoulder, "We should be back by noon tomorrow. Or you can leave the address on my machine."

Jane closed the door just as the song ended and Cordelia released Thurman from her grip. He fell exhausted into a chair.

"Now," said Cordelia, slapping her hands together and rubbing them gleefully. "It's eggnog time! And of course we have to have some of those hideous little Christmas cookies. Where'd I put them?"

Roz and Cordelia began sifting through the contents of the grocery sacks.

Since Jane didn't seem to be needed, she pulled up a chair next to Thurman. He was fanning himself with Teddy Anderson's novel. "I hear you want to talk to me," she said, deciding that, this time, she'd fire the opening shot.

He fanned himself a couple more times and then dropped the book on the floor. "Actually, I do," he said. "I thought, since you're so interested in my relationship with Arno Heywood, I'd explain to you what really went on. I'm not proud of what I did, Jane, but I had my reasons. I told Roz everything last night. It's probably too much to think you'd ever encourage our . . . friendship, but right now, I'd settle for a ceasefire. What do you say?"

She sat forward in her chair. "I guess I'd like to hear what you have to say first. As far as Roz goes, she makes her own decisions. I've simply been concerned for her safety."

"Because my gloves were found in Anderson's loft?"

"Among other things."

He folded one leg over the other, resting his hands in his lap. "I have no idea how that happened. I was at work the morning he was attacked. You've got to believe me, Jane, I had nothing whatsoever to do with it."

"All right. Let's say you're telling the truth. But that still leaves Arno. Were you blackmailing him?"

He seemed taken aback by her directness. "That's . . . an interesting theory."

"Is it true?"

He smoothed out a wrinkle in his pants. "Partially. You see, Roz and I started dating last June, just about a month after I began working at the station. One weekend I was sent on assignment to a small town in southern Minnesota. Dover Creek. Ever heard of it?"

She shook her head.

"Well, one of the cameramen and I were supposed to cover the closing of a meat packing company. We had to stay overnight at a hotel downtown because there were some people we couldn't get to see until the next day. Around eight we knocked off and drove over to a local watering hole where we settled down at a table in the back. You have to understand, by this time, Roz had already invited me to one of Arno's potlucks where I'd met Peg Martinsen. As I was sipping my Scotch and water, I spotted Peg at the bar. I was a little surprised to see her so far from home. She was sitting with another woman, someone I didn't recognize, so I figured it would be a friendly gesture if I went over and invited them back to our table. I got up and started toward the front of the room, thinking that maybe the woman with Peg was a relative. That would've been a simple enough explanation for her being in Dover Creek. About ten feet from the bar it hit me. The woman she was sitting next to was none other than Arno Heywood."

Rotten luck, thought Jane. Peg and Arno had undoubtedly driven out of the Cities because they wanted to protect their anonymity. "So what did you do?"

"After nearly swallowing my gum, I ducked behind a screen and walked around the edge of the room until I got back to the table. For the next few minutes I watched them. They talked to the bartender, ate some pretzels, and generally engaged anyone and everyone in conversation. Nothing out of the ordinary. Since the cameraman had a Nikon loaded with low-light film, I asked if he'd take a couple of surreptitious shots of the people at the bar. He was a little surprised, but since he was getting drunk, he thought it might be fun. He got a great close-up of Heywood without even knowing it was him. Later, I retrieved the negatives and had some prints made."

It was a bit more Machiavellian than Jane had suspected, but it all still boiled down to blackmail. "Then what?" she prodded.

"At that point, I don't really think I had any idea what I was going to do with the pictures. But as time went on, and I became more and more frustrated with Heywood's untouchable, golden-boy status at the station, a plan of action did present itself. You see, when I started working there in May, Heywood was all business, very professional. I could almost say I admired him. But by late August, he began missing meetings, some days not even showing up until early afternoon. All during September, he seemed sluggish and disinterested in his TV program. I thought he was becoming an embarrassment to the station, but no one else seemed to notice. The entire month of October he had the flu. Altogether, I'll bet he missed three weeks of work. That's when I got my first chance to host 'Eye

On Minnesota.' If I do say so myself, I did a bang-up job. I don't suppose you caught it?"

"Sorry."

"Well, when November came along, and Heywood was back at work again, although only marginally, I started feeling more and more resentful and frustrated. Oh, Roz defended him, as did virtually everyone else at Channel 7, but from my point of view, the guy was a complete screwup. Everybody was making excuses for him. I suppose he went through the motions of doing his job, but it only served to prevent someone with real interest and ability from taking over the helm."

"You mean you."

His eyes were defiant. "Exactly. I felt certain the management boys over at corporate wouldn't take too kindly to word getting out that their revered though somewhat aging golden-boy was a weirdo."

Jane couldn't let that pass. "Do you ever see yourself for the pathetic, judgmental asshole you are, Thurman? Your understanding of anything outside your own purview—and I'm being kind when I say this—is shallow beyond belief."

His lips drew together into a tight line. "Just back off. I've taken about as much abuse from Roz as I can stand over this issue, and I'm not taking any more, especially from you. I think the guy was weird. Nothing you say is going to change my mind. And the guys at corporate would have shared my view, don't doubt it."

"So what did you do?"

"A week or so before Thanksgiving, I took him out for a drink and we had a talk. I never asked him to resign from the station. I would never have done that. I just told him I thought he needed a vacation. He was obviously exhausted. Every time I saw him he looked worse. He even admitted that he wasn't sleeping. So I suggested he take off say, six months from his program, naming me as his temporary successor. Was that so terrible?"

"Did he agree to it?"

"Of course not."

"And so you showed him the pictures."

The question caused him some discomfort. "You know," he said, avoiding her eyes, "as long as I live I'll never forget his reaction. He looked at the pictures for a moment. I think he was shocked, but he didn't let on.

Then, without saying a word, he just dropped them over his plate of pasta and sat there. I was getting really uncomfortable when . . ." Thurman shifted in his seat. ". . . he burst out laughing! And he wouldn't stop. One of the waitresses finally came over and asked if everything was all right. That's when he made another odd move. He asked her if she'd ever been to the top of the Foshay Tower. I mean, what on earth did some building in downtown Minneapolis have to do with the subject at hand? But she was cool. She played along with him, saying she hadn't. He picked up the photo of himself, handed it to her and said, 'The woman in this picture was a child when she first saw the Foshay Tower. She didn't know it then, but that tower was to become the symbol of her life. Her omen. Her fate.' Then, without another word, he just got up . . . and left."

Her fate, thought Jane, repeating it silently to herself. She wondered if Arno was already planning his suicide.

Thurman seemed dazed, unable to make sense of it. "The next night he showed up for the taping of his program dressed like a woman. And the following day, he walked into Ted Bauer's office and resigned."

"And two days later he committed suicide."

He nodded, whispering, "He jumped—from the tower."

"And you don't feel any responsibility for pushing him over the edge?"

Thurman ran a hand across his mouth. "I don't know. That's why I couldn't keep it to myself any longer. I had to tell someone. You understand, don't you?"

"Of course I do. You want absolution. I have none to give."

Cordelia sauntered up with a tray of eggnog and set it on the low table between them. "Are you two talking about what I think you're talking about?"

Roz joined them, taking a glass and sitting down on the floor in front of Thurman. She took his hand and drew it over her shoulder.

"Arno Heywood," said Jane, in answer to Cordelia's question.

"Well have I got a news flash for you," said Cordelia, draping herself dramatically over a chair. "I forgot to tell you this when we talked earlier today, Janey, but did anyone catch Arno's illustrious sister on TV the other night?"

"I heard about it after the fact," said Jane.

Everyone else shook their heads.

"Well I watched it," continued Cordelia, "and when I heard the old boy was on anti-depressants, a thought struck me."

"He was?" said Jane, surprised at this new piece of information.

Cordelia gave a knowing nod. "You remember we were wondering how one person could make another person commit suicide. Well, it's simple, dearhearts. Mess with the poor schmuck's depression medication. The reason Arno was on it in the first place was because he'd tried to commit suicide once before. He was diagnosed as clinically depressed and, according to his sister, they tried a bunch of different drugs until he found one that worked. If someone screwed with it. . . ." She drew a finger across her neck. "Get the picture?"

"I had no idea about any of this," said Jane. She glanced over at Roz. "Did you?"

"Well, pretty much everyone around here knew he was on anti-depressants. But the attempted suicide, that's news to me."

"Me too," insisted Thurman. "I had no idea he was so . . . unstable. Not that I couldn't have guessed."

Jane gave him a withering look.

"But you're all missing the point," said Cordelia, flailing her arms in the air for attention. She got up and walked to the windows, leaning her back against them. The lights of downtown Minneapolis framed her body as she said, "Look, whether or not he was on depression medication isn't the issue. Lots of people are. The key piece of information here isn't the knowledge that he was *on* the medication, but that he'd tried to commit suicide prior to being *stabilized* on that medication. Depression is very complex, and this is an over-simplification, but if someone got it in their mind to try to murder him—and I think that's a very big *if*—it all boils down to—"

"Who knew he'd tried to commit suicide once before," said Jane. It was slowly sinking in. "Mess with his meds, and he might try it again."

"Bingo. And I think Mabel Lind answered the question of who knew on national TV."

All eyes were glued to Cordelia.

She paused, prolonging the drama. "Only the immediate family," she pronounced. "That means, other than Mabel, only Arno's ex-wife, his daughter, Kelly, and probably Peg, since she was once his therapist."

"I wonder if Teddy knew?" asked Jane.

"I doubt it," said Roz. "If Teddy had known, everyone else here would have too. You may not believe this, but beneath that eccentric exterior beats the heart of a confirmed gossip. I suppose that's what makes him such a good biographer."

Jane considered the issue. She was more perplexed now than ever.

"Kind of far-fetched, if you ask me," grunted Thurman. "If someone wanted to do away with Heywood, and quickly, it makes no sense. It's too nebulous."

"You know, I'm afraid I have to agree," said Roz.

"And anyway," continued Thurman, "I've had about as much amateur analysis as I can take for one evening. The man is dead. For God's sake, let him rest in peace."

"He has a point," said Cordelia, walking up to the tree and sniffing the boughs. "This was supposed to be an evening of fun, frivolity, and oodles of empty calories."

"But where does that leave us?" said Jane, unable to drop the subject without some resolution.

"With a Christmas tree to decorate!" declared Cordelia, grabbing Jane's arms and pulling her to her feet. "Come on, dearheart. I've saved the most prestigious, most *intellectually challenging* job just for you." She wiggled her eyebrows suggestively.

"And what would that be?" asked Jane, feeling herself being whisked over to the dining room table.

"What else," said Thurman, smiling snidely. "You get to untangle the Christmas lights."

38

By the time Roz and Thurman finally left it was nearly midnight. Now close to one, Cordelia puttered in the kitchen, cleaning up dishes and putting away food, and Jane relaxed on the couch finishing Teddy Anderson's novel. The lighted and decorated Christmas tree stood sentry by the living room windows, casting a peaceful, reflective glow over the loft's interior.

After turning the last page, Jane shut the book and let it drop to her lap.

"So, was it the great American novel?" asked Cordelia, drifting into the room and sitting down. "Or just lurid M.O.W. material?"

"M.O.W.?" repeated Jane, not having the slightest idea what she was talking about.

"That's Movie of the Week, for the uninitiated."

"When did you become such a Hollywood mogul?"

"No, dear, I'm a *St. Paul* mogul. With aspirations, but not for Hollywood." She shuddered. "So what's it about?"

Jane picked the book up again and gazed thoughtfully at the cover. "Well, it's about love and loss, and I suppose youth's hunger to create."

"Are we talking *The World According To Garp?* Or," she said, propping her feet up on a footstool, "is it more along the lines of *The Origin of Species?* Be more specific."

"Well," said Jane, amused at Cordelia's range of possibilities, "it's set in Boston in the twenties and early thirties. It's about a newspaper reporter and his love for a wild, uneducated older woman. The story follows the man until his death. He was still fairly young, mid-forties, when he took his own life. It surprised me how romanticized the story was. Somehow, I didn't expect that from Teddy. The concept of fate looms large. But it was beautifully, almost poetically written."

"All I can say," said Cordelia, stuffing a pillow behind her back, "is that I'd read the book if I had time. Which I don't."

"Perhaps you should make time, Cordelia. Teddy will be joining us for

Christmas dinner." She relayed the gist of her afternoon's conversation with Edgar. As she was finishing, she saw Cordelia's eyes dart several times to the door. "What are you looking at?" she asked, annoyed at her friend's lack of attention.

Cordelia got up and glided over to a cloth briefcase propped against the wall. "Lookey here. A small conundrum. Who could this belong to? Oh, I suppose it's probably Roz's. She must have forgotten it when she left. Then again, since I've never seen it before, we better check."

Jane recognized it immediately as Julia's. Before she could head Cordelia off at the pass, Cordelia withdrew a bunch of photographs. "Hey, look at these." She rifled through the top few photos. "Wanna see?"

"They don't belong to us."

"Oh, don't be such a moral prig." She dropped them on a table and continued to paw through the contents. "My stars and garters!" She lifted a slug of keys from the case.

Jane was disgusted with herself for not putting an end to Cordelia's unlawful search and seizure right away.

Cordelia held up the keys by a gold fob attached to the ring. "This says *AH* on it. I'll bet you these are Arno Heywood's building keys. I wonder how they got in here?"

"The case belongs to Peg's daughter."

"Really?" said Cordelia, her head rising with interest. "I didn't know Peg had a daughter."

"She does."

"How very interesting. But how did her briefcase get in here?"

"Julia stopped to say goodbye on the way to the airport. She must have forgotten it."

"Julia?" Her nose twitched.

Jane could tell Cordelia smelled a story. She was so irritatingly on target sometimes. Even though Jane was positive her tone had conveyed nothing out of the ordinary, Cordelia had picked up a scent.

"Tell me about *Julia*," she said, dropping the case to the floor and plastering on a fake smile. She stood directly in front of Jane, arms crossed over her chest.

"You look like a four-year-old, waiting to see if I'm going to read you a bedtime story."

"Indulge me."

238

"There's nothing to tell. Give me the keys, will you?"

"You're changing the subject."

"There *is* no subject. Just give them to me."

Cordelia dropped them in her lap.

"This is incredible luck, you know that?" said Jane, quickly checking them over.

"Okay, we'll talk about Julia later. Why is it incredible luck, Jane dear?"

"Because there's one critical question I have that's impossible to answer without a *key*."

"You won't look at a bunch of silly photos but you've got nothing against breaking and entering?"

"It won't be breaking and entering if we have a key." Jane dashed back to Arno's tool chest, located just behind the kitchen. She returned waving a bolt cutter.

"Hey, you really know how to get into it. But I feel I should remind you, I do not *do* demolition."

"Then you'll help me?"

"No," she said flatly.

"But I need you. You're stronger than I am."

"True."

"Cordelia, listen to me. I've had a lot of time to think in the last twenty-four hours and I've come up with a theory. This building is still keeping some secrets, I'm sure of it. I don't know where my hunch will lead, but since I've got the means now to check it out, I have to try. Are you with me?"

She scrunched her eyes closed, flattened her hands hard against her ears and began singing, "'There'll be bluebirds over the white cliffs of Dover—'"

"Please," pleaded Jane. She poked Cordelia in the stomach with the tip of the bolt cutter.

Cordelia whipped it away. "All right. It's against my better judgement, but I'll go."

"Great."

"But first—" She wiggled her eyebrows. "I have a small gift for you."

"A gift?"

Cordelia reached into her pocket and drew out a small cylinder. "It's mace. After last night, I think you should carry it with you."

Jane took it from her hand. "Thanks," she said, checking it over to see how it worked. She gave Cordelia a hug. "That's very sweet."

"An excessive show of gratitude is not necessary."

"No, really, Cordelia. I appreciate the concern."

"I'm an expert at concern, Janey. It comes from years of knowing *you*."

Jane smiled. "Now, you need to run upstairs and get the flashlight out of the bedroom closet. I'll head up to the roof to retrieve that padlock I put on the door."

"You're taking the padlock *off?*"

"We'll need it."

"You know," sputtered Cordelia, slapping a hand to the side of her face, "next time, I should pay someone to examine my *head*, not my feet."

After the elevator lurched to a stop, Jane made straight for Brandon Vachel's studio.

"It smells funny down here," said Cordelia, sniffing the air. "And it looks like a recently dry-walled dungeon." She waited as Jane searched for the right key. "What if someone's inside?" she whispered, her eyes traveling up part of a limestone arch. "I mean, we don't want to get caught."

"Kelly and Brandon are in Cannon Falls tonight," said Jane, continuing to work down the row of keys.

"How on earth could you possibly know something like that?" She crouched closer.

"Hey, don't crowd me. You're blocking my only light source."

"Just think of me as an eclipse." She glanced suspiciously over her shoulder. "I bet there are lots of bugs down here."

"Probably."

She watched Jane without interest. "You know, not that you'd care, but this bolt cutter is heavy. I think it's giving me carpal tunnel."

"Success! This one works." Jane turned the knob and pushed the door open.

"It's dark in there," whined Cordelia.

Jane switched on the flashlight and let the strong beam wash over the interior. "Just like I said, nobody's home. Come on, Cordelia. Let's make this quick."

After closing and locking the door behind them, they each moved a bit hesitantly around the room.

"So this is Brandon's studio," said Cordelia, nearly tripping over an open can of paint. "If we get caught, we certainly won't be accused of theft. There's nothing in here worth stealing."

Jane took the bolt cutter from Cordelia's hand and approached the storage room door. After several aborted attempts to cut through the padlock, she stepped back and shook her head.

"Here, let me try it," said Cordelia. She spit on her palms, grabbed the tool, and snipped through the metal on the first try. "You may thank me *properly* later."

Jane unhooked the padlock and opened the door.

The sight and smell that greeted their eyes made them both gasp.

The storage room, as Brandon had called it, was large, about half the size of the upstairs lofts. Row after row of low tables were covered with marijuana plants, all of them green and vigorous, and most about the size of a small patio tomato. Heavy stems were bent under the weight of buds as thick as fists. The stench was vegetal, sweet, and sweaty.

"This is what smells so much like bubble gum," said Jane, touching one of the plants.

Grow lights and an expensive ventilation system had been installed. A dozen or so of the tables contained new plants scarcely a foot tall, but already sending out fingers of hairy calyxes.

"It's a perfect greenhouse," said Jane, walking though the room. The value of the grass had to be worth hundreds of thousands of dollars, if not more. She honestly had no idea.

"Is this what you expected to find?" asked Cordelia, her voice full of wonder.

"I expected to find a few plants," said Jane. "Not a small industry."

Cordelia stood next to a drying table. "Marijuana is America's biggest cash crop, did you know that? The next biggest is corn. I read an article about it a few weeks ago."

Jane shook her head. "You know, when I was down here the other night, Brandon made a comment that should have alerted me, but I didn't think about it until later."

"And that was?"

"Well, first he asked if I wanted a joint. When I said I didn't, he said that was too bad, because he could give me a good deal. We could have a party, just like he and Kelly. I was so disgusted by his sexual swaggering, I missed the significance of his statement."

"Do you think this marijuana farm has something to do with Merchant's murder?"

"Don't you? Think about it, Cordelia. We're not talking simple marijuana *use* here, we're talking major felony. There are people in the country serving life terms for growing far less than this. If Arno had kicked Kelly out, what would she and Brandon have done? You don't find a sweet setup like this every day. When the electricity bill went up, no one knew but her. Merchant's interference could have ruined everything! It could have sent them to prison!"

"Do you think he knew about *this?*" She swept her hand to the tables.

Jane shook her head. "All he had to know was that Kelly was doing drugs. Teddy Anderson told him that. And that information alone in Arno's hands would have sunk this operation. I doubt that Kelly was the one who actually did the deed. Brandon probably handled Merchant's murder by himself."

"And what about Arno? Did they mess with his meds?"

Jane shrugged. "I don't know. We may never know unless one of them confesses."

Cordelia wandered through the room, touching a plant here, a clay pot there. "Look at that." She pointed to a long shelf. Three clear plastic sacks filled with marijuana buds were piled near the top. "They don't smoke the leaves anymore, you know."

"They don't?"

"No way. This stuff is almost ten times as potent as what we used in college. And by the amount they've got here, I'd say they're already in business. I wonder how they get it out of the building without being seen."

Good question, thought Jane. And she had what she thought was a good answer. "You want to take a little walk?"

Cordelia's eyebrow arched ever so slightly. "Where to?"

"It's a secret. You like secrets."

"No, I don't."

Before leaving the studio, Jane stuffed the broken padlock into her pocket. She replaced it with the one she'd removed from the roof's door. Except for the lock, it was an exact match. She pushed the mechanism only part way up the double shafts, far enough to make it look closed, but not so far that it would prevent someone from slipping it off. She wanted to give herself some time, just in case Brandon and Kelly returned before tomorrow afternoon. She had to make a decision about how to proceed with this information. And to do that, she wanted to talk with Teddy first.

After closing the door soundlessly behind them, Jane and Cordelia crept down the darkened corridor. It was only a few yards to the wooden double doors leading to the underground tunnel.

"What's this?" asked Cordelia, once again reluctant to follow Jane into the unknown.

Jane opened one side and pointed the flashlight beam at the dirt walls. "About a hundred years ago the basement housed a stable. Horses were brought out to the Mississippi through this tunnel. They were watered, and then the stable hands walked them back to their stalls." She stepped into the darkness, feeling her boots crunch on the dirt and gravel. "So," she said, glancing over her shoulder. "Are you coming?"

"Ah, no thanks, Janey. I'm really not thirsty. Besides, river water gives me gas."

"Get in here!"

"You don't have to get nasty about it."

Sticking close to each other, they covered the half mile to the end of the tunnel in a matter of minutes. The air became colder as they neared the opening. Rubbing their hands together to keep warm, they stepped cautiously out into the bitter night air. The tunnel exit was protected from casual view by pines and low evergreen shrubs. About thirty feet away, the Mississippi spread out before them, huge and undulating in the frozen moonlight.

"You think Kelly and Brandon brought the goods out this way?"

Jane ducked under a low-hanging pine bough, shining the flashlight on the snow until she found what she was looking for. "See this? Tire tracks." She gazed up at the top of the hill. "Someone probably brings some kind of four-wheel drive vehicle down here and loads up."

"At night?" asked Cordelia.

"Yes, that's probably a good guess."

"Like right about now?"

Both turned at the sound of a truck bumping through the trees several hundred yards away. Since the headlights were off, Jane felt fairly confident they hadn't been seen. "Dive!" she called, grabbing Cordelia's hand and hitting the ground behind one of the more distant shrubs. "Be quiet," she whispered. "And don't move."

"My entire body is quaking with fear and incipient frostbite and you tell me not to move?"

"Shut up!"

The truck came to a stop just a few feet away.

Jane watched in stunned silence as Eric Lind emerged from the cab, slammed the door and walked around to open the back end. He climbed in and rearranged some boxes. Then, jumping back down, he disappeared inside the tunnel.

Cordelia spit snow out of her mouth. "I thought you said this was Kelly and Brandon's operation."

Jane shook her head, too thunderstruck to speak.

"You know, you should take some sort of amateur detective correspondence course, Janey. Your skills are something less than Sherlockian."

"If I'd wanted a Greek chorus, I would have brought one."

"Am I wrong?"

"Look," said Jane, more than a little indignant, "we don't know for sure if he's gone inside for the marijuana."

"No," said Cordelia, yanking her sweater up around her ears. "He might be searching for antique horse dung."

Jane hardly knew what to say. If Eric was involved, that meant *three* people might have plotted to murder John Merchant. Had she misread him so completely? Had her empathy with his position blinded her to the kind of man he really was?

It only took a few minutes for him to reappear. Jane's heart sank as she saw that he was carrying the plastic sacks. He hoisted them into the back of the truck, tossed a blanket over them, and slammed the door. Then, looking around to make sure no one was watching, he hopped back inside the cab. In less than a minute, he was gone.

"Can we go now?" pleaded Cordelia. "I've lost feeling in everything but my lips. And they're going fast."

With a sense of overwhelming sadness, Jane stood, gazing down at the lights shining along the banks of the Mississippi. The city seemed like such an alien place tonight. Standing here now, she knew she didn't have all the answers, but she had enough to finally explain to Roz what was rotten at Linden Lofts. This was the end of the road. Turning away from the river, her eyes rose wearily to the top of the Linden Building in the distance. She felt as if she were watching some great silent ship, making its way slowly towards its doom. "Come on, Cordelia," she said, her voice full of defeat. "Let's get out of here."

39

Shortly after ten the next morning, Jane stood in front of the Boline Mansion and rang the front doorbell. After an unsuccessful attempt to contact Teddy at his loft, she'd bumped into Roz and Thurman in the freight elevator as she was leaving the building. Roz explained that she'd talked with Teddy earlier in the morning and that after he visited his wife at the nursing home, he was planning to spend the rest of the day working at the mansion. Jane hoped that by waiting until now, she'd find him in.

As she saw it, Teddy was one of the only people left who cared about Kelly Heywood. She felt he deserved an explanation of what had been going on down in the basement of Linden Lofts, and perhaps even a say in how the information was handled. Not that Jane would allow him to bury the evidence. John Merchant's murderer had to be caught, no matter if it turned out to be Kelly, Brandon, Eric, or any combination of the three. At least now, the police would have a clear motive. Jane was happy to let them, not her, pursue the evidence to a final conclusion.

She gave it a few more seconds and then rang the bell again, this time knocking loudly. Just as she was about to give up and head back across the street to her car, the door swung open and Teddy appeared.

"Jane," he said, his tone a mixture of surprise and frustration. He seemed highly agitated, his cheeks bright with color. "What can I do for you?"

"Could I come in?" she asked.

"Well, I'm rather busy at the moment." He said the words curtly, projecting a harried, businesslike image. "I'm expecting an important call and—"

She cut him off. "It's important."

He adjusted his glasses. "All right. If you insist." He shook his head in such a way that he let her know it was against his better judgement. Shutting the door behind her, he said, "You'll have to come up to my office."

"No problem." As she watched him take the stairs two at a time, she couldn't help but wonder where all this energy was coming from.

By the time she reached the third floor, Teddy was already back at his desk. The printer behind him was spewing out pages.

"Have you finished the biography?" she asked, stepping over to a window and looking down at the street.

"No, but it won't be long now." He punched some keys on the computer keyboard, glanced quickly at the screen, and then sat back, threading his fingers over his tweed vest, waiting for an explanation.

Jane was about give him one when she noticed the blue Escort pull into a parking spot in front of the house. She could make out a dark smudge in the driver's seat, but no one got out.

"Is something wrong?" he asked impatiently.

She couldn't believe she was still being followed. Who was out there? "Do you know anyone who drives a blue Escort?" she asked, her eyes boring into the side windows of the sedan.

He blinked his incomprehension. "You came to ask me *that*?"

"No, but do you?"

"Of course not. Now, if you wouldn't mind getting to the reason why you're here?" He coughed deeply, several times, wiping a hand across his mouth.

She stayed near the window, but turned to look at him. "I'm sorry to have to be the one to bring you bad news. I know you've been worried about Kelly's marijuana use."

"Who told you that?" he asked indignantly, sitting up straight in his chair.

"Your brother."

"Oh . . . Edgar. I suppose it shouldn't surprise me that he'd confide in you." Some of the color drained from his cheeks as he continued, "In my day, it was considered shameful to use drugs. It's not a subject I feel all that comfortable discussing. But . . . you're right. I have been terribly concerned."

Jane knew this would be hard for him to hear. "Last night I discovered that the young man Kelly is dating, Brandon Vachel, has installed a greenhouse in the basement of Linden Lofts. It's attached directly to his studio. He's growing marijuana plants. Hundreds of them. I have no doubt that this is being done not only with Kelly's knowledge and approval, but with her help. Eric Lind is also involved."

Teddy's mouth dropped open. He stared at her, giving himself a moment to absorb the information. "Are you sure?" he asked, his face full of astonishment.

"I saw it with my own eyes. What they're involved in is a felony, Teddy. It has to be reported to the police."

"Oh my God," he whispered, closing his eyes. His shoulders sank and his body collapsed inward, as if taking a blow. He was silent for almost a minute. Finally he said, "I've never gone down to one of those studios. I just . . . I can't believe she'd do that."

"I'm sure it all boils down to money. When you asked John Merchant to talk to Kelly about her drug use, I think all three of them panicked. If John went to Arno, as he threatened, Kelly would most likely have been kicked out of the building. Their get-rich-quick scheme would have come to an abrupt halt. Or worse. They might have gotten caught. So, feeling like their backs were to the wall, they took matters into their own hands."

His head snapped up. "What are you saying?"

"It's pretty obvious, isn't it? One or all of them was responsible for John Merchant's death."

"You go too far!"

Jane glanced back down at the car. The smudge was gone. Damn. She should have been more careful. "You and I both know it's not only possible, it's probable, Teddy. I came over here this morning because I felt you had a right to know what was going on. When we're done talking, I'm going directly to the police station."

"But Kelly *couldn't* have been involved. It had to be Brandon." His eyes pleaded with her for agreement.

"The police will sort it out. I know it hurts, but perhaps you can console yourself with the fact that you tried to help her. What more could you have done?"

His voice took on a faraway tone as he slumped forward in his chair. "You know, about a month before Arno died, I went to him. I see now that I waited too long. But since Merchant hadn't been able to get through to Kelly, and neither had I, something had to be done. I knew Arno would act."

"You actually told Arno about this?"

"You have to understand, the last weeks before he died, he was a changed man. He was depressed. We all thought it had to do with his work, but whatever the case, his normal passion and interest in living was gone. When I explained to him about Kelly—that she'd resumed her drug use—he listened, but his response was flat. I'd hate to characterize it as uncaring, but the fact is, I don't think he cared very much. Kelly knew I'd gone to him. And after he died, she accused me of upsetting him so much that in his despair, he took his own life. How could I tell her the information barely even registered?"

"I know Arno was your friend. I'm sure that was hard to watch."

"It was," he said.

Jane had a thought. "Before Arno died, he told Peg he thought he knew who murdered John Merchant, but he wouldn't name the person because he didn't have any real proof. Did he ever confide in you?"

Teddy's brow furrowed. "No," he said. "That's the first I've heard of it."

"I'm convinced Merchant's murderer thought there *was* proof. And one of them, whether it was Kelly, Brandon, or Eric, was searching through all the lofts, looking for it."

Placing his hands flat on the desk top, Teddy said, "I refuse to listen to any further insinuations about Kelly!"

This wasn't getting them anywhere. She'd done what she'd come to do, and now it was time to leave. "Do you want to come with me to the police station?"

"Jane, stop for a second and think! You must let me talk to her first. At least give her a chance to explain. We don't want to be hasty. Her entire future is at stake!"

"I've already waited longer than I should have. Maybe you'd like to drive back to Linden Lofts so that you can be with her when the police arrive."

His face grew stony, but he said nothing more.

Taking one last look down at the street, Jane said, "Will you answer one question for me before I go?"

"If I can."

"How was it you knew Kelly was smoking pot?"

He hesitated, but only for a second. "Why, I saw her."

"When was that? She said she hadn't smoked a joint in years, not until the other night."

His lips tightened. "Well, perhaps I misstated myself. I saw *evidence* in her apartment. A plastic sack containing the cannabis buds. I'm not an idiot, Jane. I know what marijuana looks like. Kelly can't handle drugs any better than an alcoholic can handle booze."

"But, I mean, she wouldn't have left it just sitting out."

"No, of course not. I discovered it . . . by accident."

"While you were visiting her?"

"Yes."

It still didn't make sense. Unlike some of the other apartments, Kelly's loft was completely open, no walls of any kind. If he'd been snooping around, she would have seen him. "And you just happened to be rummaging through her things? I guess I'm not clear on why she'd allow that."

"Why are you interrogating me? I was simply *in* her apartment and discovered marijuana. End of story."

Except, as Jane held his eyes, she knew it wasn't the end of the story. In an instant, she saw it all. She tried to cover, hoping he couldn't see the fear in her eyes. "Well, I guess I'm just glad someone cares enough about her to try to help." She glanced down at her watch. "Hey, look at the time. I'd better shove off."

"Leaving so soon?" he said, his voice growing low and mocking.

"Yeah, well—"

With deliberate evenness, Teddy pulled one of the file drawers open and drew out a gun. He stood and pointed it at her, his face looking more drained than angry. "Evidently, the man I hired to stop you from your obsessive search didn't get my message across. It's a pity. If you'd taken his advice, this might all have ended differently."

Jane just stared at him. She'd been so sure of her theory. "You're the intruder! You were the one who was searching through all the lofts. That's how you knew Kelly had the marijuana."

He moved around the desk and motioned with the gun for her to walk toward the door.

She stood her ground, looking him straight in the eye. "You murdered John Merchant. Why?"

"You don't care about my reasons. No one does."

She took a chance. "I know about your son."

"What do you know?"

"That Boline's grandson was instrumental in convicting him and sending him to prison."

"His monumental arrogance, you mean! He was so sure of what he saw. But he was wrong! My son was innocent."

"And the biography," said Jane. "That was going to be your revenge."

"Exactly! But not just the biography. That was only part of it." He walked a few paces closer, making a big show of holding the gun on her.

Her eyes darted to the door. There was no way she could get around him without being shot. Instinctively, she knew she had no choice but to keep him talking. "But why John?" She tried desperately to control her voice.

"He surprised me! He came back after our meeting that last night. I don't know why. He'd never done it before. He probably wanted to offer me a ride over to the Guthrie. But when I discovered him, he was sitting behind my desk, paging through the top files. It only took a few seconds for him to realize I had found proof that August Boline had swindled at least five well-known engineers and inventors in the Midwest. I had the original signed contracts! A great deal of the money legally owed these men for their designs was never paid."

So that was it. That's what all the numbers she'd seen on his desk had been about. She'd probably even had one of the contracts in her hand, but she hadn't understood its significance.

"Oh, Boline coughed up some of the money on a regular basis," he continued, "just to keep them satisfied that he was meeting his end of the bargain. But it was only a pittance, only a tiny fraction of what was due them. After fifty years of default, we're talking multiple millions of dollars. I've checked, and there's no statute of limitations on binding, legal contracts."

"But what are you going to do with the information?"

His eyes glowed. "Give it to the families of the men he swindled. It will reduce the Boline estate to cinders."

"You murdered a man for *that*?"

"Don't be absurd!"

"Then why?"

The hand holding the gun began to tremble. "I did it for my son!"

"But he'll be out—"

"He'll *never* be out!"

She stared at him. "I don't understand."

"I couldn't tell anyone—I was terrified it would get back to my wife. It would kill her if she knew the truth!"

He swallowed hard, wiping a hand across his mouth. "The day before Merchant discovered what I was doing, I received word that Bobby had been killed in a knife fight in the prison yard. He was dead, Jane. Richard Crawford murdered him, just as surely as if he'd held a gun to his head and pulled the trigger. My wife and my boy, they were all I had. In my whole life, they were all I ever loved! Crawford took everything from me. Even my livelihood. I couldn't write for two years after my son went to prison, not until the day I was asked to do the biography. It gave me a purpose again! I had a reason to keep going, to get up in the morning. But then, when I found out Bob was gone, I don't know how to explain . . . I just snapped. Next thing I knew, Merchant was sitting behind that desk about to take away my only means of retribution!" He clamped a hand over his ear. "I remember he spoke to me as if I'd been a naughty child. While he had his back to me, stuffing the incriminating papers into his briefcase, I stuck him with the first heavy object I could put my hand on. I wanted to hurt him. To erase him. To make him go away and never come back. All I wanted was to be left alone!"

"Heavy object?"

"Yes!" His eyes fixed on the barrel of the gun. "It was a few minutes later that what I'd done finally penetrated. I tried to get him to sit up, to talk to me, but it was no use. That's when I panicked." His eyes rose to hers. "From that moment on, my life has been out of control. I killed two more people to save my own skin. I didn't see any other way." He held his free hand up in front of his eyes and stared at it. "It's amazing how precious your life can look when it becomes threatened."

"Two more?" she repeated softly to herself. Had she heard him correctly? John. Peg. Then it hit her. "Arno," she said under her breath.

Teddy was beginning to sweat. He pulled a handkerchief out of his vest pocket and wiped his brow. "I never meant to hurt him. The day he died was one of the blackest days of my life. But he'd gotten it into his mind that I had something to do with Merchant's death. You see, I did make it to the Guthrie that night. After intermission Arno noticed some mud on my pants and shoes. And also, I couldn't hide the fact that I was out of breath and sweating like a pig. I told him I'd just gone out to get some air, and that I'd tripped, but he didn't buy it."

"Didn't anyone else notice?"

"Apparently not. I was sitting in an aisle seat next to Arno. He had the best view of my somewhat damaged state. When he found out the next day what happened, he put it together. He came to me late that night. Although he never asked outright, I know he expected some sort of confession. He didn't get one. But over the next week or so, he kept at me. Chipping away at my story. Where had I walked? What had I tripped over? He asked about my business relationship with Merchant. How was the biography going? He was like a dog with a bone. He wasn't going to let the subject drop! That's when, out of pure exasperation, I got the idea to tamper with his medication."

"But why do that?"

"I just wanted him off my back! About five years ago, he decided that he didn't need his anti-depressants any more. So, he stopped taking them. Within weeks, he was a changed man. What I remember most about that time was that he lost interest in everything around him. And that's exactly the reaction I needed."

Her eyes dropped to the gun. She had to get it away from him. "But how did you do it? That must have been really hard to do."

"No, on the contrary. It was quite simple. Eric and I took turns taking care of his cat while he and Peg were away, so I had a key to his apartment. I knew where he kept his prescription medication. The drug was administered by capsule. It was easily emptied and refilled with cornstarch."

"And that's when you got keys made to the other apartments so you'd have easy access."

"You're a clever girl. That's exactly what I did."

"But, didn't you know about his earlier suicide attempt?"

His face turned a deep red. "Of course not! I wasn't trying to hurt him, just *divert* him."

He was a fool, thought Jane, though she knew better than to say it out loud. "But," she continued, coaxing the story out of him, "what were you searching for in all the lofts?"

"Photographs. And if I do say so myself, I think I found every last one. Peg had the odious habit of making Arno take endless pictures of every event in their lives, and then she'd pass reprints out like candy. I had to find and dispose of all the shots taken the night we went to the Guthrie. Let's just say they might have become problematic if my name had ever been linked to Merchant's murder."

"Because of the mud on your pants?"

"No," he said indignantly. "Just like you, Arno thought he was clever as hell, but he missed the real proof. What he never noticed, and what I didn't notice until the next day, was that I'd lost the middle button on my suit coat while I was dumping Merchant's body under that tree. It was a fairly generic button, nothing out of the ordinary. Unfortunately, it was found at the scene. I destroyed the clothes I was wearing that night, but those pictures were proof that the button was there early in the evening, but gone before we all left the theatre."

Her mind raced as her eyes shot once again toward the door. Time was running out. "I, ah . . . I thought I should tell you that I finished your book last night."

A muscle twitched in his face.

"I liked it. It was—" She couldn't think of anything to say. "— a great read," she said finally, knowing as soon as she said the words that it was all wrong.

"I loathe half-hearted flattery, Jane. I've been damned by so much faint praise in my life that it's become the single, resonant theme of my professional existence. But no more. With the publication of this biography, that will all change. Now," he said, his voice resuming a more threatening tone, "I suggest you do as I say. Raise your arms above your head where I can see them. And *move!*"

She had little choice but to obey. She also had little doubt she was going to end up exactly like John Merchant.

Together, they walked stiffly out of the room, Jane first, with Teddy following several feet behind. As they descended the stairs, her eyes flew in every direction. On the second floor landing, she stopped and turned half way around. "What are you going to do with me?" she asked, her voice betraying her growing panic.

"What you've forced me to do." He stuck the gun into her back and pushed her forward.

When they reached the first floor, he ordered her into the kitchen. He took some twine from one of the pantry drawers and then directed her out the back door. "Put your hands down at your sides, but keep them visible," he said. "Don't be stupid, Jane. You know I won't hesitate to use the gun if I have to."

"Where are we going?" she demanded, knowing full well she had no right to demand anything. It was then that she remembered the mace Cordelia had given her last night. She had on the same jeans, so chances were it was still in her pocket. But it would be almost impossible to get at it without being seen. She moved cautiously into the bright morning sunlight, squinting at the fresh snow covering several dumpsters sitting in front of the garage. Since it was Sunday, none of the workmen were around.

Teddy kept his hand in his pocket now, urging her in a low, quiet voice to walk faster. "There's a side door near the back of the garage. It's unlocked. That's where we're going."

She moved down a wide cobbled walk, sidestepping the most obvious ice. Anyone who might be watching them from a window, or from a passing car, would have seen nothing amiss.

Entering the cold garage interior, Jane saw that there were three cars parked all in a row—two antique roadsters and a rusted Honda Civic. On the far end, the workers had left a bunch of shovels, plywood boards and dirt covered two-by-fours next to another partially open side door. Morning sun streamed in through a narrow line of windows in the main doors, brightening the interior with a kind of diffused, gauzy light.

"Put your hands behind you," barked Teddy, shoving her toward the Honda.

"Are you going to shoot me right here?" she asked, turning around and shoving her hands defiantly into the pockets of her jeans. Adrenaline shot through her body as she seized the tiny cylinder. She positioned it quickly in her hand.

"No," he said, walking to the rear of the vehicle and opening the trunk. "Get over here," he ordered. "We're going for a ride."

His attention strayed only briefly, but it was enough time for Jane to yank the mace free, point it at him and spray. It didn't hit him square in the eyes, as she hoped, but it stunned him and he staggered backwards.

"Damn you!" he screamed, wiping a hand across his face.

In an instant, she was on him. The mace tumbled to the floor as she grabbed for the gun, struggling to make him release it. But he fought back, jamming her hard against the car. The edge of the tail light caught her square in the ribs, the exact same spot where she'd been injured two nights before. Gasping in pain, she doubled up and sank to her knees.

Teddy's hand shook as he leveled the gun at her. "You never quit, do you," he said, his chest heaving as he tried to catch his breath.

She raised her eyes to his.

"I don't intend to leave this world until I finish what I set out to do. Now, get up!"

As she struggled to her feet, she saw a figure dart out from behind the second car and rush toward him, a two-by-four held high. Teddy never saw what hit him. The whack to the back of his head sent him reeling to the floor. The gun skittered across the cement, lodging next to a tire. In a second, Jane was on it, grasping it in both hands.

She held it firmly, steadying herself against the side of the car, and then turned, coming face to face with her rescuer. "What are you doing here?" she demanded. It was about all she could get out.

Amy McGee clasped the piece of wood to her chest as if it were a scepter of office. "I followed you," she said, squaring her shoulders proudly.

Jane blinked. "Followed me?"

"Sure. I've been following you for over a week."

"You mean, *you* were the one in the blue Escort?"

A pout formed. "I didn't think you saw me."

Jane had no idea what to say.

"I've been tailing you ever since you came to see me at my office. I had some vacation time coming and I thought, what the hey, why not keep an eye on you to see why you were so interested in John Merchant. You were obviously doing some kind of investigation, and I knew it wasn't for your father." She clucked her tongue. "You should be ashamed of yourself for lying, Jane, it's not nice. But back to my story. After following you a couple of times, I kind of got into it. I thought maybe I'd spy on you a little longer. See who else you were dating."

"*Dating?*"

"Other than me. I wondered about that Julia person I talked to, although since she said she was a doctor, I let it pass. But after you got clobbered the other night, I thought I should follow you a while longer. Just in case. And see," she said triumphantly, glancing down at Teddy, "I was right!"

Jane found it hard to match Amy's enthusiasm, not that she wasn't grateful. It was just, as she thought about it, it all seemed a little sick. She stepped over and kicked Teddy in the leg. He appeared to be out cold. "Amy, I want you to do me a favor."

"Sure. Anything you say, honey." She fluttered her eyes eagerly.

Jane did a double take. Very soberly she said, "I want you to go inside and call 911. Tell them to come right away—there's been an attempted murder. Do you have that?"

"Absolutely." She didn't move.

"What are you waiting for?"

"Oh, nothing," said Amy. "Except, I was thinking. You really owe me big this time, Jane. This wasn't just a *small* favor. One might almost say you owe me your life. Not that I'm the type to hold something like that over another person. But still, it's comforting." She wiped a bit of dirt off Jane's chin and then skipped off.

"*Comforting*," thought Jane, watching Amy's back disappear out the door.

Not the word she would have chosen.

40

"Poor Edgar," said Cordelia, standing next to the fireplace and warming her hands near the fire. "Have you told him yet?"

Jane relaxed on the couch in her office, sipping a lager and lime. After a hectic afternoon spent mostly at the police station talking to the detective assigned to John Merchant's murder case, the day was finally drawing to a close. When she and Cordelia had arrived at the restaurant a few minutes ago, twilight was descending on Lake Harriet. "I'll talk to him in the morning. Maybe by then I can think of just the right words to say."

Cordelia nodded, resuming her own place on the couch. She picked up her coffee and said, "I've still got a truckload of questions."

"Like what?"

"Well first, what happened to Teddy? We got as far as Amy McGee calling the police."

As Jane snuggled into the folds of her favorite ragg wool sweater, she luxuriated in the thought that never again would she have to darken the doors of the Linden building. She would sleep in her own bed tonight. And tomorrow her aunt was coming home. Even so, she was more then a little discouraged that matters had ended so badly. "The police came and arrested him. By then, he was awake. He insisted he had nothing to do with Merchant's death, or Peg's, or Arno's."

"But you said he admitted it all to you."

"Sure he did. But since he won't come clean, the police are going to have to prove his guilt. I don't think that's going to be too difficult. Norm, Dad's paralegal, told me that one of the officers found a baseball bat up on the third floor of the Boline Mansion. It was in Teddy's office. Hair fibers were imbedded near the top. They'll do some tests, of course, but I'm positive they'll confirm that the hair belonged to John Merchant. And in the trunk of Teddy's car, they found a tie clasp with the initials JM on it. It's already been identified as Merchant's."

Cordelia whistled. "But why in the trunk?"

"That must have been how Teddy transferred the body to Loring Park.

I think, once all is said and done, we'll find that Teddy first drove John's car over to the Guthrie, parked it, and then took a bus back to the mansion. Right before the performance, he drove his own car—with John's body stuffed inside the trunk—to the Guthrie and parked it near the southeast corner of the park. During intermission, he left the theatre, ran to his car and dumped the body under the pine tree where it was later found."

"So people would think it was a gay hate crime?"

"Exactly. And he might have gotten away with it except for one thing."

"What's that?"

She took a sip of her drink. "A button. And you, my dear, found the most damning evidence of all."

"I did?"

"Those photos you found in Julia's bag? It was a longshot, but I took a chance and drove back to the Linden Building to look at them this afternoon. They're clear proof that Teddy was at the scene of the crime. It was *his* button the police found. I dropped them off at the station a couple of hours ago. In the first set taken that night at the Guthrie, the button is there on his suit coat. In the later ones, it's missing. Those incriminating photos were what Teddy was searching through the lofts trying to find. And he no doubt found every last one, even the negatives, all except for the ones Peg sent to her daughter. I have no idea why she brought them with her. Probably a whim, but I'll find out later when I talk to her."

"Say, speaking of *Julia*—"

"And," said Jane, cutting her off, "thanks to your willful disregard of property rights, we had the evidence right at our fingertips."

"So what? You and your misplaced integrity wouldn't look at them."

"I repent of my stubbornness in sackcloth and ashes. Is that abject enough for you?"

"No. Now, what about the knock Teddy took on the head back at his apartment?"

"I'm sure he did it to himself. He knew Roz had called the police about a prowler. It was his way of distancing himself from any personal involvement. And by planting Thurman's glove, which I'm sure he lifted from Roz's trash, he introduced a well-placed red herring into the mix."

"Fascinating," said Cordelia, mulling it over. "The picture is becoming clearer. But what about the Linden Lofts' growers association? Simple farmers, tending the soil, making a living by the sweat of their respective brows, waiting for Mother Nature to send them rain, sunshine, and oodles of potheads to buy the produce."

"Well put."

She took a small bow, then added a bit more cream to her coffee.

"The police picked Kelly and Brandon up as soon as they got home from their all-night party. They also confiscated the contents of the greenhouse. And later, they found Eric at work over at his antique shop."

"And?"

"They demanded to see an attorney. My dad told me later that there are at least thirty people in the country serving life sentences for growing marijuana. It's a federal crime. Possession of a hundred marijuana plants carries a mandatory five to forty-year sentence without chance of parole."

"They had five times that many plants."

"I know."

"Boy, are they in trouble."

"Dad did say he thought their sentence would be mitigated by the fact that all their records are pretty clean."

"Great. Instead of forty years, they'll get thirty-five."

Jane shook her head. Her gaze strayed to the fire, watching a log shift and send a spray of sparks against the screen. Even though it wasn't a happy ending, she was glad it was all finally over. Being away from her normal routine for a few weeks had made her realize just how much this restaurant meant to her, how much a part of her blood it had become. "You know, I had a chance to talk to Eric before they took him into the lock-up. I asked him why he'd done it."

"And? What did he say?"

"Money. He said that he accepted the blame for his father's death. Because the antique business was all his mother had left—and they were having financial troubles—he felt that when Brandon and Kelly came to him with their idea, it was a great way to make some quick cash. He'd sunk about four thousand dollars of his own money into the operation. Their first crop was finally ready to sell, so, in the next week or two he would have made it all back—and then some."

"Except that we blew the whistle on them. God preserve us from friends with great ideas."

Jane thought about Mabel Lind and her effort to shield her son from the wrong crowd. Now he *was* the wrong crowd—in more ways than one.

"Eric made his own decisions," she said. "Even so, I don't think he's a bad person—that goes for Kelly too. I just think they have rotten judgement."

"What about Brandon?"

"I'll bet you anything that Brandon knew the potential dangers, but kept it quiet. He was the ring-leader, the one with the connections and the know-how. Eric admitted that to me before they took him away. I hope Kelly finally sees him for the kind of man he is."

Cordelia stared thoughtfully into the fire. "All right, but one last question, Janey. Was Arno's death a suicide, or murder?"

Jane shook her head. "Teddy called it a murder, and I think it was, though his death was never Teddy's intention. Teddy took a risk with another man's life—and he lost. To his credit, he did take responsibility for it, at least to me."

"Fat lot of good that did Arno." Cordelia shuddered. "You know, I'll never be able to look at the Foshay Tower again and not think of him. Poor man. What a tragic end to a successful life."

"I know," said Jane, softly. "But the real irony is that Arno might have been able to tolerate the withdrawal of his medication if it hadn't been for Mark Thurman. The grief he caused Arno over at the station might just have been the final nail in his coffin. In a very real sense, Thurman was also responsible for what happened to him, and I think he knows it."

Cordelia pursed her lips. "*Miserable* fellow. Lucky for Roz she isn't the marrying kind. But I suppose we should look on the bright side. Perhaps Brandon will be out of jail in thirty or forty years. By then, Roz will be looking around for a new man. I feel the powerful hand of destiny here, Janey. Only time will tell."

"Time will tell," repeated Jane softly to herself, her thoughts straying to Julia. What would *time* tell for the two of them? It was an unfortunate situation, being so far apart, not being able to resolve what had happened between them. Jane couldn't predict the future, she only knew how she felt now. She wanted a chance with this woman more than she'd wanted anything in a long, long time. But whether or not life would provide her with that chance was another story. She simply had to wait and see. She'd call Julia later tonight and tell her what had happened today. She deserved to know the reason for her mother's death. But would the conversation end there?

"So, tell me about Peg's daughter," said Cordelia, gazing at Jane over the rim of her coffee cup.

Even though her manner was casual, Jane knew Cordelia was bursting with interest. "What made you think of her?"

"You don't usually grow pensive over scumballs like Brandon and Thurman."

Jane laughed. "I guess you got me there."

"So what went on between you two?"

She stared down into her drink. "I can't talk about it, Cordelia. Not right now."

"Boy, you *are* in deep this time."

"What do you mean?"

"You only refuse to talk about someone when you've really got it bad for them."

"Who said?"

"Janey, I've known you since you were sixteen. Give me a little credit. You didn't talk about Christine until you'd been dating her for almost three whole months. That's how I knew it was serious."

"You make me sound so predictable."

Cordelia reached over and took hold of Jane's hand. "Not predictable, dearheart, but very loveable. Whoever finally grabs you is going to get themself quite a woman."

Jane was incredibly touched. "What a sweet thing to say."

"It's the truth."

"I think that sentiment calls for a fabulous dinner on the house."

"I thought you'd never ask."

As she switched off her desk lamp, Jane heard a knock on the door. She moved quickly to answer it.

"Hi, Jane," said one of the dining room waiters standing patiently outside. He seemed out of breath. "The hostess sent me down to tell you your party has arrived."

"What party?"

"There's three of them. They've already been seated. Sorry, but I gotta run. See ya." He rushed back upstairs.

Jane turned to Cordelia, a perplexed look on her face. "I don't know what he's talking about."

"Don't look at me, dearheart. I may be large but I hardly constitute a party of three." She took a last gulp of coffee. "So, let's go find out."

As they entered the reception area, the hostess walked up to Jane. "Good. You got my message."

"I did. But I haven't a clue what it's about."

She pointed to a table between the fireplace and the north windows. There, drinking a grasshopper and deep in conversation sat Amy McGee along with an older man and woman.

The hostess continued. "Ms. McGee said you'd invited them here for dinner tonight on the house. I didn't have the reservation, but she said that was to be expected. You'd had a lot on your mind today and had probably forgotten to make them."

"I *what?*" said Jane indignantly.

"When you join them we're supposed to bring in the champagne."

Cordelia's somewhat strangled laughter did not go unnoticed.

"You think this is funny!" demanded Jane.

"Of course not," replied Cordelia, her face moving from hilarity to stern sobriety in less than a second.

"Who's with her?" asked Jane, returning her attention to the hostess.

"Oh, that's Mr. and Mrs. McGee. Her parents. They introduced themselves as Biff and Tammy."

"Biff and Tammy!" shrieked Cordelia, banging Jane on the arm. She immediately covered her mouth with her hand. "Sorry."

As Jane glared, the entire party stood and marched out into the foyer.

Amy slipped her arm through Jane's and gave her a sugary smile. "I knew you'd get here sooner or later," she said, half under her breath.

"Biff McGee," said Amy's father, thrusting out his hand. "And this is the wife, Tammy."

Tammy gave them all a creamy smile.

"It's, ah, nice to meet you both," said Jane.

"Oh, we've heard great stuff about you," said Biff. "Great stuff." He spoke with bluster. He was a stocky man, well over two hundred pounds, and he looked and sounded like an athletic coach.

"Well, I'd better get going," said Cordelia, elbowing Jane in the ribs. "I wouldn't want to spoil your evening."

Spoil it, *please*, thought Jane.

"See you later, alligator," said Amy, with a dismissive wave.

Jane and Cordelia exchanged pained glances.

As if on cue, Cordelia sagged against Jane's chest. "My medication," she said, coughing and gripping the top of Jane's sweater. "I must have my medication."

"Are you all right?" said Amy's mother, her face full of concern. "Tell us what's wrong."

"It's her heart," said Jane, thrilled at Cordelia's fast thinking. "Tell me where the medication is? I'll get it."

"New Delhi," she whispered, fanning air into her face.

"What?" said Amy, a hand rising to her hip.

Rallying for a moment, but then weakening, Cordelia draped her arm over Biff's shoulder, tweaking open his suit coat pocket and extracting his handkerchief. "It's at home. In my medicine chest. Jane, you *must* drive me."

Jane plastered on a serious look. "I'll get your coat."

"No!" roared Cordelia. "There's no time. We have to leave now."

"But what about our dinner?" demanded Amy. The annoyed look on her face told everyone she had absolutely no interest in Cordelia's health problems.

"I'm afraid it will have to wait," said Jane, leading Cordelia over to the door.

"But . . . this is a special occasion!" she called after them.

"It is?" chirped Jane. She couldn't bring herself to ask what the occasion was.

"Maybe you'll get back in time for dessert," said Amy, waving hopefully.

"Try the apricot torte," called Cordelia. She coughed into the collar of Jane's shirt.

"But should we wait?"

"Oh, I'm going to be sick for a long time," said Cordelia. "Possibly months."

"But Jane!" said Amy, stamping her foot.

"Order some nice wine," smiled Jane, propping Cordelia up. She was fading fast.

"But!"

"Try the Chateau Malartic-Lagraviere 1945," said Cordelia, warming to the idea. "In fact, have three or four bottles. You'll feel just like you're in a David Niven movie!" She swirled around and then yanked a sputtering Jane out the door.

ABOUT THE AUTHOR

Ellen Hart is the author of five previous mysteries featuring Jane Lawless: *Hallowed Murder*, *Vital Lies*, *Stage Fright*, *A Killing Cure* and *A Small Sacrifice*. Formerly a chef, Hart lives in Minneapolis where she is at work on her seventh Jane Lawless mystery, *Robber's Wine*.

SELECTED MYSTERIES FROM SEAL PRESS

The Jane Lawless Mysteries by Ellen Hart. The Twin Cities are turned upside down in these compelling whodunits featuring restaurateur and sleuth Jane Lawless and her eccentric sidekick Cordelia Thorn.
HALLOWED MURDER. $8.95, 0-931188-83-0.
VITAL LIES. $9.95, 1-878067-02-8.
STAGE FRIGHT. $9.95, 1-878067-21-4.
A KILLING CURE. $19.95, cloth, 1-878067-36-2.
A SMALL SACRIFICE. $20.95, cloth, 1-878067-55-9.

The Meg Lacey Mysteries by Elisabeth Bowers. From the quiet houses of suburbia to the back alleys and nightclubs of Vancouver, B.C., divorced mother and savvy private eye Meg Lacey finds herself entangled in baffling and dangerous murder cases.
LADIES' NIGHT. $8.95, 0-931188-65-2.
NO FORWARDING ADDRESS. $10.95, 1-878067-46-X; $18.95, cloth, 1-878067-13-3.

The Cassandra Reilly Mysteries by Barbara Wilson. Globetrotting sleuth Cassandra Reilly gets herself into intriguing situations no matter where she is—from Barcelona, Spain to the Carpathian mountains of Transylvania.
GAUDÍ AFTERNOON. $9.95, 0-931188-89-X.
TROUBLE IN TRANSYLVANIA. $10.95, 1-878067-49-4; $18.95, cloth, 1-878067-34-6.

The Pam Nilsen Mysteries by Barbara Wilson. Three riveting mysteries, featuring Seattle sleuth Pam Nilsen, take us through the worlds of teen prostitution and runaways, political intrigue and the controversial pornography debates.
MURDER IN THE COLLECTIVE. $9.95, 1-878067-23-0.
SISTERS OF THE ROAD. $9.95, 1-878067-24-9.
THE DOG COLLAR MURDERS. $9.95, 1-878067-25-7.

The Maggie Garrett Mysteries by Jean Taylor. Maggie Garrett is a red-headed San Fransisco P.I. with a reputation for quick thinking and an ability to keep her mouth shut.
WE KNOW WHERE YOU LIVE. $9.95, 1-878067-62-1.
THE LAST OF HER LIES. $10.95, 1-878067-75-3. Due out May 1996.

Seal Press publishes many books by women writers. To receive a free catalog or to order directly, write to us at 3131 Western Avenue, Suite 410, Seattle, WA 98121. Please include 16.5% of the total book order for shipping and handling. Thank you!